Oxana
and the
Red
Dress

A NOVEL

LAWAYNE LENO

RIVER GROVE
BOOKS

This is a work of fiction. Although most of the characters, organizations, and events portrayed in the novel are based on actual historical counterparts, the dialogue and thoughts of these characters are products of the author's imagination.

Published by River Grove Books
Austin, TX
www.rivergrovebooks.com

Distributed by River Grove Books

Design and composition by Greenleaf Book Group
Cover design by Greenleaf Book Group and Anna Jordan
Cover image © master1305/Adobe Stock

Publisher's Cataloging-in-Publication data is available.

Print ISBN: 978-1-63299-861-3

eBook ISBN: 978-1-63299-862-0

First Edition

For Reid

Blessed be he who has passed through the world in its fateful moments.
—Fyodor Tyutchev, Russian poet (1803–1873)

I know my love for you is hopeless.
—Frédéric Chopin (1810–1849)

Part 1

Dreams

Peterstal, Ukraine

1920

Chapter 1

Oxana sat on her mother's front doorstep one late April afternoon, basking in the warmth of the sun-drenched air. Stretching her legs and leaning her head back, Oxana closed her eyes. Within moments, she was standing in a large room somewhere—she couldn't tell where—but it was dark, completely dark. She was wearing a red satin floor-length dress, and a matching ribbon held her hair. In the distance, a black grand piano was encircled in a halo of bright light. Oxana stepped toward the piano, and suddenly people—hundreds, maybe thousands of people—were clapping and cheering. The audience fell silent as she sat at the keyboard. She touched her fingers to the keys and the hall was filled with beautiful music—

"Wake up, sleepyhead." Irina, Oxana's twin sister, was poking her. "Didn't you hear Mama calling? She's ready for us. We can go inside now." Oxana sat up. The sun had become even more intense, and she blinked her eyes and tugged to loosen her damp blouse.

There was a white iced cake on the table, and their mother was standing beside it, a small wrapped gift in each hand. "You can open yours first," she said, handing one to Irina. Irina carefully peeled away the gold paper and opened the gold-colored box. She extracted a vial of perfume shaped like an egg. "Ooh," she cooed, showing the bottle to Oxana before gently pressing the silver cloth atomizer with her thumb and forefinger to spritz a mist into her palm.

"It smells nice," Oxana said while Irina rubbed the perfume across the front of her neck.

"Not too much, only a hint," her mother cautioned as the room was filled with the sweet scent of jasmine.

"She'll probably spray on the whole bottle to try to get Jakob Schweitz's attention," Oxana mumbled.

"Will not," Irina said. "Why would I want to get some boy's attention?"

"Because you're in love with him, that's why."

"Am not."

"Girls, quiet," their mother said. "Now, Oxana, open your gift."

Oxana tore away the paper to reveal a leather-bound volume entitled *The Lives of the Great Composers.* "Oh, Mama, thank you."

"Now you can read all about the people who wrote the pieces you're learning. Look inside." Oxana opened the front cover and gently ran her fingers over her mother's elegantly crafted Cyrillic script while mouthing the words:

> *For Oxana Nikolaevna Stepaniaka*
> *On the occasion of your fourteenth birthday,*
> *4 April 1920—Peterstal, Ukraine*

"And, girls, I have another surprise for you," their mother said, sinking a knife through the rich white frosting and cake. "Tomorrow we're all going to Odesa to hear a piano concert."

"A piano concert!" Oxana exclaimed. "Thank you, thank you."

"Our first trip to Odesa," Irina added. "This is the best birthday ever!"

Their mother eased slices of the cake onto plates while the girls hovered over Oxana's book.

"Irina, Jakob's never going to talk to you," Oxana whispered, carefully turning each page to gaze at the photographs of the composers. "He's so shy he doesn't talk to anyone. You should go up to him and say something."

"Girls can't talk to boys. It wouldn't be proper."

"It isn't proper for girls your age to even be thinking of boys," their mother interrupted, handing them each a plate, "much less talking to them. Now eat your birthday cake."

That night, Oxana was startled awake by a crash of thunder. Just as she sat up, a streak of lightning lit up the pitch-black room as if it had passed right through the roof and barely missed striking her. In the sudden flash of brightness, Oxana saw that her mother's bed, which stood against the opposite wall, was empty, and she noticed a glimmer of light shining under the door. She nudged Irina, lying beside her. "Wake up! Don't you hear the storm?"

"Who cares. Go back to sleep," Irina mumbled.

There was a loud crash. Something, maybe a tree branch, had fallen onto the roof, and Irina jolted upright.

Oxana whispered, "Irina, I'm scared. What if something bad happens in this storm and we can't get to Odesa tomorrow? We'll miss the concert. Mama says he's the most famous pianist in the world, and he's so old I'll probably never have another chance to hear him."

"Nothing bad is going to happen. It's just a storm. We'll get to the concert. Mama promised us."

There was another crash, this time against the side of the house—another tree branch most likely—followed by another streak of lightning and several loud claps of thunder.

"Irina, what if—"

"Go to sleep, girls," their mother said, coming into the room carrying a kerosene lantern in one hand and the dress she was sewing in the other. Elena Vladimirovna was not even forty, but Oxana watched her move stiffly with stooped shoulders, and the glow of the kerosene lamp seemed to accentuate her graying hair and the dark shadows around her eyes. "It's only a storm," she said. "There's nothing to be afraid of. We're safe for now, and I'll see in the morning if the roof has been damaged."

"But Mama, what if we can't get to the concert?" Oxana said, tears welling in her eyes.

"I'm not scared of the storm," Irina said, fluffing her pillow and leaning her head against it. "It's just wind and rain."

"Irina!" Oxana poked her leg out from under the blanket and jabbed her sister. "How can you be so calm? Things are smashing against the house. What if the roof collapses? What if the windows shatter? What if—"

"Girls, quiet!" Their mother sat on the edge of their iron-framed bed and placed the kerosene lantern on the nightstand. She patted each on the head. "Everything will be fine. I'll leave the lantern lit so you can see that there is nothing to worry about. Now both of you go back to sleep."

Irina rolled over and within minutes was sound asleep.

"Mama, I'm scared," Oxana whispered. "I want to hear him play tomorrow, but I'm worried it might discourage me. Are you sure I can be a pianist? What if I'm not as talented as you say I am? What if I'm not good enough to play concerts?"

"Hush, Oxana. Of course you're talented enough, but you shouldn't be thinking about the future. Just spend each day trying to be the best you can be and the future will happen on its own. But right now you need to go to sleep—and when you wake up the storm will be over. I'll sit here beside you while I finish this dress. Then, tomorrow, as soon as I deliver it to Naydia Rostova and she pays me, I'll have the money to buy our tickets. Everything will work out just fine."

Oxana lay for a long time listening to the rain pelting the roof. She winced with each boom of thunder and flash of lightning as she watched her mother gently but swiftly passing her needle and thread back and forth through the fabric, late into the night.

Chapter 2

Jakob was startled awake by a crash of thunder. He flinched and the hairs on his arms stood on end. Gusts of wind were driving the rain horizontally against the house, and Jakob wondered if the windowpanes might shatter. The straw stuffing in his mattress was scratching his back, and he rolled onto his side. A small kerosene lamp was casting grotesque shadows across the bare wood walls, and Jakob stared at the halting, clumsy gyrations, imagining the strange shapes were reflections of the ogres and goblins his brother had told him about when he was a small boy.

The house consisted of one large square room, with a small lean-to his father had added before Jakob was born. The addition was intended for his parents, but now Jakob had the extra space, and Pa and Wilhelm slept in the main room. His father and brother were talking, and Jakob leaned to the edge of his cot to peek around the corner to hear better.

"Damn rain's going to ruin the crops," his father mumbled, moving his cigar from one side of his mouth to the other. "Stinking Russia. I hate this place." The red glow of the lit cigar bobbing up and down resembled the baton of some conductor providing a musical accompaniment to his father's speech.

Wilhelm was bending over to remove his rubber overshoes. He was a few weeks shy of his seventeenth birthday and was now taller than Pa. His long hair was completely blond, almost white, and he had recently grown a beard, which was also light colored. The heavy farm work had toughened his muscles, and his voice had dropped at least an octave lower than Jakob's reedy-sounding boy soprano. "Rain's coming too hard to soak in," Wilhelm said, standing to hang his drenched coat on a peg beside the door. "Running through the fields like a river. The lowlands are probably flooded by now—good thing we don't live down there."

"Damn, damn," Jakob's father kept repeating, his voice barely audible over the howling winds. As each bolt of lightning lit up the room, the haze of cigar smoke enveloping his face gave him the appearance of a wispy apparition, like some ancient prophet of doom, returned from the grave. "Tall stalks. Kernels starting to fill out. Aiming to be a good harvest. And now this storm. I hate this country."

"Couldn't see much in the dark," Wilhelm said, pacing the room, "but it looks like most of the crop's been washed away."

Jakob rolled to the edge of his cot and propped his head up with his pillow, staring at his father in his chair. Pa was only forty-five years old, but his hair had already turned a silvery gray and he had recently been complaining that he had difficulty breathing and often felt dizzy.

Wilhelm continued to pace, and Pa slowly shook his head as if momentarily confused, not sure where he was. "Damn Russia," he said, his voice stronger. "We should never have come. My great-grandpa fell for all those promises Tsarina Catherine made. Sly old vixen. She knew the future tsars would never honor those promises, but she made them anyway, to lure us here. He should have stayed in Prussia."

Following another boom, Pa paused, but both boys knew he wasn't finished—they had heard it all before. Wilhelm stepped to the window and peered out, to be sure the boom really was thunder and not some explosion.

Pa took a deep breath. "In '04 they forced me into the army and shipped me off to Manchuria. I was married with a son to take care of, but it didn't matter to the tsar. Nothing mattered to him, except to keep pretending we were winning the war. Two years in those filthy, stinking trenches. Soldiers—my friends—all around me being killed. In the end we didn't even have ammunition. Did they think we were going to win the war by throwing stones at the Japanese? Like cavemen? Nothing to eat, clothes always wet, and cold, so cold—"

Jakob jumped when another crash sounded against the house. Wilhelm stepped into the lean-to. "Nothing to be scared of," he said, seeing that Jakob was awake. "It's only empty kerosene cans. I should've put them in the barn. Didn't expect there'd be a wind strong enough to blow them around. Go back to sleep." He patted Jakob's head.

Wilhelm stepped back into the main room. "Time for bed, Pa. We'll see to fixing things up tomorrow in the daylight. Nothing more we can do until this wind and rain let up."

Pa reached for his glass and downed the last of the vodka in one swallow. "And when I came home from the war, your mother and I decided it was time to leave, go to America. We had it all planned. Plenty of others were going, and we were going too. But then she got pregnant again, and we had to wait until the baby was born."

"Let's go to bed, Pa." Wilhelm held out his hand to help him out of his chair, but Pa remained sitting, staring out the window into the black night.

"And then she died while Jakob was being born."

Jakob crawled back across the cot and tugged the blanket up to his chin. He put his pillow over his head and willed himself to sleep.

Chapter 3

Oxana woke to the sound of tree branches scraping the side of the house. She went to the window and saw her mother outside, pulling the fallen tree limbs into a pile in the front yard. She glanced at Irina, still asleep, before jumping back into bed. Oxana loved mornings, the warmth of the bed with her blankets pulled up to her chin and the feeling of safety and protection, knowing as long as she had her mother and sister, nothing in the world could truly harm her.

She heard the front door open.

"Get up, girls," their mother called. "The storm has passed. Thank God we're all safe, but you're going to be late for school if you don't hurry."

Irina rolled over on her side, and Oxana jabbed her with her elbow.

"Ouch," Irina yelled. "Why did you do that?"

"To wake you. We have to get up."

As if on cue, they jumped from the bed and began to gently wrestle, pulling at each other's hair and arms.

"Stop that," their mother chided them, hearing the tussle. "Get dressed right now."

Oxana and Irina began thumbing through the rack of dresses hanging from a bar mounted above their bed. As the town's finest seamstress, Elena Vladimirovna took great pride in her daughters' clothing and made certain they were always dressed as well as she could manage, fashioning their dresses and ribbons out of the remnants of elegant fabric from the garments she created for her customers.

"Let's wear blue today," Irina said, pulling a dress off its hanger and holding it in front of her, against her nightgown.

"What is taking so long?" their mother scolded as she came into the room. "Get dressed! And Irina, how much perfume did you put on? You're not supposed to use the whole bottle. Now come and eat. It's time to be off to school, and no one leaves this house without a hot breakfast in their stomach."

The twins hustled into the main room and sat at the rectangular dining table where two bowls of steaming porridge awaited them. "I've arranged for you to leave school at noon, so be sure to come straight home," their mother continued while the girls slurped their cereal. "We'll have to hurry to catch the train."

"I'll try to pull Irina away from that Jakob boy," Oxana said as she gave her sister another jab with her elbow. "She sits and stares at him all day in school."

"I do not," Irina responded. "It's you who is staring at him, from what I can see."

"Girls, enough. Now get going. And be careful," their mother called as the girls opened the front door. "Your papa's old ginkgo tree toppled over last night. That's what you heard hitting the house. I'm sorry to lose it; he loved that tree. I'll get someone to help chop it up later—it'll make good firewood for next winter."

———

"Where's Mama?" Oxana said to Irina, checking each room and still panting from rushing home from school. Their mother wasn't in the front room, nor in the kitchen or bedroom.

"The train is already at the station. If we don't hurry, we'll miss it," Irina said, just as the door opened and their mother came in. "Mama, where were you?"

"You don't even have your hat or coat on," Oxana said. "Aren't you afraid we're going to miss the train?"

"I was at the station and I'm afraid we are going to miss the train, but not because we're late. The storm last night washed out the tracks. There are no trains to Odesa until the tracks are repaired, which the porter told me would be tomorrow at the earliest."

"We're not going to hear the concert," Oxana whispered to Irina, tears stinging her eyes.

"Or get to see Odesa," Irina moaned.

"Well, girls, it seems God has smiled on us today after all. You are correct that we are not going to Odesa, but we will hear the concert because it is going to happen right here in Peterstal."

"Here? In Peterstal?" Oxana asked. "How is that possible?"

"When I went to get our tickets, the porter told me there was a famous pianist on the train, and it turns out it is the very one we were going to hear. He was on his way from a concert in Kyiv. Since he's stuck here for the night, he agreed to play at the Lutheran church, so I had to hurry over there to get Father Vanska's permission."

"But we don't get to go to Odesa," Irina said, her lips protruding into a pout. Oxana put her arm around her sister's shoulder.

"Irina, at least we're going to hear the concert. That's what's most important," their mother said. "But of course," she continued, settling into a chair and wiping her brow, "he's a professional and is demanding a fee. I tried to get it out of Naydia Rostova, but she only agreed to pay a portion. I guess I'll have to pay the rest, although where that money is going to come from, I have no idea. But that's not something you girls need to worry about."

"Oh, Mama," Oxana said, her eyes opening wide and her face relaxing into a broad grin. "When it comes to piano, I think you can make anything happen."

"And now, Oxana," their mother said, standing and turning toward the kitchen, "you need to do your practicing, and Irina, come help me with cooking."

Oxana sat at the piano and, after a few scales to warm up her fingers, started playing the Chopin piece entitled "Fantasy." She had been working on it for several months and, despite the difficulties, had grown to love it. Even though the piece lasted less than fifteen minutes, it contained an entire world of emotion. The quiet opening pages reminded her of a solemn march by holy men as if in preparation for some mystical rite. Oxana loved how the march transformed into a whirling rhapsody of passion, like how she imagined a jubilant celebration of love must feel, and, as she played, Oxana wondered if she would ever feel that way, ever experience a love that deep, that fulfilling.

As she played the final chords, even though today, for the first time, she had played the entire piece from memory and without a single wrong note, she felt a regret, similar to the way she often wept at the end of her favorite novels, wishing the story could go on forever.

"That was excellent," her mother called from the kitchen, above the reverberation of the final chords. "You finally have it. Soon I'm going to have to figure out a way to get you to the Odesa Music Academy so you can get the sort of training a talent like yours deserves."

"And maybe I can come to Odesa with you," Irina added. "That would be fun."

"But Mama, maybe you could just continue teaching me?" Oxana called to her mother.

"My dear, even though you already play so beautifully, there is still much to learn."

Oxana sat smiling, listening to her mother and Irina chatting while chopping vegetables. *The Odesa Music Academy*, she thought. *It's so far away. I wonder if Mama could have studied there, and why she sews instead of teaching piano for a living? I've never even heard her play an entire piece. She only plays certain sections to show me how they should sound, but even then, I can hear how good she is.*

"Oxana, I'm not hearing any music," her mother called. "You're not finished yet. You still have another hour to go. Why don't you play the Fantasy again, and this time try to make the softer sections even softer. Soft playing is what is most exciting for an audience, not loud."

Oxana closed her eyes, placed her hands on the keyboard, and began again.

Chapter 4

Jakob dropped his schoolbooks on a chair and tossed his jacket on top of them. He pulled a chunk of bread from the stale loaf lying on the kitchen table and dipped a cup into the milk pail that was still sitting on the floor inside the door from the morning's milking. A few dead flies were floating on top, and he flicked them out before swallowing the entire cup in one gulp.

"What's all the hullabaloo at the train station?" Jakob asked when the door opened and his father stepped inside.

"Seems there's going to be some kind of piano concert tonight," his father said. "I came from town where that Stepaniaka woman—the twins' mother—was running around like a chicken with her head cut off, trying to set it up. Some famous piano-playing guy was on the train on his way to Odesa, but now that the train isn't going anywhere, he's going to play over at the Lutheran church."

"A piano concert? Wonder what that sounds like," Jakob said, shoving the last bite of bread into his mouth and chewing while he pulled his tarpaulin overalls over his pants.

"Don't know and ain't planning to find out," his father muttered. "Can't imagine anyone wanting to go hear a bunch of piano playing, but then there's always fools who will do just about anything to avoid work."

Jakob slipped his boots into his rubber overshoes, grabbed the pail of milk beside the door, and headed to the barn to slop the pigs. They were squealing with hunger, and he had to use the wooden handle of a pitchfork to push them back while he leaned against their pen and poured the milk into the trough. On his way to the barn, he tossed a small pail of grain into the chickens' pen. The cows were mooing—their udders were full—and he picked up his pace. Pa had long ago decreed that Wilhelm should do the morning milking and leave the evening milking to Jakob, saying, "Cows can't wait for Jakob to crawl out of bed."

After milking, Jakob shoveled the day's accumulation of manure into a wooden box mounted atop a sled and pulled the sled into the pasture behind the barn to spread it. "Keep the barn clean," Pa always said. "Animals want things clean the same as people do."

While he worked, Jakob kept thinking of what his father had said. *A piano concert? I'd like to hear that.*

The sun was already low in the sky, and Jakob hurried into the house and threw several pieces of wood into the stove. He put a pot of water on to boil and quickly peeled onions, beets, and potatoes and tossed them all into the pot. It wouldn't be much of a supper, but it was all he had time for, and besides, there wasn't anything else in the house to eat.

Jakob filled the ewer on the small table beside the front door with warm water and refolded the towel. He had forgotten to hang it outside and it was still damp. Wilhelm wouldn't like that, but Pa only wanted them to use one towel a day.

Pulling plates from the shelf above the stove, he paused a moment in contemplation. The dishes were the only things of his mother's left in the house, and each plate had a large rose in the center. He had never seen any photographs of his mother, but he was certain she was very beautiful, like the rose on each plate. While Jakob set the table, he glanced over toward the stove and imagined her stirring the pot of stew, turning to smile at him, and he would return the smile. "I'm sorry you had to die because of me," he whispered.

He was ladling the stew into bowls when the door opened. "What's to eat?" Wilhelm asked while Pa poured the warm water from the ewer into the basin so he and Wilhelm could wash up.

"Stew," Jakob said, carrying the steaming hot bowls to the table.

"Stew? Not again."

"Hush," Pa chided him. "If the boy made stew, then that's what we eat. All food's the same once it's inside your belly. Be glad you got something to fill you up."

They ate in silence, and as soon as they finished, Jakob stacked the dirty dishes and grabbed his jacket, still lying atop his schoolbooks.

"Where are you going?" his father asked.

"Thought I might go hear that famous piano player at the church tonight."

"Piano player?" Wilhelm laughed. "Why d'you want to hear a piano player?"

"Don't know. Maybe it might be nice." Jakob pulled his cap down nearly over his eyes, quickly closed the door, and hurried down the main road.

Chapter 5

Oxana and Irina walked slowly beside their mother toward the Lutheran church. The stained-glass windows were glowing in the dark, and the flickering of the candles inside made the window's figures appear to be alive and moving.

Holding the church door open for her mother and Irina, Oxana scanned the small crowd. She immediately spotted and waved to Slava and Ludmilla Domitovich, sitting off to the right, near the front. Slava, by virtue of being the oldest man in the village, was head of the village council, and his wife was the town's midwife. Ludmilla had babysat Oxana and Irina when they were small, and Oxana considered her to be like a grandmother.

Naydia Rostova and her two youngest daughters were sitting a few rows behind Slava and Ludmilla. *Thank God Fedor isn't with them*, Oxana thought. Fedor, the Rostovs' oldest child, was in the same grade as Oxana and Irina and had recently been paying Oxana more attention than she cared to receive. He had even tried to kiss her one day when no one was looking, and she had slapped him hard enough to leave a red mark on his cheek.

Father Vanska had moved the church's old upright piano to the center of the sanctuary, in front of the altar, and Oxana followed behind her mother and sister as they made their way down the aisle to the front row. Moments after they were seated, the bald, portly pianist emerged from a side door, and Elena clapped as he stiffly made his way toward the instrument. Oxana and Irina, along with the rest of the audience, followed her cue and joined in the applause. He was wearing a black ill-fitting tuxedo with long tails, along with a broadly knotted silver tie, and when he bowed to the audience, his tie tack glinted in the candlelight. *I'll bet it's a real diamond*, Oxana thought, squinting to get a better glimpse.

The pianist lowered himself onto the bench with perceptible effort. The clapping subsided, and in that moment of silence, with everyone waiting for the music to begin, the creaking of the rear door echoed through the sanctuary. Oxana turned and saw Jakob, the boy from school, dart in and slip into the rearmost pew. Oxana poked Irina and pointed to him. She frowned and poked back. Their mother scowled and put her finger to her lips to shush them.

The old musician stared at his hands, as if in prayer, before he turned to the audience and announced, "Bach." He played a loud chord, and Oxana winced at the twangy sound of the off-pitch notes. He had no reaction and continued playing. Oxana was surprised at how nimble the old man's fingers were as they danced across the keyboard. The twanging gradually faded away as the sounds coming from the instrument became beautiful and harmonious, as if the music itself were transforming the decrepit piano and the sprightly melodies were forcing the sour notes back into tune.

Oxana was not sure what the name of the piece was. She would ask later; Mama would know. It lasted less than five minutes, and while the final chord reverberated through the small sanctuary, the old man held his hands over the keyboard, seemingly reluctant to stop, as if regretting that the music had ended so soon. The small audience clapped, and the pianist stood and bowed, smiling and nodding his head in agreement that he too liked Bach.

He announced "Beethoven" and played a soft, stark arpeggio. Oxana immediately recognized the *Appassionata* Sonata. She had learned it last year, but even as she listened to him play the sparse opening notes, she understood how very far she still had to go to really know the piece. There was an authority about his playing that made the music completely convincing, as if, in that moment, his interpretation was the only possible way the piece could be played. The pianist's hands moved to the top part of the keyboard, and the colorless, emotionless opening gave way to the warmth of quiet trills in the treble. Suddenly he pounced on the keys, and the loudest music Oxana had ever heard came crashing out of the old piano. She sensed the entire audience jerking to attention.

The stormy music was sometimes so soft it was barely audible, and then the sounds would grow so loud they shook the floor, as if the piano might explode at any moment from the sheer force of the music it was producing. But Oxana was most amazed at how the music was not merely loud but was also deep and rich and noble. She had never heard an orchestra, but the variety of sounds the pianist produced made her feel that this must be what an orchestra would sound like, with violins, flutes, trumpets, and even drums.

Oxana sat staring, her mouth gaping, experiencing the true power of music, the emotional possibilities behind and beyond the notes. Through the music, the pianist was revealing something intangible yet beautiful, something she had never known before, something that was beyond words, beyond images, and could only be conveyed through the purity of sound.

The concert continued with short pieces by Chopin, and Oxana sat in dazzled awe as the magical sounds poured out of the old instrument and filled the small, dimly lit, unadorned church. After each piece, the audience erupted in a roar of applause—at least as much of a roar as the small crowd could make—forcing the old man to stand and bow several times. With each succeeding piece, Oxana became more and more determined that this was what she wanted—no, needed—to do for the rest of her life. She had been playing the piano for as long as she could remember. Her mother, who claimed Oxana was already trying to play at age three, started teaching her soon after she turned four. Oxana had always loved playing the piano, partly because it made her mother happy, and partly because she loved the beautiful sounds, the pretty dresses she wore . . . and the applause. But this was not merely making pretty sounds. This was about creating music so powerful it transformed people—lifted them out of the dreariness of their daily lives to show them beauty and joy. Mama kept telling her she had the talent to become a concert pianist, but tonight, for the first time, she herself believed it to be possible, and she vowed she would do whatever it took to make it happen.

"For my final piece," the pianist announced, "I would like to honor a request made by this, I must say, unusually intrepid woman who organized tonight's concert, Elena Vladimirovna." He pointed to Oxana's mother. She stood and turned to the audience, nodding several times while everyone clapped. "I am told she has a very talented daughter, and so this last piece I play for her." The old man pointed to Oxana, and she also stood and faced the audience while everyone clapped even louder.

He played the soft, slow march-like opening theme of Chopin's Fantasy in the lower part of the keyboard. *Mama told him!* Oxana nearly said aloud. She closed her eyes, leaned her head back, and was bathed by the most beautiful music . . .

Chapter 6

Jakob sat motionless, listening intently to the beautiful sounds the old pianist's fingers were producing. He closed his eyes and inhaled deeply, imagining he was moving in step with the soft, steady music while gazing toward some fog-enshrouded horizon. The music grew in intensity, and Jakob, keeping his eyes closed, imagined a large red feather on his path, and he knelt to pick it up. He stood, with the feather in his hand, staring, as the fog evaporated, gradually revealing the vague outline of some figure, until at last he recognized her—the Firebird, from his fairy tales—with feathers as bright red as any Jakob had ever seen, while those on her head were gold-colored.

The piano music gradually transformed into a turbulent rhapsody, and the bird began to warble, rich and melodious and in perfect tune with the piano. Keeping his eyes closed, afraid of breaking the spell, Jakob heard a single tone sound three times across the keyboard. The Firebird turned away and covered her body with her wings. The pianist intoned a series of sweet, hymn-like chords, and the Firebird turned back to face Jakob, slowly unfolding her wings to reveal her face, now transformed into a human visage. She was young and beautiful, and Jakob sensed, instinctively, that it was his mother. She was mouthing words to him—he couldn't hear what she was saying—but he felt a peace welling up inside him. Jakob leaned forward, straining to hear, when he was startled out of his trance by the audience's roar of applause.

He rushed out the door before anyone could see him wiping his eyes.

With only the glistening stars to light his way, Jakob slowly made his way home. What was the Firebird trying to tell him? He had heard something more than mere music—something strange and powerful, as if the notes were a secret code—and he suddenly felt an overpowering need to learn to play the piano, for he was certain that if he could play that music, no matter how difficult it was or how long it took him to learn it, he would unlock the hidden messages and mysterious voices buried deep within the sounds.

———

Jakob arrived at school early the next morning and waited inside the door for the twins to come up the steps. As usual, they were wearing identical dresses, today yellow with white collars and thin white belts, their hair tied back with white ribbons. He had to stare to tell them apart, they were so indistinguishable. Both had pale, smooth skin and long brunette hair hanging below their shoulders. Jakob thought their oval-shaped faces and dark eyes gave them a half European, half Asian appearance, as if they might have been the favorite daughters of some ancient Cossack warrior prince—or maybe twelfth-century Byzantine priestesses. Before he lost what tiny shred of self-confidence he had managed to rouse, he quickly strode toward them. "Hello, Oxana Nikolaevna and Irina Nikolaevna," he said, bowing stiffly.

Oxana giggled, and Irina, blushing, stared at the floor.

"Please, call us Oxana and Irina," Oxana said. "You don't need to be so formal."

"I saw you at the concert last night," he said to Oxana, and almost too nervous to even breathe, he quickly added, "Do you happen to know the name of the last song the man played? I figured you'd know, being a piano player yourself." He could smell Irina's perfume, and by the time he finished speaking, his voice was quivering. He instinctively put one leg ahead of the other to try to cover the hole where his bare knee was exposed, while discreetly lifting his books to hide the stain on his shirt.

"It's called Fantasy, and it's by Chopin," Oxana said.

"Who's Chopin?"

"Chopin was a pianist from Poland, and Fantasy doesn't really mean anything specific. It's whatever music came into his mind at the time he was writing it."

"Oxana can play it," Irina said. "Would you like to hear her?"

"Irina." Oxana glared at her. "I'm sure he has better things to do than to listen to me. Besides, I'm still learning the piece."

"You can play that?" Jakob responded.

Irina giggled and Oxana scowled at her.

"Why don't you come by our house after school," Irina said, "so you can hear her."

"Sure," Jakob blurted out as Fedor Rostov came up behind them.

"*Privyet*, Oxana. *Privyet*, Irina," Fedor said, putting his arm around Oxana's waist. She pushed it away.

"Can I come along with Jakob? I'd love to hear you play too."

"I'm afraid you'll have to wait to hear me," Oxana said, folding her arms across her chest. "Mama says I'm not yet ready to give public performances. Maybe in a few years."

"So why does Jakob get to hear you?"

"Because he was at the concert last night and wants another hearing of one of the pieces that was played. And besides, Irina invited him, not me."

"Students, time for class," one of their teachers called.

Oxana and Irina headed down the short hallway, and Jakob overheard Irina whisper, "He's tall—and so handsome."

"Seems like Schweitz's got himself two girlfriends," Fedor said, putting his arm around Jakob's shoulder.

"Do not," Jakob mumbled, clutching his books against his side.

"Don't be embarrassed, old pal. Who wouldn't want a pair that pretty? I just hope you'll be a friend and let me have one of them, because I don't think Father Vanska will let you marry them both." Fedor laughed.

"I'm not marrying anybody." Jakob pushed Fedor's arm off his shoulder and hurried into the classroom.

———

Jakob waited at the bottom of the school's front steps. He would have to think of some way to explain to Pa why he was late getting home, but right now the only thing on his mind was that he was about to head out with the two most beautiful girls at school. Oxana and Irina emerged from the schoolhouse and descended the steps. Without saying a word, the three crossed the road in front of the school, took a shortcut across the Orthodox cemetery, went around the side of the Orthodox church, and walked into the village's main square.

"That was our papa's," Irina said, pointing to the blacksmith shop on the west side of the square.

"I know," Jakob said. "My pa told me your mother sold it after your father died."

"Mama had to sell it," Irina said. "There was no one to run it. She had only Oxana and me to help her, and girls can't run a blacksmith shop."

"Girls could if they wanted to," Oxana corrected.

"But what girl would want to run a blacksmith shop?" Irina said, and after a pause added, "We never knew our papa. He died when we were still little."

A wagon pulled by two horses rolled into the square, kicking up a cloud of dust, and they covered their faces with their hands.

"What made you come to the concert?" Oxana asked when the air cleared.

"Guess I thought it might be nice," Jakob said, staring at the ground.

"Why were you all alone?" Irina asked.

"My pa and brother weren't wanting to hear piano playing."

"If your mother was alive, maybe she would've liked to come to the concert with you," Irina said.

"Do you know about my mother?" Jacob was surprised, and for the first time he looked directly at her face.

"Everybody knows everything in this town," Irina said.

There was silence, and all three stared at the ground. Jakob traced a circle in the dirt with his toe while Irina and Oxana fidgeted with their dresses.

"I hope you're not mad at me," Irina whispered. "I didn't mean to say anything bad."

"I'm not mad," Jakob said. "Besides, it's not like it's some kind of secret or anything. Everyone knows I killed her."

"Don't say that," Oxana said. "You didn't kill her. Babies don't kill their mothers. She died while you were being born, that's all—it's not your fault."

"But if I hadn't been born, she wouldn't have died, so it's one and the same."

"No, it's not," Oxana said. "Not at all. Sometimes it happens. It's just an accident."

"It's so sad, you never even knowing your mother," Irina said. "And her never knowing you."

"Come on, we'd better hurry," Oxana said. "Mama's going to be mad if we don't get home soon."

The three crossed to the south side of the square, went past the general store and the butcher shop, and around the corner. Elena was standing with the door open, waiting, when the three came into the yard. "Mama, this is Jakob Schweitz," Irina called to her. "He wants to hear Oxana play."

"Privyet, Jakob, nice to see you." Elena extended her hand and Jakob shook it. "How's your father doing these days?"

"Do you know him?" Jakob was surprised.

"My, yes! We go way back, but now is not the time to talk about all that. Come in and have a seat."

Jakob stood in the doorway, staring, trying to see the entire room at once. The walls were painted white with gold flower-patterned drapes hanging across the windows. The pine plank floor was scrubbed and waxed so shiny he could see a reflection of himself in it, and several hand-braided rugs were lying about. But most impressive of all was the tall dark-brown upright piano against the wall opposite the front door. Jakob had never been in a house that had a piano, and he went toward it, with Oxana and Irina following behind.

"Oxana, why don't you get started?" Elena said. "I'll be in the kitchen if you need anything." Jakob listened to the sound of her shoes clattering across the pine floor. *Had his mother's shoes made sounds like that?*

"Do you know all of these?" Jakob asked, pointing at the pile of music lying on a small table beside the piano.

"Yes, or at least I will, eventually. This is all the music I'm learning. Here's Chopin's Fantasy." Oxana handed the score to Jakob.

"There are so many notes," he said, turning the pages. "Like hundreds of ants crawling on the page. How can you learn all this?"

"You just have to practice until you know it," Oxana replied.

"Where do you get all this music?"

"Mama orders it from a music store in Odesa."

"It must cost a lot!"

"Not that much—maybe ten or fifteen rubles for each."

"That's a lot to me," Jakob whispered.

He sat on the sofa and gently pushed his hands into the soft down-filled cushions. The chairs in his house were straw-filled, if they had any filling at all. Irina sat beside him, and Oxana took her place on the piano bench.

As soon as Oxana played the slow, somber opening, Jakob recognized the sounds. Soon her fingers were flying across the keyboard, and Jakob was astonished. He knew Oxana played the piano—everyone in town knew it—but he had no idea she was this good. He shifted his weight to spread his legs into a more comfortable position and accidentally brushed up against Irina. They both immediately pulled away.

Jakob clapped wildly when she finished, the way the audience had at the old pianist's concert. Oxana stood and bowed. "That was fantastic," he said. "Play some more."

Oxana thought for a moment and then played a shorter piece. Jakob stared at her hands with his mouth open, and again clapped when she finished. "More, more," he begged as Elena brought in a tray with glasses of milk and plates of plum cake.

"Jakob, you must be tired by now." She set the tray on the table beside the sofa.

"No, ma'am, not at all. I love piano music."

"Well, enjoy this and then you'll have to be off. Oxana still has to do her practicing and Irina has her chores to do."

Irina handed Jakob a plate of plum cake. He picked the cake up with his fingers but put it back down when Irina handed him a fork. "Sorry," he mumbled, jabbing the fork into the cake and taking a big bite. "Do you think I could learn to play the piano?" he asked, his mouth full of cake.

"Everyone can learn to play," Oxana said, handing him a glass of milk, "if they're willing to practice."

"Oxana can teach you," Irina said.

"I'd really like that," Jakob said.

"But Irina—Mama's the teacher, not me."

"Who taught your mother to play?" Jakob asked, swallowing his last bite of cake.

"Her mother," Oxana said. "All the girls in our family learn to play the piano, except Irina, because she's too lazy to practice."

"Am not," Irina said. "I'm just not any good at it."

"It's time for Jakob to be getting home," Elena interrupted, coming back into the room, "and for you girls to get busy."

"Thank you for the milk and cake," Jakob said, standing and heading toward the door. "And thanks, Oxana, for playing for me. You're really good." Oxana bowed. "And thanks, Irina, for sitting beside me," Jakob called out as he stepped out the door.

———

As soon as he woke the next morning, Jakob counted the money he kept in a tin can beside his bed. There were thirteen rubles. He wrote a note explaining that he wanted to buy some music called Fantasy, written by a guy named Showpan—he had forgotten to ask how the name was spelled but figured this was close enough. He tucked both the note and his money into an envelope and stuffed it into one of his schoolbooks, hoping Pa and Wilhelm wouldn't notice it before he left the house.

On the way to school, Jakob stopped at the general store and got in line behind a woman standing at the post office window. "Next," the postmaster called. Jakob was fingering his envelope. "You, boy. You're next. What are you waiting for?"

Jakob stepped to the window and pushed his envelope under the iron grill partition. "Do you know the address for the music store in Odesa?" he whispered.

"Speak up, boy. I can't hear you," the postmaster said. Jakob's hands were shaking. He glanced around to see if anyone was watching.

"I need the address for the music store in Odesa," Jakob said, trying to speak louder.

"Which one? There are two."

"Don't know," Jakob said, his voice dropping back to a whisper. "I guess the one Frau Stepaniaka sends to."

"That'll be the one on Primorsky Boulevard." The postmaster hastily wrote the address on Jakob's envelope. "One ruble."

Jakob's knees were shaking. "I don't have a ruble," he mumbled. He had forgotten about money for postage.

"Then you don't mail a package." The postmaster pushed the envelope back under the iron grill partition.

"Here's your ruble."

Jakob spun around and saw the store owner coming around from behind the counter.

"Let the boy mail his package," he said, handing the money to the postmaster. "I've known his father my entire life. They're a good family, always pay their debts."

Jakob pushed his envelope back under the grillwork. "Thank you, sir."

"Consider it a loan."

"I'll pay you back, I promise. Just please don't tell Pa or Wilhelm," Jakob pleaded.

"Don't worry, I can keep a secret. A boy your age is entitled to his secrets, especially when it involves the Stepaniaka twins." The store owner grinned, and Jakob took off out the door as fast as he could go.

Jakob thought about his music order while he did his chores that afternoon. He wasn't sure exactly how he was going to learn to play it once the music arrived, but he would start by studying the pages to try to figure it out on his own. Then, if he had any questions, maybe he would ask Oxana to help him. He wasn't sure how he would practice; maybe Father Vanska would let him practice at the church. He'd figure that out later.

Jakob rushed to the general store each day after school. He was too shy to ask if his package had arrived, so he stood beside the post office window, and each day the postmaster shook his head at him. He had nearly given up hope when, one afternoon, the postmaster called, "Came in this morning," and shoved a large brown envelope under the iron grill partition.

"*Spasiba*," Jakob muttered, and he hurriedly tucked the envelope inside his shirt. He tore out of the store and down the road, ran into the house, and shoved the unopened package deep into his mattress's straw filling.

That night, and most nights after, once his father and Wilhelm were asleep, he pulled out the parcel. He quietly untied the brown string, undid the brown wrapping paper, and carefully opened the book to stare at the pages. The tiny lines were densely packed with what seemed like millions of notes along with all sorts of other markings. Even the few words here and there were in some foreign language, and no matter how long or hard he stared, it all remained completely indecipherable. *How can music be so complicated?* He lay awake clasping his music book, dreaming of what it would be like to sit at a piano and make beautiful sounds, like Oxana . . . beautiful Oxana.

Chapter 7

"Quick, come inside," their mother shouted from the door when Oxana and her sister came into the front yard from school one afternoon. "I've had a telegram from Vera Fedorovna Veranitzskaya."

"Who's Vera Fedorovna?" Oxana asked as she and Irina entered the house and took off their hats.

"She's the lady in Odesa I sew for. Don't you remember? She wants to hear you play. She wants us to come tomorrow, and I wired back and said yes."

"Yay!" Irina shouted, twirling around the room like a ballerina. "We finally get to go to Odesa. I can't wait to see what a big city looks like."

"Irina, dear," their mother said, "I'm afraid only Oxana can go."

"But why, Mama?" Irina stopped in the middle of the floor, her hands still in the air.

"Irina, I'm sorry, I know it's only the cost of a train ticket, but after helping to pay for the concert, there isn't enough money left for all of us to go. Please try to understand. Your father was a wonderful man and provided us with a good living, but when he died his wages died with him. No matter how fast I work, my sewing can't keep up."

"It's not fair," Irina sobbed. "It was a birthday present for both of us. You promised, Mama. Why do I have to stay home?"

"Irina, please don't cry," Oxana said.

Their mother reached out to take hold of her hands, but Irina pulled away. "We're only going so Oxana can play for Vera Fedorovna and then we will come straight home. We're not going to do any sightseeing."

"But it's not fair."

Oxana put her arms around Irina's shoulder. "Don't feel bad."

"You always get to do things, and I never do," Irina wailed. "It's not fair."

Irina ran out of the room and Oxana followed into their bedroom. "I'm sorry, Irina," she said softly. "Please don't cry. We'll go another time."

Irina pulled a pillow over her head and bawled while Oxana sat rubbing her back.

───

Oxana and her mother set out for Vera's mansion as soon as the train pulled into Odesa's main station. It was a long trek, but by sparing the cost of the streetcar, they could afford a meal before their return.

The sky was clear with bright sunshine, and they were thirsty and sweaty by the time they approached Vera's imposing estate. Oxana's mother pulled the silk cord to ring the bell while Oxana peered through the grillwork of the wrought-iron gate. She squinted to get a glimpse of the grand house, set far back from the street and nearly hidden by the tall old oak trees. A footman approached, unlocked the gate, and, without saying a word, walked them down the long, curved gravel driveway. Oxana slowed her pace to stare at the meticulously maintained flower beds. She recognized some of the flowers—roses, lilies, petunias, dahlias, marigolds—but there were so many others she had never seen before. Some housewives in Peterstal grew flowers, but only along the edge of a garden or the side of a house, certainly nothing on as grand a scale as this.

Oxana hurried toward the wide stone steps leading to the double-doored front entrance but stopped when her mother and the footman veered off to the side. Her mother scowled and shook her finger as Oxana ran to catch up. "Servants never enter through the front door," she hissed in Oxana's ear to keep the footman from overhearing her.

The footman unlocked a side door and held it open. Oxana and her mother went down a short, narrow corridor and into a small vestibule where her mother hung her coat and hat on the coat tree. She adjusted her primly fitted black dress and ran her fingers across her hair—braided and coiled around her head in typical Ukrainian style—to flatten any stray strands.

Oxana took off her hat and coat and hung them beside her mother's. She was wearing a green dress with a lace collar and the arm cuffs folded back, revealing a lace lining. Both her belt and the ribbon in her hair matched her dress. Her mother pulled a brush out of her travel bag and handed it to Oxana. "There's a washroom. Brush your hair and get yourself ready. I'll have Xenia tell Vera Fedorovna we're here."

Closing the door, Oxana stared at the pristine floor tile, laid in a black-and-white alternating pattern, and the white porcelain fixtures. She tried the faucets above the sink and water came out of both, and one was hot! *Ooh*, she thought, pulling her hand away. *No house in Peterstal has anything like this.* She hoisted her skirt and sat on the toilet, giggling at the tinkling sound. *Wait till I tell Irina what it's like to go in a real indoor outhouse.* The bar of soap on the washbasin smelled of roses. *Wonder how you get soap to smell so nice? Our soap just smells like soap.* The white towel hanging on a rack beside the sink was soft—and even ironed. *Do I dare wipe my hands? I'll wrinkle it.*

"Oxana, what's taking so long?" her mother called through the door. "We mustn't keep Vera Fedorovna waiting—and be sure to flush."

"I'm ready, Mama," Oxana said, opening the door.

"But I didn't hear you flush."

"I don't know how," Oxana whispered in her mother's ear.

Elena stepped inside and pulled the porcelain knob at the end of the chain attached to the reservoir of water mounted above the toilet. Oxana watched the yellow water whoosh away before fresh water flowed back into the bowl. "Oh, my dear child," her mother muttered. "I have to get you out of Peterstal."

Xenia was waiting outside the washroom. "Madame Veranitzskaya is ready to receive you," she said and motioned them through a door. Oxana gasped. They were standing at the end of a long, wide central hallway with a large winding staircase wrapped along one wall. Xenia led them down the corridor, and Oxana glanced into the rooms as they passed by them. One had walls paneled with a dark wood and was filled with books, and another was decorated in pastel green. Carpet, chairs, wallpaper—everything was green. Another room was decorated entirely in blue.

"Ah, come in, come in," Vera said as Xenia led the two women into the music room. "How wonderful to see you again, Elena Vladimirovna." She gave her the traditional three kisses on her cheeks.

Oxana stared at the old woman—as if she were admiring a statue. Vera was short, but her snow-white hair was piled high atop her head, giving the appearance of being taller. She was wearing a blue satin dress with a string of pearls and matching earrings. Her dress hung above her ankles and Oxana noticed she wore silk stockings. Oxana tugged her dress lower. She had never seen women wear anything but cotton.

"And this must be the young *wunderkind*," the old lady said, extending her hand.

"Vera Fedorovna, allow me to introduce my daughter, Oxana Nikolaevna."

Oxana awkwardly took hold of Vera's hand to shake it, before realizing she should be bending over and giving it a light kiss.

"My, my. Tall, and very pretty," Vera cooed. "You'll do well with the boys, I dare say. And your mother says you are an excellent pianist. Feel free to try it out." Vera pointed to the ebony piano stretching across one entire wall of the room.

"It's a *grand* piano," Oxana whispered. A twinge of nervousness was roiling her stomach, and her hands were cold, despite the warm room.

Vera chuckled. "It is indeed a grand piano, a concert grand, the biggest they make, and it's a Steinweg, from Germany. The very best."

"I've never played a grand piano," Oxana said, turning to her mother for some kind of reassurance.

"Go ahead, try it," Vera said.

Oxana sat on the bench and rubbed her hands together to warm them while Vera picked up a small bell on a side table and rang it twice. Moments later, the maid appeared.

"Xenia, please lift the lid for our young virtuosa," Vera told her.

Xenia stepped to the bend in the piano. "Careful, careful, it's heavy. Don't drop it," Vera said as Xenia hoisted the top and rested the open lid on a stick she raised from inside the piano.

Oxana played a scale with both hands to adjust to the feel of the keys and the volume. "It's in tune," she whispered to her mother.

Vera laughed. "Of course it's in tune. I keep my piano in top condition. Do you know Beethoven's 'Moonlight Sonata'?"

Oxana nodded and waited for Vera and her mother to settle into their chairs, Vera beside the piano and her mother across the room, before she began the slow rippling notes of the opening movement. Her hands quickly warmed up and her fingers practically did pirouettes through the middle minuet movement. Then, with hardly a pause, she launched into the tempestuous, difficult third movement. Each time the main theme repeated, she ever so slightly increased the tempo, so that by the final section she brought the piece to a tumultuous climax. "Brava, Maestra!" Vera shouted as Oxana played the last crashing chords.

The session continued for over an hour, with Vera naming a piece and Oxana playing it, glancing, after each song, at her mother, who was beaming with pride.

"Beautiful! Beautiful!" Vera exclaimed. "But you must be completely exhausted. Let's have lunch." The three ladies stepped into the dining room across the hall, where plates mounded with cucumber sandwiches, thin pancakes with sour cream topping, and Russian tea cakes were awaiting them. While Oxana and her mother ate, Vera talked nonstop, telling all about her days when she was a student at the Moscow Conservatory. As the old lady prattled on, Oxana sat staring at her empty plate. She wanted to ask for more cucumber sandwiches and pancakes, but her mother's glare silenced her.

"But enough about me!" Vera sat up. "You, young lady, are more talented than I am, and I am offering you a scholarship so you can attend our music academy."

"A scholarship!" Oxana's mother exclaimed, putting her hand over her mouth. "How wonderful. Thank you very, very much. You have no idea what this means to Oxana, and to me."

"Furthermore," Vera continued, peering directly into Oxana's eyes, "you must live here with me and do your daily practicing on my piano."

Oxana smiled and nodded, not quite sure if what she had been offered was a blessing or a curse. She wanted to study at the music academy—it was what she had been dreaming about for years—but to live here, in this big house, with an old lady she didn't even know? "But I'll hardly ever see Irina or you, Mama, if I live here," Oxana blurted out.

"Of course you'll see us," her mother said, and leaning over, whispered, "Don't be ungrateful." Raising her voice, she added, "But this is all premature. First you must pass the audition, and the standards at the academy are very high."

"Oh, there's no need for an audition," Vera interrupted. "Your demonstration today was audition enough. I'll drop by the school tomorrow and speak to a few people. From what I've just heard, there is not a teacher in all of Russia who would not be thrilled to have this young lady as their student."

As they were saying their goodbyes, and with her mother still thanking Vera for her enormous generosity, Vera grasped Oxana's hands. "There is one thing more I want to tell you, young lady. You are not the first to play for me. Others have come before, in hopes of impressing me, and they all went away empty-handed. But your playing is unique. Your mother has told me about you, and I understand your situation." Vera paused. She released her grip on Oxana's hands and held out both arms. "I did not always live like this. I too came from a small village and know what it is to struggle, but I married a very successful businessman. Today, hearing you play, I can, at last, repay my good fortune."

Elena wiped her eyes, struggling to hold herself together, while Oxana stared, awestruck and a bit frightened.

———

Elena and Oxana arrived at the station with plenty of time for a sandwich. While waiting for their train, a group of soldiers, maybe thirty or more, with rifles slung over their shoulders, staggered in. They had obviously been drinking—several were singing with their arms around each other's shoulders. Oxana leaned in close to her mother.

"There's nothing to be afraid of," her mother whispered. "They won't bother us."

The train pulled into the station and the soldiers jostled their way toward the doors—pushing and yelling. Her mother nearly fell when she and Oxana were stepping into a car and one of the soldiers pushed them aside and entered ahead of them. Oxana was taking a seat next to her mother when one soldier shouted, "No Ukrainians in this car. Only Russians."

"Be quiet, you swine," her mother hissed at him.

The soldier came down the aisle with his rifle pointed toward her. "What did you call me?" he shouted.

"I called you swine. Any man who accosts a widow and her young daughter is swine."

"Out! Out of this car!" the soldier yelled. "Before I shoot you both."

"Leva!" one of the soldiers shouted. "Why would you shoot such pretty women before at least trying them out? The young one is ripe as a peach. How about letting us have a taste?" The entire troupe roared with laughter.

"Filthy Bolshevik swine, all of you," Oxana's mother shouted, standing and grabbing their bags. "Come, Oxana. We'll move into another car." The soldiers jeered and prodded them with their guns as they forced their way down the aisle and out the end door.

"It's a shame to let something that sweet slip away, Leva," Oxana heard one say as the doors closed behind them. "You sure I can't at least have a little sample?"

"Forget them," her mother said as she and Oxana slipped into empty seats inside the door of the next car. "They are nothing but a rowdy bunch of scum."

They sat a long while in silence as the train rumbled along. It was completely dark outside, and the inside was dimly lit by several oil lamps hanging from the ceiling. Her mother began talking in a low voice, and Oxana stared out the window as she listened. "You are being offered a great opportunity—an opportunity that was denied me. I've never told you, but I was once accepted to the National Academy. I was only a year older than you now are. But unfortunately, I did not have a Vera Fedorovna Veranitzskaya to help me, and my father refused to allow me to go. He believed the only thing a woman was fit for was marriage, and so I obliged him. But that is no matter now. You are more talented than I was. But Oxana, you must not squander this opportunity. It will be hard, but you are strong."

For a while, they rode in silence.

"I know what rich people are like," she continued. "You can live among them, but don't forget that you are not one of them. Vera will pamper you, but you must not become filled with envy. Money is not a goal. Money is nothing more than a convenience and will not guarantee success. Even your talent will get you only so far. It is hard work that will get you to your final goal. Never forget this, and never be deterred. Your future is to be a concert pianist. I've done all I can for you—now the rest is up to you."

Tears were streaming down Oxana's cheeks, and her mother handed her a handkerchief. Oxana stared out the window into the black night, wiping her eyes, hoping that all the right decisions had been made and that this really was what she wanted.

Chapter 8

"Do you remember that today is May Day, Pa?" Jakob asked while they ate breakfast. May Day was the biggest holiday of the year, and Jakob had been watching the preparations over the past few days. A Maypole had been erected in the center of the main square, and the younger schoolchildren had decorated it with all sorts of trinkets and ornaments—colorful ribbons tied into bows, bouquets of flowers, twigs woven into wreaths, even fruit tied to long pieces of string hung from the top of the pole.

"Hmm," his father grunted. "I suppose there's no harm in going to town and getting some supplies we're running low on."

"Thanks, Pa," Jakob said and quickly downed the rest of his breakfast.

The sun was bright and warm. The overnight rain had made the air smell fresh and clean and had washed the dust away so that even the grass seemed greener and brighter. The apple tree beside the house had burst into full bloom, and Jakob inhaled deeply.

He made a quick stop in the outhouse while Wilhelm helped Pa hitch the horse to the wagon. Pa took hold of the reins, and Jakob climbed into the passenger side. Wilhelm, who had absolutely no interest in any May Day fun and was staying behind to do chores, waved them off. They rode in silence until they reached the bend in the road and his father pointed to the land across the pond. "All this once belonged to our family. There, from that wheat field all the way to the lake, and all the way across to the forest. That was all ours once."

Jakob stared across the expanse of wheat swaying in the breeze.

"It was bad times in Prussia when my great-grandpa Johann and great-grandma Magdalena came. They loaded four wagons with everything they owned, and the trip took ten months. But it was good times once they got here. The village was getting started, with farmsteads all around the town center. Great-Grandpa Johann claimed land along this road. Of course, in those days, the roads were nothing more than ruts in the grass. It was damn near all trees back then, all the way to the lake. The early farmers cleared the timber to where the forest now stands."

Jakob had to strain his eyes to see the trees to the west, and across, the large lake to the east.

"Your great-great-grandpa worked hard. He added more land, until he had quite a spread—built the town hall in 1808 from the money old Empress Catherine gave the village. They added on to it later . . . it was the biggest building in the area. And then things started going to hell."

His father slowed the wagon to let another pass, and the dust was so heavy they covered their eyes and mouths. "There was drought so bad some years you couldn't even grow a crop, but that never stopped the tax collectors," he continued when the dust settled. "They claimed our wheat for the tsar no matter how little there was. We had to sell land to stay alive. Us men were forced into the army, and the women were left to do the farm work. They didn't give a damn if we lived or died."

Pa turned the corner and stopped in front of the general store. Villagers had set up small tables along all four sides of the square and were selling whatever they had—fresh vegetables, meats, handicrafts, needlework, wood carvings, soaps, clothing, baked goods . . . anything that might be of use to someone else.

"I'm going to get us some salt, sugar, tobacco, and vodka," Pa said. "Those are the only things anyone needs to pay good money to a Russky for. The rest we got on the farm." Pa gestured dismissively at the basket-laden shoppers thronging about. "If a man can't live off his farm's produce, he may as well lie down and starve." Pa handed Jakob several rubles. "Here's some money. Go enjoy yourself, but be back here in one hour."

Children were swinging on a rope hung from the top of the Maypole. Some men were playing *garmoshkas*, their right-hand fingers running up and down the accordion-like keyboard while their left hand squeezed the bellows, their knees bouncing in time to the music. People were singing and dancing, while others were beating drums. One man's drum was made from a piece of cowhide stretched across an old wooden keg, and another had stretched cowhide across a wagon wheel rim. The drummers liked to start each song slowly and then gradually speed up, forcing the singers and *garmoshka* players to keep up, while the dancers went faster and faster around the Maypole, holding on to the strings and ribbons until at last everyone collapsed into a heap of laughter.

Jakob wandered into the crowd and spotted Irina. "Hello," he said, catching up to her. She spun around and smiled.

"How's Oxana?" he asked. Irina had told him all about the trip to Odesa and playing for some rich old lady, and that Oxana was now living with the old lady.

"She writes almost every day. She says she's happy, but I think she misses us."

"Is she coming home for the summer?"

"I think she'd like to, but Mama said she needs to stay and get as many lessons from her teachers as they are willing to give. Mama says coming home would be a big waste of time."

"Do you want a fizzy soda?" Jakob asked.

"I'd love one."

Irina and Jakob ambled to the end of one row of vendors, where an old spinster was selling glasses of seltzer water.

"Plain or flavor?" the old woman rasped.

"Want some cherry syrup stirred in?" Jakob asked. "I always have cherry."

"I love cherry."

"Flavor costs extra," the old woman barked.

"We'll take two cherry fizzy sodas," Jakob announced, trying to sound as if his pockets were full of cash.

The old woman handed over the glasses, and Jakob handed her the rubles Pa had given him, praying it was enough. They walked to a bench in front of the Orthodox church and sat.

"Do you miss Oxana?" Jakob asked. "It's odd, not seeing you two together all the time."

"Of course I miss her, but Mama says we can go and visit her once in a

while and maybe she can come home a few times, so I'll still get to see her."
It was obvious she was trying hard to sound cheerful, and Jakob reached
for Irina's hand. He held it for a moment, but when he squeezed it slightly
she pulled away and tucked both hands under her dress.

"I've never been to Odesa." Jakob slurped the cherry syrup from the
bottom of his glass.

"Me neither," Irina said. "Sometimes it feels like Oxana always gets to
do fun stuff, and all I get to do is stay home and work."

Irina handed him her glass. They stood and, after returning the two
glasses, began strolling through the crowd.

"Over there. It's her—Olga," Jakob whispered, pointing to an old hag
talking with two other babushkas. All three women were dressed in black
and had reputations as the town's most vicious gossips. "Let's see what
she's saying."

"Mama says we should never go near her. She's evil, like a Baba Yaga,
and they say she hunts at night for children to bake and eat."

"That's just a silly old fairy tale. Let's sneak up a little closer." They both
tiptoed until they heard her raspy voice. At first it was just the usual complaints and gossip, but then the conversation turned to Oxana.

"Old lady Stepaniaka must have a mighty heap of cash buried somewhere to send her all the way to Odesa," Olga was saying.

"I heard she stole the money," one of the other babushkas added.

"I heard that Oxana isn't going to play piano at all but is going down
there to be doing all sorts of favors for the menfolk," the third one said.

"Well, I know for certain," Olga replied, "that the devil's got something
to do with this."

"Let's touch her and see what happens," Jakob whispered. "Fedor says
you'll turn into a pillar of salt, like in the Bible, and Arkady says she's hot
as the devil and you'll burn your hand."

"Jakob, I think we should go and leave her alone."

"Aw, come on, Irina—let's have a little fun."

"I'll watch you. I'm not going near her."

Jakob crept up and grabbed a piece of Olga's dress. He tugged on it, and
the old hag spun around. "Be gone, vile scamps," she shouted. "A hex on
you all, you evil fiends."

Jakob and Irina ran away, laughing. They paused, completely out of breath, and Jakob noticed his father.

"I gotta go. Pa's waving to me. I liked talking with you."

"I did too," Irina said, "and thanks for the fizzy soda."

Jakob took a few steps but turned back and quickly kissed Irina on her cheek. "Tell Oxana good luck from me," he whispered and ran.

Pa was already seated in the wagon, and Jakob climbed in beside him. He steered the horses out of the square and onto the main road.

"Pa?" Jakob said softly. "I was wondering something . . ."

"What?" his father answered in a loud voice, to make himself heard above the noise of the hoofbeats.

Jakob cleared his throat and spoke up. "I was wondering if we might get a piano."

"A piano! What put that idea in your head? I suppose this has something to do with that Stepaniaka woman and you going to hear that guy at the church."

"I was thinking I might like to learn to play the piano, Pa. That's all."

"I'm not buying a piano, son. We got to be thinking of getting to America, and there's no use spending good money on something we're going to leave behind."

Jakob stared straight ahead, saying nothing.

"And I don't want you hanging around those Stepaniaka girls anymore."

"Why?"

"'Because they are putting foolish notions in your head, that's why. I don't want you having anything to do with them."

They rode the rest of the way without talking, until they pulled into the yard and his father muttered, "Your ma always wanted a piano too. I told her the same thing—no sense buying something we're going to leave behind, and here we are, fourteen years later and still in this stinking place."

"My ma wanted a piano?" Jakob suddenly sat up and turned to face his father. "Could she play?"

"No," Pa responded, "and this is the last I want to hear of any talk of pianos and piano playing." Pa climbed down and shouted for Wilhelm to come help unhitch the horse, but Jakob remained seated in the wagon a long while, staring, with his hands folded in his lap.

Chapter 9

Oxana sat at the small writing desk in front of the window in her bedroom. Vera had already retired for the night and the house was quiet. It seemed ironic how important silence was to musicians, and how much she had come to appreciate it. What a relief to finally listen to . . . nothing.

She had only been at the academy a few weeks but already understood how rigorous the program was going to be. First-year piano students were expected to learn all twenty-four Chopin etudes—some of the most difficult music ever written—as well as twenty-four preludes and fugues from Bach's Well-Tempered Clavier. Oxana had never played a Bach fugue and was surprised at how tricky they were. She had already been given a list of concertos to learn, as well as Beethoven sonatas and other pieces. She worried Vera would grow tired of listening to her practicing, but on the contrary, it seemed the more she practiced, the more Vera enjoyed it.

Oxana looked around her bedroom—the large bed with satin sheets, the window with satin drapery, and from the window, the view of the front grounds of Vera's estate. She still couldn't quite believe it was all real, and yet—

There was a light rap on her door. "Yes?" Oxana called out.

Xenia eased the door open and poked her head around it. "Can I come in?"

"Of course," Oxana said. "There's no need to knock. You're welcome to come in anytime."

"But Vera Fedorovna says a maid must always knock before entering a lady's bedroom."

"Xenia, don't think of me as a lady or you as a maid. We're friends. You are almost like a sister to me, and believe me, my sister would never even think of knocking before coming in."

Oxana had draped her dress across a chair, and Xenia picked it up to put it on a hanger and into the closet.

"Xenia, you don't have to be my maid all the time. Come sit here," Oxana said, patting the edge of the bed, "and we can talk."

"I enjoy listening to your piano practicing," Xenia said, sitting on the bed and smoothing out her skirt. "It makes the days seem short, and my work is easy when I can hear your music."

"Thank you, Xenia. I worry that maybe you and Vera will get tired of hearing me."

"I'll never get tired of hearing you. You play so beautifully."

"Maybe you would like to play?"

"Oh, no . . . well, maybe I would, but I'm sure I wouldn't be any good at it."

"How do you know until you try? I could teach you."

"I would love that, but I don't think Vera Fedorovna would look too kindly on it."

"Why not? She loves piano music."

"Playing the piano is not for a maid to be doing. It's not proper."

"Xenia, you are not only a maid. Why wouldn't it be proper for you to learn to play the piano?"

"It's just that we all have a job to do and we need to know our place in the world. That's what my father always told me: Know your place in the world. It's not for maids to sit around playing the piano. I'd best be going. It's getting late and I still have the dishes to wash and one of Vera Fedorovna's dresses to iron before I leave."

"Thank you for stopping in," Oxana said as Xenia tiptoed to the door. "And," as Xenia eased the door shut, "thank you for being my friend."

The door closed so gently Oxana did not even hear the latch click. She sat at her desk a moment before picking up her pen.

Dear Irina,

I hope you like getting my letters as much as I like getting yours! I love being here. I really like my teachers. I'm learning so much, and Vera is so kind. Every morning, she calls for the horseman and he drives me to school in her carriage, which is pulled by two identical white horses. I feel silly because almost no one goes by horse and carriage anymore, but Vera refuses to ride in automobiles. She says they are not dignified enough.

She also insists that we "dress for dinner," so every evening we both go to our rooms to put on our fancy dresses. It doesn't take me too long to choose one, since I don't have that many, but I know Mama will be sewing more for me. I don't know how many dresses Vera has, but I've never seen her wearing the same one twice, so I suppose quite a few! When I'm dressed, I wait at the top of the stairs until Vera emerges from her boudoir (she says that's what a fancy lady's bedroom is called in French). Then I take her arm and we slowly descend the wide grand staircase.

Dima, one of her footmen, helps us with our chairs. (Vera explained to me that footmen are the servants who help with serving dinner.) She has two footmen so that when one has a day off, we are not left to fend for ourselves! I don't know what she would do if she had to push her own chair up to the table!! (That's a joke, Irina, so you better be laughing!)

The dining table is laid out with more silver and china than I even knew existed, and I had to learn how to eat properly. Xenia explained it all to me, and I will show you how when you come with Mama. It's all a bit silly, but I'll warn you, if you start laughing during dinner, I'll kick you under the table to make you be quiet.

I know I'm making all this sound like a great deal of fun, and it is, but I really miss you and Mama. I'm happy I'm here and I'm glad for this opportunity, but still I can't help feeling like I'm missing out on a lot back home.

Love,
Oxana

Chapter 10

Summer proved hotter than usual, and early one morning, with the sun barely above the horizon and both the temperature and humidity on the rise, Jakob stood at the stove, frying eggs and sausage for breakfast.

His father was staring out the window. "Goddamn it," he suddenly shouted and ran out the door. "Rostov's cow is on the loose again and heading toward the field," he yelled to Wilhelm, who was coming out of the barn with a pail of milk. Jakob stood in the doorway watching his father making his way across the pasture, waving his arms and yelling. His movements were clumsy, and he bobbed from side to side, his knees stiff and unable to bend properly. Wilhelm quickly put the milk pail inside the front door and followed behind.

Before long, breakfast was ready, and Jakob pulled the frying pan away from the heat. He wondered what was taking so long—Wilhelm wouldn't like it if the eggs were dry, and Pa wouldn't like it if they were cold. He heard Wilhelm shouting and went to the door.

"Jakob! Come help! It's Pa," Wilhelm was yelling, running toward the barn.

"What is it?" Jakob called out as he stepped outside the door. Wilhelm stopped and pointed toward the field but said nothing, as if searching for words but unable to formulate a sentence. "What's happened?" Jakob again called across the farmyard. "Where's Pa?"

"I think he's dead!" Wilhelm yelled. His voice was quivering, and his arms were twitching. "Just fell down. I thought he tripped, but when I got to him, he wasn't breathing. His heart must have given out. I tried to lift him, but I couldn't move him by myself. You've got to come help me."

Wilhelm disappeared into the barn and a moment later emerged with the sled Jakob used to haul manure. He kicked at the box nailed to the sled, and it went flying. "Maybe we can get him on this and pull him home."

Jakob stood frozen. Pa dead? Had he heard Wilhelm correctly? People don't just die without first getting sick.

"Come on, Jakob. We've got to get going. Pa's lying out in the field."

They sprinted past the barn and across the pasture. Jakob saw his father up ahead, lying on the ground. He had never seen a dead person before, and his heart was pounding in his chest.

"We've got to get him back home," Wilhelm said, gasping for air. Jakob began to whimper, struggling to hold back tears. Wilhelm put his arm around Jakob's shoulder and patted him on the back. "Let's try to lift him." Wilhelm took hold of Pa's arms, and Jakob grabbed his legs. Their father weighed nearly a hundred kilos, and they could barely hoist the body high enough to get it on the sled.

Both boys stood a few moments, and Jakob stared at the gruesomeness of his father lying on his back, his feet and arms hanging off the sides of the sled, his eyes staring at the sky and his mouth open, like he was begging for water. Jakob reached down, his hand trembling, to close his father's eyes.

They each took hold of one of the sled's ropes. It was hard to get started, but once they were moving, the sled was easier to pull. They went only a short distance when the sled hit a furrow and dipped. Pa's body rolled off, face down in the dirt, and suddenly a wet stain appeared on the seat of his pants. The corpse had emptied its bowels. The stench was overwhelming. Jakob's stomach clenched.

"Goddamn," Wilhelm said, wiping the sweat from his brow. "Pa's crapped his pants. I didn't know that could happen." Jakob retched, dropping to his hands and knees and spewing the contents of his stomach onto the ground. "Holy Christ," Wilhelm said. "You okay?" Wilhelm knelt and patted him on the back while Jakob heaved several more times, his empty stomach spewing bitter bile.

"Don't cry, little brother," Wilhelm whispered, continuing to gently rub his back. "It's going to be alright." Jakob wiped his mouth on his shirt-sleeve, and they hoisted the corpse back onto the sled.

"It'll be better if we go slower," Wilhelm said, as if trying to reassure himself, and they again set off across the pasture. A light breeze stirred the air, which was not only a refreshing relief from the heat but also wafted the stench away. The sled caught several more times in the ruts, but they were careful to keep it from tipping.

The brothers slowly made their way back to the farmyard with neither saying a word. The light breeze dissipated almost as quickly as it arose, and the hot sun was more oppressive than ever. Pulling the sled's runners across the sun-dried soil had taken every bit of strength they had, and Jakob and his brother were soaked with sweat, gasping for air and needing water by the time they slowly pulled the sled into the farmyard and up to the front door.

"What do we do now?" Jakob asked, staring at the ashen, lifeless face.

Wilhelm put his arm around his shoulder. "Don't know. Never thought about anything like this."

"Maybe we should try to get him in the house and lay him out on his bed?" Jakob whispered.

"Don't know," Wilhelm repeated.

"We should go get Father Vanska. He can tell us what we're supposed to do and help us plan a funeral."

"Jakob, there isn't time for laying him out or any of that funeral stuff. We should go ahead and bury him right now. The wheat's ripe and ready for harvesting—what little's left after that spring storm, and now Rostov's cow. If we lose any more, there won't be enough to get us through the winter. We need to get on with cutting the grain."

"But Pa's got to have a funeral so people can come and say goodbye," Jakob pleaded. "It wouldn't be right to bury him without a service."

"Jakob," Wilhelm raised his voice. "Funerals are nothing but a bunch of people sitting around pretending to be sad while they wait for the free lunch afterward. We don't have time for sitting around staring at a dead person. There's spare wood in the barn—I can nail together a coffin and get to digging a grave while you go into town and fetch Father Vanska."

"But he's our father. We need to show him respect and give him—"

"Jakob," Wilhelm said, his voice suddenly more firm and resolute, almost cold sounding, "we're burying Pa now because that's what he would want. It's what he did to her. You didn't live through it, but I did, and I've had to live with it every day since. I was only four, but I remember every second." Wilhelm's face was red, and Jakob had never seen him so agitated. He was pacing in a circle while words spewed out, like water once a dam has burst. "Ma was in her bed in the lean-to, where you sleep, and Pa and I were in the main room. She had been screaming from early morning. Frau Domitovich was trying to help, but the baby—you—wouldn't come out. I'd never heard anyone scream so loud. I stood, listening to that horrible yelling, while Pa paced the room like a wild animal trying to break free. Finally, he told me to go outside. I stood by the door. He and Frau Domitovich were talking, and she was sobbing. He came out the door and took off for town, running. I stood there. Not moving. Waiting. Pa came back with Elena Vladimirovna Stepaniaka—yes, her, the mother of those twins you're so in love with. Pa and Frau Stepaniaka went right past me, into the house, and I waited outside. And then the screaming stopped. Pa came out and headed straight for the barn. I opened the front door and peeked in. Both women were crying, and Frau Domitovich was trying to clean up the bedding—red . . . dripping with blood."

Wilhelm paused to catch his breath. "Elena was holding you, and now you were the one screaming. She was trying to calm you down, but you kept on yelling at the top of your lungs. Pa came out of the barn and went back in the house. He went right past me and didn't say a thing. He was wild, crazy, out of his mind, yelling that he couldn't stand to see her anymore, that she had to be buried now. Frau Domitovich ran out the door, toward town, and Pa grabbed a shovel and started digging, right over there." Wilhelm pointed to the apple tree beside the house. He was sweating, and his shoulders and arms were shaking.

"But Pa said Ma is buried in town, in the cemetery. He even showed me her grave," Jakob whispered.

"That ain't Ma's grave. That's her cousin's. They had the same name, Amelia, and they were about the same age."

"You mean our mother is buried here? But why did Pa tell me that was her grave?"

"Maybe he didn't want you pining away, being all sad. You were always asking questions, and Pa didn't want to answer. He wanted you to shut up. So now you know. She's right here, under this apple tree, and that's where we're burying Pa."

"Then what happened?" Jakob stammered.

"See. There you go, always asking your damn questions. Well, I'll tell you what happened next. Pa dug so fast that, by the time Frau Domitovich came back with Father Vanska, the grave was ready. Vanska tried to stop him, told him to put the shovel down, that it wasn't Christian to bury a warm body, but Pa ignored him and went back inside. I was still standing by the door and could see everything. You had quieted down, and Elena Vladimirovna laid you on the table. Her hands were shaking and she didn't say anything, just did what Pa told her, and together they carried her out. They carried our Ma right past me. She was wrapped in one of the sheets . . . still dripping blood . . . limp . . . legs and arms hanging down, almost scraping the ground. There wasn't even a coffin. Father Vanska prayed while Pa shoveled the dirt over her."

Wilhelm took off his shirt and wiped his head. His undershirt was soaked with sweat. He went over to the well and lowered the pail, pulled it back up, and took a long drink before bending over and pouring the rest of the cold water on his head.

"When he had the grave covered," Wilhelm continued, more slowly and softer, "Pa went back into the barn and slammed the door shut. No one dared go near him. Elena Vladimirovna took both of us to her house. Her twins were newborn and she had enough milk to feed you too. But I didn't stay. I told her, 'Thank you, ma'am, but my place is at home with Pa,' and I went back home. No one stopped me. I was already a big kid, even if I was only four, and I'd have put up a fight if anyone had tried to stop me. Pa stayed in the barn for two days, not coming out to eat or anything, just sat in the barn, and I was in the house, alone, for those two days. Then the door opened, and he came into the house but didn't say a thing, only looked at me and shook his head. He gathered up all her stuff—clothes, pictures, furniture, doilies, blankets, curtains, everything that reminded him of her—carried it all out back and threw it into a big pile, never saying one word. When he had everything on that pile, he lit it and it burned to ashes. I never saw a tear, and he never said a word; he just stood there until it was all burned. I may have been little, but that day I knew Pa would be hurting for the rest of his life."

"What about me?" Jakob whispered. "Who took care of me?"

"Who do you think? Elena Vladimirovna, that's who. She raised you for nearly two years. You and those twins were like brother and sisters. They would come visit and bring you to see us. And then one day, Pa brought you home, and from then on, we raised you, me and Pa. So now you know the whole story. You can stop asking questions. Pa would want to be buried the same way as he buried our mother. We're doing it now, so go fetch Father Vanska. Hurry up!"

Jakob ran out of the yard and down the main road into town. "Father Vanska, Father Vanska!" he called as he neared the church, panting, with sweat streaming down his face.

Father Vanska came around the side of the church. "What is it, my boy, that's got you so worked up?"

"It's Pa," Jakob shouted between gasps. "He's died. Wilhelm is wanting to bury him today—now. You gotta come."

"Holy Mother of God," Father Vanska whispered. "Yes, yes, let's go."

Father Vanska followed Jakob down the road. He tried to run but soon was completely out of breath. "Slow down, my boy, or you'll give this old man a heart attack."

Jakob paused to allow him to catch up. "I told Wilhelm it's not right, but he won't listen to me." Jakob was speaking so fast he struggled for air. "He says it's what my father did to my mother, and we have to do it the same way." Jakob covered his face with his hands to hide his tears.

"Don't worry, son. Let's keep going." They hurried along the road, Jakob running ahead of Father Vanska and then waiting for him to catch up, until they rounded the last bend and entered the farmyard.

Wilhelm was standing beside the grave, leaning on his shovel.

"This isn't proper," Father Vanska said. "You can't atone for one sin by committing another."

Wilhelm let the shovel fall to the ground and stood with his legs spread, ready for a fight. "We're doing it the way he would want."

"That is probably true," Father Vanska said, "but it doesn't make it right."

"Nor does it make it wrong, Father."

Wilhelm's makeshift coffin was sitting beside the hole, under the shade of the apple tree.

"Come and help me, Jakob," Wilhelm said in a firm, loud voice.

"It's okay, son, help your brother," Father Vanska said, lifting his hand in the air and making the sign of the cross. Jakob and Wilhelm bent over and hoisted their father's body into the coffin.

"This is where she is." Wilhelm pointed to a spot on the ground to the left of the tree trunk. "Right here."

"Yes," Father Vanska quietly responded. "I remember it only too well—a terrible, sad day. Now they can lie together."

They stood beside the coffin and made the sign of the cross three times across their chests. Wilhelm, and then Jakob, bent over and kissed their father's lips, in the old Russian tradition, before Wilhelm placed the top on the casket and nailed it shut.

"We'll need to use these," Wilhelm said, handing the ends of two rough hemp hay ropes to Jakob. They slipped the ropes under the casket, one rope near the head and the other near the foot. It was a strain to lift the coffin even a few inches off the ground while keeping it from tipping over. They hoisted it over the grave and slowly uncoiled the ropes until the coffin lay at the bottom.

The sun was setting, and a cool breeze was now blowing. Father Vanska began to intone, "Our Father, who art in heaven . . ."

Jakob stared at the hole in the ground, thinking, *What father in heaven—some old man who never shows himself?* And where was heaven? His father was here. In the ground. Dead.

"Hallowed be Thy name . . ."

Hallowed be *her* name—Amelia. The name Pa never spoke.

". . . Thy will be done, on earth as it is in heaven."

Except that it was always your will, Pa, that was done, and no one else's.

". . . and forgive us our trespasses as we forgive those who trespass against us."

He had so desperately needed his father's forgiveness. If only they could have talked about it. *Why wouldn't you talk about her? I'm sorry she died giving birth to me. Why couldn't you forgive me?*

A light rain began to fall, and Jakob wept, the rain combining with the tears streaming down his cheeks.

"And lead us not into temptation," Father Vanska concluded, "for thine is the kingdom, the power, and the glory, forever and ever. Amen."

I forgive you, Pa. I forgive you. Can you please forgive me?

The rain was getting heavier, and they hurriedly shoveled the dirt before it turned into mud.

That evening, Jakob and his brother sat in silence. It was odd not having Pa in the room, and Wilhelm kept glancing toward the door, as if expecting him to come in from his chores.

"Suppose everything's up to us now," Wilhelm finally said, pointing to the small chest of drawers where their father kept his papers. Pa kept the chest locked, but both boys knew the key was on the ledge above the doorframe. Wilhelm inserted the key and turned the lock. Jakob's father had never opened any of the drawers while he and Wilhelm were in the room, and they would never have dared open the chest on their own. The top drawer was filled with old letters. "They're all from our mother and postmarked either '04 or '05," Wilhelm said, shuffling through them. "She must've written him when he was in the army."

"Wonder why he saved them?" Jakob asked, staring at the bundle. "Maybe he wanted us to read them someday?"

"Well, I'm not reading them. All this has been dead and gone long ago." Wilhelm stuffed the letters back into the drawer and opened the second one. It, too, was full of papers, mostly about the farm. "Suppose we need to be hanging on to these, in case there's ever any questions." Wilhelm replaced the papers. He opened the bottom drawer and pulled out a large tin cash box. He opened it and gasped. "There's got to be three or four thousand rubles here," he said, lifting the neatly stacked bundles out. "Pa always said he was saving to go to America. Guess this must be it." At the bottom, underneath the money, was an envelope. "It's got your name on it," he said, handing it to Jakob. "Wonder what it says?"

Jakob turned the envelope over in his hands. The handwriting was neat and the paper was crisp and clean. "Probably nothing important. I'll read it later." He stuffed it in his pocket. He couldn't imagine why Pa would write him a letter, or what it might say, or why it was some secret Pa had hidden in his cash box, but he definitely knew he didn't want to read it with Wilhelm staring at him.

"Suit yourself." Wilhelm put the rubles back in the tin box. "So that's that." He closed the drawer, locked the cabinet, and put the key back on the door ledge. They sat for a long while. The sun had set and the room was almost entirely dark, but neither of them lit the kerosene lamp on the table.

"Pa had a tough life, but he was a good man," Wilhelm said, lighting one of Pa's cigars. The smoke wafted across the room. "You can't blame someone for becoming cold and hard when they went through what he did." Wilhelm's face was lit by the dim glow of the cigar, and Jakob noticed, for the first time, how much Wilhelm resembled their father. "I'll miss him," Wilhelm whispered.

Jakob rose from his chair and went into the lean-to. He lay on his bed, without undressing, and pulled Pa's envelope out of his pocket. It contained a letter and a small wadded-up package. He undid the wrapping. Inside was a gold ring. He unfolded the letter:

Dear Jakob—

Guess if you're reading this, I'm either dead or it's your wedding day, which is when I plan to give this to you. It's your mama's wedding ring.

You have no idea how much like your mother you are. You're a spitting image of her, and every day when I look at you it kills me. It was terrible to see her going out of this world while you were coming in. But it's more than looks. You talk like her and think like her. You see and love all the beautiful things, like she did, and you're gentle and kind, like she was. But Jakob, I want you to know I don't hold her death against you. It wasn't anybody's fault. It was damn, rotten luck.

I've been hard on you. I hope you can forgive me. I only wanted to toughen you up. If she'd been tougher maybe she would have come through the birthing and lived. I want you to live and not die like she did, and in this world you got to be tough if you're going to make it.

I'm giving you her ring. I want you to give it to the
woman you love, and I hope you'll love her as much as I
loved your mama.

You're a good boy, Jakob. God bless you—
Your Pa

Jakob lay for a long while, clutching the letter and ring, listening
to the silence, and reliving the horrible images of his mother's suffering and death that Wilhelm had described. As he was drawing his first
breaths, she was being carried, lifeless and bloodied, to her grave. He
thought of his father and the gruesome image of his strong, muscular
body lying helpless on a sled, being pulled home. Both were now resting
a few feet away from each other, under the shade of the apple tree, and
he felt a peace he had never known before—an acceptance that he would
never know his mother, never see her, never hear her voice, and also an
acceptance that the only way Pa could deal with his suffering was to lock
himself inside a rock-hard shell, closed off from the world.

Jakob thought of the concert at the church and the last piece the old
pianist played. Fantasy, Oxana said it was called. He thought of the fantasy he had seen—the Firebird—while listening to the beautiful music. It
didn't matter if the Firebird was real or imagined. He finally understood
that he was not responsible for his mother's death, nor for his father's grief.
Life moved in a circle, like a wheel, and with each revolution, change was
possible—forgiveness and redemption, too. In a few years, he might be a
father. He would give to his sons the love his father had withheld from him,
and his wife would be to his children the mother he never had. His family
would not live in the shadow of death, as he had been forced to, but would
live in the sunshine of life.

"I love you, Pa," he whispered and kissed the letter. "I love you, Ma,"
he whispered, carefully slipping the ring and letter back into the envelope and placing it beside the music book hidden inside his mattress.
He drifted off to sleep just as the sun was beginning to rise above the
eastern horizon.

Chapter 11

Dear Irina,

Something really terrible happened today and I was so scared I'm still shaking. I want to tell you about it, but I don't think you should tell Mama. It might make her worry, and I'm safe, so she doesn't need to.

Vera and I were shopping along Primorsky Boulevard when we saw a small parade of people, men mostly, coming toward us, carrying signs and shouting slogans against the Bolsheviks. All of a sudden, soldiers came around a corner and started shooting. Everyone took off running and some fell.

Vera and I and some other people near us ducked into a shop. The shopkeeper locked the door as soon as we were inside and pulled the blinds so no one could see into the store. We waited until the street was quiet before the shopkeeper opened the door. The soldiers were gone, but there were dead bodies everywhere. Some of the people on the sidewalk looked like they had been trampled on, and about half the marchers were lying right in the street. There was blood everywhere.

Irina, I've never seen a dead person before, and it was really upsetting. Vera said I should avert my gaze, but I couldn't help but stare. I didn't cry. Maybe I should have, but I didn't know who any of the people were. I just felt shocked at the horror of it. The soldiers didn't even try to arrest anyone, they just shot at them with no warning. We had to wait a long time before Vera's coachman could get through the street to pick us up and, of course, we went straight home.

Vera says I must never go out alone, but I never do anyway. I always have either her coachman or a butler with me.

I don't know what is going to happen next. Vera says there has been unrest ever since last winter when the Bolshevik army entered the city. I'm glad I wasn't here then. Vera said there was lots of fighting in the streets, and she never went outside the entire time there was shooting. Vera hates the Bolsheviks. She said that after the tsar abdicated, she was certain we would have peace, but now the Bolsheviks seem even more brutal than the Tsar's army was. There are also rumors that grain has been confiscated and that people in the country are starving.

At least you and Mama are safe. I thank God that nothing like this will ever happen in Peterstal. Remember how I used to laugh and say that the farmers seemed to find happiness going through every day, knowing that tomorrow will be exactly like yesterday. But now I'm glad Peterstal is so small and poor and unimportant.

Please don't worry about me. I'm going to focus on my piano practicing and my studies at school.

Love,
Oxana

Chapter 12

Jakob pulled his music book out of his mattress, wrapped it in a kitchen towel, tucked it inside his shirt, and stepped outside. The summer's heat was finally relenting and soon school would be starting. He went around to the side of the house where his mother had once grown a flower garden. Most of the flowers had disappeared long ago, choked out by weeds, but there was still one rosebush up against the house. He snapped off a perfectly shaped bud on the verge of opening. A thorn stuck his thumb, and he wiped the blood on his pant leg before heading out the front gate and slowly down the main road, clutching the rose in one hand while holding his music book inside his shirt with the other.

"For you, Frau Stepaniaka," Jakob said, handing her the yellow rose when she opened the door. His shirt was sweaty and clinging to his chest, and his thumb was still bleeding. He brushed it on his pant leg, hoping she wouldn't notice.

"Ah, Jakob Schweitz," Elena said.

Jakob pulled the music book out of his shirt, unfolded the towel, and showed it to her. "Do you think you can teach me to play this?"

She took the book in her hands. "It's Chopin's Fantasy."

"Yes. After the old pianist played it and then Oxana played it for me, I ordered this from the music store. I know I won't ever play it as well as Oxana does, but I really want to learn it. Will you teach me?"

"My dear boy, you must study many years, and even then, you can only play this music if you have a God-given talent."

"But I want to learn."

"Well, how well do you play?"

"What?"

"How well do you play? What pieces do you currently know? That will give me an idea of how much you need to learn."

"I don't know any pieces," Jakob whispered.

"You don't know *any*? Surely you must play something, even if only by ear."

"I can't play anything, and, um . . . what is playing by ear?"

"It's playing what you hear, without reading the music. You must at least be able to pick out a few tunes on your piano?"

"I don't know how to read music, and . . . I don't have a piano."

"Well, I'm not surprised to hear your father never bought a piano. Parting with even one ruble was always a hard thing for him. But Jakob, if you don't have a piano, don't know how to play or how to read music, and can't even play by ear, how can you possibly expect to learn this piece?" she said, handing the book back to him.

"But I really do want to learn," he mumbled. "I'll work hard."

"Well, come in," Elena said, stepping aside. "I can at least show you how to begin."

She motioned Jakob to the piano bench. He sat down, and she demonstrated the most basic elements of piano playing—how to use the two black keys to locate all the Cs, and how to play a five-finger pattern in both hands. Then she drew the notes on a sheet of paper to show him how they correspond to the piano keys. "This will at least get you started."

"Jakob," she said, when he stood to leave, "I was sorry to hear about the loss of your father. I knew both your mother and father quite well. Your mother was a friend of mine."

His lower lip quivered. "I know what you did for me," he said quietly, "how you took me in when I was born and fed me and cared for me. Wilhelm told me. I want to thank you for doing that. That was real nice of you."

"Jakob, your mother was not only my friend—she was my best friend. She loved piano music, and when she came to visit she would ask me to play for her. I can see she passed that love of music on to you. That makes me happy, and I'm sure it would please her too."

Jakob turned away from her, wiped his eyes with his shirtsleeve, and blew his nose into his handkerchief. "You were a sweet baby, Jakob. You never cried, and you and my twins got along beautifully, until the day your father came to get you. He walked into this room, right past me without saying a word, picked you up out of the bed, wrapped you in your blanket, and took you home. He could be as hard as a stone when he set his mind to something."

"I'm sorry for how my pa acted. He went through hard times."

"But he wasn't always like that. He was a lot of fun when he was young. He and your mother were married about the same time as me and my husband, and the four of us spent time together. Oh, I remember how your parents really kicked up a storm when we went to barn dances."

Jakob again wiped his eyes and blew his nose.

"It was only a short while after your mother died that I lost my husband. I always admired your father, handsome and hardworking, and I figured, my girls needed a father—and God knows, you boys needed a woman's touch in your lives. I called on him one afternoon, but when I suggested we might get together, and, you know, maybe form a family one day, he became angry. I guess he was still grieving your mother and not ready to think of those kinds of things. He told me to leave and never come back. Well, you can be sure I got out of there as fast as I could. And that was the end of our friendship. He never spoke to me again. I was sorry about that. And I was sorry I couldn't do more for you boys."

Jakob turned to go and was surprised to see Irina in the doorway. "I didn't know you were here," he said.

"I finished in the garden," Irina replied and began to cry.

"Irina, what's wrong?" her mother asked.

"I heard what you were talking about. Jakob lived with us. He's practically our brother. Why didn't you tell us, Mama? Why didn't you tell us?"

"I didn't think it mattered. It was so long ago—you were only babies."

"But still, you wanted to *marry* his father, and then he really would have been our brother. How could you not tell us?" Irina ran out the front door and slammed it behind her.

"I should be going now," Jakob whispered.

"Yes, we can be done for today. I hope I haven't said too much. I thought you should know the whole story. But come at this time each week and we can spend a half hour on a lesson. I'll sort through Oxana's earliest pieces and find something for you to learn—then you can spend an hour practicing before you go back home. And don't worry about Irina. She's upset, but nobody has done anything to be ashamed of. She'll come around once she's had time to think about it."

Chapter 13

Dear Irina,

I was shocked when I read your letter. I am writing right away to tell you I agree with everything you said about being angry with Mama. But I don't agree with you saying you are going to stop seeing Jakob and have nothing more to do with him. Irina, think about it! Even if Jakob lived with us as babies, he's not our brother. It was a nice thing for Mama to take in a baby who had no mother. There is absolutely nothing wrong with the feelings you're having for Jakob. You and he should spend time together and keep going for walks so you can get to know each other better.

Since I've been here, I've started to see things differently. Sometimes people are lonely, and no one should be alone. I'm sure Mama has been lonely not having Papa, and maybe Jakob's father was lonely not having his wife. I think even rich old Vera is lonely. That's why she likes having me around.

I'm sometimes lonely too, and when I'm really missing you and Mama I cry at night before I go to sleep. One night, Xenia, Vera's maid, came in to see what was wrong. When I told her, she said that she cries at night too, because she misses her mother and sister. Xenia told me her parents were Russian, but they lived in a small town in France, and during the war their house was bombed. Both her parents and her sister were killed. She said she was sent to an orphanage until they figured out how to contact her aunt who lived here in Odesa. Xenia was sent here on a train from France, all alone when she was only ten years old! Her aunt died, so now she works for Vera and lives all by herself, even though she is only our age. So now Xenia and I are friends, and I'm not so lonely anymore. And besides, the piano is also my friend, but of course you will always be my best friend. Irina, I hope you listen to me!! I am technically your older sister, since Mama says I was born first!!

Love,
Oxana

Part 2

Love and Loss

Peterstal, Ukraine
1924

Chapter 14

Leaning forward in her train seat, Oxana stared out the window, watching the wheat fields passing by. It had now been four years since she had gone to study in Odesa. *Four years.* It felt like a lifetime. Her thoughts turned to the recital she was to play that evening at the Lutheran church. Her mother was calling it her special graduation celebration, but Oxana was sure what she really wanted was to show her off. It seemed sort of dumb to want to impress a tiny village of peasants who didn't know anything about music. There was just so much jealousy and gossip in Peterstal. She was glad she didn't live there anymore.

Graduation—Oxana repeated the word in her mind several times—*and then what?* She had worked hard, and everyone was saying she was the best pianist at the academy and that she needed to go to the Moscow Conservatory. Maybe, once there, she could play a debut concert, and if she got a good review maybe an agent might be willing to represent her, or maybe a teacher would recommend her to a conductor and she could start her career.

"Next stop, Peterstal, fifteen minutes," the conductor announced. Oxana pushed her nose against the window and exhaled a puff of air. The window fogged over, and she drew several random shapes. *How exciting Moscow must be,* she thought, *like Odesa only ten times better.* Odesa had seemed so crowded and noisy when she first arrived, but Vera showed her how wonderful life in a city can be—concerts, elegant restaurants, expensive shops—and of course Vera always paid. *Vera Fedorovna—I owe her everything. She taught me how to live. I only wish Irina could've done it all with me.*

Wiping the window clean with the sleeve of her dress, Oxana leaned back in her seat. It was obvious from Irina's letters that a marriage proposal was imminent. Irina seemed so happy with Jakob, but marriage was a big step. They would probably live their entire lives in Peterstal, Jakob a farmer and Irina a housewife. Oxana sighed and leaned sideways to adjust her dress, trying to get comfortable in the hard unupholstered seat. *I'm not saying don't marry him, just maybe wait a while and do something with your life first?*

Before the locomotive even came to a complete stop, Oxana pushed the carriage door open and jumped onto the platform. Her mother and Irina ran toward her, and the three of them hugged and kissed, hugged some more, and somehow even managed to cry and laugh at the same time.

"Here, let me carry that." Her mother took hold of Oxana's small suitcase. "You don't want to strain your hands."

"Still the same dusty old town," Oxana said as they stepped off the station's wooden platform and onto the dirt street.

"What did you expect?" Irina replied. "That we would become another Odesa?"

"Irina, I only meant that maybe something would change. Don't you want a new store so you can buy hats or shoes, or one of those brand-new ready-made dresses, instead of always having to sew your own?"

"How will I make money," her mother replied, "if everyone starts buying ready-made dresses?"

"Mama, women will always want your dresses," Oxana said. "They're the best."

"There's lots of new things," Irina said. "We have a doctor. His office is where the old cobbler used to be. And some of the buildings have those new electric lights. You pull a cord and the bulb lights up. And, best of all, they installed a telephone in the general store. Some days, people are even standing in line to make calls."

"You can call me," Oxana said. "Vera had a telephone installed in her house and I've heard her talking on it. I'm sure she wouldn't mind if you called me."

"I will mind," their mother interrupted. "You pay for every minute, and once you girls get to talking, I'll go broke in no time. But enough chattering. We'd better hurry so we can start getting ready. Oxana, I hope you brought the blue dress I sent you. I was planning it for tonight."

"Don't worry, Mama, I have a very nice dress. I think you will really like it."

"Please don't tell me you tried sewing a dress on your own."

"Wait and see, Mama. It will be a surprise."

———

Oxana went to the church early to warm up while Irina and her mother stayed home to finish getting ready. She was curious if the piano had, by some miracle, improved, but when she played a chord, she winced. *Same out-of-tune clunker it's always been, but if that old pianist could manage, I can too.*

Father Vanska had turned his vestry over to Oxana. After changing into her concert dress, she opened the door enough to peek through a crack. A jolt of adrenaline coursed through her veins. Every seat was taken—even the extra chairs along the rear and side walls—and she was eager to play for them. The crowd quieted as Irina, in a white dress, and her mother, elegant in a navy blue dress with her hair braided and coiled around her head, made their way to the seats Oxana had reserved for them in the front pew.

Jakob came bounding down the aisle, sat beside Irina, and kissed her cheek. Oxana had not seen him since she had left for Odesa and hardly believed the transformation—from a gangly fourteen-year-old boy to an eighteen-year-old man. He had to be over six feet tall, with blond shoulder-length hair combed back to reveal his high, square forehead, an unmistakable trait of his German ancestry. His blue eyes sparkled against his traditional white tunic with red embroidery—*probably Mama sewed it for him. He looks like a medieval Cossack warrior out of a fairy tale, just off his horse and about to sweep some lady off her feet.*

Oxana pushed the door open and stepped into the sanctuary. In a rush of energy, the audience jumped to their feet and clapped wildly; some even whistled and shouted. She was wearing a sleeveless, low-cut, red satin dress, floor-length but with a slit up one side so that her legs were visible up to her knee. Vera said she looked beautiful in it, and she had to confess, she felt very pretty when she wore it.

Her heart gave a little flutter, however, when, while bowing, she glanced at her mother and saw she was scowling and leaning over, whispering in Irina's ear. *I knew it . . . she doesn't like the dress.*

Oxana steadied herself, made a second deep bow, and proceeded slowly toward the old upright piano. She sat on the bench and, out of the corner of her eye, noticed a woman in the back row, off to the side. Her head was wrapped in a black scarf, pulled down so low her face was hidden, as if she were nothing more than a shadow. It was *her*—Olga. What was *she* doing here? Oxana shifted her eyes back to the piano. *Stay focused,* she told herself. She lifted her head, placed her hands on the keyboard, and filled the small church with sound.

The concert lasted well over an hour, and prior to playing her final piece, Oxana stood and motioned for silence. The clapping subsided and she stood gazing for a moment. She was among the people she had grown up knowing, yet she felt, somewhat strangely, like an outsider, as if she no longer was one of them. "Ladies and gentlemen," she addressed the audience, "I thank each and every one of you for coming tonight. It is a long journey from the discovery of middle C to the performance of Beethoven's great C Major *Waldstein* Sonata, which I played for you. All along the way, I've had tremendous support and encouragement from many of you, but none more so than from my dear mother and sister." Oxana pointed to Irina and her mother, and the audience shouted and whistled. "In tribute to them," Oxana continued, "I would like to close with a piece that is not only my favorite, but theirs as well—Fantasy in F Minor, by Chopin."

The moment she played the opening notes, a silence fell over the audience so complete it was as if they were no longer there, and Oxana played with the ease and freedom she had come to understand was a special gift granted to very few performers. Unlike so many of her friends at the music academy, she was at her best when playing for an audience.

The moment she sounded the final chords, the silence was broken by a roar of applause. Ludmilla and Slava Domitovich, sitting in the front pew next to Irina and her mother, rushed over to shake Oxana's hand and congratulate her.

Fedor Rostov, with his mother, Naydia, and his two little sisters, stepped up behind them. "I loved your concert," Fedor said. "I confess I don't really know anything about music, but I loved it. I knew I would. You've always been the best, Oxana. The best." His black hair was still curly but much longer now, and he had a full beard, which made him surprisingly handsome. Fedor held out his right hand, and as she shook it, he gently pressed his left palm against her lower back. *Not much has changed; still the same old Fedor.* "By the way, you look—" he started to say when another young man stepped in front of him.

"Congratulations, Oxana," the man said. "We've not met, so allow me to introduce myself. I'm Ilya, the new doctor here in Peterstal."

"Nice to meet you," Oxana said, extending her hand and shaking his.

"Your playing was—" Ilya started to say.

"I was just telling Oxana how much I enjoyed her concert," Fedor interrupted.

"Do you two know each other?" Oxana asked.

"No, I don't believe I've had the pleasure of meeting you," Ilya said, extending his hand to Fedor.

"I've seen you around. New faces tend to attract attention," Fedor said without extending his hand, and Ilya slipped his outstretched arm back against his side.

"It will be a long while before this town hears another like you, Oxana," Ilya said, "unless of course you are willing to play for us again."

"She would love to play again, wouldn't you?" Fedor said, his palm still against her lower back.

"I'm not sure I will be able to," Oxana replied. "I'm soon to graduate, and beyond that, my plans have not yet been finalized."

"You'll want to come back here and spend time with your family, and it sure would be nice for you and I to get reacquainted. It's been a long time since I've seen you." As Fedor was speaking, Oxana gently removed his arm from her lower back.

"Why would anyone as smart and talented as Oxana ever want to return to this town?" Ilya responded. "There's nothing here for her."

"There's me," Fedor said. "Me and Oxana go way back. She's always been special."

"I'm not sure what you mean by special, Fedor," Oxana said, "but yes, we have known each other since we were children."

Someone stepped in front of Fedor and Ilya.

"If you will excuse me," Oxana said, turning away.

"Of course," Ilya mumbled, while Fedor said nothing.

Oxana continued shaking hands, smiling and nodding, until Irina pulled her aside. "I'm dying to introduce you to my new friend Maria, but I don't know what's happened to her. I know you'll love her, and she was so eager to meet you. She was here with Arkady . . . I don't know why she slipped out without saying hello. And, big sister," Irina's voice dropped to a whisper, "I saw you talking to our new doctor. Isn't he one handsome catch? If you want him, you'd better move fast. Every girl in town is after him."

"Irina, is that all you ever think about?"

"Just giving you some sisterly advice," Irina said, and she turned away to allow the well-wishers to shake Oxana's hand.

As soon as the last of the evening's audience drifted away, Irina and Jakob left to prepare for the after-concert party. Oxana's mother helped Father Vanska tidy up the church while Oxana changed back into her street clothes.

"Ready whenever you are, Mama," Oxana said, emerging from the vestry with her concert gown draped across her arm.

Her mother nodded silently and they went out the door.

"You haven't said anything about the concert, Mama. Did you like my playing?"

"Where did that dress come from?"

"What do you mean, where did it come from?"

"Don't be evasive. I asked where it came from."

"It was a gift from Vera, Mama. She bought it for me."

"I should've known. That dress is scandalous."

"It's not scandalous, Mama. It's only a dress."

"It is not only a dress," her mother shouted, stopping and pointing her finger at Oxana. "It is a scandal! Bare arms! What were you thinking? It's not appropriate. No woman in Peterstal has ever exposed her arms in public. And a slit all the way to your knees, and red, no less! What has gotten into you girls? Even your sister insisted I raise the hem on her dress. I taught you both to be respectable and decent, not to be like loose women who go around showing off their bodies to impress men."

"Mama, you're so old-fashioned. All the women in Odesa wear dresses like this now."

"You are not in Odesa. You are in Peterstal and you need to be proper."

"I *am* proper. And besides, Vera loved the dress. She said that on stage I need to look like a young woman, not like an old nun."

"Oxana, I am your mother, and I say that on stage you need to look like an artist, not some hussy."

"But Mama—"

"Quiet. I will hear no more. And I never want to see that rag of a dress again." They walked the rest of the way in silence.

"Ta-da!" Irina shouted, pointing to the table when Oxana and her mother came through the door. "Mama made all this to celebrate." There was a bowl of fresh fruit, traditional cakes—a *medovik*, with honey and sour cream, and a *skazka* in the shape of a log, with candied fruit and soaked with rum—and a bottle of sweet rosé wine was uncorked, with four glasses poured. Jakob handed each a glass of wine.

"A toast," Irina said, holding her glass in the air, "to my sister, who plays like a goddess, dresses like a goddess, and I guess . . . is a goddess!" All four laughed as they chinked their glasses and took their first sip.

"And I want to propose a toast," their mother spoke up, "to the wonderful concert you just played, Oxana. It exceeded all of my hopes for you. It is quite apparent you have used your time in Odesa wisely and your talent has flourished." They all chinked glasses, and Elena bowed to Oxana.

"Thank you, Mama," Oxana said with tears in her eyes, giving her mother a hug. These were the first words her mother had spoken since they got home, and Oxana was relieved the tension over her dress had dissipated.

"And now," Irina said, "another toast." Her voice quivered when she tried to continue, and Jakob reached for her hand and put his arm around her waist. "Jakob," Irina began again, "has asked me to marry him . . . and I said yes."

"Wonderful news," their mother said, while Oxana embraced Irina. "I was wondering when you two were going to make it official."

The evening proceeded with hugging, crying, Oxana proposing another toast, more hugging and crying, until Jakob insisted Oxana play something. "To celebrate!" he shouted.

"More music?" Oxana held out her hands and wiggled them as if her fingers were wet noodles. "I just played an entire concert for you."

"One song," Jakob pleaded. "Something for Irina and me."

Oxana sat at the piano. Her mother pulled a chair beside her and sat while Jakob and Irina settled into the sofa. As she played, Oxana glanced over at them. Jakob had undone the top buttons of his tunic, exposing a bit of blond chest hair. He had a slight hint of beard, also blond, and Oxana noticed how the muscles in his arms flexed when he reached to wipe away the beads of sweat on his forehead.

When she finished, she closed the lid over the keyboard, saying, "And that is definitely the last of the music for tonight. I am exhausted."

"So am I," Irina added. "Mama, I'll help you carry everything into the kitchen and we can wash the dishes in the morning."

While Irina and Elena ferried the plates and glasses, Jakob came over and sat beside Oxana on the bench. "I'm sorry I haven't even had time yet to say a proper hello," he said, and lightly kissed her cheek. "It's been four years, but Irina has kept me so well informed, I almost feel as if she and I were in Odesa with you."

"I wish you could have been there with me," Oxana said, and she felt her face reddening into a blush.

"Your music was beautiful. Just how I remembered it from the very first time you played for me, right here in this room."

"I hope I've improved somewhat while at the music academy." Oxana laughed. "We've all changed. In fact, I hardly recognized you when I first saw you tonight."

"I'm sure you've improved, but what I mean is the beauty of your music has not changed. It's still there, and you haven't changed either. You're still as beautiful as you've always been." Jakob pulled her against his body and held her in a long, firm embrace.

"Thank you for playing tonight," he whispered in her ear. "You've made a perfect day even more perfect." A sensation rippled through Oxana that she had never before felt.

"Jakob, how much wine have you had?" Irina said, emerging from the kitchen after depositing the last of the dirty dishes. "Have you decided to marry Oxana instead of me? I know we look alike, but I hope you can tell which one of us you actually proposed to."

"Don't you worry about that," Jakob said, standing and taking Irina into his arms. "I don't think I could ever be drunk enough to forget you. You are the love of my life."

"And now I am off to bed, and you girls should be too," their mother said, also emerging from the kitchen. "It has been a big day."

It was nearly midnight by the time Oxana and Irina, totally exhausted, fell into their old bed beside each other like they had while growing up, with their mother sound asleep on her cot across the room. "You're on your way to being a pianist, and I'm on my way to being a wife," Irina whispered as both stared at the ceiling. "Life has worked out so wonderfully for us."

"Well, you may be about to get married, but I'm still a long way from being a concert pianist." Oxana rolled onto her side. "So tell me all about it. How did Jakob propose? Was it all gushy and romantic?"

Irina turned to face her sister. "I've been dying to tell you. It was a perfect day, warm with a clear blue sky, and Jakob asked if I wanted to go for a walk. We went a little way down the main road, and then Jakob took my arm and led me into one of the lanes bordering the fields. The wheat was tall, and I picked a couple of stalks and began to play with them." Irina sighed, again rolled on her back, and stared at the ceiling.

"So did Jakob get down on one knee when he asked you?"

"No, that's not at all how it happened. While we were strolling along, I wove my wheat stalks into a ring, like a wreath. Jakob put his arms around my waist, took the wreath from my hands, and put it on my head. 'Do you remember the old tradition of Ivan Kupala Day?' he said. 'The girl wears the wreath when they go into the forest, but if the boy is wearing it when they come out, they're engaged.' I didn't say anything, only ran ahead of him. He came running to catch up, and I lifted the wreath off my head and placed it on his."

"Oh, Irina, that is so romantic," Oxana whispered.

"And then Jakob said, 'I love you, Irina Nikolaevna Stepaniaka. Will you marry me?' And I said back, 'Yes, Jakob! Yes! I love you and I want to be your wife.'"

"Irina, I'm so happy for you."

"It was the most beautiful day of my life," Irina whispered. "The best day ever."

Chapter 15

While milking the next day, Wilhelm received Jakob's happy news with slightly less euphoria. "You're not marrying her," Wilhelm said.

"Why not?"

"Because she's Russian."

"She's not Russian, she's Ukrainian, and besides, what's that got to do with anything?"

"There are no Ukrainians," Wilhelm said, his tone growing hostile. "There will never be Ukrainians because Ukraine will never be free from Russia. They are all Russians."

"Then we are also Russians, since we live here the same as they do."

"We are not Russians," Wilhelm growled, stopping the milking and turning to face Jakob. "We will never be Russians. We are Germans, and you need to find yourself a nice German girl, like I did. Or better yet, wait until we get to America. I'm sure there are lots of German girls over there."

"Wilhelm, I'm going to marry the woman I love, and that happens to be Irina, and I don't care what you want to call her."

"Jakob, try to be reasonable. Yes, she's pretty, I will admit that. Take her into the barn some night for a good roll in the hay if that's what you're needing, but don't marry her."

"Enough, Wilhelm. Enough," Jakob said. "I won't listen to you slander the woman I love."

"If you won't listen to slander, then listen to reason. What do you think she'll say when it's time to leave for America? With Pa's money plus what Greta and I have saved, there'll soon be enough. Pa always said we need to leave, and he was right. There is no future here. Our future is in America, and when we go you need to come with us. What will your Russian wife say to that?"

"Go to hell, that's what I say to that." Jakob slammed the barn door and stomped toward the house. He kicked an empty bucket, and it went flying across the barnyard. *Why is Wilhelm so harsh and narrow minded?* he thought. All his brother could see was Germans and Ukrainians against Russians, angry and jealous of each other, always wanting to fight. Why couldn't he see Irina as simply a young woman who was as beautiful on the inside as she was on the outside?

Chapter 16

Dear Irina,

I'm glad you are writing to me almost every day. I like getting your letters. I'm sorry I don't write back as often. I'm busy getting ready for graduation, so I hope you will forgive me.

What a surprise to read about your big argument with Mama. Are you really going to convert to Lutheran and have your wedding in the Lutheran church? Don't listen to what Mama says. You are not betraying our papa and our family or abandoning the Orthodox church. Of course your children should be raised in the church of their father and his ancestors. I'm really proud of you for standing up to Mama. You're braver than I thought you were! (Don't take that the wrong way. I mean it as a compliment!)

Now I want to tell you about my good fortune. Mama always says don't worry about the future, it will happen on its own, and I guess she's right. It seems my chance to go to Moscow is going to happen after all and I'm just so thrilled. It was announced only a few days ago that Heinrich Neuhaus is coming. Five students have been selected to play for him, and I am one of them! Neuhaus is the most famous teacher at the Moscow Conservatory and one of the greatest musicians in Russia, maybe even in the world. Pretty impressive, don't you think?

My teacher says that if Neuhaus hears someone he likes, he might invite them to Moscow to study with him. Plus, he can arrange for a full scholarship and housing if he really likes them! I'm sure it won't be like living with Vera, but that's alright with me. I really, really want to go, and everyone here says I'm the best, so I think it will happen. Nevertheless, I'm practicing extra hard.

As soon as I finish this letter, I'm writing Mama to tell her all about Neuhaus too.

And one last thing: I'm going to wear my red dress when I play for Neuhaus. Mama hates it, but I like it, and Irina, if you can turn into a Lutheran, then I can wear a red dress. Mama is no longer in charge!

Love from your "older" sister and best friend!

Oxana

———

The audience stood and applauded when Oxana, along with the other four performers, entered the hall and made their way down the auditorium's side aisle. The clapping continued while the five of them sat in their front-row reserved seats in the order in which they were to perform, with Oxana designated last.

Moments later, Neuhaus slowly made his way down the aisle, rather stern faced, nodding left and right. The applause ceased only after he climbed the steps to the stage and sat in the chair placed for him to the left of the piano's keyboard.

The first performer came onstage, but after playing only a few minutes, Neuhaus stopped him, thanked him, and called for the next student. Oxana watched with a growing sense of unease as, one after another, each performer was stopped before they finished their programs and the next was called for.

When her name was called, Oxana quickly walked up the six steps and onto the stage, trying to ignore the tightness in her stomach. She adjusted the bench and glanced toward Neuhaus. He nodded and she began a Bach fugue. After playing only a few notes, her muscles relaxed and her nervousness eased. As she proceeded through her program, the audience's applause became more and more enthusiastic, while Neuhaus remained silent, only dipping his head slightly after each piece, indicating for her to go on.

He's going to hear my entire program. I'm the only one. He must like me.

Oxana placed her hands on the keyboard for her final selection, Chopin's Fantasy. She began to play and almost immediately felt an eerily overwhelming sensation of lightness, as if she had been transported into some otherworldly dimension of pure sound. Her body felt like nothing more than a mere conduit through which the music was flowing directly from her soul into the hall. She played without any awareness of the passing of time—seconds might have been stretched to hours, or hours contracted to mere minutes—and she was jolted back to reality only as she was playing the final chords. Neuhaus rose from his chair and patted her several times on her back while Oxana bowed to the audience's ecstatic clapping and shouting.

Neuhaus held up his hands and the applause was replaced by a deafening silence as everyone strained to hear what the old musician was going to say. He paused a long while before saying, softly, "You are very talented. Tremendously talented." Again, a long pause. "If you continue to work as hard as you have, you can become an excellent pianist." Turning to the audience, he announced, "And now I must be going—I don't want to miss my train. Thank you all for coming. It has been most enjoyable."

There was a stunned silence as Neuhaus made his way down the auditorium's center aisle. He kept his head low, looking neither left or right, and some later claimed he was mumbling to himself. He went out the rear door; it closed behind him, and he was gone.

Many tears were shed that day, but they didn't change the fact that an invitation to Moscow had not been extended. Oxana finished out the final weeks of school, played her senior recital, graduated with top honors, and returned to Peterstal to her mother's home. Gone was the coach driven by identical white horse; gone were the footmen and the formal dinners served on bone china with sterling silver flatware; gone was practicing on a concert grand piano; gone was the huge mansion; gone was life in the big city with concerts, shopping, restaurants. Oxana's fairy tale had come to an end.

———

In her first days back home, Oxana tried talking with her mother, but whenever she initiated a conversation, her mother abruptly left the room, until finally Oxana gave up. Her mother said nothing about the Neuhaus audition, or her graduation, or the fact that Oxana had not touched the piano since returning home. A curtain of ice had dropped between them.

But what hurt most of all was knowing she deserved her mother's cold indifference. No one had believed in her more strongly or encouraged her more, and she had not lived up to her mother's expectations or fulfilled her dreams. So many had high expectations, and she had disappointed them all.

Oxana spent as much time out of the house as she could, telling her mother and sister that she needed time alone to think, but in truth she was trying to avoid them as much as possible. She was an utter failure and keenly felt the paradox that just when she desperately needed friends, she was too embarrassed to face people. She had not seen Jakob since the night of her concert. Ludmilla had come by to visit, but Oxana stayed in her room and left it to her mother to entertain her.

Her afternoons were spent on long walks through the wheat fields surrounding the village, endlessly reliving the Neuhaus audition, replaying her pieces in her mind, trying to think of what she had done wrong, remembering over and over his kind comments, and then . . . nothing.

———

Oxana was sitting outside one day, reading, when she looked up and saw Fedor leaning against the fence. "Fedor, you scared me. What are you doing here?"

"Watching you," he replied. "And I wanted to bring you these." He stepped toward her and handed her a bouquet of daisies.

"You don't need to bring me flowers, or anything."

"I know I don't need to. I do it because I want to."

"Fedor, I'm sorry, but I'm afraid I'm not really in the mood to be entertaining you."

"That's fine. As long as I can watch you, it's entertainment enough for me. Oxana, it's great having you back in town."

"Fedor, I really think you need to leave me alone."

"I'll leave, if you want me to . . . for now."

"Yes, please."

"Bye, Oxana," he called, closing the garden gate behind him.

She went in the house and Irina met her inside the door. "Maria will be here any minute now and she's dying to meet you. Can't you at least try to show some excitement? I'm soon to be married and all you can do is mope around the house. Can't you at least pretend to be happy for me?" Irina paused when she heard the knock on the door. "It's Maria," she whispered. "Will you at least try to like her—and be excited?"

"Privyet!" Maria almost sang when Irina opened the door.

Oxana frowned. Maria's hair lay flat against her face, without any curls, and she definitely could lose a few kilos.

"Privyet, Maria. Come in." Irina hugged her.

"I can't stay long—I only came to meet this famous sister I've heard so much about," Maria said, clasping Oxana's hand and shaking it.

"Hello, Maria. Nice to meet you," Oxana said, forcing herself to smile.

"Irina has told me all about your piano playing and you being in Odesa. I was at your concert. It was really good. 'Course I don't know anything about music, but I loved it just the same. But at the end, it was too much— you were dressed so elegantly, and what with me in my plain dress. I said to Arkady, we have to get out of here before she sees us and thinks we're nothing but country bumpkins . . ."

But everyone in Peterstal is a country bumpkin. Why would you be any different, Oxana thought as she continued to smile at Maria.

"Maria and Arkady Mikhailov are going to be married in the fall," Irina said.

"Why does everyone seem so eager to get married?" Oxana said. "Why not try to do something with your life first?"

"Oxana." Irina frowned at her. "Maybe getting married *is* doing something with our lives—"

"Fall was my idea," Maria said, interrupting. "Arkady wanted to do it right away when he asked me, about the same time as Jakob proposed to you, Irina, but I told Arkady right out that while I want to marry him in the worst way, I didn't want our weddings to collide. Weddings are so special . . . you've got to savor them one at a time!"

She sure seems to talk a lot. I wonder what Irina sees in her? Oxana thought. It was clear from Irina's smiling face that she enjoyed Maria's company. They both seemed so happy and excited. Oxana supposed that was what being in love felt like. Would she ever know that feeling?

"And now I want to hear about this *rushnyk* so I'll know how to do mine," Maria continued.

Irina held up the piece of cotton fabric about the size of a hand towel. "First, Mama said we had to take it to Father Vanska to be blessed. We did that yesterday."

"I didn't know you and Mama took it for a blessing. You didn't tell me. I would've come along," Oxana said, trying to mask her hurt feelings. While they were growing up, she often felt sorry for Irina, and even somewhat guilty, sensing that she always seemed to receive preferential treatment from their mother, but since her return home she had become acutely aware of a subtle shift in her mother's attention. Now she was the one being slighted.

"You were reading. I didn't want to disturb you," Irina said, "and besides, you haven't exactly been a lot of fun to be around since you came home."

"Well, we're here to have fun today," Maria said. "So tell me all about this."

Irina explained that the red thread symbolizes a life with fertility and good health and that her mother had told her to start by embroidering diamond patterns around the edge to represent a sown field as protection against evil, but to work slowly and carefully since mistakes can bring bad luck. Irina stitched another red diamond. "See, like this." She held it out for them to see.

"That's pretty," Maria said, feeling the stitching. "You sure know a lot about the tradition of these rushnyks."

Oxana held the fabric in her hand. It was beautiful. Irina was as fine a seamstress as their mother.

"Mama says a bride's rushnyk is one of the most important things if you want to have a happy marriage, and then, eventually, when I die, my rushnyk will be put with me in my coffin."

"Eeew," Maria said. "Let's not think of dying and coffins quite yet."

"So why did Mama tell you all about this and not me?" Oxana asked.

"Because you're not the one getting married. I suppose if you ever do decide on someone she will probably tell you everything, the same as she's told me."

"Do you think you would like to get married?" Maria asked Oxana.

"It's not something I think about," Oxana said, *which is a lie. I think about it a lot. I just can't see myself tied down. Is it wrong to want to travel, see new things, have new experiences?*

"Oxana thinks boys are silly," Irina said. "Isn't that what you've always said to me?"

"I don't think they're silly. I just don't think a husband would add anything to my life right now."

"What about, you know, the nighttime stuff?" Maria giggled and covered her mouth with her hand. "Don't you want any of that?"

"Maria!" Irina shot her a look of mock indignation. "I'm surprised you're thinking about that."

"Don't blame me. It's just that Arkady is always, you know, putting his hands on me and, you know, wanting stuff whenever we're alone. I keep saying no, but he says it's fine to do it, now that we're engaged. But I want to save it for our wedding night."

"What's next?" Oxana interrupted. "What do you sew in the middle?"

"Mama says I should embroider a pair of birds swimming. The birds represent me and Jakob, and the water symbolizes us enjoying a peaceful family life. She said it can be geese or swans, but I'm going to embroider ducks."

"Ducks?" Oxana asked. "Why ducks?"

"Ducks are pretty, and they're Jakob's favorite bird. I suppose you'll sew swans or something more elegant and refined on yours someday, but ducks are fine for Jakob and me."

Oxana leaned back in her chair as if she had been physically pushed. Irina had never said anything like this to her before, implying that she felt inferior. Oxana was deeply embarrassed and ashamed that Irina had such thoughts. "Why do you think I need something elegant and refined?" she said, her voice sounding strained and tense. "I'm not trying to be any different from you."

"What birds do you think you'll sew to represent you and Arkady?" Irina asked, ignoring Oxana and turning toward Maria. But before Maria could reply, their mother entered, carrying a bolt of fabric she had taken to Naydia Rostova to be sure she liked the colors before starting on her dress. Oxana stood and took the heavy bolt from her mother, who was panting from the exertion of having carried it. "I need to lie down," she said, and went into her bedroom.

"I'd better be off," Maria said. "Can't be sitting around here all day. There's too much work to be done."

"Oxana, how could you?" Irina said as soon as Maria was out the door.

"How could I what?"

"Don't act innocent. You were rude, and I'm sure you made Maria feel uncomfortable. I begged you to be nice. Was it too much to at least do that for me?"

"I'm sorry. I didn't intend to be rude, but if I was it's because I don't think she's as great as you made her out to be. Are you sure you want her as a friend?"

"Maria is nice, and honest, and warmhearted, and caring." Irina wiped tears from her eyes. "Just because you lived in a palace and wear fancy dresses and get applause doesn't give you a license to act high and mighty. And in case you haven't noticed, while you were off living like a princess in a fairy tale, I was living in the real world. And unlike you, who only thinks about yourself and your problems, I have a man who loves me and wants to marry me and spend the rest of his life with me, while you have no one." Oxana tried to console her with apologies, but she couldn't shake off the fact that what Irina had said was true. *Maybe I'm jealous.*

———

"Mama, I want to bake Irina's wedding bread. It will be my gift," Oxana said the next day, as soon as Irina left to help Jakob prepare their home. "I want to help. You're already working too hard."

"It's about time you stop sulking and do something to help out. It's going to take me every minute to get this dress finished in time."

"Will you show me how?"

"I'll get you started." Laying Irina's wedding dress aside, she pulled mixing bowls and spoons from the cupboard while explaining how to measure the flour and to dissolve the yeast in warm milk to make the bread light and airy.

"Careful—not so much flour. You're getting it all over the floor," her mother called from her chair while Oxana worked at the kitchen table. "You're not at Vera Veranitzskaya's any longer. Here we can't afford to waste. Careful, you're heating the milk too hot. It will kill the yeast. You're using too much flour; I already told you—my God, this *korovai* is going to be the talk of the town, the toughest and driest anyone ever ate."

Oxana worked half the day, mixing the dough, waiting for it to rise, and then punching it down and letting it rise a second time. She rolled the dough into long tubes and wove them into heart-shaped braids. While they baked, she cut pieces of dough into the shapes of birds, animals, flowers, and even a sun and moon, and baked these separately. She decorated each loaf with the flowers and animal and bird figures, and then coated the loaves with a clear sweet sugar glaze.

"Ooh! Ooh!" Irina clapped her hands when she came in that evening. "They're too beautiful to eat. You've turned each braid into a little Garden of Eden. Aren't they wonderful, Mama?"

"Well, at least they aren't a complete disaster." Their mother stood and carried Irina's wedding dress into the bedroom.

Chapter 17

On the eve of the wedding, Jakob worked until it was too dark to continue, but the house was still not ready. For furniture, he had only had time to nail together a table, two chairs, and a rough platform to serve as a bed. Irina had sewn several gunny sacks together to use as a mattress, and Jakob was stuffing it with straw when he heard the sound of roosters crowing outside the front door. "Hmm, roosters crowing at night," he said aloud. "I think I know what this is all about." The door flew open. Arkady and Fedor, his two best friends, stood in the doorway, crowing.

"We heard there's a wedding about to happen, and the rooster can't have his hen without a party," Arkady said, while Fedor tied a rope around Jakob to hold his arms tight against his waist. They led him outside to Fedor's wagon and laid him in the back.

"Let's get us some hens for this rooster!" Fedor shouted. He snapped the reins and the horse pulled the wagon onto the road toward town.

As soon as they stopped in front of Elena Vladimirovna's house, Arkady and Fedor began making loud clucking sounds. Before long the door opened and Irina, Oxana, and Maria were all standing in the doorway, Irina and Maria laughing, while Oxana frowned. "We got a rooster needing a hen!" Fedor yelled, and he and Arkady began tying ropes around the girls and lifting them into the back of the wagon beside Jakob.

"So where are you taking us hens and this sad, lonely rooster?" Irina called out.

"Just you wait and see!" Arkady yelled.

Before long the wagon pulled up to Fedor's front door.

"Time for a party," Arkady and Fedor announced, helping the wedding party into the house. Fedor lit the samovar and opened a bottle of vodka while Arkady untied the ropes. "Tea for the ladies and vodka for us men," he announced. He poured three shots and handed them around. They downed their shots in one gulp. "Now let's see if this rooster knows which hen is his."

The game was an old bachelor's tradition, and while everyone knew exactly how it played out, they all pretended to be completely mystified as to what was about to happen. Arkady wrapped a cloth around Jakob's eyes to blindfold him and put him in a chair, explaining, "If you're correct, you get to kiss your bride. If you're wrong, you have to drink a shot of vodka."

"Now, ladies," Fedor continued, "which of you is first?"

Jakob flailed his arms in the air, pretending to be completely disoriented, until the first girl approached. He placed both hands on her head and began to run his fingers through her hair. "Hmmm, not sure if this is my bride or not. I'll have to go further." Everyone laughed as his hands moved lower, feeling her face and neck. "Hmm. Still not sure. I think I need to keep checking." He put one hand around her waist while his other hand slowly drifted down her back. "Yup, she's the one," he called out. "This is my bride, but just to be sure, let me make one final check."

"Okay, okay," Arkady called out, just as Jakob's hands began to touch Maria's breasts. "This one's not for you. I've got my eyes on this pretty little lady." Everyone laughed as Arkady removed Jakob's blindfold and handed him a shot of vodka.

"Next," Fedor called, tying the blindfold back on Jakob.

The second girl stepped up, and Jakob placed his hands on her head. The moment he touched her hair he was certain it was Irina. He could even smell a hint of her perfume, but he decided it would be fun to play along—feeling first her hair, her face and neck, and then her back and waist. Her muscles twitched and she leaned into him. He reciprocated, enveloping her in a tight embrace and feeling her hot breath on his neck.

"Yup, no doubt, she's the one," Jakob called out as his hands made their way toward her breasts and began lightly massaging them. He felt her body tremble slightly.

"That one's not for you either," Irina suddenly called out, "so you better stop before you get yourself in trouble."

"Oxana?" Jakob said, removing his blindfold. "I'm sorry. I thought you were Irina."

"You're so drunk, you'd probably even think fat old Ludmilla Domitovich was your bride," Fedor said. The momentary tension in the room was dispelled and everyone laughed. Arkady gave Jakob another shot of vodka. "Let's see if you can get it right this time," Fedor said, tying the blindfold on a third time. Irina stepped toward Jakob, and he began feeling her from the head down, claiming that this one had to be his bride.

"Correct, at last," Arkady called out, ripping the blindfold away. "As your reward you can kiss the lovely lady." Everyone clapped while Jakob and Irina embraced.

Another round of vodka was poured. Jakob and Irina sat beside each other at one end of the sofa, and Arkady and Maria settled, arm in arm, at the other end.

Fedor stepped over to Oxana and put his arm around her waist. She removed it, but a few moments later he put it around her again. She again removed it and stepped away from him. He moved toward her and this time put his arm around her shoulder.

"No," Oxana insisted and pushed his arm away.

Fedor grabbed Oxana and moved in to kiss her.

"Stop," Irina shouted, standing up, and Jakob lifted himself off the sofa. Maria and Arkady also both stood.

Oxana pulled away quickly, just as Jakob lunged toward Fedor, nearly tripping as he tried to punch Fedor's face. "Can't you hear, you Russian idiot? The lady said no."

"How dare you call me a Russian idiot," Fedor shouted, flailing at Jakob with his fists, but both men were barely able to stand, much less fight.

"Party's over," Arkady said, stepping between them. "Time for these hens to go home. There's a wedding tomorrow, and no one wants the groom showing up with a black eye."

He led the women out to the wagon and drove them home.

"Sorry," Fedor said to Jakob, who was bent over and panting for air. "Didn't mean to cause a ruckus. Did I hurt you?"

"I'm okay. No harm done, but next time when a lady says no, she means no. Don't forget it."

"Guess you're right, I am sort of a Russian idiot," Fedor admitted.

"Maybe I am too," Jakob said, and he began laughing. He put his arm around Fedor's shoulder. "My brother certainly thinks so."

Chapter 18

At precisely ten a.m. the next morning, Oxana, seated at the piano, watched Jakob walk to the altar with Wilhelm beside him. Jakob was wearing the blue suit the twins' mother had sewn for him, with a white shirt and blue silk tie. He was even more handsome than Oxana remembered from her concert when she first saw him after four years. He turned toward her, and she smiled.

Everyone stood, and Oxana, turning to see Irina standing in the doorway at the back of the church, began playing a wedding march to accompany her procession down the aisle.

Irina arrived at the altar, and Jakob took hold of her hand. Oxana was stunned at Irina's beauty. Her dress was made of a traditional brown brocade that matched her brunette hair, and it was gathered at the waist to accentuate her trim figure. Her mother had embroidered floral designs across the front of the bodice and trimmed the sleeves and hem with lace.

Oxana slipped into the pew closest to the piano to watch the ceremony and glanced over at her mother, sitting in the front pew, smiling. Oxana could not help feeling a twinge of sadness. Everything had worked out for Irina while nothing had worked out for her, and she wondered if she and her mother would ever again regain the closeness they had once known.

Father Vanska, standing behind the altar beaming, motioned for the couple to approach. There was a pause. According to tradition, Irina's rushnyk was on the floor in front of the altar, and the old lore held that the first to step on it would be the one to make the decisions in the marriage. Suddenly Jakob lurched sideways, as if he were about to faint. Irina instinctively stepped forward to catch him and was now standing on the rushnyk. Everyone laughed as Jakob bowed to her before placing his foot on the cloth.

Father Vanska blessed the korovai, making the sign of the cross three times to symbolize the couple's union with the Father, Son, and Holy Ghost. Oxana felt proud of how well the bread had turned out. She wanted everything to be perfect for Irina and Jakob. Father Vanska broke off pieces from the loaf and placed them in Jakob and Irina's mouths. He recited another prayer and then asked Jakob to recite his vow.

"Irina, I give you this ring," Jakob said, his voice cracking. "This ring—my mother's wedding ring—" Again his voice cracked, and he wiped tears from his cheeks. "This ring—as the most powerful symbol of love I can think of." He paused and this time reached to brush tears from Irina's cheeks as well as his own. "With this ring I thee wed."

Irina repeated her vow, and Father Vanska wrapped a symbolic cloth around the couple's hands, fastening them forever in an eternal bond. He declared them husband and wife. Putting his arm around Irina's waist, Jakob and Irina both smiled at Oxana when they heard the first notes. Instead of some lively wedding recessional, she was playing their favorite, the quiet opening of Chopin's Fantasy.

The wedding party and guests made their way across the square to the town hall for the reception, where the food Oxana and her mother had spent days preparing—sandwiches, Russian salads, cakes, as well as Oxana's korovai—awaited them. Several village men played balalaikas and garmoshkas and others beat drums. There was dancing and singing while Oxana rushed about, replenishing empty wine and vodka bottles and removing dirty plates, until finally, as the sun set, the guests offered Jakob and Irina one final toast. Oxana, standing apart from all the others, watched and waved as the newlyweds made their way toward their new home.

Her sister was now Irina Schweitz; Irina Stepaniaka was no more. The late-night talks, the sisterly confessions, the commiserating—were no more. Irina now had a husband for the late-night talks, confessions, and commiserating—while she had no one.

"That's not how you peel potatoes," Oxana's mother said, coming into the kitchen one day. "Didn't you learn anything from me? You have to put them in a bowl of cold water or they'll turn brown."

"Mama, I know how to peel a potato. It's not exactly difficult."

"What would you know about difficult? You've had it easy your entire life. Everything is handed to you."

"Mama, what are you talking about? I'm peeling potatoes for soup."

"Yes. Soup. I'm talking about soup. Here you are back home, peeling potatoes, making soup. I worked day and night to give you a better life. I spent every ruble I had to give you everything you needed. You had every opportunity in Odesa. You lived like a queen in a palace, and you threw it all away, and now you're back here making soup."

"Mama, I didn't throw it all away. I did my best. Neuhaus didn't ask me to Moscow, that's all. I don't know why. I guess he didn't like my piano playing. I don't know what I'm supposed to do or where I should go."

"You can't stay here. Your sister is now married, and you need to think about finding a husband too. What about Fedor Rostov? He's had his eyes set on you for years, plus he's got plenty of money and is decent enough to look at."

"All he ever talks about is his farm, his crops, and the weather. I'm not about to tie myself to some yokel who doesn't know Bach from bacon. I don't want a life of cooking meals, milking cows, and popping out babies."

"While you're busy being snooty, the good ones are being grabbed up."

"Maybe I don't need a husband."

"Don't be stupid. Every woman needs a husband. That's how the world works."

"Mama, I refuse to listen to any more of this." Oxana threw down the knife and potato and went out the door. It was nearly three kilometers to Jakob and Irina's house, and she strolled along slowly, mulling over the plan she had been formulating over the past few days.

Irina was in the yard, pumping water. She waved as Oxana approached. Oxana joined her by the pump. "Mama's whining at me again."

"Don't worry about Mama." Irina put her arms around Oxana's shoulder. "She's disappointed for you, that's all. Give her a little time. Come inside and we can talk. Jakob's gone to help Wilhelm."

"These are nice," Oxana said, fingering the draperies hanging around the bed. "Did Mama sew them?"

"I did, I'll have you know. Since we only have one room, I thought it would be a way to separate the bed from the rest of the space. Jakob likes how they brighten up the room. He says I have an eye for decorating."

"And this is the piano I've been hearing about," Oxana said, stepping to a small spinet pushed against the wall opposite the bed. Oxana ran her finger across the keyboard. The ivory was missing from some of the keys. She played a chord and winced. "Where did you find this?"

"Jakob got it at an auction sale," Irina said, wiping her hand across the top as if dusting it. "It's our first purchase together, although Mama paid for half of it. But we're going to pay her back as soon as the crop is harvested and we sell some grain. I know it isn't much, but hopefully in a few years we can get a better one."

Irina picked an apron off the counter and handed it to Oxana. "You can try it out later, but right now I need your help. Jakob asked Wilhelm and Greta to come to dinner tonight, and you know I'm a bad cook. They already don't like me, and by the time they endure my dinner they'll hate me."

"You're not that bad, Irina, but sure, I'll help." Oxana tied the apron strings behind her back. "We'll put that snooty Greta in her place. We'll make a meal so good, even tough old Wilhelm will be forced to compliment you. So, what's there to work with?"

"You can start by chopping these onions and then cut up the chicken."

Soon Oxana and Irina were laughing and joking. "This is fun, like the old days," Oxana said, rolling out a pie crust.

"I've heard you're spending time with Fedor." Irina nudged Oxana with her elbow and winked. "Any *news* you want to fill me in on?"

"I'm not *spending time* with him; he keeps wanting to go for walks and I've run out of excuses for refusing, so I'm stuck."

"Maybe stuck is where you need to be," Irina said, and laughed. "He adores you, and you have to admit he's good-looking."

"Irina, there is more to a man than good looks, and for your information I'll never marry Fedor. He's helping me, that's all. I need to get away from Mama, and I've come up with a plan. His grandmother's house is empty now, so I'm moving into it, and to pay the rent I'm going to teach his little sisters. He's arranged it with his mother. Then hopefully I can get more students, and once I have enough money saved, I'm going to Moscow. I don't care that Neuhaus turned me down. I can find another teacher. I know it's not ideal, but it's the best option I have."

"I'm glad to hear it, sister. Now you're sounding like the old Oxana."

"Now that we've talked about my life," Oxana said, shoving a pie tin in the oven, "tell me about yours. What's it like?"

"What's what like?"

"Don't act so innocent with me. What's it like—you know—with Jakob?"

"Oxana, shame on you." Irina covered her mouth with her hand to suppress her laugh. "You're prying."

"Oh, come on. You can tell me. What's it—he—like?"

"Well, he's big."

Oxana covered her mouth in imitation of Irina, and both laughed.

"So how often have you done it?"

"Oxana, you really are prying. I'm not sure I'm going to tell you any more."

"We're sisters. We can tell each other everything."

"Well, if you must know, so far it's been every day, and somedays more than once," which brought on another bout of laughter from both of them. Then Irina blushed deeply. "Oxana—you're the first to know . . . I'm going to have a baby. I haven't even told Jakob yet. I plan to tell him tonight, after dinner."

"Irina, congratulations. Jakob will be so proud. I'm truly happy for you both." Oxana hugged her. They stood embracing for a long while and Oxana could sense a spiritual aura emanating from within her, illuminating her eyes and filling the space around her body with an unearthly warmth. "I am truly happy for you both," Oxana repeated. "You've gotten exactly what you wanted in life. My sister . . . a mother . . . so very lucky."

Oxana was pulling the pies out of the oven when the door opened. Jakob shook his head, pretending to be confused. "Am I seeing double?

Or did I marry two identical wives? I must be the happiest man in the world."

"Oh, shush," Irina said and kissed him. "Hurry and get washed up. They'll be here any minute."

"And I need to make a hasty exit before they arrive," Oxana said, taking off her apron. "I certainly wouldn't want Wilhelm and Greta to think you're shacking up with two wives."

"Wait a minute," Jakob said. "You haven't said what you think of my piano. Don't you want to give it a try?"

"Ahh," Oxana mumbled, trying not to laugh. "It's . . . ah . . . well, it's a piano. I think I'll leave the pleasure of playing it to you."

"He plays it all the time, and Mama still helps him once in a while," Irina said. "He can even play Chopin's Fantasy."

"I play *parts* of it, Irina. I play what I can, and I skip over the hard parts."

There was a knock.

Too late, Irina mouthed to Oxana.

The door opened and Wilhelm entered, followed by his wife, Greta. Oxana was always amazed at how different Jakob was from his brother. Both had blond hair, but Wilhelm had a beard that hung nearly to his chest and was as large and muscular as the proverbial Russian bears, while Jakob was clean-shaven, and tall and wiry. "Come in, come in; have a seat," Jakob said. He shook his brother's hand and kissed Greta on the cheek.

"Hmmm, *gut*," Greta said, sniffing the air.

"Now you will see that Ukrainian food is as good as German food," Jakob said, motioning for Wilhelm and Greta to sit. Wilhelm sniffed and muttered, "*Ja, vielleicht wird es nicht zu schrecklich sein.*"

Oxana had no idea what he had just said, but from the frown on Jakob's face, she was pretty sure it was not a compliment. "See you tomorrow." Oxana waved and brushed past Greta as she hurriedly closed the door behind her.

"Mama, I'm moving," Oxana said while they sat drinking tea.

"Moving? Where are you going? You don't have any money. Are you planning to put the piano in the back of a hay wagon and play your way to Moscow?"

"Mama, please. Fedor's arranged for me to live in his grandmother's house and teach his little sisters. I can get more students, and when I've saved enough, I'm going to Moscow."

"So now you've gone begging to the Rostovs. They're already the richest family in town. I suppose they can afford one more servant."

"I won't be a servant. I'll be a teacher, like you were to me. I can manage by myself." They sat staring past each other. "I need one last thing from you. Can I take the piano with me?"

"Yes, take the piano. It's yours. You can do anything you want with it." Her mother stepped to the doorway but turned to face Oxana. "Just don't come back crying to me. I've done all I can for you," and she slammed the door.

Jakob arrived after dawn the next morning, with Arkady, Fedor, and his younger brother Gregor.

Oxana's mother was already outside, in her garden, and refused to even look toward the house, as if nothing was occurring. The men maneuvered the piano out the door and into the back of Fedor's wagon. Oxana watched, and sighed. *All those hours of practice*, she thought, *and where did they get me?* She picked up her hat and coat and stood a moment. She was leaving her home, the home where she and Irina had grown up, the home where she had dreamed such lofty dreams, the home that was filled with music, with joy and love and hope, but now felt like little more than an empty shell. She gently pulled the door shut behind her.

━━━━━

The Rostov house was only one room, smaller even than Irina and Jakob's, but at least it was hers. There was a small table with two chairs in one corner, a kitchen counter with a sink against one wall, and a stove in another corner. Her bed was against the wall opposite the kitchen counter, and the piano stood against the wall opposite the entry door. Mama had stopped by once to bring some dishes and towels, and Irina stopped in as often as she had time.

Oxana was finishing Fedor's little sister's lesson one afternoon, writing instructions into her music book, when the door opened. "Privyet, Naydia. Come in," she called without looking up, assuming the little girl's mother had come to take her home.

"Privyet."

"Fedor!" Oxana swung around. "I thought it was your mother."

"Run along," Fedor said, holding the door for his sister. "Mama's waiting at home, and I want to talk to Oxana."

"Talk?" Oxana asked. "About the house?"

"No, not about the house—but first I'd like to offer you these." Fedor handed her the large bouquet of red roses he was holding behind his back.

"They're beautiful. Thank you very much." Oxana stepped to the counter for a jar to put them in. "Are you celebrating something?"

"Well, sort of—Oxana, it's wonderful having you in my grandmother's house. It almost feels like you're a part of the family. And now that your sister is married, I thought . . . I've been thinking . . . maybe it's time for you to become a real part of the family. I was thinking that maybe . . . What I'm trying to say is that, ever since I can remember, Oxana, I have liked you. Actually, I've loved you." Fedor paused to wipe sweat from his forehead. "Do you mind if I sit down? It's really hot in here." Fedor dropped onto the sofa and Oxana sat on a chair beside the table, afraid of what was about to happen and trying to pull her thoughts together.

"So there—I said it. Oxana, I love you. I know you maybe don't feel quite that way about me, but if you would give me a chance, I think you would come to. I'd be kind to you and treat you the way a lovely lady like you deserves. And I'd love to listen to you playing the piano. You could play all day long."

Fedor again paused and wiped his brow. Oxana sat stone-faced, her mind racing, groping for thoughts, struggling for a reaction. He dropped to one knee. "Oxana, would you marry me? Would you agree to be my wife?"

Oxana remained sitting, her heart pounding. "I . . . I . . . I," she stuttered.

"I know this may seem sudden to you, but it isn't to me. I've known for years that I wanted to marry you, and now, seeing you around nearly every day this whole summer, I don't think I can stand to wait any longer. Oxana, I love you."

"Fedor, I'm very flattered, but I can't marry you. I'm not ready to settle down and be a wife. I'm not planning to stay here in Peterstal. I may go to Moscow, or maybe Kyiv. I want to play concerts and teach. Maybe one day

I can become a professor at the Kyiv Conservatory . . . or I might return to Odesa."

"I'll work it out to go with you. When my father died he left half the farm to me and half to my brother, Gregor. It's a big farm, almost too big to keep up even with the two of us. I'll sell part of it and we'll live off the money until you get settled. And then, after a few years, we can come back. Once we have kids I'm sure you'll be wanting to quit music to be a mother."

"Fedor, music is not some hobby. It's my career—my life. It's what I want to do forever, even if I do have children. I'm sorry, but I'm not ready for marriage."

"Won't you at least think it over?"

"I'm afraid I don't need to think it over."

"You're not making this easy, Oxana. I hoped you would at least agree to think it over."

"I'm sorry, Fedor. I truly am."

"But you owe me, Oxana. You're living in my grandmother's house, because of me." Fedor grabbed Oxana by the waist and pulled her against him.

"Let me go!" she shouted.

"Oxana, you know you have feelings for me." Fedor pulled Oxana closer and kissed her mouth.

"Stop!" Oxana screamed. "You need to leave."

"My leaving won't change how I feel about you." He let go of her but hesitated, and she could see he was struggling to contain his emotions. "Please, Oxana, you're driving me mad—if only you loved me as much as I love you, we would be happy."

"Goodbye, Fedor."

He wiped his eyes and then slowly stepped into the bright sunshine. Oxana closed the door behind him.

She sat breathing deeply, trying to calm down. Why couldn't Fedor understand that she was never going to marry him? But he was persistent, she thought. You had to give him that. She supposed she should be flattered, but still . . .

"Wait until Irina hears about this," she said aloud.

Chapter 19

"*Gott hilf mir!*" Jakob shouted, throwing the letter to the floor. "I'm going to chop his head off."

"Maybe not such a bad idea, but please not today," Irina said. "I just scrubbed the floor."

"Oh, no, it won't be today. I just sharpened my ax. I'll wait until the blade is good and dull so I can hack at his neck—it'll give him maximum pain."

"Such is brotherly love. I'd hate to see what would happen if you two were enemies. What does the letter say?"

The door flew open, without a knock. The sunshine behind Wilhelm's huge torso cast a long, broad shadow across the wooden floor. "Good morning, my brother," Jakob said, and he quickly stood. "Come in, come in—we weren't expecting you so soon." He reached out to shake Wilhelm's hand, but his brother was staring at the pile of dirty dishes covering the counter under the small window opposite the door.

"Take a seat." Jakob pointed to the empty chair beside him at the small table. His brother's eyes shifted to the bed in the corner. It was a rumpled mess of sheets and pillows. Jakob quickly grabbed the drapes hanging from the ceiling and pulled them around to conceal the bed.

"My Greta always has the bed made before the sun is up," Wilhelm muttered. He eased his brawny torso into the raw pine-wood chair and glanced at the paper lying on the floor. "I see you got my letter," Wilhelm said, pushing aside the breakfast dishes still on the table.

Wilhelm had always been large, but now as he neared his twenty-third birthday he was practically a giant. He stood six feet six inches tall, and his sandy blond hair hung down to his broad shoulders. His blond beard reached almost to his chest, and even his hands were thick and muscular, nearly twice the size of his brother's.

"Yes, I got your letter—only a short while ago," Jakob replied. "But come now, brother, do you need to send letters? We only live five kilometers apart; there's no need to waste money on postage. Besides, if Irina had known you were coming, she would have baked a pie to have with our coffee—wouldn't you, Irina?" Jakob glanced at her. She had turned her back and was furiously washing the pile of dirty dishes.

"I don't need pie," Wilhelm replied. "My Greta makes the best pies—German pies. Irina, maybe you could come over one day and Greta could show you how she makes her pies."

There was a crash as a cast-iron skillet fell to the floor. Jakob jumped out of his chair to retrieve it. Tears were streaming down Irina's red face and her shoulders were shaking.

"Irina doesn't need help with her pies!" Jakob tried to give voice to his inner fury, but he knew that around his brother, he always sounded weak and subservient.

"I sent you a letter," Wilhelm said, "because you no longer seem to hear me when I speak to you. Maybe reading will help clear your mind. So, will you sign?"

"You expect me to sign the papers today, selling everything I have, and by the end of summer we're supposed to be ready to board the ship to America? You don't leave much time to think about it!"

"You've already thought for too long. It's all decided. Greta and I and the boys are going. Old Ivan Lenyoff has agreed to buy everything and has already given me half the money. He gives me the other half just before we go. Thanks to me, he has agreed to a very good price for your land too, so are you coming with us?"

"Wilhelm, we've already talked about this—how can we leave our home? How can Irina leave her mother and sister? She'll never see them again."

"She can write letters; it will be enough."

"How does Greta feel about leaving her family?"

"What does it matter what Greta feels? She's a good wife. She does what I say. She doesn't try to have feelings, like these Russian women."

Another pan clattered to the floor. Jakob turned in his chair. Irina was shaking uncontrollably. "Why don't you get some air," Jakob offered.

The two men sat in silence as Irina flew out the door.

"Irina is not Russian, she is Ukrainian, and furthermore, she is my wife. Do you have to be so blunt around her?"

"If I'm blunt it's because I need to be. Jakob, you have your head in the clouds, and it's preventing you from making wise decisions. Just look around. This entire place is falling apart. You don't repair anything. That stone wall you put up is leaning so badly, I was scared to even go near it. And I will not dignify this filthy hut by calling it a home."

"That's enough, Wilhelm. You've said enough. You should leave now."

"I have not even begun to say what I came to say, and I will not leave until you hear me out. We are Germans, and we've lived here in stinking Russia for too long. It's time to leave. It's past time to leave—Pa knew it and he was right; we should have gone long ago. We had the tsars, and then Lenin, and now Stalin. Each is worse than the one before. Now they say we are the USSR—the Union of Soviet Socialist Republics. Union of Soviet Socialist Rats is what I say. These Bolshevik thugs will not stop until Ukraine is completely crushed, and we will be crushed too. It's time to get out while we still can, while we are young and can start over—in America."

"I'm tired of listening to you, Wilhelm. You say the same things every time we talk—always Germans hating Russians, Ukrainians hating Russians, and Russians hating everyone. In the end we're all the same, we're all peasants, and we're all poor. You're right, our ancestors came from Germany, but they also came from mud huts! At least here we have houses and enough land to make a living. How can you be so sure things will be better in America?"

"Here we sit, like two old women, wasting time when there's work to do," Wilhelm bellowed. "Go ahead, love your Ukraine, love your Russia, I don't care, but Jakob, it's time to leave. Come with Greta and me, to America. We will have freedom. We won't have to worry about the government taking half our grain for taxes, or soldiers showing up in the middle of the night to haul you away because you didn't kiss Stalin's photo properly.

You mark my words. Soon those Bolshevik henchmen will take away what little we do have. They won't stop until they either turn us into obedient communists or kill us—and they will not care which it is. You must sign the paper—now!"

"I'll talk it over with Irina."

"Maybe if you play that foolish piano it will help you come to your senses." Wilhelm stood and pointed at the spinet pushed up against the wall near the bed curtains. "You barely have enough money to feed your wife, but you have money to buy a piano. It's a good thing our pa didn't live to see this day." Wilhelm opened the door and stepped back into the bright sunshine. "And could you at least fix that stone wall? Maybe Lenyoff would add a few more rubles to his offer if it didn't look as if it could fall over any minute. I left you a bag of cement powder over there."

Jakob stood in the doorway, staring, as his brother mounted his horse and rode off. He was furious, but he also knew Wilhelm was right. There was no future here. *Wilhelm is always right.*

Jakob went inside the barn but didn't see Irina. *She's gone to Oxana again, like she always does when she's upset.* Jakob gazed a moment at his tiny farmyard and had to agree, it was a mess. Why was Wilhelm so good at everything while he couldn't seem to do anything? The barn roof leaked, and birds flew in and out of a broken window. Weeds were growing in the front yard, and the stone wall he had put up between the barn and the chicken coop did look like it was about to collapse.

Yet as Jakob stood gazing, he felt the pull of nostalgia. This was home for his little family, Irina and, maybe, he hoped, soon a son. *Tonight Irina and I will decide.*

That evening, with the room lit only by a single kerosene lamp, Irina sat sewing and Jakob went to the piano. He had never let up in his quest to conquer Chopin's Fantasy, and while much of it remained beyond his ability, he played the parts he could and skipped over the sections that were too hard.

Tonight, as he softly played the mournful opening, he wondered if what he was feeling was what Chopin had felt when he left his home in Poland to live the rest of his life as an exile in France. If Irina agreed to go to America with Wilhelm and Greta, they too, like Chopin, would be abandoning their beloved Ukraine for a new life in America and, like Chopin, they would never return.

Jakob's hands hovered over the piano keys while the chords quietly faded into silence. He reached from the piano bench to Irina's chair and wrapped his arms around her. He kissed her gently as he caressed her arms. "We will remain together always, no matter where we live," he cooed into her ears. "As long as we are together, we will be happy." Jakob slowly massaged her stomach and she relaxed into his embrace. "And now we will be a family. I can hardly wait for the baby. Maybe I will have a son." He slipped his hand beneath her dress and gently slid it up along her inner thigh. She quivered at the tingling sensation.

"You men are all alike," she said drowsily.

"And that's why you women can't stay away from us," he whispered as his hand reached its destination and began a slow and gentle massage.

Chapter 20

Oxana heard rapid hoofbeats and opened her front door. "Something's wrong—I'm getting Ludmilla!" Jakob shouted and rode off, kicking his horse in the flanks. It was only minutes past sunrise. Oxana grabbed her hat and ran toward her mother's house.

"Oh God, it's too early for the baby to be coming," her mother moaned. She grabbed her hat and they headed down the main road, half running, reaching the farmyard just as Jakob came riding in with Ludmilla Domitovich hanging on behind.

"Probably morning sickness or something she ate," Ludmilla said as Oxana helped her off the horse. "These babies can mess up your insides something awful."

Oxana followed her mother and Ludmilla into the house, leaving Jakob to lead the horse to the barn. Irina was lying in bed, panting, her face pale, her eyes wide open. "It hurts," she screamed, clutching her stomach. Oxana pulled a chair to the side of the bed and held Irina's hand while their mother pulled a chair to the opposite side of the bed, grabbed a rag, and wiped Irina's forehead. "There's nothing to be scared of, sister," Oxana said softly. "Mama and I are here. Everything is going to be fine." Jakob entered and stood at the foot of the bed, saying nothing, only staring.

"Now, now, my sweet child," Ludmilla said. "We'll have you back on your feet in no time." Ludmilla pulled back the bed covers and shrieked. "Holy Mother of God! There's too much blood. My God! Jakob! Go for the doctor!" Jakob stood staring at the blood-soaked bedding. "Jakob! Go for the doctor! *Now*!"

His face was white, and he was shaking. "I already did," he whispered. "The doctor's out, won't be back until tonight."

"No doctor?" Irina said, so feeble she was barely able to whisper.

"You're going to be fine," Oxana reassured her, gripping Irina's hands tighter to try to calm her shaking. "Ludmilla is here and she knows what to do."

Ludmilla tried massaging her stomach, but Irina wailed every time she touched her. Oxana massaged her arm to get her to relax. "It's alright, sister. Don't be afraid."

"I've got to stop the bleeding," Ludmilla muttered. "I'm afraid she's lost the baby."

Oxana stood and paced the room, alternately clenching her fists and running her hands through her hair. The mention of losing the baby brought back horrid memories of the dead bodies she had seen while shopping with Vera the day of the Bolshevik massacre in Odesa. She remembered how she was shocked but had not cried because she didn't know the people. But today . . . her thoughts trailed off when she heard Irina moan.

"My baby? What's wrong with my baby?" Irina lifted her shoulders, as if trying to get out of bed. Their mother wiped her brow and eased her head back onto the pillow, which was soaked with sweat.

Jakob knelt beside the bed and kissed Irina's cheek. "Don't worry, my love. We can make another baby."

"Listen to Jakob," Oxana whispered in Irina's ear. "We need to get you healthy and then you can become a mama."

"Oh my God, the pain. God, don't take my baby away."

"I'm sorry, my sweet child." Ludmilla leaned over Irina. "Everything has to come out so we can stop the bleeding."

Oxana squeezed Irina's hand. "We're here, sister . . . Mama and I. Everything is going to work out. You just need some bed rest."

"My poor child," their mother moaned.

"The doctor would know better what to do," Ludmilla muttered. "My God. Oh my God."

Oxana gripped Irina's arm and felt her pulse weakening. Her body temperature seemed to be dropping, yet her screams became even louder.

"Hold on, my child. Hold on," Ludmilla kept repeating, grabbing more rags and applying pressure.

"I love you," Jakob sobbed, with his head on Irina's breast. Oxana knelt beside him and embraced him. His hands and arms were trembling.

"I love you," Irina whispered back to him, her voice now so weak she could hardly be heard.

"Jakob, it's best you go outside," Ludmilla said. "Oxana can be with you while Elena and I take care of this."

He remained immobile, his face buried in Irina's breast. Oxana kept her arms around him. His shirt was wet from sweat. "Come with me, Jakob," she said. "We can get some air while Mama and Ludmilla take care of her. She's going to be fine. She just needs time to heal."

"Is she going to make it? Is she going to live?" Jakob asked, more to himself than to Oxana as she led him into the farmyard, her arms around his waist. "There's so much blood." Irina's screams were becoming fainter. Jakob pushed her away and began pacing. "It's my fault. I killed my mother and now my baby is dead, and my wife is dying. This is God's punishment. God hates me."

"This is not your fault, and Irina is not dying. We have to let nature take its course. Ludmilla knows what to do."

"You had better come now," Ludmilla called from the front step, and Jakob and Oxana hurried inside.

"I'm sorry, Jakob, but—" Ludmilla was sobbing, almost too hard to speak. "I couldn't do any more. She lost too much blood . . . Oh God, I tried . . . I tried . . . I couldn't do any more. You must go for Father Vanska."

Oxana and Jakob both knelt beside the bed. Oxana brushed Irina's hair, wet with perspiration, away from her eyes just as their mother reached to also wipe. Their hands met. Oxana looked at her mother and saw a face that no one should ever have to see—her mouth contorted into a grimace, eyes staring blankly, cheeks wet with tears—the face of a mother losing her child.

Oxana kissed Irina. "Jakob," she whispered. "Let's go for Father Vanska . . . I'll come with you."

"No. Stay . . . with Irina." Jakob's voice was barely audible. "I'll go."

Oxana sat beside Irina, massaging her hands and arms, feeling her muscles tightening and her body losing its warmth. Their mother reached over and closed Irina's eyes. "My baby, my baby," she wailed. "My baby."

"God have pity," Ludmilla repeated several times. "Have pity on our poor Irina."

The minutes ticked by as if each lasted an hour until finally the door opened and Father Vanska rushed to the bedside. "May the blessing of God be upon this house," he intoned and made the sign of the cross before opening his bag and pulling out a prayer book and vial of holy water.

Oxana moved to the front door to make room. Jakob knelt beside the bed and took Irina in his arms. Father Vanska placed his hand on Irina's forehead. "Through this holy anointing may the Lord, in his love and mercy, help you, with the grace of the Holy Spirit."

She heard muffled voices outside and opened the door. Wilhelm and Greta were standing in the front yard. Fedor, Maria, and Arkady stood quietly next to them.

"Is she . . . is she—" Maria tried speaking. Oxana shook her head. Maria and Greta fell to their knees. Oxana stepped outside and knelt with them. At first she cried silently, dabbing her eyes with the edge of her dress, but soon she was sobbing. Maria and Greta put their arms around her, weeping, silently consoling her.

Jakob came outside and stood beside the group, saying nothing. The men held their hats in their hands and bowed their heads.

"We came to help, brother," Wilhelm said, patting Jakob on his back. "You don't need to see what comes now. We can take care of everything." He turned to Oxana. "Why don't you take Jakob into the barn."

"No," Jakob said. "I need to be with my wife." He went back inside and Oxana followed him. He knelt beside Irina and took hold of her hand. Oxana also knelt beside the bed. She grasped Jakob and Irina's hands and held them tightly. "You will be together forever," Oxana whispered. "Forever," she repeated.

"Jakob," Father Vanska said, tapping him on his shoulder, "there is nothing more you can do. Irina is with God now. Please go with Oxana. We can see to matters."

Oxana was suddenly filled with rage. She wanted to hit Father Vanska. Her sister had just died. How could he be so calm and speak of God? Was God so evil as to allow this to happen, or was he simply absent and uncaring? Irina was young, innocent, and soon to be a mother. How could God take her away? She turned her back to Father Vanska and watched Jakob, leaning over and kissing Irina. Oxana gently tugged him away. He stood a moment with his arm outstretched, still clasping Irina's hand. Oxana reached out, and the three hands were once again interlocked.

———

"Are you here?" Oxana called as she opened the door to Jakob's house later that afternoon. He was sitting in his chair beside the table, staring at the floor. "I thought you might be with Wilhelm and Greta."

Jakob did not speak.

"You should not be alone," Oxana said quietly. She took the chair beside him and held his hands. "Irina is with me," Oxana whispered, trying not to weep. "Mama wanted her, but I said she had to be with me. We're twins. Wilhelm made a coffin, and I washed her and dressed her in one of my dresses. She is very beautiful." Oxana pulled her chair closer and put her arm around Jakob. "She will not be alone. Mama and I will be with her, day and night. Please come and sit with us."

"I can't . . . can't bear it."

"Do you want Father Vanska to do the service?"

"No—not Lutheran. Orthodox—her church."

They sat a long while, holding hands, saying nothing, until Oxana slowly rose and closed the door behind her on her way out.

———

Jakob was still sitting in the chair beside the table, still wearing the same clothing, when Oxana returned the next morning. She put her arm around his shoulder. "Everything is arranged. The priest comes tonight for the Orthodox prayer service. Please come and say the prayers with us."

Jakob stared uncomprehendingly, as if she were speaking a foreign language. She put a basket of food on the table. He shook his head. "Not hungry."

"Tomorrow is the funeral, Jakob. You should see her—one last time."

"Yes—I'll . . . yes."

Oxana turned when her front door opened. Jakob's silhouette was outlined by the gray, cloudy sky. Wearing his wedding suit, his white shirt neatly tucked into his blue trousers, and blue silk necktie carefully knotted, he cradled a bouquet of roses in his arms. Oxana went to him and Jakob fell against her, weeping.

The coffin, draped with bedsheets to hide the rough-hewn pine, was on the table. Elena was sitting beside it, and Jakob nodded to her as Oxana clasped his hand and slowly led him in. Irina's hands were folded across her chest, and Oxana had placed pillows to make it appear as if she was lying in bed. Jakob placed the roses under Irina's arm and laid her hand across the flowers. He pulled Irina's rushnyk out of his pocket and tucked it under the roses. "Take this with you, while you wait for me," he whispered, bending and kissing Irina's lips. "Goodbye, my love. Goodbye."

The priest entered and the pallbearers stepped in behind him—Wilhelm, Arkady with Maria beside him, Fedor, and his younger brother, Gregor. Swinging a censer and chanting prayers, the priest circled the coffin three times, filling the air with sweet-smelling incense, while Oxana folded the bedsheets across Irina until only her face—pale, young, beautiful—was visible. Taking hold of each corner, the pallbearers lifted the coffin off the table and hoisted it onto their shoulders. Except for the soft intoning of the priestly chanting, there was total silence. Jakob, Oxana, and Elena put their arms around each other's waists and followed the procession out the door.

A throng of villagers were gathered outside and sang the Trisagion prayer—Holy God, Holy Mighty, Holy Immortal, have mercy on us—repeating the words over and over, their thin, reedy voices barely audible, their feet in time with the solemn dirge as they proceeded to the church. "Even the angels in heaven are in mourning," Oxana whispered to her mother as a misty drizzle moistened the air.

Each person reached for an unlit candle as they filed into the church and waited silently while the pallbearers lowered the coffin onto the funeral bier in front of the altar. Chairs were placed around the perimeter, but everyone remained standing. The priest lit a candle and passed it to Jakob. He lit his and passed it to Oxana, and she in turn lit one and passed it, until everyone was holding a lighted candle.

In accordance with ancient tradition, the priest placed a floral wreath on Irina's head, and Jakob broke down sobbing. Oxana kept her arm around his waist, holding him tightly, remembering Irina's description of their engagement, when she had fashioned a wreath and Jakob had placed it on her head.

While the priest intoned prayers, the mourners filed past the open coffin, many stooping to kiss Irina's lips in the customary fashion of offering one last loving goodbye. Oxana held her mother's hand as she bent over to kiss her beloved daughter, her tears wetting Irina's cheeks. Oxana bent and kissed her twin sister, her other half. Jakob was the last to offer a kiss before Wilhelm placed the lid on the casket and everyone made the sign of the cross across their chests.

Oxana gripped Jakob's hand in her right hand and her mother's in her left as the congregation again sang the Trisagion prayer, lifting their voices to drown out the dull thud of Wilhelm's hammer striking each nail three times, in honor of the holy Trinity. The pallbearers lifted the coffin off the bier, and the priest led the procession out the door and around the side of the church to the cemetery.

Jakob, Oxana, and her mother stood beside the grave, holding hands. While the priest recited the final prayers, the pallbearers lowered the casket into the ground and the crowd slowly dispersed. Wilhelm had invited everyone for lunch, and many headed toward his farm.

"It's time to go," Greta said, extending her hand to Jakob. He began to sob.

"Irina loved you," Oxana whispered in his ear. "You were the most important person in her life; now all we can do is hold her memory and love in our hearts." He embraced Oxana and her mother and slowly stepped away with Greta.

Oxana remained, arm in arm with her mother, her lips trembling, her tears flowing—her last moment with Irina, the final goodbye.

Oxana rose before sunrise. She had tried to sleep, but every time she closed her eyes, her mind was flooded with memories, memories of small things, odd things—the way Irina laughed, how she would cock her head to one side when she disagreed with you, how she would tug on her dress and shift from one foot to the other when she was angry.

Hoping it would relieve her sore, bloodshot eyes, Oxana splashed cold water over her face before pulling on a dress and going out the door. The air was cool and she inhaled deeply, trying to lift her body out of the numbness of her grief. She rounded the corner of the Orthodox church and was surprised to see Jakob sitting cross-legged beside Irina's grave, still wearing his wedding suit.

"May I join you?" Oxana asked.

"Please."

"Did you spend the entire night here?"

"This is the only place I want to be. I loved her so much."

Oxana sat on the ground beside him. "I loved her too, but I didn't always show it. I assumed we would always have each other. I took so much for granted."

"I did too," Jakob whispered. "I tried to tell her I loved her as often as I could, but it wasn't enough."

"You didn't need to say it. Irina felt your love constantly. I know she did."

Jakob turned to face Oxana. "What am I going to do? She died because she was going to have my baby. My mother died while I was being born, and now God has punished me by taking my wife and my baby. I killed them all."

"Jakob! No one killed Irina. She had a miscarriage and died. It's not anyone's fault." Oxana put her arms around his shoulders. "Don't talk like this. No one is blaming you, not for your mother's death, or for Irina's, or for your baby's."

"But it's true. If I hadn't been born, my mother would still be alive and Irina would still be alive."

"You're hurting now, but give yourself some time," Oxana said while Jakob sifted his fingers through the freshly dug soil.

"I'm so lost, Oxana. How am I going to live without my wife, my Irina?"

Oxana reached over and they embraced. "I know, Jakob, I know. I'm lost too. How am I going to live without my sister and best friend?" she whispered, a knot forming in her chest. She had always known that as long as she had her mother and her sister, life would be complete. But Irina was gone, and her life would never again be whole. There would always be a missing piece. Oxana stared at Jakob, his wedding suit stained from the freshly dug dirt, and for the first time she felt she fully understood him. Life had never been complete for him and never would. He had never had his mother, and now his wife was gone.

They sat a long while, embracing tightly, warmly, lovingly.

———

Oxana eased open the door to Jakob and Irina's house as she had every day since the funeral, and, like every day, Jakob smelled of alcohol. She was about to berate him but stopped. *Who am I to judge? God only knows what hell he's living through.*

Jakob said nothing as she set the small pot she was carrying on the table and ladled the stew into a bowl. He pulled his chair closer to the table and swallowed a few spoonfuls. "Thanks for bringing this. I guess I am hungry." He poured a shot of vodka and swallowed it in one gulp. "I feel I'm locked in a prison and I can't escape," he said. "But it doesn't matter. I don't want to escape. I want to feel grief because Irina is in that grief. That's all I have left of her."

"Jakob, you have your memories. Irina is also in those, and you can hold on to those for the rest of your life."

"I don't want a future if it means a life without her. I want the past. I want Irina."

"I want her back too. I'd do anything to bring her back."

Jakob wiped his eyes with his shirtsleeve. Speaking as if lost in a dream, he said, "You and Irina were the most beautiful girls in school. Sometimes I couldn't even tell you apart, and I wasn't sure who I loved more. But you went off to Odesa, and eventually I knew Irina was the girl for me—so kind and sweet and gentle. I loved her completely . . ." Jakob's voice trailed off. Oxana put her arm around his neck and rubbed his back, not sure if he had finished and was expecting her to respond. "But I never stopped loving you," he said, so weakly it was nearly inaudible. "Is it wrong to say that? Is it a sin?"

Oxana laid her head on Jakob's shoulder. What could she say? It was only now, in retrospect, that she could admit to herself that she too had always loved Jakob, but she also fully understood and accepted that he was not for her. He was for Irina, and she never would have violated that unspoken agreement. She never could have taken him away from her sister. It would have destroyed Irina. "No, it's not a sin," Oxana said. "We were a team, the three of us. We all loved each other."

Jakob held Oxana's face and caressed her cheeks and mouth. "Yes, we were a team," he repeated. He gazed into her eyes and Oxana turned away, lips trembling. Jakob reached for her hand. "But I love you too," he whispered. "I love Irina so much, but I also love you."

"We were a team," Oxana whispered.

Jakob leaned in and kissed her on the lips. He kissed her cheeks and eyes, and his lips returned to her mouth. Oxana knew he could feel her trembling. "Is this wrong, Oxana?" Jakob whispered. "Is it a sin?"

"No, Jakob, no," she whispered. He took another gulp of vodka. Without saying another word, Oxana stood and reached for her hat. *Yes, Jakob, I love you*, she thought, *and No, this love is not a sin. But I cannot violate my sister's wedding vows. It would be a desecration of her memory.*

Without looking back at Jakob, Oxana stepped out the door and into the bright sunshine.

———

That evening, hearing her front door open, Oxana turned to see Jakob standing, or rather leaning, in the doorway. Even from across the room she smelled vodka. "Oh, Jakob." She put her arm around his neck to steady him while glancing over her shoulder to be sure no one was watching. She got him through the door and eased him into a chair. Jakob pulled a vodka bottle from his pocket and gulped the last of it. "Play Fantasy . . . please," he mumbled, cramming the bottle back into his pocket.

"Yes, of course, for you, and for Irina too."

Oxana sat at her piano, and as the opening bass notes sounded, Jakob staggered over to the piano and squeezed onto the bench. Oxana continued playing and he put his arm around her waist. He leaned against her, his hot breath warming her neck as his lips touched her skin. "I love you, Oxana," Jakob cooed into her ear, reaching a hand under her blouse and cupping her breast.

Oxana stopped playing and put her arms around his waist. She hoisted him to his feet and helped him back to the chair, but when she tried to help him sit, Jakob leaned against her, fumbling with his belt. "No . . . bed . . . lay with me, please." She eased him toward the bed and he fell backward. Oxana, not sure if he had fallen asleep or passed out, put a pillow under his head and covered him with a blanket.

Oxana tiptoed out the door, into the cool night air and into the town square. The Orthodox church, lit only by the dim moonlight, looked cold and forbidding, like a tomb, Irina's tomb.

She felt her way around the side of the church and into the cemetery. Oxana knelt beside Irina's grave and made the sign of the cross across her chest. *God, please help me. Irina, forgive me.* She remained on her knees a long while, shivering, as if she were before a precipice, about to fall over the edge, her mind saying "step back" while her heart screamed "jump."

———

Jakob opened his eyes and lay watching when she came into the room. She slowly removed her dress, and he lowered his pants to his ankles. She eased herself beside him and pulled the blanket over their bare bodies. Jakob snuggled against her and put his arms around her. His muscles felt strong and firm, and a warmth pulsed through her body as her fingers caressed his chest and stomach. He nuzzled his nose against her breasts and kissed her nipples. Oxana lowered her hand and gently massaged. Jakob moaned.

She had never been with a man before and tensed when he rolled on top and eased into her. Jakob began a rhythmic thrust, slowly at first, and Oxana's body relaxed, instinctively responding with her own rhythmic gyration. His movement became more forceful, until Oxana felt his muscles tighten into a jerking spasm. Jakob, moaning, breathing deeply, lay against her as if in a trance, their nakedness entwined, their sweat intermingling.

He rolled onto his side and the vodka bottle in his pants pocket fell to the floor and smashed. Jakob was startled. "No, no," he mumbled. He tried to stand but stumbled. Oxana quickly wrapped herself in the blanket before grabbing his arms and hoisting him to his feet. He staggered to the door, struggling to pull up his pants. "No. No, Irina . . . I'm sorry, it's wrong . . . sorry." He was barely out the door before he bent over and heaved. Oxana stood in the doorway, weeping, watching him staggering toward the main road. Was Jakob right? Had she—they—committed an unpardonable sin? But it was not Jakob's fault. He was drunk. It was her fault. Jakob's confession had allowed her to convince herself that maybe she could have Jakob, but she was wrong and could never be forgiven. She had forever stained her memories of Irina.

Chapter 21

Jakob yanked open his front door and lurched over the threshold. He began alternately pushing and pulling on his piano, until he managed to force it out the door and into the farmyard. He staggered to the barn, grabbed his ax, and frantically hacked at the piano until it was reduced to a heap of splintered wood and clanging wires. Hobbling into the kitchen, he grabbed a cast-iron skillet and scooped several lumps of red, glowing embers out of the stove. He blew on the embers to reignite the flame as he carried them to the pile of splintered wood. The small fire gradually grew until the pile was completely ablaze, and Jakob stood without moving, as though he were witnessing the funeral pyre of a beloved friend.

He grabbed a burning stick and tromped to the barn. He threw the stick into the hay and quickly untied his horse and cow and shooed them out the door. Within minutes the flames spread across the barn walls and reached the roof.

Jakob slowly returned to the house. He tore away the curtains Irina had hung around the bed. Her dresses were hanging on a peg on the wall above the bed, and Jakob took down the front one, a yellow dress with buttons down the back and a small tie at the waist. Irina had only recently finished sewing it and had not yet worn it. Jakob laid it on the bed. He took down her dark navy blue dress with a white crocheted collar, Irina's favorite, the one she always wore on Sundays. *You were so beautiful in this, Irina.* Jakob laid it on the bed, atop the yellow dress, and smoothed out the wrinkles.

He lifted Irina's two cotton calico-patterned dresses from the wooden peg and held them to his nose to inhale her lingering scent. She had sewn in side panels so she could wear them while she was pregnant. Jakob laid them both atop the other dresses and ran his fingers over the seams—seams she had stitched by hand.

Jakob lifted Irina's wedding dress from the back of the peg and felt the smoothness of the rich brown brocade. He caressed the embroidered design and the frilly lace trim, remembering how it fit Irina's slim body perfectly. The dress was a surprise—Irina had followed the tradition of not allowing the groom to see the bride's dress until the wedding. Irina had smiled as she proceeded toward him, at the altar waiting for her—wanting her so badly he could hardly breathe while he held her hand during their wedding ceremony. She had not worn the dress since that day.

She had been so beautiful. He had never deserved her; she should have married someone better. Jakob laid the wedding dress across the others on the bed and bent over to kiss the hem. *Goodbye, Irina. I am so sorry.*

He reached to the shelf above the bed, removing her underclothes, one piece at a time, sniffing each for one last faint inhalation of her scent before gently placing each piece beside her dresses. He carefully smoothed everything out one last time to ensure nothing was wrinkled.

I am so sorry, Irina. You deserved silk and I gave you cotton. You deserved a husband and I am nothing. You deserved a life, and I took it from you. Forgive me, Irina.

Jakob went to the stove and scooped out the last, barely lit ember and carried it to the bed. He gently laid the hot red coal on Irina's wedding dress and folded the dress around it, as if wrapping a present for her. A flame emerged from the fabric, and Jakob stared at the strange beauty of the iridescent orange-red as it almost floated in midair. Soon the bed itself was in flames. The fire spread from the bed to the flimsy paper covering the wooden walls, and before long the counter in the kitchen area was ablaze. Jakob slowly eased himself into a chair and laid his head on the table, inhaling the black smoke in hopes of bringing about the end as quickly as possible.

A hand pulled him out of the water tank and Jakob coughed, struggling to breathe. He spit water, gasping for air.

"It's time to go."

Jakob opened his eyes and looked into Wilhelm's face. It was the first time he had ever seen his brother cry.

Chapter 22

The air was unseasonably cool, and Oxana, shivering, buttoned her sweater. The large golden cross atop the bright red onion dome of the Orthodox church glinted in the sunlight. She had passed by the church all her life without ever giving it a second thought, but now she couldn't help but think of it as Irina's final home, where she lay for the last time, where her last goodbyes were said.

Irina's grave was the same as the day she was buried, the dirt still black and freshly dug, the flowers not yet wilted. Oxana sat with folded hands on the small stone bench that workers had installed at the foot of the grave, silently staring. She had so much she wanted to say but could not find the words. She watched two ducks waddle into the small pond at the edge of the cemetery. For a moment, they were in the same position as the ducks Irina had embroidered on her rushnyk. Oxana buried her face in her hands and sobbed.

I'll go to Jakob today, but later, not now.

She made her way across the square to the general store and opened the door. Olga was standing inside with another seemingly ancient babushka.

"*Dobroe utro,*" Oxana said, briefly glancing at the two old women as she wished them a good morning. Both were wearing long black wool dresses, their heads wrapped in brightly colored kerchiefs. Olga's old dog was lying at her feet. It had, long ago, lost the use of its hind legs, and Olga carried it with her wherever she went, doting on it like a child. Oxana passed by them quickly but still smelled the stench of perspiration and urine.

"They say Jakob Schweitz left," Oxana overheard Olga say. Her body tensed. *What? He left?* "The whole family went," Olga continued. "Took the first train out."

"Going to America, someone said," the other woman added.

"I'm glad he's gone," Olga rasped in a low-pitched, gravelly voice. "That Jakob Schweitz brought nothing but bad luck to the entire village."

Oxana could feel her face redden with anger.

"He was cursed by God!" Olga continued. "God punishes babies who kill their mothers, and evil like that always comes in threes. So now the devil has taken his wife and baby too."

"You fiends," Oxana shouted, coming around the corner. "You should be ashamed."

"Fie, she's always been a sassy one," Olga hissed, a hideous gap-toothed grin spreading across her face. "Thinks she's better than the rest of us."

Oxana ran out of the store. The last thing she wanted was for them to see her tears. It would give them even more mud to roll around in.

She hurried to her mother's house and found her sitting at the kitchen table, a cup of tea in her hand. "Mama, Jakob's gone," Oxana said, taking a cup off the shelf and pouring herself some hot tea. Her mother's eyes were red. "Olga said it at the store. Do you think it's true?"

"It's true," her mother replied quietly. "Jakob's gone. He stopped by early this morning on his way to the train." She pulled a handkerchief out of her apron pocket and dabbed her nose and eyes.

Oxana dropped into a chair. "He's gone . . . to America?" She could hardly utter the words. Her heart was racing. "Irina never said anything about going to America. She would've told me if they were planning to leave."

Her mother fidgeted with her handkerchief. "He said they wanted to wait until they were sure and that they were planning to tell us, but then—"

"Did he say for how long?"

"No, but I'd reckon forever."

"Forever? Surely he'll be back."

"Oxana, he isn't coming back."

"But he didn't tell me."

"He said he couldn't tell you. He could barely tell me. He kept saying he was sorry, that this would hurt us, and we already have enough hurt in our lives." Her mother gazed out the window while she brushed her wet cheeks with the back of her hand.

"He never even came to say goodbye," Oxana whispered.

Oxana went home dazed, as if she had lost all feeling in her body. She unlatched the lock, opened her door, and stepped inside. She could envision Irina's coffin still lying on the table, like a shadow that would never go away. Her piano stood against the far wall, staring, accusing, like a witness at a crime scene, while her small bed, sheets still rumpled, smelled of him—his arms around her, embracing her, the weight of his body against hers, the contrast between his firm, hard muscles and the gentleness of his hands. She stood in her tiny, miserable hut with tears streaming down her cheeks. Her love for Jakob would never fade; she would never love another man.

———

Memories of Irina and Jakob hung in the air like a fog that summer, and at times her grief was nearly overwhelming, but Oxana found comfort in the dreariness and monotony of routine—waking, cooking a bit of food, taking long walks, teaching her students, and finally going back to bed. And she found comfort in sensing that Irina and Jakob were never far from her—as though they were in the next room, or behind a tree, or around a corner, watching, listening. She would find herself calling aloud, "Where are you? I know you're here, why won't you let me see you?"

Frying eggs one morning, she barely managed to pull the chamber pot out from under the bed before throwing up. When it happened again the next day, she suspected she had picked up a stomach flu. Her illness continued until its source finally occurred to her. Oxana's face went white. "Oh no," she moaned, sinking into a chair and rocking back and forth. *Oh no.*

That afternoon, Oxana went to the cemetery and sat on the stone bench at the foot of Irina's grave. *Privyet, Irina.* Her forehead was feverish. She pressed her hands into the black soil to absorb its damp coolness and held her palms against her forehead. *Irina,* Oxana spoke silently to her sister, *do you remember after my concert when you and Jakob announced your engagement? And how you and Jakob sat on the sofa while I played? And Jakob smiled, with his blond hair and blue eyes, wearing that tunic Mama had sewn for him?*

Irina, that was the moment I became jealous of you. That was the moment I wanted what you had. God forgive me, Irina. I wanted Jakob. After you died, he came to me. He was drunk—too drunk to know what he was doing, but I knew. Irina, I'm so sorry. I've taken your husband.

A knot was forming in her stomach, and Oxana buried her face in her hands. Her arms were shaking, and she felt she might faint. *Oh God, Irina, I'm in trouble . . . Oh God . . .* She pitched forward onto Irina's grave and her knees sank into the soft soil. *Irina . . . I'm going to have a baby.* Oxana leaned her arms forward to steady herself. *If only you were here, none of this would have happened. I'm not blaming you—I blame me—I know you hate me, and you should. I can never ask for your forgiveness; I'll never deserve it. Oh Irina, my sister, what have I done to you? Oh God—Irina, help me. I'm all alone and I need you.*

Oxana wandered down the main road as if she were blind and groping for her way, her mind filled with fear and anxiety. Her decision was made, and while it was not what she wanted, she had no other choice; it was best to get it over with as quickly as possible. Several people waved as their wagons passed, but none stopped to offer a ride. At last she recognized the farmyard. Fedor was coming out of the barn and ran to open the gate.

"Oxana! It's great to see you." Fedor grabbed her waist and hugged her. "I'm sorry about Irina. I wanted to come and talk to you, but I didn't know what to say."

"Can we sit in the shade? It's a long way out here."

"Yes, yes, of course, shade. Come over here and sit. Do you want some water?"

"Fedor, I've come to talk about the proposal you made to me. I know I said I didn't need to think it over, but I was wrong. I have thought it over, and well, to be blunt, if your offer still stands, I am prepared to say yes."

"What are you saying, Oxana? That you will marry me? Of course the proposal still stands. Is it true? Will you marry me?"

"Yes, Fedor. I will marry you."

"I can't believe my ears or my good fortune. You've made me so happy." Fedor held her against him and kissed her lips, and Oxana, for the first time, did not push him away.

Fedor, his brother Gregor, and his mother were waiting when Oxana and her mother arrived at the Orthodox church. Fedor was wearing a suit and necktie, the first time she had seen him dressed up, and she had to admit he was handsome. He kissed her and introduced his brother. They all shook hands. Gregor and Naydia offered condolences and their understanding that any celebrating was out of the question, given the circumstances.

The ceremony was brief—a few prayers and the exchange of vows. There was no rushnyk to step on, no korovai to be blessed. The priest pronounced them husband and wife, they kissed, and the wedding party emerged into the sunshine.

Naydia invited them all for at least a slice of cake and a wine toast, but Oxana's mother declined. The two mothers wiped tears as they hugged, said their goodbyes, and wished Fedor and Oxana well before heading back home. Gregor shook both their hands, congratulated them and also turned to leave.

Fedor reached for Oxana's hand, and the newlyweds began walking. "I'm sorry we're not having a celebration," he said. "My mother was really hoping for a big wedding, and I guess I was too, but of course with Irina and all, plus this all came on sort of suddenly—you changing your mind—I had almost lost hope. Don't get me wrong—I'm very happy you did change your mind, but still, a wedding ought to be celebrated."

"I couldn't possibly celebrate," Oxana said.

It was nearly five kilometers to Fedor's farm, which lay north of the village, the opposite direction of Jakob and Irina's house. The land was flat and, except for the lake to the east and the forest to the west, was covered by green wheat fields separated by narrow paths of short grass. Oxana was surprised at how the monotony of the landscape somehow had an allure to it.

"There's Arkady Mikhailov's place," Fedor said, and Oxana's gaze followed his pointing finger. "He bought it before marrying Maria. And that there's the Domitovich place." Fedor pointed to the farmyard on the opposite side of the road. The buildings were dilapidated, and the paint had faded to a dull gray. "There isn't much happening there these days. Slava's near eighty already, and Ludmilla's not far behind him. And this is my place, and yours now too," Fedor announced, pointing up ahead. The house was a long, low rectangle, like most of the houses in Peterstal, and like the Domitovich house, in need of paint. The red barn was larger than the house, and several outbuildings were scattered about.

He unlatched the gate and, still holding Oxana's hand, led her into the farmyard. "Bet you haven't seen one of them before," he said, directing her gaze to a bright green tractor parked in front of the barn door. "It's practically brand new, came from America. There aren't too many tractors in Russia. Cost too much for most folk. Gregor and I went half and half and it still set us back quite a bit, but it sure is nice not to do all the field work by hand."

With his left hand still clasping Oxana's, he pointed toward the wheat field behind the barn. "That's where my land begins, stretches all the way to the forest, and Gregor's is over there. It's a big spread, I don't mind saying. One of the biggest in the area. My father worked hard to pull it all together, and me and Gregor keep it going."

Oxana had no reaction, only staring, knowing that she had to accept the reality that this strange new place was now where she would spend the rest of her life—a wife to Fedor and a slave to a farm.

Fedor led Oxana to the steps of the house and opened the front door. He lifted her into his arms.

"Don't be silly." Oxana tried pushing him away.

"Welcome to your new home, my lovely bride," he said, carrying her across the threshold. He set her down and Oxana tugged on her dress, speechless. The windows were covered with a gray film, probably the accumulated result of years of cigarette smoke, and the floor had not been scrubbed in a very long time. There were food stains on the tablecloth, and the sofa was so faded and threadbare that she wasn't quite sure what color it had originally been.

"I tried to clean up for you, but I guess I'm not much for housekeeping," Fedor said as Oxana gazed at the room. "It was clean when my mother was here, but after my father passed on, she moved into town and, well, there isn't much need for a bachelor to keep things clean."

There was a knock at the door. "Privyet! Privyet!" Ludmilla sang out. "Congratulations on your wedding. I brought you a basket of food."

"Ludmilla, how sweet of you," Oxana said, taking the basket.

"Ya, a heap of thanks," Fedor added.

"Don't mean to disturb you, but I don't want you two to starve on your first night together. I know how it takes a bit of time for a bride to find her way around a new kitchen."

As soon as Ludmilla was out the door, Oxana started to cry.

"I know this is a big change—for both of us," Fedor said, rubbing her back, "but you'll get used to me and the house. It'll take some time, but I know we'll be happy."

That evening, after consuming every bit of the bread, sausage, and cheese in Ludmilla's basket, Oxana and Fedor sat on his sofa, holding hands. "I want you to know how lucky I feel," Fedor said softly. "A lot of men had their eyes on the Stepaniaka twins over the years, but I always knew you were the girl for me, and I can't tell you how long I've waited for this night." Fedor leaned over and kissed her. "I love you. I'll try to be a good husband." He put his arm around her waist, pulled her to her feet, and led her over to the bed.

Oxana, too numb to feel either pain or pleasure, obediently followed his lead. She was his wife and she would do her duty, do whatever it took to protect the baby she was now carrying.

"Let me do that," he whispered when she started to fumble with the buttons on her dress. He pulled her hair back and licked her neck with his tongue as he slowly undid the buttons and slipped her dress from her shoulders, letting it drop to the floor. He massaged her breasts and abdomen as he nuzzled her hair. Slowly he turned her around to face him. "I'd like it if you would undress me," he whispered.

Oxana undid the buttons on his shirt, and he held out his arms so she could slip it off him. He had a small triangle of black chest hair which trailed down his stomach. Oxana opened his pants. He was already fully erect and squeezed his body against her, thrusting himself between her legs, and began a slow dance before he picked her up off her feet and laid her on the bed. He was slow and gentle, and despite her anxiety, she relaxed as their bodies joined.

He quickly reached his climax and rolled onto his back. "Are you hurt? I hope I didn't hurt you," he whispered.

"No, I'm not hurt. You were gentle. It felt like you've maybe done this before," Oxana said with a soft laugh.

"Same with you," Fedor responded.

"What do you mean?"

"There's no blood. But don't worry." Fedor also laughed. "I don't mind. I figured a woman as beautiful and talented as you must've learned a little bit more in Odesa than how to play the piano."

"I have no idea what you're talking about," Oxana said and rolled onto her side.

"All the same, that was mighty fine," he whispered, stroking her hair. "As fine as any man could ask for."

As soon as Fedor was asleep, Oxana slipped out of the bed and grabbed her dress off the floor. She pulled it across herself and sat on the sofa, gazing out the window. The full moon's soft light was illuminating the trees. The room was chilly and she shivered, clutching her arms around herself. In her home, she had at least felt Irina and Jakob's spirits, but in this foreign house she had no sense of them. It was as though when Fedor carried her across the threshold, he had carried her into another world. An unbridgeable chasm had opened, and she could never again cross back.

Oxana was up early, before sunrise and before Fedor. A coffeepot sat on the stove, but the bottom was caked with old coffee grounds. She found a knife and scraped, trying her best to remove the dried-on dregs. The stove's fire chamber was filled with ashes, and she had to scoop them into a bucket to make space to add wood and light a flame to start the coffee. She noticed several cups on the shelves, but all had dried coffee residue in the bottoms. By the time she had heated a small kettle of water for the washbasin and washed the cups, Fedor came into the room.

"Morning," he said, nuzzling her neck.

"Good morning," she replied, without turning toward him.

"Suppose you'll be wanting to bring your things here as soon as we can fetch them."

Oxana picked up a towel to dry the cups. It was damp and smelled musty, and she tossed it back on the counter. She wiped the cups with her dress and poured coffee.

"We can do it today. Gregor can help."

She picked up a half loaf of bread lying on the counter but threw it back down. The bottom crust was green. She picked it up again, tore away the moldy part, and pulled off a chunk. They sat in silence while Fedor chewed the bread and slurped his coffee.

After Fedor left to get his brother and she finished washing the rest of the dirty dishes, Oxana went into town but paused in her former front yard, working up the courage to step inside her home for the last time. She undid the latch and opened the door, gazing at the table where Irina's coffin had lain. *Will I eventually forget you? Forget the sound of your voice? Forget your smile and your laughter?*

She brushed her hands across the quilt covering the bed. *And will I forget you, Jakob, as well? Your strong hands, your beautiful blue eyes and blond hair? And will you also forget me? It's Irina you'll remember, not me.*

Her dresses were hanging from the rack beside the bed. *How many hours did you work for me, Mama?* She felt the softness of the fabric, tracing the intricate needlework with her finger. *How many hours of eye-straining, finger-numbing work, just so I could have a pretty dress?* Oxana folded each into a square. At the back was her red concert dress. *Mama hated you. Maybe Neuhaus did too. Why didn't he like my playing? Why didn't he invite me to Moscow? Was it me? Or was it you?* Oxana folded the dress and opened her steamer trunk. *I won't be needing these anytime soon*, she thought, laying the dresses inside. She removed her hair ribbons from the bedside bureau and placed them on top of the dresses. Belts, hats, gloves . . . she put everything into the trunk, even her perfume bottles, remembering how Irina loved perfume. She wore so much it made people's eyes water—except Jakob's. For him, it was never too much. She closed the trunk lid and snapped the lock.

Fedor and Gregor arrived as Oxana was packing her kitchen dishes. She didn't have much to move. The furniture belonged to Fedor's mother and would stay with the house. Fedor and Gregor loaded the steamer trunk and the few boxes into the back of the wagon. The last to go was the piano. Fedor and Gregor groaned as they pushed it out the door. Taking hold of it from the bottom and hoisting, they had it almost high enough to slide into the back of the wagon when Gregor lost his grip. The piano nearly fell to the ground before he regained his grasp. Oxana had no reaction. *Let it fall. Let it smash. Maybe in the end it's better to be rid of the burden. That part of my life has ended.*

"That's the heaviest thing I've ever lifted," Gregor gasped, once they had the piano in the wagon box. "What do they make these things out of? Bricks?"

Fedor cranked the tractor engine several times and climbed into the seat. Gregor crawled into the back of the wagon and Oxana walked alongside, clutching her prized possession, a small gold icon inlaid with semiprecious stones, her graduation gift from Vera Fedorovna Veranitzskaya.

Oxana spent her first days of married life cleaning, starting with scrubbing away the layers of accumulated soot on the stove. Like most Russian peasant homes, the stove was the most prominent feature of the main room and took up an entire corner. A small wood-burning chamber heated the stove's cooking surface, and beneath it was a larger open-fire chamber, which heated a baking oven and served as the sole source of heat for the house.

It took her several days to scrub the walls, wash the windowpanes inside and out, and polish the floor. She stripped Fedor's grungy bedsheets and replaced them with hers, boxed up Fedor's old, chipped dishes and put her dishes on the shelf above the kitchen sink, and knit a spread to cover the dirty sofa. As she worked, she glanced toward the piano as if it were staring at her, demanding attention. *Don't stare at me like that. And stop pouting. We're not friends any longer.* She placed her mother's tatted lace runner across the top and hung Vera's icon above it. *At least you can look nice.* But she could not bring herself to touch the keys.

"Sure is pretty in here," Fedor said one evening, putting his arms around Oxana and kissing her cheek. "I didn't know floors got this shiny. They're too clean to even walk on."

Once she had the house cleaned to her standards, Oxana went outside to investigate what appeared to be a vegetable garden, despite being completely overgrown with weeds. Starting at one end, she worked her way across the bed, pulling up pigweed, thistles, nettles, and dandelions and soon discovered a nice array of vegetables—potatoes, carrots, onions, beans, pumpkins, squash, and even a couple of melons.

"I see you've discovered my vegetable patch," Fedor said, swinging the gate open. "I plant it every spring, but it always gets away from me. With all the field work, I've got no time for weeding a garden."

Oxana stood and rubbed her sore back.

"It was my mother's," Fedor continued. "She loved it. That's why I keep planting it." Fedor put his arm around Oxana's waist. "Sometimes me and Gregor helped her when we were little, but our father didn't take kindly to us doing gardening. 'That's women's work,' he'd say, and he would take a strap to us. He was a mean one, our father—a hard worker, but mean. Always had his strap ready if we took a wrong step. I got it more than Gregor, but he got his share too. He could make our mother cry half a day when he started beating on her. But she always brightened up when she came out here. I want you to be like my mother. I want you to find happiness in this garden, like she did. Oxana, you're the best thing that ever happened to me."

Fedor had tears in his eyes and, for the first time, Oxana initiated a kiss.

Oxana had never worked in her mother's garden. That was Irina's job to do while she practiced, but while it was exhausting, she found she enjoyed gardening. Once the weeds were cleared, she began pulling away the invasive vines covering the trees at the far end and discovered fruit trees—apple, cherry, apricot, and even one yellow plum. The apple and plum trees were loaded with ripe fruit. When Fedor came home that evening, she had a pie waiting for him.

———

The Saturday market was a village tradition stretching as far back as anyone could remember. Farmers brought vegetables, meats, handicrafts— whatever they had for sale. Oxana recalled her mother bartering for their weekly supply of food, as well as the fragrant aroma as her mother and Irina prepared the fresh meats and produce while she did her practicing. Oxana wanted to continue this tradition, and she went into town to shop every Saturday as soon as she finished washing the breakfast dishes.

She was purchasing lamb chops one Saturday morning when a voice called, "*Dobroe utro.*" She turned. Maria was waving and pushing her way through the crowd. "I miss Irina terribly," Maria said, giving Oxana a hug before wiping her eyes with her dress, "but I guess all the crying in the world won't bring her back, though I sure wish it could. I'd cry a river for Irina if I thought it would help."

"I think between you, me, and Mama, we've probably already cried a river," Oxana said.

"By the way, I want to congratulate you on your marriage," Maria continued.

"And I want to congratulate you, Maria, on your marriage. I'm sorry I wasn't able to come. It's been too—"

"I know," Maria said. "Me and Arkady did like you and Fedor—a small, quiet wedding, nothing more. Anyway, I hope you won't be offended, but me and Arkady are putting on a dance tomorrow night to celebrate our wedding and we'd love it if you and Fedor would come, and sort of celebrate your wedding too. Of course, I understand if you and Fedor are not wanting to. It's tough to be celebrating with Irina still so fresh in our minds, but just in case, you and Fedor are welcome. Anyway, tomorrow night, in case you want to come. Gotta run. *Poka.*" Maria waved.

━━━━━

The dance was already underway when Oxana and Fedor arrived. A table of drinks was set up inside the door, and Fedor downed a shot of vodka. Everyone was circling with arms entwined in a traditional round dance, and Fedor led Oxana onto the dance floor to join in.

Ilya, the town doctor, came over. "Mind if I steal her away?"

"Fine with me. I've got no reason to be jealous," Fedor said. "I'm about ready for another drink anyway."

Ilya put his arm around her waist. The band started another dance, this time a mazurka. His eyes were glassy and his speech slightly slurred. He had obviously gotten a head start on the vodka. "Thank you for dancing with me," Ilya said. "I know we hardly know each other, but I've been hoping for a chance to talk to you ever since your concert. It was the best piano playing I've ever heard." He lifted her arms and twirled her around. Oxana was surprised at how firm and strong yet at the same time gentle and light his touch was. His black, curly hair was combed back, and she smelled a hint of spicy cologne.

"I like this music," Oxana said.

"You caught yourself quite a handsome husband," Ilya said.

"Beg your pardon?"

"I mean, I didn't think you were planning to marry and stay here, but if I had known, I might have thrown my hat in the ring too."

Oxana laughed. "I wasn't aware that marriage was a boxing contest." They twirled several more rounds across the dance floor. She sensed a naturalness about him, as if he was utterly relaxed and at ease without a care in the world, and she leaned into him, feeling as if his ease and calmness were transferring itself into her tense body.

"I'm only saying your husband is one lucky fellow." Ilya grasped her tighter around the waist and leaned his cheek against her face. "You are a very beautiful woman," he cooed into her ear.

"What the hell are you doing?" Fedor said, coming up behind Ilya and pushing his arm away from Oxana. "This is my wife you're getting all fresh with, not some cheap whore."

"Calm down. I was only—" Ilya started to say, but Fedor smacked him with his fist and Ilya fell to the floor.

"Fedor!" Oxana screamed. The band stopped playing and everyone stopped dancing, staring in utter silence.

"Let's get out of here," Fedor shouted. "I hate this music." He grabbed Oxana's hand and pulled her toward the door, grabbing two shots of vodka and downing them before they stepped outside.

"What was that all about?" Oxana asked.

The air was cool, with a light breeze, and Fedor put his coat around Oxana's shoulders. "That doctor had his eyes and hands all over you."

"What are you saying? We were simply dancing."

"I'm not saying anything—except that you'd think you were married to him instead of me, the way he was acting."

"What difference does it make how he acted? You're my husband, not him. And besides, we're going to have a baby."

"What did you say?" Fedor said, stopping and turning Oxana to face him.

"I said we're going to have a baby."

"Holy Christ!" Fedor shouted. "A baby? I'm going to be a father? Are you sure? Holy Christ!" He wrapped both arms around Oxana's waist, lifted her off her feet, and swung her around in a circle. "I love you." He kissed her. "Now we'll be a real family." Fedor held Oxana's hand the rest of the way home, squeezing it and muttering every few minutes, "Holy Christ! I'm going to be a father."

Chapter 23

Stepping off the train platform, Jakob pulled his coat up and his hat down, leaving only his eyes visible. He was back in Peterstal and did not want anyone to recognize him. He had spent the past months thinking of nothing but this return, going around in circles, one day planning every detail, every word he intended to speak, and then the next day abandoning it all.

He had gone with Wilhelm and Greta to Odesa, but at the last moment he could not board the ship to America. There had been a ferocious fight, with Wilhelm demanding he come along and at one point even putting up his fists, threatening to sock Jakob in the jaw, but Jakob's mind was made up. He would not go to America. He would not abandon Irina's grave, and he would see Oxana.

Quickly crossing the town square, he hurried around the Orthodox church and into the cemetery. Someone, Irina's mother he assumed, or maybe Oxana, had planted flowers on Irina's grave, and they were in full bloom. Fingering Irina's wedding ring in his pocket, his mother's ring that his father had given him, and remembering his father's letter telling him to give it to the woman he loved and to love her completely, he knelt beside the grave and inhaled the rich scent of the flowers.

"Irina," he whispered, "I'm going to ask Oxana to marry me, and I'm going to give her your ring. I beg you not to be angry with me. I loved you completely, and I will never stop loving you, but you are gone and I have to go on living. I know you loved Oxana at least as much as you loved me, so I hope you can allow me to love her too. It's not a sin. A man can marry his sister-in-law . . ."

A shadow fell across him, and Jakob turned to see Irina's mother standing beside him.

"Elena Vladimirovna! I didn't expect to see you," he stammered.

"Nor I you," she said, appearing to be equally startled. "I thought you had gone to America with your brother."

"I couldn't"—he continued stammering—"leave Irina . . . or Oxana."

Elena stepped over to the stone bench at the foot of the grave, and Jakob quickly stood and took her hand to help her. Her knees were stiff, but she managed to ease herself down and Jakob sat beside her.

"Jakob," she began to speak, "you know I love you like a son. Remember, I raised you when you were a baby. I taught you to play the piano. I would have done anything for you, just as I would for my own daughters. And when you and Irina married, I could not have been happier. Irina had found the perfect husband, and I had the perfect son-in-law."

Jakob turned toward her and she took hold of his hand.

"But Jakob." Elena paused and swallowed uncomfortably, as if something were stuck in her throat. "But Jakob," she began again, "Oxana is married."

"Married? To who?"

"To Fedor Rostov."

"That cannot be true. She hates Fedor."

"That is not for either you or me to say. Maybe once she did not care for him, but she has made her decision and they are married."

Jakob balled his hands into a fist and dug into the soil. "So it is true," he said.

"Yes. And Jakob, Oxana is going to have a baby."

"A baby?" Jakob wiped the dirt from his hands and covered his face.

"Yes, a baby," Elena Vladimirova said, putting her arms around his waist. "Jakob, I am so sorry for you, but you must put the past behind you. Irina is gone, and Oxana is now a wife and soon to be a mother. A marriage is sacred and cannot be violated. There is nothing more for you here. I wish it were otherwise, but it's not."

"A baby," Jakob repeated.

"I'm sorry, Jakob. I really am."

"The last thing Wilhelm told me, as he was threatening to hit me, was to never return to Peterstal. 'Don't go back there,' he said. 'There is nothing there for you.' I was so certain he was wrong."

"I'm afraid he wasn't," Elena said, rubbing his back. "There is nothing here for you."

"Yes, I understand," Jakob whispered. "Wilhelm is always right."

"I will leave you here to say your final goodbye," Elena said, rising with difficulty. "I wish you well, Jakob. You will find happiness, one day. May God be with you." She turned her back, slowly crossed the cemetery and went out the gate, disappearing around the church.

Jakob sat a long while until finally he found the strength to utter, "Goodbye, Irina. I suspect you didn't approve of my plan to marry Oxana after all. It's fine. It was stupid of me to even think of such a thing. You are my wife, and always will be."

He rose to go but paused at the gate when he noticed a pair of ducks swimming in the pond at the edge of the cemetery. "Goodbye," he said, lifting his arm in a feeble wave toward the ducks, tears streaming down his cheeks.

———

Again covering his face to avoid being recognized, Jakob made his way across the square to the Lutheran church. Father Vanska was sweeping the steps outside and said hello, not recognizing him.

"Hello, Father Vanska," Jakob said, uncovering his face.

"Jakob! I heard you went to America."

"Not yet, Father, but perhaps I will, soon. May I come in?"

"Of course, of course," Father Vanska said, laying his broom aside and opening the church door.

"Father, I wish to make a confession, and to ask your forgiveness."

"Yes, go on."

"Father, after Irina . . . after my wife . . . died . . . Father, I went to Oxana. I was drunk, but I knew what I was doing. Father, I slept with my sister-in-law."

"I see," Father Vanska said, rubbing his hands together.

"Can you forgive me? Can God forgive me?"

"Jakob, what you did was not a sin. Your wife is gone. You are free to marry again if you choose."

"But Father, I broke my marriage vow."

"Jakob," Father Vanska began, "I forgive you, and I know God forgives you as well, but you must dig deep into your soul and find forgiveness for yourself. Neither I nor God can do that for you. And when you can forgive yourself, you will also find peace and eventually happiness. Pray to God. He will help you along your journey."

"Yes, Father." Jakob sat with his hand in his pocket, fingering the ring. "May I ask one final favor?"

"Yes, of course."

"Can you give me a sheet of paper and an envelope? I would like to write Oxana a letter. I left without saying goodbye, and I owe her at least this much."

"I'll be right back," Father Vanska said, and he quietly went down the aisle and into his vestry.

Jakob stared at the upright piano in the corner. He would never forget the old pianist's concert when he had first heard Chopin's Fantasy and experienced his vision of the Firebird. Was it his mother? It didn't matter. He remembered Oxana's concert, how beautifully she played, and in her red dress, how beautiful she looked. He remembered how he had sensed that the Firebird was directing him to a new life, and even though he desperately wanted that new life to be with Oxana, he realized that he had to accept that it was not possible. He would need to find another path.

"Here is paper and a pen," Father Vanska said, interrupting his thoughts.

Jakob quickly wrote the letter and slipped it into the envelope. He took the ring from his pocket and dropped it into the envelope as well. "For Oxana," he whispered, handing the envelope to Father Vanska. "My goodbye."

"Yes, my son." Father Vanska leaned over and kissed Jakob on his forehead. "Go in peace, for God is with you."

Jakob stood and paused to glance one final time at the old piano, sitting silently, innocently, yet magnificently aware of its power to create love and beauty. He nodded toward the instrument, mouthing the words "thank you."

Chapter 24

"Ouch!" Oxana muttered, wiping her pricked finger while sewing side panels into one of her dresses to make it hang more loosely, the way her mother had shown Irina. "Mama makes this seem so easy."

Hearing barking and shouting outside, Oxana went to the door. Fedor was kicking at a stray dog and had injured its hind legs. The dog was trying to pull itself along by its front paws, but Fedor kept kicking. "Stop," Gregor yelled. "Can't you see she's going to have pups? She probably needs food and water."

"I don't give a damn what she needs," Fedor screamed. "The bitch is a stray." He picked up a sledgehammer.

Oxana watched Gregor run toward him, shouting, "Jesus! Stop it!" but Fedor swung the sledgehammer and the dog fell to the ground. He threw the sledgehammer aside and stomped toward the barn.

"I'm sorry you had to see that," Gregor said, seeing Oxana standing on the front steps, her hand over her mouth. "He's like our father when he gets mad."

"Get the hell away from my wife," Fedor shouted from the barn door, "or I'll take the hammer to you next."

"Oxana, I think you need to know, there's some vicious gossip going around, and Fedor has gotten wind of it," Gregor said once Fedor was inside the barn.

"Gossip?" Oxana arched her back, despite the tightness in her stomach. "What sort of gossip?"

"About you, and the baby—it's mean people saying mean things, that's all."

"About me and the baby?" Oxana instinctively rubbed her stomach, as though she felt a sudden stab of pain. "What about me and the baby?"

"It's nothing but lies—some are saying the baby isn't Fedor's—I know it's not true—but it's got Fedor all worked up."

"I said get away from my wife," Fedor bellowed, coming out of the barn and picking up the sledgehammer.

"Put your hammer away. I'm leaving," Gregor yelled back. Before stepping away, he whispered, "If he ever lays a hand on you, you tell me. I'll beat the hell out of him. I won't allow him to beat on you the way our father beat on our mother." Gregor went out the gate and down the main road while Oxana stood staring.

———

The next days passed mostly in silence. Fedor ate breakfast and went out to the barn, returning to the house in the evenings, only to eat supper and go to bed. Oxana slipped in beside him after washing the dishes, but their nightly routine had ended. Fedor no longer touched her. He lay facing the wall, with his back to her, until he fell asleep, while Oxana lay awake, staring into the darkness, fearing what the future might hold.

On Saturday, Oxana pushed through the crowd at the market, wiping sweat from her forehead. The odors were making her dizzy and her stomach was upset, but she was determined to finish her shopping. She wanted to prepare a nice meal, despite Fedor's coldness.

"Privyet, Semyon Tromvich," Oxana called out. "My husband and brother-in-law loved your chops, so I'll take three more."

"I got no lamb for sale," he said.

"But isn't this your lamb?" Oxana pointed to the freshly slaughtered carcass, still dripping blood.

"It's not for sale."

"What do you mean, not for sale?"

"I mean what I say. It's not for sale. I don't sell to a woman like you."

Oxana stared at him blankly, unsure what to say, when she felt a tug on her sleeve and turned. "Don't pay him no mind. You don't need his smelly mutton. It's probably old and half rotten anyway. I'm Inna Sherpoka—here, take this." She handed Oxana a jar of honey. "I heard you play at the church. It sure was good."

"Thank you," Oxana said, trying to hold back her tears.

"You got lots of friends in this town. Don't forget that."

Oxana turned to go. Villagers were thronging around, and she was afraid she might vomit. "Are you sick?" a young boy asked. "You're kind of pale."

"I'm fine—a bit hot, that's all," Oxana said and hurried across the square to retreat to the quietness of Irina's grave. She sat on the stone bench and massaged her legs.

"Do you mind some company?" Maria said, coming toward her. "I was in the square and saw you going around the corner. Am I intruding?"

"No, not at all. I'd love some company right about now."

Maria awkwardly eased herself onto the stone bench. "Carrying these babies around ain't easy."

"When are you due?" Oxana asked.

"I thought it should have been about a month ago. Ludmilla's wondering if it'll ever come out, or worse, it may take one glance at this dusty old town and turn around and crawl right back in." They both laughed. "I think of her every day," Maria said, pointing to Irina's grave. "How she was the first of us to get married. There was never any question about her and Jakob, how she loved him, how we all loved him. Don't get me wrong. I love my Arkady, but that Jakob was something special. I told Irina she got the cream of the crop. It's probably best he went off. There'd be too many painful memories for him here."

"Yes," Oxana said quietly. "There probably would be."

"But it's funny how, once people you've known your whole life are gone, you get to wondering, were they ever here? Or did we make them up?"

Maria paused and fingered the hem of her dress while Oxana sat with her hands folded. "Things always seem to have a way of working out," Maria said. "Me and Arkady, and you and Fedor. You kept saying you didn't want to be married, but I always suspected you two would end up together."

Softly, almost whispering, she continued, "For some reason a baby didn't come right away for us . . ." Maria's voice drifted away, and she and Oxana sat listening to the breeze stirring the oak leaves. "Not having a baby right away was hard for me and Arkady. It certainly wasn't for lack of trying, I can tell you, but it didn't happen. I worried there was something wrong with me. What good is a woman if she can't give her husband a baby? I even told Arkady he could divorce me if he wanted. It was hard on him, I could see it—and now here I am, big as a house!"

"Maria, a woman is good for a lot more than giving her husband babies. You're smart, you can do whatever you want, be more than a farm wife—be a schoolteacher, or a nurse, or open a store and sell things."

"Oxana, you're so strong. I admire you, but I'm not like you. I wish I were, but I'm not. I don't have the courage to up and do something."

Oxana continued gazing at the grave, wondering what should be a woman's place in the world. Irina had wanted to be a wife and a mother, and so did Maria. Was that wrong? Oxana simply wanted more than that. She wanted a career as a pianist. Did that somehow make her superior?

"Well, I'd best be going." Maria stood. "With my luck, my water will probably break any minute and I'll end up delivering right here in the cemetery, with God and the whole village watching. Wouldn't that be a good way to bring a baby into the world—in the land of the dead."

Oxana laughed.

"I was wondering," Maria said but paused. "I know I'm not up to your level, you being so smart and talented, but since Irina and I were such good friends, maybe we could be friends too. Would it be alright if I came by once in a while to visit? It gets lonely at home all day with Arkady always working. And to be honest, I'm a little scared about having a baby after what happened to Irina. It frightens me, not knowing what it's going to be like when the time comes. It'd be nice to have someone to talk to."

"Maria, I would love nothing more than for you to come and visit. When you're around, I almost feel like Irina is here too." Oxana wrapped her arms around Maria and hugged her long and tight, embarrassed at how badly she had at first misjudged Maria. *Maria is a fine person and a great friend. Irina could see that, but I couldn't.* "I also need a friend right now."

Oxana had the usual Saturday meal ready when Fedor came in. They sat at the table in silence, avoiding eye contact. Fedor shoveled his food into his mouth while Oxana barely touched her plate. She cleared the table as soon as Fedor finished and was standing with her back to him, slicing an apple pie, when he came up behind her. He belched and she turned away from the hot, breathy odor. He put his arms around her waist and turned her around to face him, swaying as if he wanted to dance. "Is this how the doctor put his hand around your waist?" Fedor pulled Oxana against his body. "And is this how he kissed your neck? Am I doing it as nice as the doctor does it?"

"I don't know what you're talking about. You can't possibly be jealous of one short dance with someone I hardly know."

"You're right," Fedor said, and twirled Oxana in a circle. "It was only one short dance. I just want to make you happy, the way other men make you happy." Fedor gripped her tighter around the waist.

"Other men do not make me happy." Oxana pushed him away. "And the doctor means nothing to me."

Fedor stood in the middle of the room, with his arms wide open, waiting to resume the dance. "Don't you think it's awful early for you to be getting so big?" He pulled a vodka bottle out of his pocket and swallowed a few gulps.

Oxana stared at him, furious, unable to utter a word.

He slammed his fist on the table. "It's the damn doctor's, isn't it?"

"What are you talking about?" Oxana shouted.

"I only want to know if the gossip is true. Is it his?"

Oxana glared at him.

"You whore. You goddamned whore. God cursed me the day I married you. You're carrying another man's child and you tried to pass it off as mine. You stinking slut." Fedor lunged at her, slapping her face and shoulders. He held her tightly and punched her belly. Oxana screamed, but he punched harder. She tried to pull away, but he was too strong and held on. She bit his hand, and he loosened his grip enough that she broke free and ran out the door. He came after her but tripped and fell. She kicked the gate open and ran blindly, not sure where she was going, while Fedor rolled on the ground, hurling vulgar profanities into the black night.

She bent over, panting, terrified the baby might be injured, but she didn't feel any pain. *Please, God, please. Please save the baby.* Oxana lurched and staggered down the road, stumbling several times, until she was standing at her mother's door.

———

The sun was just lifting above the horizon when Oxana woke. She pulled on an old sweater to hide her bruised arms, but there was no hiding her black eye or the gash on her cheek. She stepped into the kitchen and poured a cup of coffee. Her mother came in from outside, took off her coat, hung it on a hook, poured coffee for herself, and sat at the table, saying nothing. Oxana sipped at the hot black coffee and tried to swallow a bit of her mother's dark rye bread.

Her mother broke the silence. "You're going back to him."

"He tried to kill my baby."

"A woman must be with her husband. You're going back today."

"Mama, look at me. He beat me. He'll kill the baby. I can't go back."

"You are a wife, and you are with child. You will go to your husband, and you will do what he says. You think I don't hear the gossip? I can hardly hold my head up any longer. Now we know why you were in such a rush to marry Fedor." Her mother slammed her cup on the table hard enough to spill the coffee. "I didn't raise you to be like this. I raised you to be an artist, a concert pianist, with morals and character, not some two-timing hussy. Oxana, I am ashamed of you."

"I'm sorry, Mama, but if you will listen, I can explain. He was drunk and—"

"Stop!" her mother screamed. "I do not ever want to know who the father is. That can rest on your conscience—if you have one." Her mother stood, her finger pointing, her arm shaking. "You will obey me, and you will obey your husband. You married Fedor, and now you will live with him."

"Mama—" Oxana said, but her mother, in a flat monotone, interrupted her.

"You are no longer my daughter. I disown you."

"Mama, please," Oxana said, standing and stepping toward her mother. "You can't possibly mean what you just said."

"I always mean what I say," her mother said, backing away from Oxana and turning toward the window.

Oxana sat back down and stared at the hot coffee cup in her hand. "I'm sorry I'm an embarrassment to you," she said, but her mother said nothing.

"You can disown me if you want," Oxana whispered, almost as if speaking to her cup of coffee, "but I will not disown you. You are all I have, but don't forget that I am all *you* have. Without me you will be alone." Oxana stood to leave but turned back. "Bye, Mama."

Her mother did not move.

"I love you," Oxana said.

Her mother's shoulders twitched, and she lowered her head.

Oxana closed the door behind her.

She walked to the cemetery but stopped outside the gate. *Not today, Irina. I'm too ashamed for you to see me like this.*

———

Oxana was standing at the stove when Fedor came in. She kept her back to him while she dished up their dinner. She set the plates on the table and sat in her usual chair. The meal passed in silence, both avoiding eye contact.

"Sit down," Fedor said when Oxana stood to remove the empty plates. He glared at her, and his voice was low and severe. "You've made me look like an utter fool. The entire village is talking—laughing at how Fedor Rostov sure got taken in by that pretty harlot. I do not take kindly to this. It's time you understand that I am the man of this house, not some henpecked half-wit. From this point on you will do as I say. You will not leave this farm except to go to the Saturday market. You and I will never be seen together in public. You will continue to be my wife, but in name only. You will no longer share my bed. You can sleep on the floor over there by the stove, like the dog that you are." Fedor pointed to a spot between the stove and the room's outer wall. "You will raise your bastard as my child, and it will carry my name. Whether a boy or girl, it doesn't matter, I will have nothing to do with it. When it turns sixteen it will leave this house with nothing."

Oxana stood and with a scowl of utter contempt, locked eyes with Fedor's. "I am forced to accept your terms, not because I agree to them but because I have no other option. You may control my life, but you will never control the life of my child. My child will grow up with dignity and pride, with or without your name. And as to your bed, I have no intention of ever again sharing it with you," Oxana said, grabbing a folded bedsheet from a pile of clean linen and spreading it on the floor beside the stove.

Chapter 25

Oxana's contractions began on a cold late-winter morning while she was cooking breakfast. Fedor was in the barn, and she called to him from the front door. He came out of the barn and, without a word, headed toward the Domitovich farm. Oxana was leaning over the kitchen table, clutching her stomach, when Ludmilla arrived. She helped Oxana out of her clothing but was surprised when Oxana insisted she lie on the straw mattress on the floor beside the stove. Oxana was embarrassed to tell her the truth but was more afraid of what Fedor might do if he found her in his bed.

The labor pains steadily increased until, by early afternoon, Oxana was screaming and drenched with sweat. "It's only for a while," Ludmilla said, putting wet rags on Oxana's forehead and wiping the sweat from her face. "Once you set eyes on this little baby, you'll forget all about the pain."

"Ludmilla, I'm afraid. I've done something bad, and I'm afraid—" Oxana screamed as she clenched her muscles to endure another spasm.

"You've done nothing bad, my child," Ludmilla said, massaging Oxana's arms and legs, "and you've got nothing to be afraid of."

"But I have done wrong." Oxana moaned, inhaling deep breaths. "Everybody knows the baby is too soon. There's talk—" She grabbed her stomach and shrieked.

"Oxana, you listen to me. You've done nothing wrong. I hear the gossip, but I don't pay it any attention. You can't stop people from talking. You go on with your life and ignore the talk." There was leftover soup on the stove, and Ludmilla poured a cupful and handed it to Oxana. "I know your husband is going through a rough patch right now. You give him a little time. You're not the first couple this has happened to, and I'm sure you're not the last, either. Lord, if I let my tongue start wagging, half the women in this town would have to hang their heads in shame. Once Fedor sees this beautiful baby, he'll come around and, before you know it, the past is forgotten and everyone keeps going forward."

The winter winds were howling, and a light snow had begun to fall. Ludmilla added several logs to the stove.

By late afternoon, the baby's head had emerged. "It's coming," Ludmilla shouted. "It's coming—it's a boy! Oxana, you have a boy." She tied the ends of the umbilical cord with a damp rag and cut it, wiped the baby with a warm rag, and handed him to Oxana.

Oxana lay cradling her son while Ludmilla cleaned up, said goodbye, and left, taking the soiled bedding with her to launder. The house was quiet and she dozed but woke when the door opened. Fedor staggered in. He sat at the kitchen table and pulled a bottle of vodka out of his pocket. He did not prepare food for himself, did not ask if she wanted anything to eat or drink, and did not even look toward her, only sipped vodka until his head drooped into his chest.

"Your name will be Nicholas," Oxana cooed, holding the baby tight against her breast, "after my papa, and I will call you Kolya, the way we do when we love our little Nicholas very much. I never knew my papa, and you will never know yours either. But I will take care of you, and you will grow up to be as beautiful as your papa. Who knows—maybe you will eventually play the piano? Maybe you will be better than me and maybe one day you will be invited to Moscow and will become famous."

She glanced at Fedor, sprawled across the table, snoring.

The next morning, while Oxana was making coffee, Kolya woke and started to cry. "Kid sure does make a racket," Fedor said, stumbling out of bed. "Can't you keep him quiet?"

"It's a boy. Do you want to hold him? He's adorable."

"Why would I want to hold some bastard kid?"

"I've named him Nicholas, after my father."

"Suit yourself. Makes no difference to me." Fedor grabbed his coat and went out.

———

Kolya was colicky, and Oxana was sitting in a chair, rocking him, when Fedor came in one evening. He took a few steps toward her, stumbled, and paused to steady himself before leaning over her. He reeked of alcohol and cigarette smoke, his eyes were glassy, and his face was red. "Let me see him," Fedor slurred, reaching his arms out.

Oxana stood and began to back away.

"I said, let me see him," Fedor shouted and lunged at her, grabbing hold of Kolya's blanket and pulling the baby away.

"Give him back. Give him to me," Oxana screamed.

Fedor had his arm around Kolya's stomach and held him tight. "Won't shut up, will you, you little bastard? I'll make you shut up." Fedor punched him.

"Stop it. Stop!" Oxana screamed, diving toward Fedor. She got her hands around the tiny body and tried to pull, but Fedor slapped her across the face. The sudden pain was excruciating, and blood gushed from her nose. She lunged at Fedor, clawing at his face, trying to wrest the baby from his grip. He slapped her again, harder, and she fell backward and hit her head on the chair. Kolya's blanket fell to the floor, and Fedor stood grasping the naked baby with one arm while he steadied himself against the table.

Oxana grabbed a cast-iron frying pan. "If you harm Kolya, I'll kill you, I swear I'll kill you." She hurled herself at him, waving the frying pan.

Fedor slapped her again and she fell. "I'm supposedly his father. I can do anything I want to the little bastard." Oxana lay on the floor writhing in pain and was afraid she might faint.

"You little son of a whore," Fedor yelled. "This whole damn town is laughing at me." Oxana struggled to her knees.

Fedor slammed his fist hard against the baby's legs. "How about I give you something to help you remember your old dad." Kolya was screaming more loudly than Oxana had ever heard a baby cry. She leapt to her feet, lunged at Fedor, and whacked the frying pan against the side of his head. He fell backward against the table and released his grip. Oxana dropped the pan in time to catch the baby. With one hand grasping Kolya, she picked up a ceramic water pitcher and smashed it over Fedor's head. He leaned against the table, moaning, holding his head with both hands while blood streamed through his splayed fingers and across his face.

Clutching the baby against her chest, Oxana grabbed Kolya's blanket off the floor and ran out the door. The night air was cold, and she paused to drape the blanket over him to keep him warm. She held Kolya's legs with her right hand and headed across the open wheat field. It was closer to town than going along the main road, and the fields, now during the winter months, were nothing but stubble with a light snow covering. She was terrified that jarring movements might do Kolya even more harm, yet she had to get him to the doctor quickly. The sky was cloudy and it was completely dark. Oxana shivered. She was wearing only a thin dress and could see her breath. She was afraid of dropping Kolya if she twisted her ankle or tripped over a rut, but she rushed across the frozen ground, trying her best to hold him steady.

The clouds cleared enough for the moon to light her way as she rounded the corner of the Orthodox church, ran across the main square, and pounded on the door of the doctor's office. The front windows were dark, but she continued pounding until a light came on and a moment later the door opened. "Come in, come in—Oxana! What has happened? You've been beaten up."

"It's not me. It's my son." Oxana handed over the swaddled bundle. She was too out of breath and upset to say anything more. The doctor laid the baby on the examination table and unwrapped the blanket. Kolya's legs were swollen and red. "Ah, yes, this is serious. Sit here," he said, pointing to a chair inside the door, and he reached to switch on the new overhead electric lights. Kolya had been screaming while Oxana ran into town, but now was exhausted and merely whimpering. The doctor held both of Kolya's legs with one hand while feeling them. He filled a syringe. "This is to put him to sleep but will not take effect immediately. Because of the swelling I must work quickly, and I'm afraid the baby will have more pain."

Oxana sat in silence beside the examination table, gently caressing Kolya's forehead and arms. Kolya screamed as the doctor slightly jerked each leg, and Oxana clenched her fists against her stomach, fighting back an urge to throw up.

The doctor carefully ran his fingers along the injured area before tugging on each leg again. "It's the best I can do for now," he said, wrapping both legs in cotton bandages. "Tomorrow I will put splints on to hold the legs in place. There must be no movement or disturbance until they are completely healed." The painkiller was taking effect and Kolya fell asleep.

"Doctor, will he be able to walk?" Oxana had calmed down enough to speak without gasping for air.

"Oxana, please call me Ilya. This injury is serious and I cannot guarantee anything. Fortunately, an infection is unlikely since the skin has not been pierced." Oxana buried her face in her apron and sobbed. "The legs may be permanently deformed, but at this point it's impossible to know. My best prognosis is that the child will be able to walk but may need to use crutches. There is most likely nerve damage, and he might experience periodic spasms of pain. All we can do is wait to see how the legs develop."

"Can I please hold him for a little while?"

"Yes, but you must keep his legs very still." Oxana gently lifted Kolya into her arms and rocked him back and forth. "And now let me see about you. Your face is swollen." Ilya touched her nose and Oxana winced in pain. "I'm afraid it's broken." He wiped away the dried, caked blood, put cotton swabs into her nose, and wrapped a bandage to hold them in place. "That should do it for now, although you will feel pain for the next few days."

"How were the baby's legs injured?" Ilya asked while he washed his hands in the basin of water beside the examination table.

Oxana had not anticipated his question and hesitated. If she told the truth, Fedor would surely hurt Kolya again, maybe even kill him . . . and even kill her. "He fell off the bed," she said.

Ilya turned and looked directly into her eyes. "This baby did not fall off the bed. Please tell me the truth. How were his legs broken?" Oxana was silent. "Did Fedor do it?"

Oxana sobbed into the bloodstained apron she was still wearing.

"Please tell me the truth, Oxana. I can help you. I have known cases like this before. My uncle is a high-ranking member of the Politburo and has many friends in the secret police. I only need to make one phone call and your husband will be dealt with."

Oxana remained silent, staring, her trembling hands tugging at her apron. "Did Fedor do this?"

"Yes," Oxana whispered. "Yes."

"The bastard," he muttered. "Tonight you can sleep here on the sofa. I'll fix food and give you blankets. By tomorrow you will have nothing more to fear; however, you are free to remain here for as long as you like. You are safe here, and it might be nice to have your company."

———

When Oxana woke, the office was empty but for a pot of fresh coffee on the table. She poured herself a cup and held Kolya in her lap, caressing his head and arms while sipping the steaming hot liquid.

"Good morning, Oxana," Ilya said, coming into the room. "I trust you slept well?" He sat at the table and poured himself a cup of coffee.

"Yes, thank you."

"I've been on the telephone and been assured the matter is taken care of. Oxana, you and your child are safe. The OGPU agents have already been here and arrested your husband. By now, he is on a train to Siberia. I can assure you he will not be returning, but as I said last night, you are welcome to stay. I'd love to hear all about your time in Odesa. Perhaps you don't know that I attended medical school in Odesa. We might find we have much in common."

"Thank you, Doctor, but—"

"Ilya, please."

"Thank you, Ilya. Your offer is generous, but I prefer to be at home with my child." Oxana wrapped Kolya tightly to keep him warm, and Ilya loaned her a coat and scarf. A strong, cold wind was blowing, and Oxana held her head down to protect Kolya while she returned to the farmhouse. She opened the gate. The front door was ajar and the shadow of a figure moved inside.

Was the doctor mistaken? Had Fedor returned? *He'll kill us both if he has a chance.* She gently nudged the door open, ready to flee, but to her complete surprise, her mother was sweeping the floor. "Mama, what are you doing here?"

"I've heard . . . Fedor is gone."

"Yes, he's gone."

"He hurt the baby?"

"He broke both of Kolya's legs."

Her mother put her arms around Oxana and the baby and held them in an embrace. Oxana wept on her shoulder.

"I'm sorry for what I said to you." Her mother also began to cry. "And I'm sorry for how I've treated you. I've caused you too much pain."

"Don't cry, Mama."

"I need to cry. It was not your fault that you did not get to go to Moscow, and I should not have blamed you. I was angry and hurt and I pushed you away. I should not have said the things I said to you. Oxana, I love you. I wanted so much for you. I had such dreams. You are talented and you worked hard. You deserved success. It was wrong of me to disown you."

"It's not your fault, Mama. I've always known you loved me, and I've always loved you."

"I've become a lonely, bitter, cruel old woman, and that is not who I want to be." She sobbed on Oxana's shoulder. "I can't bring Irina back, but I can bring you back. I can't bear losing both of my daughters, and I can't bear being alone any longer." They held each other in a tight embrace for a long while. "I want to be a grandmother and I want to be a mother again. I want you to come back to me. Can you forgive me, Oxana?"

"Of course, I forgive you. I, too, made mistakes."

Her mother wiped her eyes. "It will be better for you without Fedor. I came to clean up in case you want to stay here, but you can come and stay with me if you prefer."

"I will stay here, at least for now. I have my son to think about. I must now build a life for him. Maybe he will not be a disappointment. Maybe he can become the great pianist I never was."

"Hush, child. You are not a disappointment. To me you are a great pianist, and you always will be."

While Oxana washed the evening dishes, her mother sat on the sofa, rocking Kolya. He was fussing and would not sleep. Oxana joined her and they sat, gazing into the glowing embers in the stove. "Please play for me," her mother whispered. "It's been too long. Play for me the way you used to."

Oxana stepped to the piano and lifted the lid covering the keyboard. She sat on the bench, wiped the dust from the keys, and stared at her hands. Her skin was red and chapped from the endless washing—dishes, clothing, bedding, beets. Could she still play? Would her fingers ever again move with the speed and agility she had once commanded? Could she even remember the notes?

She lifted her hands and began the slow opening of Chopin's Fantasy. She was stiff and clumsy, but soon her muscles relaxed, and as her fingers found the notes, tears dripped onto the keys. The sound calmed Kolya, and her mother sat with her eyes closed, cradling him in her lap, while the soft, sweet music wafted through the room.

———

The next day, Oxana bundled Kolya into his blanket and carried him into town. "Privyet, Oxana Nikolaevna," Father Vanska called when the light from the open door illuminated the dark interior of the Lutheran church. "How can I help you?"

"Father, I would like you to baptize my son."

"Yes, of course."

"Before you do it, Father, I want to explain, in case I'm making a mistake or committing a sin that God will punish my baby for. You performed the ceremony when my sister converted to the Lutheran faith. Therefore, even though I'm Orthodox, I would like you to baptize my son so I can raise him in the same tradition my sister and brother-in-law would have raised their child."

"Oxana Nikolaevna, you can rest assured you are not committing a sin. I'm very happy that you wish to raise your son in the Lutheran tradition, but in the end it doesn't matter. God is in all churches, if we only take the time to search for him." Father Vanska motioned Oxana to the baptismal font and began the brief ritual with a prayer.

He concluded the rite by making the sign of the cross on the baby's forehead, and Oxana began wrapping Kolya in his blanket. "Can you please wait a minute?" he asked. "I have a letter for you. You must forgive me because I should have given it to you long ago, but I didn't want anything to come between you and your husband." Father Vanska disappeared into his side office.

He emerged a few moments later and handed Oxana a small envelope, sealed, with no writing on the outside. Oxana laid Kolya in the pew beside her and turned the envelope over in her hand. "Jakob asked me to give this to you."

"Jakob?" Oxana was shocked. It had been months since she had heard his name spoken aloud. She opened the envelope, and as she slid the letter out, the gold band fell onto the wooden floor. The clatter echoing through the small empty sanctuary startled her, and she quickly retrieved the ring and clasped it in her palm while she unfolded the letter.

> Dear Oxana:
>
> I hope you are well and happy. I am giving you Irina's wedding ring. My grandfather gave it to my grandmother, my father gave it to my mother, and I gave it to Irina. Please keep it as a memory of her. Please pray every day for Irina, and especially pray that she can forgive me. I also pray every day that you can forgive me too. I'm sorry I left without saying goodbye, but I didn't want to cause you any more pain. I won't be coming back. It is for the best that we never see each other again, at least not on this earth, but maybe someday, Irina and you and I can all be together again in heaven.
>
> Jakob

Oxana's lips were trembling. She was embarrassed to have Father Vanska see her cry and she tried to control herself, but soon the paper was damp and the ink became smudged.

"There, there, my child." Father Vanska put his arms around her. "You weep as long and loudly as you want. It is the only way to heal."

Oxana's hands were shaking and she was afraid she might tear the thin paper. She laid the letter beside Kolya in the pew but continued to clasp the ring in her hand.

"Oxana," Father Vanska began, "your church is splendid with its gold icons and your priest in rich velvet robes spreading sweet-smelling incense while intoning the liturgy. Here we are plain. We've only our stained-glass windows and our small painting of the Virgin Mary. Yet our humble way of knowing God is also beautiful. You can enjoy both churches. Bring your son to services anytime. He will be welcomed—and so will you. And don't forget, Oxana, we still have the piano you once played so superbly." He pointed to the old upright in the corner. "Remember what our great Dostoevsky said: 'Beauty will save the world.' Maybe you can create some beauty for us. Maybe play for our services once in a while? People would like to hear you. Oxana, you were given a gift, and it is not right to hide God's gifts."

Oxana nodded and wiped her tears, still clasping the gold ring.

"I will leave you now. You may stay as long as you wish."

Oxana remained, with Kolya beside her, in the empty sanctuary, staring at the painting of the Virgin Mary, rereading Jakob's letter and clutching the gold ring until her fingers began turning white and numb.

———

The next day, after gathering the eggs and milking the cow, Oxana eyed Fedor's green tractor with its huge rear wheels and tall exhaust pipe, mulling over how a classically trained pianist was going to commence her education in farm management. She needed to learn quickly. Fedor's winter wheat would soon be ready for harvesting—and after that the spring wheat would need to be planted.

Oxana crawled into the tractor seat and tugged at the various levers and handles. She knew she had to open the throttle before turning the crank and yanked what seemed the most likely candidate before going around to the front of the tractor to turn the crank. At first she did not pull fast enough to fire the engine. After several more tries, straining to pull faster and harder, the engine sputtered and took off. It immediately came to a full roar. Realizing she had opened the throttle too much, she rushed back into the tractor seat to slow it. She pulled on the shift lever to ease the tractor into gear and it moved forward. Oxana nearly rammed into the barn before she yanked back the shift lever to disengage the flywheel. Pulling the throttle to stop the engine, she was shocked to see Gregor standing beside the tractor.

"Privyet," he called, trying to stifle his laughter.

"Privyet," she said and climbed down.

"That was . . . um . . . interesting. I've never seen a tractor driven like that." Gregor burst into laughter.

"Oh, hush up," Oxana said.

"Oxana, I'm sorry about what Fedor did, and I'm sorry I listened to him and stayed away. I should've come by to check on you."

"It's not your fault, Gregor. And you certainly didn't need to babysit me. I can take care of myself."

"But he harmed the baby?"

Oxana nodded.

"I'm sorry about that. I want to help you. The farm is too much work for one person, but if we work together we can make a go of it."

"I can't afford to pay you."

"We can share the crop, like Fedor and I did. Please, let me help you. Fedor's not a bad man, but he sometimes does bad things. I don't ask you to forgive him, but maybe I can make it up to you by helping you."

"Thank you, Gregor. Your offer is generous, and yes, you're right, I certainly do need help."

"Good. I'll start tomorrow."

Oxana smiled and waved, watching him go down the road. She liked Gregor. He was humble and modest, unlike Fedor, who was always so cocky and aggressive.

She went inside the house. Kolya was lying in Fedor's bed—now her bed—cooing. "We will make this work," she said, picking him up and holding him against her chest. "You and me, and Grandma Elena, and now Uncle Gregor. We are going to be a family, a happy family, I promise. And one day you will make me and your papa Jakob very proud. I promise," she repeated, gently patting Kolya's head while he suckled at her breast. "I promise."

Part 3

Death by Hunger

Peterstal, Ukraine

1931

Chapter 26

Oxana and Gregor's friendship grew until, before they realized it, seven years had passed—and over those seven years, Oxana, her mother, Gregor, and Kolya had indeed become a family.

Saturday meals remained the highlight of the week, and Oxana had worked hard to make this one extra special—borscht from beets saved from last summer's garden, fresh fish from the lake served with Oxana's horseradish sauce, beef with fried onions, and a creamy Russian salad with peas and carrots. "That was delicious," Gregor said while Kolya ate his last forkfuls.

Gregor gathered up the dirty dishes, while Oxana pulled a steaming hot kuchen out of the baking chamber. She inserted seven small candles in the shape of the number seven and lit them. Kuchen was a favorite among Peterstal's ethnic German community, and Oxana had worked to perfect her recipe—a thin layer of sweetened yeast dough covered with fruit and baked with a custard filling of cream, eggs, and a pinch of her prized cinnamon—to give Kolya a connection with Jakob's German heritage, even if only in this small way.

"Happy birthday, dear Kolya, happy birthday to you," they sang as she set the dessert on the table.

"Make a wish before you blow out the candles," Gregor said. Kolya took a deep breath and blew as hard as he could.

"You nearly blew the kuchen off the table," Oxana's mother said, and everyone laughed.

"I have a joke for you," Gregor told Kolya while Oxana sliced the kuchen into generous wedges. "What's the difference between a bad year and a good year?"

"I don't know, Uncle Gregor."

"In a bad year, the government can't find any bread to take from the peasants, and in a good year the government takes all the bread they can find from the peasants."

"That's not funny," Kolya managed to say as he shoved a forkful of dessert into his mouth.

"That's the point, my boy. Russian jokes aren't supposed to be funny. We like to cry when we tell jokes."

"That's dumb, Uncle Gregor."

"Boys," said Oxana, "enough with the jokes. Kolya, why don't you walk Grandma home. There's something I want to discuss with Uncle Gregor while he helps me wash the dishes. Button up. It's cold out there. And be sure to come right back; you still need to do your practicing."

"Do I have to practice even on my birthday?"

"Even on your birthday. I want you to be the best, and no one becomes the best by skipping their practice, so hurry along."

"Aw, Mama." Kolya grabbed his walking sticks. His knees were permanently stiffened, and Oxana never failed to notice how his mouth tightened in pain as he swung each leg while leaning on his sticks.

"He's a strong boy. He'll be fine," Gregor said, standing with Oxana in the doorway with his arm around her shoulder, watching Kolya and his grandmother go down the road. "So, what is it you want to discuss with me?" Gregor picked up a dish towel. "Are you going to fire me?"

"Fire you?" Oxana handed Gregor plates as she rinsed them. "Of course not. I want to ask you a question, and I want you to be honest." Oxana paused, holding a plate and looking at him. She was always struck by how dissimilar Gregor was from Fedor. Both were tall, but Fedor had been thin, almost wiry, with thick, curly black hair, very much like his mother, while Gregor was stocky with sandy-colored hair. Oxana had never met their father—he had died long ago—but she wondered if Gregor maybe took after him. Or someone else?

"Are you happy?" Oxana asked.

Gregor set the plate he was drying on the table. "Of course I'm happy—at least as happy as a poor farmer living in Peterstal can be."

"That's not what I mean, Gregor. Is there someone else in your life? Someone, besides us, you care about and who cares about you?"

"Oxana! Where did that question come from?"

"Gregor, I won't lie to you and I don't want you to lie to me. You're handsome and hardworking, and you are also a very kind person. I know people gossiped about you being here working with me."

"I used to hear that in town, especially in the bar, but that talk has died down."

"I don't care about the town talk. I care about you and your happiness. Are you happy?"

"I guess I haven't found the right lady yet."

"Gregor, I said no lies. I've heard that when you're not here working yourself half to death, you're spending time with a friend."

Gregor laid the damp dish towel on top of the dried plates and sat down but said nothing.

"Please understand I'm not trying to pry. I'm asking because I care about you."

Gregor sat stone faced, fidgeting. "I think you mean Yuri Markovich. Does that bother you?"

"Bother me? Of course not. Gregor, we're friends. I would like to think we're best friends and that there are no secrets between us. Nothing about you would make me dislike you. I'm glad you're spending time with Yuri. Furthermore, I want you to start bringing him to our Saturday dinners. Any friend of yours is a friend of mine. Now, would you like a cup of tea?" Oxana held a small piece of kindling over the fire in the stove until the stick was blazing, and she lit the samovar.

"Sure, tea sounds good. And then I think we should go into town to hear the speakers from Moscow. The poster says they'll be making important announcements."

"How can announcements from Moscow have anything to do with us here in Peterstal? Nothing here ever changes. Besides, those fat bureaucrats already take nearly everything in taxes. What more can they want?"

"Oxana, you're sounding like old Slava Domitovich. Maybe nothing ever changed when we had the tsar, but times are different. There's talk of change. I think you should hear what they have to say."

"Alright then—if you insist, let's go when Kolya gets back. It will be amusing to see what crazy ideas they've come up with now."

As soon as Kolya returned, Oxana gave him instructions on which pieces to practice and how long to spend on each one. He had shown an interest in the piano when he was only three, and Oxana had given him short lessons nearly every day since then. She had quickly realized how talented he was as he rapidly moved into an ever more difficult repertoire. Oxana's mother claimed he was progressing even more quickly than she had, and Oxana was beginning to believe that her mother might very well be correct. He was already well on his way to becoming an excellent pianist.

Once Kolya was ensconced at the piano, Gregor and Oxana set out for the town center. Upon entering the square, they were surprised at the number of people assembled. The entire village appeared to have gathered. A truck with speakers mounted on the back was blaring music so loud that conversation was impossible. The songs were the usual patriotic mishmash, and Oxana shook her head in disgust. She waved to Slava and Ludmilla, who were standing near the Orthodox church.

The music stopped, and a young man climbed into the back of the truck. "Attention. Attention!" he shouted. He was tall and gangly, with long hair, wire-rimmed glasses, and pasty skin. He was about twenty years old, at most. "Comrades, attention!" The crowd quieted, but he continued shouting to be certain all could hear. "Fellow comrades, fellow workers, fellow Bolsheviks—a great day is upon you. For centuries, the tsars enslaved you, the churches continue to enslave you, and capitalism wishes to enslave you, but Communism will set you free." He paused, probably expecting applause, but there was none. After an awkward moment of silence, he continued, "Our great Comrade Stalin has ushered in a new era of prosperity. Henceforth you will farm collectively as a *kolkhoz*. You will use the latest scientific methods. You will use the most modern farm machinery. You will all work together, and production will increase tenfold. You will share collectively in the abundance. Famine will no longer exist! Poverty will no longer exist! Long live Stalin! Long live Communism! Long live Mother Russia!"

There was a smattering of applause, and he stood adjusting his glasses and running his fingers through his hair before he bowed and jumped to the ground. A young woman climbed into the back of the truck and shouted, "Comrades! Daniil"—she pointed to the boy who had spoken—"forgot to tell you that we come from Moscow and are representatives of the Regional Commission for Collectivization. We have been sent by the People's Commissariat for Agriculture, and it is my distinct pleasure to introduce your very own Alexi Karpenko, who will be the head of your kolkhoz."

"Alexi!" Oxana said aloud, and she laughed, watching the girl taking hold of Alexi's arms to help him climb into the truck box. Oxana hadn't seen him since they were in school together. He'd been corpulent as a boy, but he'd gained so much more weight he could barely walk, much less hoist himself up.

"Shhh, Oxana," Gregor said. "These days, even the stones under our feet have ears."

"Let them hear me. I've nothing to hide."

"Tomorrow," the girl continued, "Alexi will be here in the square, beginning at nine a.m. It will be a great honor for you to be among the first to sign over your property and swear your oath to your newly established kolkhoz. You may now come to speak to us if you have any questions." She bowed, although there was no applause, and nearly fell when she jumped out of the truck box. Alexi continued standing, smiling an idiotic grin, while the villagers turned their backs and drifted out of the square. No one approached with any questions.

"What was that all about?" Oxana said to Gregor as soon as they were out of the square and heading down the road. "We're supposed to sign over our land and get nothing in return except a few vague promises from a couple of bug-eyed university students? And they expect us to swear an oath to a kolkhoz that's run by Alexi Karpenko? His idea of work is opening a bottle of vodka. He's exactly the sort of sycophant the Bolsheviks adore— obedient enough to do what he's told, but too stupid to understand the ramifications of his actions."

"From what he says, he was once your boyfriend." Gregor smiled.

"Ha! Maybe in his mind," Oxana shot back. "He was convinced every girl in school was in love with him, but he never even managed to get any- one to dance with him."

They reached the fork in the road, and Gregor headed to his place while Oxana continued home. *Are they crazy?* she thought, mulling over the speech she had just heard. *They won't be getting anything from me.*

A cold wind was blowing, and she wrapped her scarf tighter around her head and hastened her pace. Even before she saw Fedor's house—she could never quite bring herself to think of it as hers—she heard Kolya's piano music.

Jakob would be very pleased, she thought, if only he were here to hear it.

———

After an unusually cold winter, spring came early. Oxana stepped outside as the sun was rising above the horizon to enjoy the mid-March breeze. She inhaled deeply and walked across the yard to her flower garden, just inside the front gate. Green shoots from the dormant bulbs were already poking through the soil and before long would be bursting with color and fragrance. *Soon you will once again be beautiful,* she thought. The garden was small, but ever since seeing Vera's gorgeous beds, she had wanted to grow flowers.

Oxana stood at the foot of her vegetable garden. It was time to start planting, and she was eager to get to it. She loved working with the soil and grew everything she could—potatoes, beets, onions, and carrots to store for the winter months, cabbage for sauerkraut, cucumbers for pickling, tomatoes, peas, beans, squash, and pumpkins. She planted garlic, along with a variety of herbs—dill, basil, thyme, rosemary, and oregano—but melons were her prized produce. She grew all sorts—watermelons, honeydew, cantaloupe—and they were the sweetest and juiciest of any in the village.

She gazed at the burgeoning buds on her beloved fruit trees. *You'll soon be blooming too. I can hardly wait.*

Oxana went back inside but left the door ajar to let in the fresh breeze. Kolya was eating his breakfast. "Finish up, it's time for your lesson."

"Mama, why don't you ever play anymore?" Kolya asked, scurrying to the piano.

"Kolya, you are asking a complicated question and I'm afraid there's only time for a simple answer. My playing is no longer important. It's more important that *you* develop your abilities. Now, let's get to work before we run out of time." Oxana sat, listening, as the beautiful music flowed out of the piano. Kolya played with such ease and freedom—qualities that couldn't be taught.

People once said I had those qualities, but did I? I thought I did.

"Did you like it, Mama?" Kolya asked when he finished.

"Of course. I liked everything. There was not a single wrong note, and the music is perfectly memorized. But do you realize how many pianists can play all the notes? Playing the notes is not enough. You must go deeper into the music. This is Beethoven, don't forget. He's very precise in his markings, and you must do everything he tells you to do. Now, let's start again, and this time try to be more careful."

He began, but after one page Oxana stopped him. "Kolya, what does this 'P' mean?

"Mama, I'm not stupid."

"Then prove it. What does this 'P' mean?"

"Soft."

"So why didn't I hear soft playing? You must pay attention to the details. Now start again, and less pedal. The pedal should be the final addition that makes the music even more beautiful, like putting frosting on a cake. Your pedaling makes the music sound thick and blurry, like the porridge you just ate for breakfast."

They worked for an hour—slowly and meticulously, starting and stopping, repeating passages, until Kolya played the final fortissimo chords and applause came from the other side of the room.

"Gregor! I didn't hear you come in," Oxana said.

"Did you like my Beethoven, Uncle Gregor?"

"I loved every note."

"See, Mama—Gregor likes my music, even when you don't."

"That's because Uncle Gregor is a softie when it comes to his nephew." Oxana glared at him in mock indignation.

"Guilty as charged." Gregor laughed.

"Get going, Kolya," Oxana said, "or you'll be late for school."

"Bye, Mama. Bye, Uncle Gregor," he said, closing the door behind him.

"Another group of Komsomols was in the square," Gregor said.

"I'm not surprised. There seems to be a new group every few weeks. Where were these from?"

"Leningrad."

"Leningrad? A long way. They must be getting desperate. And I suppose it was all the same speeches."

"Actually, Oxana, I came to tell you . . . I . . . ah, I signed the papers."

"You didn't! You joined the kolkhoz? And gave your land to the collective?"

"They promise us wages, and we will all work together, and they are going to bring in the latest machinery so the work is easier."

"Does this mean you can no longer work with me?"

"No, Oxana. It means I can do more with you—if you also choose to join. About half the village has signed up already. You should think about it."

"Never," Oxana said. "I don't trust the Bolsheviks, and I don't believe their guarantees. I will never give them anything. If they want my farm, they can buy it from me."

Chapter 27

The beautiful warm spring, with ample rainfall, gave way to an unseasonably hot and dry summer, and the wheat started ripening prematurely, with grain heads only partially filled out.

"I thought you might be busy harvesting the kolkhoz grain," Oxana said when Gregor unlatched the gate and came into the farmyard one afternoon.

"Alexi says the Central Committee is telling us to wait for rain so the grain will grow more."

"What do the experts in Moscow know about farming?"

"Alexi thinks they know everything. He doesn't ask for our opinions," Gregor said, relatching the gate and coming toward Oxana.

"Alexi is an idiot. Only a fool would wait and risk losing what little grain there is. I have no intention of waiting for permission from some Central Committee."

"I agree with you. In this heat everything will soon dry up."

"You'll have to go into town to get gasoline for the tractor, and then we can start the harvest as soon as you get back. The gas can should still be in the barn."

───

"Where's the gasoline?" Oxana asked when Gregor returned empty-handed. "Don't tell me you forgot about it?"

"Well, Oxana, that's the problem. Alexi refused to sell me gasoline. He says it's a new rule. Fuel is only for the kolkhoz. He even confiscated the gas can, saying it was kolkhoz property."

"How dare he!" She pulled off her apron, quickly washed her hands in the water tank beside the barn, and without another word took off down the main road.

She found Alexi Karpenko sitting at a desk in the town hall. "*Dobryj dyen*, Oxana," he said, standing. His shirt was too tight and clung to his body almost as a second layer of skin. His pants were hanging so low it looked as if they might fall off, and he tugged to get them up somewhat near his waist.

Oxana marched in and placed both hands on his desk and, leaning forward so she was only inches from his face, stared into his eyes. "Is this true?"

"Ah, it is so nice to see you again. Have you come to congratulate me now that I'm head of the kolkhoz?" Alexi said, leaning back. "I'm coming up in the world. Maybe the authorities will eventually promote me to a nice post in Odesa or Kyiv or even in Moscow."

Oxana wanted to reach forward and strangle him. Instead, she removed her hands from the desk and straightened. "Alexi, I demand to know why you refused to sell gas to my brother-in-law."

"I'm afraid Gregor was mistaken." Alexi sat back into his chair and placed his hands behind his head, interlacing his fingers. He smiled. "I did not refuse to sell him gas. I told him he can have all the gas he wanted—for harvesting kolkhoz crops."

"I will never join your kolkhoz."

"Then you will not have gas for your tractor."

"Alexi Karpenko, let me remind you that my family goes back centuries, long before Peterstal was founded. I demand you honor my heritage."

"Oh, Oxana, you're even prettier when you're mad. You and your sister always were the most beautiful girls in town."

"Alexi, you were always an idiot, and you are still an idiot. I demand fuel for my tractor."

"Oxana, Oxana, it is very simple—join the kolkhoz and you can have gas. No kolkhoz, no gas. Those are the rules. I'm simply following the rules."

"Go to hell, you and your rules!" Oxana shouted, slamming the door behind her.

Oxana was pacing in the front yard when, just after sunrise, Gregor came through the gate. "What took you so long? I've been waiting." Oxana handed Gregor an old scythe she had retrieved from the barn.

"What's this for?"

"We harvest the way the poor farmers do. Alexi Karpenko will never get the best of me."

The wheat field extended nearly a kilometer from behind the barn all the way to the edge of the forest. Gregor went ahead, rhythmically swinging the long, sharp scythe back and forth to cut a swath. Oxana came behind with a large rake, gathering the grain from the left and right into a center windrow. The heat was stifling, with the temperature hovering near forty degrees Celsius, and the dust, mixed with their perspiration, made them both seem covered with mud. The mosquitos, grasshoppers, and horseflies were all but unbearable; Gregor and Oxana had wrapped rags around their faces but were still swatting every few seconds. Despite her heavy cotton stockings and lace-up boots, the sharp grain stalks cut into Oxana's legs.

At the end of each row, they turned to work their way back, Gregor bending over every few feet to gather an armful of the cut grain and hold it upright while Oxana tied a piece of twine around it to form a sheaf. She wore gloves, but they provided little protection from the rough twine, and before long they were soaked with blood. Once they had tied five sheaves, Gregor held one upright and Oxana leaned the other four against it to form a shock to keep the grain dry until it was gathered for thrashing. They continued this process for the entire day, despite the heat. Only as the sun was dipping below the horizon did they quit, and as they headed home, completely exhausted, Oxana turned to assess their progress and felt a twinge of pride at how much she and Gregor had managed to accomplish. In the fading twilight, the shocks took on the appearance of an army of short soldiers, evenly spaced and stealthily advancing.

The next morning when Gregor saw Oxana step out of the house, he grabbed his knees and doubled over with laughter. "They're Kolya's," she tried to explain, but Gregor couldn't stop laughing. He had never seen a woman wearing pants before.

"If anyone sees you dressed like that, they'll never stop talking."

"They talk plenty about me already," Oxana said as she twirled around. "So . . . how do I look?"

"All I can say is you're the prettiest man I've ever seen." Gregor broke into another roar of laughter.

"Well, I'll take that as a compliment."

By the time they had their third shock of wheat standing, Oxana's gloves were already bloodied. Gregor gathered up an armful of grain and, instead of holding it for Oxana to tie, he handed the armful to her. "From now on, you gather and hold the grain and I'll tie the twine."

"But the tying is a woman's job," she said.

"Oxana, I can't stand to see you suffering with cut hands. Of all people, your hands are the most precious. What does it matter what is men's work and what is women's? You're wearing men's pants, so you can do men's work. From now on, I do the tying."

It took Oxana and Gregor nearly a month of working twelve-hour days with scorching sunshine and relentless heat to get all the grain cut and bundled.

Oxana stood beside Gregor one evening, contemplating the field dotted with nearly a hundred shocks, when he half-jokingly asked, "So now, how are we going to transport all this grain back to the farm and get it thrashed?"

"That, Gregor, is a very good question," Oxana replied.

"I was hoping you might have come up with some sort of magical solution." Gregor grinned at Oxana. "Like maybe you wave a wand and the grain flies home and thrashes itself?"

Oxana grinned back. "That might be one option, but a rather unlikely one. There are plenty of people in this village who think I'm a witch, but I'm afraid neither flying sheaves nor self-thrashing grain is in my repertoire."

"I will try to think of something. We can talk more tomorrow," Gregor said, and he turned to head back to the farmyard. "Right now we both deserve a good night's sleep."

―――

"Where did you get that?" Oxana asked when Gregor rode into the farmyard the next morning.

"What do you mean?" he said, smiling. "It's my horse—I've always had it."

"But you signed everything over to the kolkhoz," Oxana said.

"Yes, I did, but we need a horse to pull the wagon so we can bring the sheaves in for thrashing."

"But how did you manage to get Alexi's permission?"

"What permission? I took it."

"You stole from the commune. If they find this horse here, they will arrest us both."

"They certainly will. That's why we'd better work fast, so I can get him back before they figure it out." He hitched the horse to the hay wagon and they headed into the field. Gregor insisted Oxana do the man's work of slowly walking the horse down the rows of shocks while he did the woman's work of tossing the sheaves into the hay wagon with a pitchfork. Once they had a wagonful, they went back to the farmyard and Oxana stood in the wagon box, pitching the sheaves out while Gregor stacked them beside the barn. Fourteen hours later they unloaded the last of the grain. Gregor and Oxana, and the horse, were all so exhausted they could barely move, yet Gregor hurried the horse back to the kolkhoz barn.

The next day, he reappeared with the horse, explaining that when Alexi confronted him the night before, he said he was harvesting grain in the kolkhoz field. "Alexi didn't even ask which field." Gregor laughed. "And this morning all he said was that tonight I shouldn't be so late."

"That sounds like Alexi," Oxana said. "He thinks he's in complete control when he has no idea what's happening."

Gregor hitched the horse to Fedor's old stone roller, which was still lying against the barn. The stone had not been used in many years but fortunately was still intact, not cracked and broken as happened to so many. He retrieved a large canvas cloth that was stored in the barn and laid it in an open area near the piled-up wheat sheaves. Oxana cut the twine and spread the sheaves on the cloth while the horse, with Gregor walking alongside, slowly pulled the stone over the grain stalks three or four times to loosen the kernels. Gregor and Oxana then held the ends of the canvas cloth and shook it to separate the wheat from the chaff, stacking the straw chaff for winter food for the cow, and shoveling the wheat kernels into grain sacks.

The summer's scorching heat and lack of rainfall had taken its toll, and the harvest had yielded barely enough to supply flour for the coming months and seeds for the next crop. Oxana hoped the authorities would go easy when it came time to collect the grain taxes.

Chapter 28

A battered old truck drove in the farmyard one late fall day while Oxana and her mother were working in the garden. The truck was missing a muffler and the noise was earsplitting. The driver cut the engine, and two Komsomol youths wearing baggy, dirty uniforms jumped out of the back. Without any greeting, one of them marched toward Oxana and her mother while the other stood guard. "Oxana Rostova, former property owner," he intoned in a loud monotone voice, "is ordered to appear tonight at the village council meeting. Failure to attend will result in arrest and imprisonment." He turned, and both boys climbed back into the truck box. The driver revved the engine several times and they took off.

"What was that all about?" Oxana said to her mother as they drove away. "Arrest? Imprisonment? How dare they threaten me. Slava is head of the village council. Why wouldn't he come to tell me about this meeting? You stay here, Mama—I'm going to find out what's going on."

Oxana washed her hands in the water tank beside the barn, wiped them on her skirt, and headed down the road toward the Domitovich farm.

"Slava, I've been summoned to a council meeting tonight," she said when he opened the door.

"Privyet, Oxana," he said.

"Privyet, Slava. I apologize for my rudeness, but what is this about a council meeting—and that I will be arrested if I don't attend?"

"What meeting? I know nothing about any meeting."

"But you are in charge of the council."

"Yes, but I know nothing about any meeting."

"So, it's as I suspected. Alexi Karpenko is behind this threat."

"Tonight, you said? Don't worry, Oxana, I will certainly get to the bottom of this."

———

A crowd of men were gathered around Slava when Oxana arrived for the meeting, and as she joined them, Alexi Karpenko came across the square with two soldiers accompanying him. He had grown even more obese, and his pants hung below his waist, revealing several inches of bare abdomen and buttocks. "Dobryj dyen," he said. "Step inside, gentlemen, and you too, Oxana. The meeting's about to begin."

"By whose authority do you call a meeting?" Slava yelled. "And why indoors? It is tradition to be outside. Council meetings always occur in the open."

Alexi ignored him and kept walking.

The small, windowless room was crowded and already stuffy and foul smelling. Alexi stood before the crowd and motioned for silence. "I am now the village secretary," he announced.

"Under whose authority?" Slava shouted. "As the senior elder, I am in charge, and I say this meeting is illegal."

"Shut up, old man," Alexi admonished.

"I will *not* shut up," Slava roared. "Alexi, you know as well as any that the customs and traditions of our village stretch back to the Middle Ages, even before the time of the tsars. By tradition, we are self-governed by the oldest members of our village council. I am the eldest."

The crowd erupted into loud applause.

"Your old traditions are over!" Alexi shouted over the noise. "We are beginning new traditions under the leadership of our Central Committee and our great and wise Comrade Stalin." Alexi paused and the crowd quieted down.

"The village's grain quota, as set by the District Communist Party Committee, has not been met," Alexi continued. "Therefore, all farms delinquent in their grain taxes will be visited to collect the delinquent amount. Furthermore, all excess grain will also be confiscated so that the village quota can be paid as soon as possible. The central authorities are growing impatient with you lazy farmers."

Slava again jumped to his feet. "You have no authority over taxes," he cried. "Only the village council is empowered to make decisions concerning the levying and collection of the grain taxes."

"He's right," one old man shouted. "We are poor peasants. We've already given all we can."

Alexi, his eyes slowly drifting across the room as if he was gathering his strength, began speaking in a low solemn tone. "You are nothing but swine who take from Mother Russia and give nothing back. As the secretary of this village council and a member of the District Party Committee, I order you to give us your grain, and I order you to give us your land and join our kolkhoz or you will die resisting."

No one said a word.

"Read the inventory," Alexi shouted to the young Bolshevik soldier beside him. The officer began to intone the roll call. As each villager's inventory of property and tax levy was announced, the landowners sat silent. Oxana stared straight ahead when the officer recited, "Fedor Rostov, now absent. Farm worked by his wife. Owns land of sixty *dessiatins*, one cow, one tractor, several chickens. Is delinquent on grain tax."

A hissing was heard and everyone turned to see where it was coming from. Olga was pushing through the crowd. "She's a witch, that one is," she shouted, working her way to the front of the room, a heavy crucifix dangling from her neck. "She's got riches hidden in that house. I know it for sure. She's a high and mighty one who lived in a palace in Odesa and stole everything she got her hands on." Standing in the front near Alexi's table, Olga pointed a dirty, crooked finger at Oxana. "Oxana Rostova," the old hag shouted. "I call you by name. You are a demon. I read it in the cards. Everyone knows you were not married but seven months when your bastard son was born. Now you're living in sin with your husband's brother. You are an adulterer and a fornicator! Bewitched by the devil!" Raising both arms high in the air and shaking them, as if calling down a curse from heaven, she shouted, "I say we cast her out." Oxana smelled Olga's horrid stench and winced when a wad of the old hag's spit hit her face.

"Yes, cast her out," some shouted, while others threw whatever they could grab—wads of paper, apples, whatever they had in their pockets—at the old woman. Oxana was red with embarrassment and turned to leave, but as she was making her way toward the door a power began to grow within her. She would respond to the accusations. They would not take her down without a fight.

"Alexi." Oxana held up her hand for silence. "We have known each other since we were children in school together. We are a small village and, like all small villages, nothing escapes the notice of our gossipmongers. So be it. I am no saint. If I deserve punishment, please do so." Turning to face Olga, she pointed her finger. "I only wish to remind you what the Bible teaches: Let whoever is without sin cast the first stone." Oxana paused, but there was no reaction, only stunned silence. Turning back to face Alexi, she continued, "Alexi, why should I join your kolkhoz? Show me your successes. My farm produces more grain than your kolkhoz. Russia's farm collectives are designed to empower failures and punish successes, which is why you are sitting there and I am standing here."

Several people laughed, and Alexi slammed his fist on the table. "Enough," he yelled.

"Enough indeed," Oxana shouted back as she made her way to the door. "I leave you to your business, which is of no concern to me."

As soon as Oxana got home, she pulled a loose brick out of the stove and stuck her two most valued possessions—the gem-encrusted icon Vera Fedorovna Veranitzskaya had given her and Jakob's gold ring—into the empty space to hide them.

———

Late that night, following a loud thud, the door flew open. Alexi Karpenko staggered in with several of the soldiers who had been at the meeting.

"Get out!" Oxana yelled. "You are not welcome here."

"Nice to see you again, Oxana," Alexi said. He stank of vodka. Oxana stood firm as he stumbled toward the table. Kolya hoisted himself out of bed, reached for his walking sticks, and stood beside his mother.

"Oxana Rostova," one of the soldiers said, "we've come to collect your delinquent taxes." They grabbed the sacks of grain stored behind the stove.

"Why are you taking our food?" Oxana said as the men hauled the grain sacks out to the truck, but the men did not reply. "Alexi, I demand you order your men to stop."

"We are only following the rules, Oxana," Alexi said. "You are behind on your grain tax, so we take your grain. It's simple."

The soldiers pulled down the vegetables hanging from the rafters that Oxana had harvested from her garden—potatoes, carrots, parsnips, turnips, and rutabagas—and hauled them out the door. "I owe only the grain," Oxana said. "Why are you taking my vegetables? Alexi, stop this. I demand your men stop stealing my food."

"We are not stealing, Oxana," Alexi calmly responded despite Oxana's growing rage. "We are taking what belongs to us. Everything belongs to us."

"My mother and I spent the entire summer preserving this!" Oxana cried when the soldiers gathered up the sacks of dried fruit—apples, cherries, apricots, and plums—and heaped them in the back of their truck as well. "What are we going to eat this winter, or do you want us to starve?"

"Join our commune and you will have all the food you want," one of the young men sneered, carrying jars of pickles and jams out the front door. He threw them on the ground and the jars shattered. The large crock of sauerkraut was so heavy, it took two Bolshevik agents to lift it. They hefted it across the threshold, dumped the sauerkraut on the ground, and smashed the crock. The pungent smell of vinegar drifted into the room.

"Stop destroying our food!" Kolya shouted, but Oxana shushed him, realizing the futility of further opposition. "Don't worry," she whispered. "If we keep quiet, they will not harm us." The hoodlums ransacked the house, opening drawers and overturning the furniture.

"Anything more?" one of the thugs asked.

"That ought to do it, for now anyway," Alexi mumbled. "Close the door on your way out. There's some business here needs my attention." Alexi stumbled toward Oxana, slurring his words. "Your husband's been gone a long time. You must be lonely." He stepped forward and nearly fell against her. Oxana turned her face to avoid his breath. "You and your sister always were the prettiest girls in town." Alexi put his arm around her waist. "Too bad she isn't here. You know they say two are better than one."

"Leave my mother alone," Kolya cried out.

"You sound brave for a little cripple who can't do nothing but play the piano." Alexi laughed. "I doubt you can stop me."

Oxana grasped Kolya's hand and again whispered for him to remain silent.

Alexi leaned toward her and kissed her on the mouth. "I hear you're an easy lay," he slurred. Oxana stood rigid, refusing to step back.

"Get away from her!" Kolya shouted. Alexi grabbed him around his chest, pinning both arms so he could not hit back.

"You little son of a bitch," Alexi growled, holding Kolya against him as he stepped over to the door and opened it. Before either Oxana or Kolya understood what was happening, Alexi shoved Kolya's right thumb into the doorframe and slammed the door shut. Kolya screamed as blood spurted from the crushed fingertip. Alexi laughed. He pressed Kolya's right hand into the doorframe. "Either you crawl into bed with me or I smash the little asshole's entire hand, gently of course, one finger at a time."

"Stop!" Oxana shouted. "I'll do what you want. Whatever you want. Just stop. Don't hurt his fingers."

Alexi shoved Kolya. He fell to the floor, and when he struggled to stand, Alexi kicked his stomach. Kolya curled into a ball, whimpering in pain. "Maybe the little piano-playing bastard would like to watch; he can learn how it's done."

Without his sticks, getting up was difficult, and Kolya had to hold on to a chair to steady himself. "Kolya, do not listen to Alexi!" Oxana shouted. "Go to the barn and wait there until I come and get you." Kolya did not move. "Go to the barn! Now!"

Oxana was terrified Alexi would stop him, but he didn't. As soon as Kolya was out the door, Alexi began tearing at her clothing. She stood like a stone, staring past him, while he ripped the buttons off her blouse and pulled at the fabric until it tore.

Suddenly a bullet whizzed past Alexi's head and lodged in the wall behind him. Kolya was standing in the doorway with a rifle aimed at Alexi. "You leave my mother alone and get the hell out of here right now or I'll shoot you dead," he yelled, trying to hold his aim steady despite his shaking hands.

"You're a bastard and she's a whore," Alexi shouted. "Everyone knows Fedor ain't your father. Your father's probably some drunk soldier who was passing through town one night." He went out the door and slammed it behind him. Kolya lowered the gun and bolted the door. He pushed a chair against it for added security, while Oxana held her torn blouse against her chest to cover herself.

Both stood frozen. Oxana was not sure if Alexi was gone for good or if he and his thugs would return—with guns loaded.

"Where did you get that gun?" Oxana asked, breaking the silence.

"It's Dad's. I found it in the barn, and Uncle Gregor taught me how to shoot. He told me I should keep it in the barn. That you probably wouldn't like me having a gun."

"Gregor was right, but for tonight I'll make an exception. I'm glad you had it and knew how to use it."

"But is it true, Mama? What he said? Fedor is not my dad?"

"Oh, Kolya, my boy, of course Fedor is your father." Oxana rubbed Kolya's hair and patted him on the back. "Alexi is a mean and horrible person. Don't believe anything he says."

"But why did he say those things if they aren't true?"

"Kolya, put it out of your mind. Who knows why people say the things they say?

And now I am the liar, Oxana thought as Kolya went back to his bed while she pulled back the sheets on her—Fedor's—bed. *Am I truly any better than those Bolshevik thieves if I can't even be honest with my own son?*

Chapter 29

Several days later, Oxana heard a commotion outside the house. She grabbed the ax she had brought inside, holding it behind her as she opened the door, fully prepared to use it if she had to. Gregor was standing there, panting. "There's been an uprising and we've all left the commune and declared it dissolved. Everyone is angry. We're taking the animals into the forest to hide them, and we can take your cow, but we must go now."

He paused to catch his breath. "We were lied to," Gregor continued while Kolya, wide awake, leaned over the edge of his bed and quickly pulled on his pants. "They promised food and wages, but they've given us no money, only coupons for the commune store, which has nothing but tins of old army rations and used clothing they bring in from Moscow."

"I can take the cow, Mama," Kolya said.

"The Bolsheviks have called for soldiers from Odesa," Gregor said, "and they'll be here soon. Oxana, we are prepared to fight."

"Kolya, no. You'll fall."

"Uncle Gregor needs help and I can do it." Kolya grabbed his walking sticks.

"He'll be safe, Oxana. I'll watch him," Gregor said. "We have to move fast, before the soldiers get here."

Later that morning, as the hours wore on, Oxana grew increasingly more agitated and worried. She tried to stay busy mending one of Kolya's shirts but could not focus her mind and kept tearing the thread. She gave up and went outside to dig through the soil in the garden, hoping there might still be something, anything—potatoes, onions, carrots—she might have missed when harvesting. She found a few sorely needed vegetables, which she carried into the house. She stood, trying to think of a secure hiding spot, when she heard a knock. "Oxana. Open up. Quick." She undid the bolt. Gregor was holding a large bundle wrapped in a blanket, and his hands were dripping blood.

"Kolya!" Oxana shrieked.

"No, it's not Kolya, thank God. I'm afraid this is your cow. The Bolsheviks discovered the animals in the forest." Gregor unwrapped the blanket and laid a chunk of meat on the table. Kolya came in behind Gregor, and Oxana hugged him. "We slaughtered all the animals," Gregor continued. "It's better we have the meat than those bastards. I'm afraid we wasted quite a bit, but if you cook this and dry it, it'll last a while. But you've got to do it now, and then hide the meat. They'll come looking for it. I'm heading back to the commune to reclaim my tools. And, Oxana, we only meant to scare them off, but two soldiers were killed. I'm afraid there will be retaliation."

Oxana immediately threw more wood into the stove.

That afternoon, Oxana was in her garden digging through the soil again, desperate to find any vegetables that might have been missed, when her mother came running into the farmyard. "Gregor's been arrested," she said, gasping for breath. "They're holding a group of men in the square. I don't know what they're planning to do."

Oh God, Oxana thought, standing and brushing the dirt from her dress. *Will they never leave us in peace?* "I'll go. You stay here with Kolya. I don't want him left alone."

Angry villagers, shouting and pumping their fists in the air, were streaming into the square where nearly two dozen men were surrounded by soldiers. A group of village men lunged forward, and it appeared the crowd was on the verge of assaulting and overpowering the soldiers when several turned their rifles on the crowd, warning them to stay back. The villagers quieted down, and Oxana spotted Gregor among the corralled men, standing alongside Arkady. Gregor waved and shouted that he was not injured. An officer who appeared to be in charge opened the back of the truck, and soldiers jabbed the men with their rifle barrels to force them in.

Suddenly, Maria emerged from the crowd and ran toward the commanding officer. "These men are innocent!" she shouted. Arkady called to her to be quiet.

"Listen to your husband," the officer bellowed, aiming his rifle at her, "before I shoot you."

"No!" Maria shouted. "I will not be quiet. You've arrested innocent men. How will I feed my boys without my husband?"

"Silence, woman!" the officer shouted. "This village has defied orders to join the kolkhoz. As far as I'm concerned, the entire village is under arrest." He fired shots into the air.

Oxana rushed over to Maria just as a soldier came around the corner with Alexi in handcuffs. "Alexi Karpenko is under arrest for failing to carry out the collectivization of this village," the commanding officer announced to the crowd, while soldiers forced Alexi into the back of the truck. The truck roared to a start and drove out of the square, the assembled villagers quietly watching, wondering.

"I am Andrei Bilyik, from the District Party Committee in Odesa," the commanding officer continued once the truck was out of sight. "The People's Commissariat for Agriculture has grown tired of waiting for results. The Peterstal Village Council is disbanded and has no further authority. I am now charged with implementing the final collectivization of this village. Beginning tomorrow, each house will be searched by one of our buksyr brigades. Make no mistake, comrades, our brigades are well trained. By the time the search is complete, every house will require refurbishment. It will have no stove and no roof. If you are hoarding food, we will find it and you will be arrested. If you wish to avoid this search, you must step forward and sign the papers to join the collective now. This is your last chance."

No one moved. No one spoke. An eerie silence hung over the assembled villagers. One of the Bolsheviks called out, "Come on, what are you waiting for?" Still, no one moved or spoke.

Finally, the commanding officer, glaring at the blank faces staring back at him, lost patience. "Do you have any idea who you are resisting? You are all enemies of Russia. Do you think you matter to us? You can all die—we do not care." He stared in disbelief while the villagers quietly and grimly filed out of the square.

Oxana and Maria, with arms around each other's waists, headed down the road toward their farms. "My Arkady, my Arkady," Maria kept saying. "Where will they take them? What am I going to do?"

Oxana grasped Maria's hands when they reached her farm. "You were brave. I'm proud of you for standing up to that officer."

"What good did it do? My Arkady's still gone."

"You did a lot of good, Maria. You showed the officer that you can see right from wrong. You showed your courage and your principles."

"Oh, Oxana, I don't think I have much courage. You gave me the courage to do it. I spoke out because it's what you would do."

"That's not true, Maria. You have a great deal of courage. And don't forget. You're not alone. You can come talk to me anytime."

———

Elena and Kolya were waiting when Oxana came into the farmyard. "Is Gregor coming today to help us?" Kolya asked. "Grandma says he was arrested."

"Oh, Kolya, my boy." Oxana put her arms around him. "Gregor has been taken away." Kolya leaned his face against her dress and she hugged him tightly.

"What is happening, Mama? Are we going to be alright?"

"I don't know, my son." Oxana buried her face in his hair. "I don't know."

The next day, Oxana was stepping out of her outhouse when a soldier approached, ordering her to follow him. The soldier stepped in front of her, blocking her way, when she went toward the water tank to wash her hands. "You must come now, without delay." He led her to the town hall, where the commanding officer was seated at a desk.

"Oxana Nikolaevna Rostova, I presume?" he said, laying aside the newspaper he was reading. "Allow me to introduce myself. I am Andrei Bilyik, from the District—"

"I know who you are. I was in the square yesterday." Oxana stared, unblinking. He was surprisingly young, only about twenty-five years old, and without his hat, his blond hair was so thin Oxana could see the pink skin of his scalp. "Where have the men been taken? My husband's brother, Gregor Rostov, was one of them. He is innocent, and I need his help farming my land."

"Oxana, Oxana, you don't seem to understand. You have no need for Gregor Rostov. You have no need for any help because you have no farmland. You will join our collective and your farmland will belong to the state—to everyone."

"Where have you taken the men?" Oxana raised her voice.

"Oxana Nikolaevna, I am a very busy man with no time for your idle questions. Let me get to the point of why you were brought here. As I'm sure you know, two of our comrades were brutally murdered by the insurrectionists, and tomorrow we are having a memorial service to honor them. We have invited the entire village, and I think no one will want to refuse our generous invitation. Your piano playing is well known. I was told that in all of Odesa, no one is better. It will set a nice example for the villagers and for all of the loyal party members to hear you play and see that even someone as—how shall I say it—obstinate as you understands the importance of honoring our fallen comrades."

Oxana glared at him, not saying a word.

"I take your silence as your approval. The service will be at ten a.m., here in the square." Andrei Bilyik opened a desk drawer, took out a revolver, and slowly turned it over in his hands as if inspecting it. "You have a young son. His name is Kolya, if I am correct? He too plays the piano quite well, I am told." The officer spun the revolver around on his finger. "It would be a shame if something were to happen to him."

Oxana struggled to maintain her composure. "If you've finished with me, I will get back to work. There is much to be done on *my* farm, even though I notice that very little work is happening on the land owned by *your* kolkhoz."

Andrei Bilyik laid the revolver on his desk, "Yes, yes, we are finished—for now, Oxana Nikolaevna. Thank you for taking the time to visit with me. I'm sure we will see each other again."

As soon as she returned home, Oxana told Kolya to bring Fedor's gun into the house and to keep it loaded, just in case.

———

Oxana's mother was already in the square waiting when Oxana and Kolya arrived the next morning. A small dais was erected in front of the Orthodox church, with a dozen chairs arranged in a half circle on it. In front of the chairs stood an ebony grand piano. Oxana climbed the short flight of steps onto the stage, and the worker positioning the piano recognized her. "They had it brought in yesterday from Odesa," he said. "Just for you, Oxana Nikolaevna. Just for you." As he stepped off the dais, Oxana heard him mumbling, "Imagine, bringing a piano all the way from Odesa. She's famous." Despite what was clearly intended as a compliment, Oxana felt a stab of pain. *Nothing could be further from the truth*, she thought. *If only I were famous, famous for my interpretations of Chopin, and Beethoven, and Bach. If only I could have gone to Moscow and had a chance at a career. If only . . .* Oxana took a handkerchief out of her handbag, wiped they keys, and sat down to try out the piano.

Kolya and his grandmother stood with the other villagers while Oxana sat on the dais, among the group of Bolshevik dignitaries. After nearly an hour of laudatory speeches, one of the men nodded to her. Oxana stepped to the piano, sat on the bench, folded her hands in her lap, and bowed her head.

If Irina were here, would she have acquiesced, or would she have stood her ground and refused to play? And Jakob—he would never have given in to these bullying hoodlums. He was right to have escaped when he had the chance.

Oxana lifted her hands and placed them on the keyboard. She raised her head, gazing upward into the blue sky, and began the soft, slow opening of Chopin's Fantasy, playing as if in a trance without looking at her hands, only staring heavenward.

After the service, Oxana, Kolya, and her mother walked to the town hall, where she had been invited to join the dignitaries for lunch. "Special guests only, not you two," the soldier guarding the door said, and he pointed his rifle at Elena Vladimirovna and Kolya.

"They *are* special guests," Oxana sneered at him. "*My* special guests."

"Special guests only," the soldier retorted. "Those are my orders."

Andrei Bilyik approached, chatting with a group of men. "Oxana, my compliments," he said, reaching to shake her hand. Oxana did not reciprocate, and he stood a moment with his hand extended before returning it to his side. "It is nice to know that the professors in Odesa were correct. Your playing was exquisite. The best I've ever heard."

"This soldier is barring my son and my mother from entry."

"My apologies, a minor misunderstanding." Bilyik held his arm in front of the soldier and motioned for Oxana's mother and Kolya to enter. "Of course you are welcome. There is enough for everyone."

An elegant buffet was laid out across several tables along the front of the room. Oxana was stunned to see such plenty when the entire village was nearly starving. Her mother and Kolya got in line, and Oxana whispered that they should take as many of the sandwiches and cakes as they could fit on their plates. They sat at the table farthest from the head table, and while the obligatory speeches and vodka toasts were offered, Oxana discreetly stashed all three platefuls of food in her bag.

Once home, Oxana divvied up the food into small amounts, wrapped each portion in paper, and tied them with string. The packages would be discovered if she hid them in the house and she dared not dig a hole. Freshly dug dirt raised an immediate alert with the raiders. She went into the barn and slipped the packages under a pile of hay alongside the dried beef from her cow.

———

Kolya was practicing several days later when Maria's oldest son, Aloysha, came running into the house. "Something bad is happening. Mama's crying and they're tearing our house apart. I think you should come."

Oxana and Kolya followed Aloysha across the field. A buksyr brigade truck was parked beside the house, and Maria was outside, screaming at one of the soldiers while others were hauling furniture out of the house and throwing it onto a pile in the yard. Oxana ran toward the soldier, shouting for them to stop. He turned, and Oxana was shocked. It was Andrei Bilyik.

"Oxana Rostova! I didn't expect to see you rushing to the aid of criminals."

"These are not criminals. Why are you raiding their home?"

Maria was on her knees. "Help me, Oxana, help me. They're taking everything and they say we have to leave."

"Do not have pity on these worthless liars," Bilyik bellowed. "They have hidden grain that belongs to the kolkhoz."

"There is no grain. My boys are starving and you took my husband away." Maria pulled on Bilyik's coat. "What can we do?"

"You are a liar. My comrades found grain in your attic."

"My husband must have hidden it. He didn't tell me. Please take the grain. Take it. But let us keep our house. We have nowhere to go."

"I've no time for liars and thieves." Bilyik pushed Maria's hands away and stomped toward the house.

"Stop!" Oxana screamed. "Stop this desecration. These people are innocent. How dare you throw them out of their home!"

Bilyik spun around and came toward Oxana. His face was red and his hand was clenched in a fist. Maria gasped as he swung at Oxana's face. She stood firm, without flinching, and he stopped short of hitting her. His hands were shaking. "This house, this land, this village, it all belongs to the kolkhoz. It is *you* who is heaping desecration on our holy Mother Russia." He spit on Oxana's face. "Destroy everything," he shouted to his men. "There is nothing here to be saved."

Oxana put her arms around Kolya and Aloysha and his brothers, Maxim and Oleg, while Maria remained kneeling, wailing, beating her hands against the ground. Aloysha began speaking, as if to himself: "They told us to stand in the middle of the room. Mama tried to stop them, but they hit her. They had iron crowbars and they poked holes in the walls. They pulled up the floorboards. They smashed the stove. They tore off the roof. And then they found papa's grain—" He started to cry, and Oxana patted him on the back.

The soldiers continued until the entire contents of the house— furniture, beds and bedding, dishes, pans and kettles, clothing . . . everything—was in a heap. They poured gasoline over the pile and lit it. They smashed the windows and tossed in pieces of burning wood. The fire spread rapidly, and soon the house was engulfed in flames. Oxana and

Aloysha helped Maria to her feet, and with the boys following behind, they turned away from the smoky blaze and slowly made their way across the field.

Kolya helped Aloysha and the two younger boys make up beds in the barn while Oxana retrieved the last strips of dried beef along with the remaining onions and potatoes she had hidden under the hay. Oxana put water on to boil while Maria chopped the small amount of food. They worked in silence. There was nothing to say, or rather more to say than either could possibly put into words.

Oxana could hardly bear to watch the half-starved boys lifting spoonfuls of the watery soup to their mouths. From the first moment her town had been overtaken by the Bolsheviks, she had managed to take each assault and hardship in stride, but this moment was somehow too much. The gaunt faces of the boys she had known since they were happy little babies disarmed her. No longer able to bottle her feelings inside, she fled out the door, trying to stifle her sobs. She stood a moment gasping, inhaling the cool air, before she retrieved the packages from the Bolshevik service she had hidden. It was the only food she had left, but she could not endure the children's looks of hunger.

Kolya found only a note when he went to the barn the next morning to check on the family:

> Mama says we must leave. We can't be a burden to you.
> Wish us luck.
>
> Aloysha
> P.S. Mama says thank you for all you've done for us.

———

Oxana knew Andrei Bilyik would have his revenge and was not surprised when, the next day, she heard a truck approaching. She was very surprised, however, when the truck pulled into the farmyard and the familiar head of curly black hair emerged from the driver's door.

"There she is, boys. That's her," Fedor shouted, and the men began piling out of the back even before the truck had come to a stop.

"Stop right there," Oxana shouted. She stood in the doorway with the front door open. "What are you doing here, Fedor?"

"I've come to reclaim my property, Oxana. I'm glad you still remember my name."

"You are correct. This farm is your property, and I'm still your wife. If you're needing a place to stay, you are welcome here, but not this gang of ruffians."

"Listen to that, boys. She's calling you all a gang of ruffians—always did like to use them fancy words. Well, my sweet wife, it's you who'll be needing a place to stay. Let's move her out, boys." The brigade started toward the house. "And there he is, boys," Fedor called out when Kolya appeared in the doorway beside his mother. "Let me introduce you to my bastard son." Oxana watched anxiously as Fedor went up to Kolya and stood staring at him, as if assessing him.

"Are you my father?" Kolya asked.

"Yeah, sure, I'm your father, like my brother's your father, and who knows how many other men the whore's had here for you to call dad."

"But you *are* my dad."

"Hasn't she told you? You're a bastard. You'll have to ask your mama who your damn father is, but it sure as hell ain't me. Now get out of my way. We've got work to do." Fedor shouldered past him, and Kolya turned toward his mother, staring.

Fedor joined the others already throwing things out the door. Kolya continued staring at his mother while their belongings were tossed past him, some almost hitting him. Finally, Oxana could endure it no longer and fled into the garden. Kolya followed her, not saying a word, only staring, wide-eyed, blank-faced. Several men carried Oxana's steamer trunk into the yard. "Let's see what's inside," Fedor bellowed. "Probably filled with all the stuff she stole from that rich old kulak woman she lived with in Odesa." Fedor pulled a revolver out of his pocket and shot the lock. The men flipped open the lid and pulled Oxana's dresses out.

"Take a look at this," Fedor said, holding up Oxana's red concert dress. "I sure do remember that night. No wonder every man in town was after her." He tossed the dress onto the accumulating pile and tipped the steamer trunk over, dumping everything on the ground. "Any of you see something you wanna take home to your ladies? They might like some of this fancy stuff she's got here."

Oxana broke into tears when the piano—the last remaining item in the house—appeared in the doorway. Two of the men pushed it out the door and across the front yard alongside the pile of their belongings. "We'll get an auctioneer out here tomorrow and start selling this off," Fedor bellowed. He smashed a hole in the wall with an iron hammer and another hole in the door, wrapped a chain through the holes, and snapped on a padlock before they all jumped into the truck and drove away.

Kolya stood staring at his mother for a long while. Finally, unable to endure his icy gaze any longer, she whispered, "I'm sorry. I should have told you."

"Yes, you should have. You lied to me. If Fedor is not my father, then who is? Who am I?"

"Yes, I lied to you. I'm sorry, but I lied to protect you." Oxana reached to put her arm around Kolya's neck, but he stepped back to avoid her touch.

"Your father was a friend of mine, but this place had become a place of sorrow for him and he came to me for comfort from his grief. I had feelings for him and thought he had similar feelings for me and that, possibly in comforting him, he and I might marry. Things happened—you happened—but it didn't work out as I had hoped. Instead he left, without even saying goodbye. I never saw him again. Please believe me, Kolya, I never meant to hurt you. I married Fedor so you would have a father. I didn't know it would turn out like this."

"But you should have told me."

"Yes. I should have told you. Please try to forgive me."

Kolya stepped toward his mother and held out his arms. "I forgive you, Mama." He embraced her. "I love you."

They gathered up armfuls of clothing and headed into town.

"Oh, God," her mother said when she opened her door. Oxana quickly explained about the sudden appearance of Fedor and their subsequent expulsion, and the three headed back to the farm.

"Forget about everything else," Oxana said as they stood staring at the pile of their belongings. "The piano is most important. Kolya has to have it for his practicing."

After a few moments of thinking, Oxana pointed to Fedor's hay wagon standing beside the barn. "We'll have to use the wagon. That's how it was brought here." She went into the barn and reappeared with braided ropes. She tied them to the wagon while her mother and Kolya watched, silent, not sure what she was planning.

"And now we pull," Oxana said, handing the rope ends to each of them.

"Oxana . . . " her mother started to say, but Oxana interrupted her.

"You don't need to pull if you don't feel you can. Kolya and I will do it ourselves."

Her mother quickly grabbed a rope end. After a few tugs they got the wagon moving and managed to pull it over to where the piano stood.

"But Mama, the piano's too heavy for us to lift," Kolya said.

"Yes, I know. We need some sort of inclined ramp to roll the piano into the wagon box." Standing with her hands on her hips, Oxana noticed that several of the boards on the barn were loose. *The siding boards might be long enough*, she thought. Oxana went back into the barn to search for a crowbar. Kolya helped her wedge the crowbar between two pieces of siding. The wood was dry and the nails were rusted, but after several jerks on the crowbar the board gave way. It was long enough, but the wood was too thin to support the weight of the piano. They would need many pieces layered on top of each other. Oxana and Kolya pried away more of the siding until they had a ramp that appeared to be sturdy enough. Oxana, Kolya, and Elena all got behind the piano and pushed. At first it did not even budge, but eventually they managed to move it forward and slowly the piano ascended the slanted ramp. The boards sagged under the weight but did not snap.

Kolya had not uttered a word about any pain in his legs but seeing his clenched teeth grimace as he struggled to maintain his balance confirmed her fears. Afraid his strength might give out, causing both him and the piano to come crashing to the ground, Oxana impulsively began to sing the opening notes of Chopin's Fantasy. Soon all three were singing the march-like tune while they heaved the piano upward and into the back of the wagon.

They loaded the planks into the wagon as well, since they would need them to unload the piano. Like three human horses, they tied the ropes around their waists. "I hope no one sees us—I'm sure we're a sorry sight," Oxana said as they pulled the wagon down the dirt road toward town.

"I hope someone does see us; maybe they will help," Kolya replied, but they were not that fortunate. They pulled the cart along with only the creaking of the wagon wheels to break the silence.

By the time they reached Oxana's mother's house, the sun was setting and they were exhausted, but they had to get the piano inside. Oxana was certain Fedor would come for it. They tied the ropes around the piano and all three stood in the wagon box, slowly unfurling the ropes to ease the piano down the ramp. They laid the ramp planks on the ground to form a pathway and rolled the piano to the front door, giving it one last push to get it over the threshold and inside the house—and out of Fedor's reach— before they all collapsed into chairs. They were too exhausted to even try it out to see if any damage had occurred.

That night, Oxana sat for a long while, fondling the gem-encrusted icon from Vera and the gold ring from Jakob she had sewn into a cloth pouch inside her dress. Caressing the treasured items, she gazed at the piano. It had come full circle, back to where it had stood all the while Oxana was growing up, back to the house that had heard so many hours and days and years of her relentless practicing in her quest to be the finest pianist she could possibly be—and to escape Peterstal. With Kolya on the floor, curled under a blanket, sound asleep, and her mother asleep in the next room, Oxana leaned her head back and closed her eyes. All that was most precious to her was safe.

Chapter 30

Oxana woke before sunrise. She lit the stove and, turning, was surprised to see her mother standing in the kitchen doorway. "I'll make breakfast," she said, putting a pot of water on to boil. *Surely there must be something here to eat.* Oxana opened cupboards and drawers while her mother stood staring, saying nothing.

"I'm hungry." Kolya appeared in the doorway, stretching his arms and yawning.

Oxana ladled hot water into cups and handed them to Kolya and her mother. "This will have to do for now. Play for Grandma while I find something to cook."

Oxana put on her hat and coat and stepped outside. It was late fall and there was an icy coldness in the breeze. Coming around the corner of the house, she flinched and stepped back. Fedor was standing in the front yard, only a few steps from her. He had red eyes, as if he had not slept, and his hair was matted down, as if he had not bathed in a long while. His fingers were twitching, and he seemed nervous.

"I suppose you've come for the piano?" Oxana said.

"No. I've come to explain, and apologize."

"Explain! Apologize! After you ran us out of our home?"

"Oxana, please hear me out. I had to do it. They would only let me out of the gulag if I agreed to join the brigades, and I had to get out. I had to come back and see you. Oxana, I still love you. I've always loved you. You're the only thing I've ever wanted."

"Why are you saying all this? What do you want from me?"

"I want us to start over," Fedor pleaded. "Get rid of the kid. He can stay here with your mother or he can be on his own. He's old enough, and you and I can get away from here, have our own children, start a new life."

"Fedor, I will never abandon my son, and it is time for you to go. There is nothing here for you."

"I brought this for you." Fedor handed her the red concert dress. "I'll never forget that night. You were the most beautiful woman on earth, and you played the piano better than I thought it could be played."

"Don't be ridiculous, Fedor. It's only a dress."

"Maybe to you—but to me it was a vision of what I wanted most: a happy life with a wife and children."

"I'm sorry, Fedor, I really am. I wish it all could've worked out, but it didn't, and it's too late now."

"But Oxana, please. I need you."

"Fedor. No. I'm sorry . . . goodbye . . . and take the dress with you. I have no use for the past. I am now living for my son's future."

He stood a moment staring at her, as if he might start to cry, before he tucked her red dress under his arm and slowly wandered out of the yard and around the corner.

Oxana watched him go and, for a brief moment, felt as if she too might cry. Fedor had, at times, been so loving and caring, but then he could fly into a rage and be cruel and violent. *Is Fedor mentally ill,* she wondered, *suffering from some sort of split personality disorder?* She thought about the story of Dr. Jekyll and Mr. Hyde she had read while a student in Odesa. It was her only explanation for his wild mood swings. But she also knew she was partly to blame. What she had done was not right. Had she pushed Fedor over the edge, into madness? She tugged on her dress, as if by straightening her dress, she could also straighten her mind.

Oxana had no idea how or where to find food, but she had to find something. *It's a mother's job,* she repeated to herself as she crossed the street and went around the corner. *Kolya and Mama are starving.* The square was deserted. The Orthodox church was covered with obscene graffiti, and the Bolsheviks were using it to store grain. One of the hinges on the front door of the general store had come loose and the door was hanging sideways, flapping in the breeze. The store had stayed open until there was nothing left to sell and the owners gave up and wandered off. The door to the doctor's office was ajar, and Oxana was not sure if he was still in town or not. The mill across from the doctor's office had closed when it became illegal to grind flour and was now boarded up. Her father's blacksmith shop was also boarded up, but she could still make out the lettering above the entrance: STEPANIAK.

She wondered what kind of man her papa had been—her mother never spoke of him. Would he have found food for them if he were here now? Would he have kept them alive?

A light rain started to fall, and Oxana pulled her scarf over her head. She slowly trudged toward the building that now housed the kolkhoz kitchen, her empty stomach making her feel lightheaded, as if she might faint. She stopped to peer inside a window where a young girl was standing at a counter, peeling potatoes. Smiling broadly, the girl opened the window and tossed out a bowlful of potato peels before quickly closing the window and continuing her work. Oxana knelt to gather the peels into her apron and hurried home. She was opening the gate to her mother's house when a man darted out of the outhouse and across the street. *Fedor?* She went to investigate and on the floor, in the corner, lay a small bag of beets and onions.

The next day, Oxana returned to the kitchen. An older woman was at work beside the window. Oxana stood, unsure if it was safe. The woman glanced out the window and stepped away. A few moments later a soldier came around the corner waving his rifle. "Be gone, or I'll have you arrested for trespassing and stealing," he shouted.

Oxana returned to her mother's house and stood in the front yard, mindlessly fingering several brown, dried-up flowers, remembering how Vera's chef had garnished their vichyssoise with colorful nasturtiums and how she had giggled at the thought of eating flowers.

"Privyet, Oxana Nikolaevna. You remember me?"

Oxana turned. "Inna—the honey lady! From the Saturday market." In truth she was so thin and emaciated Oxana hardly recognized her. Inna pointed to the pigweed growing along the house. "You can boil that and eat it." She pointed to other weeds, *svyrypa* and *kozelsky*. "Mash those into a pulp and make borscht or fry them into *lyaposhky* cakes. You take some and maybe I can have some too?"

"Of course, take what you want," Oxana said, sensing the desperation in her voice.

"Spasiba. It's only me and my daughter at home and we don't have much to eat these days." Inna quickly gathered an armful. "Spasiba, Oxana Nikolaevna. Spasiba. Tomorrow I will show you where to get more." She waved and hurried down the street.

Oxana gathered an armful of the dried plants and took them inside. Following Inna's suggestion, she chopped them into a fine meal, mixed in enough water to form small patties, and heated them.

"Thanks, Mama, for making us pancakes," Kolya said before swallowing his last bite, while Elena licked her finger to moisten it, in order to gather up the remaining crumbs on her plate. "They were delicious."

Oxana coughed, trying to keep her tears in check. "Thank you, Kolya, although I'm not so sure about the delicious part."

"Everything you cook is delicious, Mama."

Oxana quickly rose from her chair, wiping her eyes. *What mother serves weeds to her mother and son?* She wrapped two remaining cakes in a towel and headed down the main road. Slava and Ludmilla were sitting beside each other on their sofa when Oxana came through their door. They had covered themselves in blankets, despite the warm room, and both appeared to be wearing several layers of clothing. Ludmilla struggled to her feet. "Don't get up. Conserve your strength," Oxana said, handing each a small cake. "I came to give you these."

"Spasiba," Ludmilla whispered. Slava tried to speak but was too weak, only uttering a soft rasp as he moved his lips. Oxana sat watching while they slowly chewed their dry patties. They ate in silence, Slava and Ludmilla pausing only to show their appreciation by smiling. "Spasiba," Ludmilla whispered again when Oxana stood to leave, and Oxana knelt and embraced her in a long hug. Oxana reached to shake hands with Slava, but she was overcome with emotion and hugged him as well. Again attempting to speak, he uttered only a hoarse rasp while tears poured down his leathery cheeks.

Before heading back home, Oxana stood a moment on Slava and Ludmilla's doorstep. She could not bring herself to venture the short distance to Fedor's house—her former home. It now belonged to the kolk-hoz. She had no idea how many people might be living there—maybe Fedor as well? She didn't want to know.

Oxana stepped to the window the next morning when she heard Inna calling to her. She was with several other women and each was carrying a towel. Oxana stuffed a towel into her apron pocket and joined them. The women trudged to the forest and made their way along the perimeter. Other villagers were already there, pulling up roots or gathering dried grass, and they nodded to each other, but no one spoke.

"You can boil this," Inna said, pointing to the bark of an acacia tree. "It doesn't make you sick." Oxana turned her head away. Inna put her arm around Oxana's waist. "We're all hungry. No reason to be embarrassed. Here, let me show you." Inna stripped a few pieces of bark. "Like this." Oxana started stripping bark as well.

Inna took Oxana by the arm and eased her through a section of dense undergrowth. There was a small clearing with nearly a dozen large anthills, and Inna poked into them with a tree branch until the ants were swarming about. She scooped handfuls into a small jar she extracted from her apron pocket. "You take some too," Inna said, pointing to the towel in Oxana's apron pocket. "Wrap them tight so they don't crawl all over you." Inna laughed, but Oxana only stared at her. "You have a boy to feed, and I have my daughter. These will keep their bodies from swelling."

Oxana bent over and scooped several handfuls into her towel.

Inna showed Oxana a large dark patch of moss on one of the tree trunks. "Take this too. It doesn't taste good, but at least it's something." Inna handed a chunk to Oxana, and she tucked it into her apron pocket along with the towel full of ants and the tree bark.

On their way home, Oxana and Inna were watching a young girl in one of the wheat fields, on her knees, gathering chaff, when a Bolshevik agent rode up on horseback and began beating her with a stick, yelling at her to stop stealing kolkhoz property. The little girl ran down the road, screaming and crying. Oxana and Inna continued walking, saying nothing.

Her mother was sitting at the table when Oxana came into the kitchen, and Kolya was reading. He no longer went to school. It had closed when Andrei Bilyik had all the teachers arrested. Oxana asked him to try to do one hour of practicing. "I know you're tired and hungry, but you must keep up your playing." Oxana begged her mother to lie down for a rest, and as soon as they were out of the kitchen she put a pot of water on to boil. She chopped the acacia bark into small pieces and added it to the pot, but when she stirred in the moss, the water turned dark green and thickened almost to the consistency of pudding. She carefully untied the towel and shook the ants into the pot, smashing them with a fork so no one would know what they were.

They ate their soup in silence. It tasted terrible, and Oxana hoped it would not make them sick.

After eating, Kolya went out without saying where he was going. He was gone for a few hours, and when he returned, he handed Oxana a towel with something wrapped inside. "Mama, we can put this in our soup tonight."

Oxana opened the towel and shrieked. "It's a rat."

"They're the only animals left in the forest. I trapped and skinned it the way Uncle Gregor taught me to skin rabbits."

"Kolya, I don't want you to worry about food. Your job is to keep up your piano playing. I can take care of things."

"Mama, we have to eat meat or we will get sick. Grandma has to have more than watery soup. Stop pretending everything is fine." Kolya grasped hold of Oxana's hand. "You don't need to protect me. We can do this together."

Oxana's hands were shaking. She tossed the meat into the boiling water and grabbed Kolya into a tight embrace. "Oh, my son, my boy. I'm so sorry you have to see this. I'm so sorry I can't take better care of you. I am so sorry. So sorry."

Inna did not come by for several days, and Oxana decided to go foraging by herself. She was nearing the forest when a Bolshevik soldier rode up on horseback. "No one is allowed in the forest," he shouted.

"Says who?"

"Andrei Bilyik says, that's who. The forest belongs to the government. No one is allowed to enter." He pointed his rifle at her. "Go back home."

The Bolsheviks were now using the Saturday market to sell the goods their buksyr brigades had confiscated. Oxana wandered in, hoping someone might have food to barter. She was carrying her mother's most prized possession, a pair of silver candlesticks that her father had given to her mother as a wedding present. Oxana had not told her mother she was trying to barter them away. She knew her mother would agree but wanted to spare her the agony of having to make the decision. The candlesticks were wrapped in a towel, and Oxana wandered amid the small crowd, opening the towel to show the candlesticks, but no one was interested.

A group of villagers were huddled around an oxcart loaded with items— an antique gun, a couple of icons, a samovar, a rug, and several blankets. An officer was holding up a frying pan, begging for bids. He announced "sold" and handed it over. He picked up a piece of women's underwear and called for bids. Oxana turned away in disgust and saw Inna. "Oxana Nikolaevna, please, would you like?" She was holding a gold icon and appeared even more emaciated. "Please, can you give me anything for this? Any food?" She shoved the icon toward Oxana. "It's gold, my grandfather's. Please. I'll trade for any food."

"I'm sorry," Oxana said. "I have no food either."

"Please. My daughter is almost dead. She needs food, anything. Please help me." Inna began to weep.

"I am so sorry, but I have nothing to give you," Oxana said, leaning over and kissing her forehead. "God bless you, Inna. God bless you." It was all she could do for the poor woman. Oxana turned away and crossed the square.

Andrei Bilyik looked up from his desk when she entered. "Oxana Nikolaevna, what a surprise."

"I have come to join your kolkhoz."

"Well, this is indeed a surprise. I always knew you would come to your senses eventually."

"You've taken all our food. My mother and son are starving. I will sign whatever papers are necessary."

"Ah, Oxana Nikolaevna, I am afraid it is not quite that simple. If only you had come earlier. Now you have no land, no animals, no machinery or tools. You have nothing to offer us."

"You already have everything. When my husband returned, everything was given over to you."

"Yes, indeed, you are correct." Bilyik rose, came around the desk, and stood face-to-face with Oxana. "But that is in the past. Do you think we are here only to give alms to the poor?"

"I'm not poor, and I am not asking for alms. I can work. My mother and son can also, if only you will allow us to eat so we can regain our strength."

"I'm afraid you have wasted both your time and mine today. I can be of no help to you."

"Please. I beg your mercy." She dropped to her knees and clasped her hands. "My mother and son are dying. Please help me, please."

"Leave this room. You and your kind are nothing but vermin. We don't need you in our kolkhoz."

"Is this what you want?" Oxana shouted, undoing the buttons down the front of her dress and exposing her breasts. "Is this what it will take to get food?"

"Petya," Bilyik called to a guard outside the door. "Please show Oxana Nikolaevna out. She seems confused. I am afraid she is no longer in her right mind."

———

Life became very quiet for Kolya, Oxana, and Elena. Entire days passed with the three of them sitting, saying nothing, lost in their thoughts, conserving their waning strength, almost as if each was rapt in a grotesque fascination, watching their bodies waste away. Oxana wondered how much longer they could go on.

She obsessively searched her mother's house, opening drawers and cupboards, in case anything had been overlooked. Knowing she would face arrest, and possibly death, if she was spotted and reported, she snuck into her mother's garden at night to dig through the soil, searching for anything that might still be there—a potato, a carrot, an onion—anything. She boiled pieces of leather cut from belts and old shoes in hope of extracting some nourishment for their starving bodies.

One afternoon, she was sitting quietly when a mouse darted across the floor. Oxana slowly picked up a broom, and when the mouse scampered across the floor again, she slammed the broom to the floor. She quickly reached under the thatch, grabbed the tail, and flung the mouse into the pot of boiling water she had going on the stove.

Kolya's legs were beginning to swell, and his face was so gaunt and pale he looked as if he were an old man. He often sat holding his stomach, and Oxana reduced his practice time to a half hour each day, and only soft, slow music. Her mother spent most of her days lying in bed curled into a fetal position, whimpering like a small child.

Sleep for Oxana became a near impossibility, and she lay awake for hours racked by remorse and guilt, reproaching herself for all she had wasted over the years, meals where she had not eaten everything on her plate, food that was allowed to spoil, vegetables that were left in the garden because there was too much to make use of. Surplus, excess, waste—the words hung in her mind like accusations. If only she had some of it now. If only she had saved more—hidden more away—maybe they would now have food and Kolya and her mother would not suffer.

Oxana took a jar of watery soup to Slava and Ludmilla one afternoon. The walk was exhausting and, stopping to rest, she noticed something sticking out of a freshly dug mound of earth off to the side of the road. She stepped closer. It was a child's arm protruding from a shallow grave. She shuddered and hurried down the road.

There was no answer when Oxana called to Slava and Ludmilla from the front door, so she went in. They were huddled together in bed and Slava was no longer breathing. Ludmilla opened her eyes and moaned when Oxana knelt beside her and took her hand. Oxana tried to give her soup, but after a few swallows she coughed and retched. A truck pulled up outside and two workers came through the door. "We work for the kolkhoz," one of them said. "Our orders are to remove the dead bodies."

Oxana pointed to Slava. One of the men took him by the arms and the other by his feet, and they carried him out. They tossed him into the truck box, which was already piled high with corpses. The two workers came back into the room. Oxana shook her head. "She's still alive."

"We need to take her now, lady. We only come by this way once a week and she won't last that long. We don't have the time to make an extra trip out here, so we need to take her now, or else by next week she'll be stinking up the place."

"For God's sake, have you no heart?" Oxana raised her voice. "She is still alive, a living human being. Can't you treat her with some dignity?"

"I'm sorry, lady. It's tough times now, but we've got a job to do. We bring in the bodies and they give us a hot meal. I'm not saying I like things how they are now, but I have children at home too. If I don't bring in the bodies, they don't eat, and they're damn near starved to death already. Bilyik's been pestering us to clear this place out. Says the kolkhoz's got a family all set to move in here soon as these two are gone. The new family won't like it if they come to a place that's been stunk up by a dead woman; we need to take her now."

Oxana kept her grip on Ludmilla's hand when the workers lifted her by her arms and feet. Ludmilla's grasp tightened. "Help me," she whispered, opening her eyes. "Help me." The workers jerked their hands apart, carried her out the door, and tossed her into the truck box, on top of her husband.

On her way home, Oxana heard screaming. She turned a corner and saw Olga in her front yard, surrounded by a group of boys. "Stop, stop it right now!" Oxana shouted, running toward the group. "Have you nothing better to do than harass an old woman?"

"She stole potatoes," one of the boys said. "I saw her take them."

"And what if I did?" Olga yelled back. "A hungry woman needs to eat."

"She stole potatoes. She has them stuffed in her pocket." The boy grabbed Olga's dress and yanked hard. A seam tore open and several small, half-rotten potatoes fell out.

"See, the witch stole potatoes and here they are," he shouted, picking up the mushy tubers.

"A hex on you all," Olga shrieked. "I curse you all. I call the devil down upon your souls, you evil fiends."

The boy pulled her dress again and it tore away, exposing the leathery, yellowed skin of her legs and buttocks.

"Stop!" Oxana screamed. She knelt to help Olga to her feet and retrieved her torn dress.

"She's a thief! She stole potatoes," the boys yelled.

"Since when is it a crime to gather a few half-rotten potatoes?" Oxana shouted back.

One young man stepped forward. "We are members of the Young Communist League. These potatoes belong to the kolkhoz, to the people. To take them is a crime against the people."

"And you are an impudent idiot who needs to learn to respect his elders," Oxana shouted into his face. "How dare you thugs tear the clothing from an old woman. Picking a few potatoes out of the ground is not a crime."

"Respect elders?" The young man sneered. "Let me show you what happens to elders who steal potatoes." He pulled a pistol from his pocket and aimed. A shot rang out. Olga's crippled old dog lying beside her fell backward with blood spewing from its stomach. A second shot sounded, and Olga clutched at her chest and let out a hissing sound before falling face forward to the ground.

"Take the chain, too," said the youngest boy, while another ripped the crucifix from around her neck. "Maybe we can get something for it."

The group ran off.

Oxana knelt beside Olga and laid the torn dress across her naked flesh. She wanted to call for help, but there was no one to call. She decided to go into Olga's house in search of a blanket to at least cover her, but when she opened the door she was assaulted by an overpowering stench. Trash was piled everywhere. The old hag must have spent her entire life collecting other people's cast-offs. Oxana glanced about the room. A dilapidated piano stood against the far wall. *She could play the piano?* There was an old, tattered volume of music on the music rack. Oxana stepped around the trash to get a better look and recognized the piece, a Chopin waltz.

A photo of two very pretty women was on top of the piano. Oxana held her nose and stepped closer. The frame was broken, part of it was missing, and the glass was cracked, but the image was clear. One of the figures appeared to be in her early twenties and the other was a teenager, and both were seated at a piano with their hands on the keys, smiling into the camera. It took Oxana a few moments to realize that the young girl was her mother, and the older one was Olga. *Olga and Mama playing piano? Together?* Oxana picked the photo up, and another photo, tucked into the back, fell out. *Papa?* Her mother had the same photo. She turned it over. "To my darling Olga, from your Nicholas" was written on the back. *Darling Olga? From your Nicholas? Papa knew Olga?* The stench was overpowering. Oxana stuffed both photos in her dress pocket and gasped for air as soon as she stepped outside.

Kolya was sitting on the front steps when Oxana got home. She patted him on his head, saying nothing, and went inside. Her mother was lying in bed. Oxana warmed soup and fed her a few spoonfuls. "Olga died today," Oxana said. "Some Bolshevik boys shot her." Her mother looked up but said nothing. "I went inside Olga's house to get a blanket. She had a piano, with music on the rack, and she had this photo on top of the piano." Oxana handed the photo of the two piano players to her mother. "It's you with her, isn't it?" Her mother eyed the photo, saying nothing. "She also had a photo of Papa." Her mother took the photo when Oxana handed it to her and held it in her hand. "It's the same one you used to have on top of our piano." Oxana reached for her mother's hand and turned the picture over, showing her the writing on the back. "To my darling Olga, from your Nicholas," Oxana read aloud. "Why would she have this photo, and why would Papa call her his darling?"

"I'm not surprised she kept it," her mother whispered.

"You knew Olga? And Papa knew her too? You've never said anything about this."

"What's to say? It was all so long ago."

"But you and Olga were friends? And she played the piano?"

"Yes, we were friends," her mother said slowly. "She was my teacher."

"But you said my grandmother taught you."

"Yes, at first my mother taught me, and then later, Olga. We played four-hand music together."

"So what happened?"

"She became angry with me, spread rumors that my father didn't pay her for all my lessons, that I stole music from her. Finally, we stopped talking to each other." Her mother laid her head back and closed her eyes.

"But why would she have a picture of Papa? And why did he write 'To my darling Olga'?"

Her mother lay a long while with her eyes closed, and Oxana thought she had fallen asleep.

"Because she was his darling," her mother whispered, "until I came along." She coughed, and Oxana got her a glass of water. "Your father was in love with Olga, I guess. They were planning to be married. And then your father and I met, and the wedding with Olga was called off." Her mother was speaking so faintly Oxana had to lean in to hear. "After your father broke off the wedding plans, Olga went away . . . was going to have a baby. People pretended to not know, but it was no secret. She had to give it up . . . was never the same again. And when you were born, Olga couldn't forgive me."

"Maybe I have a brother or sister somewhere?" Oxana whispered.

"Maybe." Her mother laid her head back and closed her eyes, breathing deeply and with difficulty.

"Oxana, Jakob did not go to America," she continued, her eyes still closed.

Oxana felt her breath catch in her throat at the sound of his name. She wondered if her mother might be hallucinating. "What are you saying, Mama? We were talking about Olga."

"Jakob . . . didn't go. He came back. I saw him at Irina's grave."

"Mama, you need to rest and save your energy. You're having a bad dream."

"No dream. Oxana—is Kolya his?"

"Mama . . ." Oxana tried speaking but fell against her mother, weeping.

"Don't be ashamed—I always knew."

Oxana held her hand.

"There's more I must tell you," her mother said. "When he came back I sent him away." Oxana let go of her hand. "He was planning on staying. I overheard him talking to Irina, at her grave. He wanted to marry you, but you were already married and going to have a baby."

"Mama . . ." Oxana started but could not find the words.

"I am so sorry. I thought it was for the best."

"Mama . . ." Oxana began again and stopped. "Mama, rest now. You don't need to say anything more."

"Yes, I do," she whispered. "Oxana, I'm glad you kept Kolya. You did the right thing. Maybe God was trying to fix his mistake. Maybe Kolya is the boy Irina couldn't have." Her mother again closed her eyes. "I always felt sorry for Olga . . . I wish she could have kept her child. I wish God had done more for her."

Oxana held her mother's hand and could feel her pulse weakening. "If only Jakob could know his son," her mother whispered. "He's a fine boy, Oxana, a fine boy."

"Sleep well, Mama." Oxana covered her mother with a blanket.

Later, when Oxana went to check on her, her mother was no longer breathing. "Goodbye, Mama," she whispered. "I forgive you. You did your best. You've always done what you thought was best. It's in the past now. Everything is in the past." Oxana closed her mother's eyes and wrapped the blanket tight around her. She leaned in and kissed her mother. "Now you can be with Irina."

She called Kolya inside. "Grandma's gone," she said. They held her hands.

"Mama, are we going to die too?" Kolya asked. Oxana put her arm around his shoulder and hugged him tightly. She could find nothing to say.

Oxana walked across the square, into the cemetery. The cross at the head of Irina's grave had long ago been stolen and the stone bench smashed. "Hello, Irina. Mama has died, but maybe you know that. Maybe she is already with you." She knelt and ran her fingers across the smooth, silky grass that now covered the grave. Except for a slight dip in the ground at the edges, it had become impossible to even see that a grave was there. "Mama did everything for us, gave us everything she had. All her hard work, her dreams, her hopes . . . was it all for nothing?" Oxana plucked several blades of grass and fingered them. "Irina, you should have lived. Your baby should have lived. You and Jakob should have had many more children and grown old together . . . and I should have been the pianist Mama dreamed of. I'm so sorry nothing worked out."

Oxana sat for a long while. "Mama told me that Jakob came back. She said he wanted to marry me but she sent him away. Irina, I'm not angry at her. I was shocked, but I'm not angry. He was your husband and I had no right to take him. He will always be yours.

"Irina," Oxana continued, "I love you, but I no longer think of you every day. I know I should, but I don't, and I'm sorry about that. It feels as if you are slowly drifting away—everything seems to be drifting away. Is this to be our fate? Mama, Jakob, you, and me? Will we all fade away, forgotten?"

Two ducks landed on the grass at the edge of the cemetery and waddled toward the pond. They slipped into the water and swam in circles, quacking to each other. Oxana buried her face in her hands and wept.

She looked up when she heard wings flapping. Oxana watched the ducks fly off and disappear into the horizon. "Goodbye, Irina; goodbye,

Jakob," she said, and impulsively lifted her hand and waved. She stood and wiped her tears before crossing into the square.

She approached the small hut beside the pile of ashes—all that remained of the Lutheran church after the Bolsheviks deemed it too small for grain storage and burned it down. "Too many deaths, too many," Father Vanska muttered, when Oxana told him her mother had died. "Holy God, Holy Mighty, Holy Immortal," he intoned and made the sign of the cross. "Have mercy on your faithful servant Elena Vladimirovna."

"Oxana," Father Vanska said when she turned to leave, "when Jakob came to me with his letter for you, he also told me he had been with you. He wanted to clear his conscience and begged me for forgiveness. Oxana, I blessed him. I told him that God forgave him, and I hope I did not speak improperly when I also assured him that you forgave him as well."

She lowered her head to avoid his eyes. "There is no need for me to forgive him," she whispered. "It is I who did wrong. Kolya is his."

"I know," Father Vanska said. "After your trouble with Fedor, I knew."

He has known? All these years? Oxana was embarrassed.

"Who knows what is right or wrong? Sometimes God sees things differently. Oxana, I forgive you, and God forgives you. You must try to forgive yourself."

"Thank you, Father, for everything."

"And now we should say our goodbyes, for you must leave as soon as you can find a way. There is nothing more to keep you here. You must leave for Kolya's sake. He will have a bright future, but it will not happen here." Father Vanska stood and clasped her in a tight embrace. "Go in peace—the love of God will protect you."

"Yes, Father, now must be goodbye," Oxana whispered, and tears ran down both their cheeks. "Thank you so very much."

Chapter 31

Getting to Odesa to try to make contact with Vera Veranitzskaya was Oxana and Kolya's only hope. At first, it was hard to decide what to take, knowing they would never return, but in the end, the decisions were quite easy. They had each other and they had their memories, and that, along with a few pieces of clothing packed into one small suitcase each, was all they needed.

Oxana did not even attempt to buy train tickets. The Bolsheviks' internal passport system required permission to travel, and everyone knew permission was never granted. Walking was their only option.

They started out before sunrise. To go along the road risked arrest for violating the travel restrictions, so they followed the train tracks, where others were also slowly making their way, but beyond a simple greeting, no one talked. Bodies in various stages of decomposition, some swollen to nearly twice their size, lay along the way, and the stench was horrible. Oxana held Kolya's hand tightly and tried to reassure him that nothing bad was going to happen to them.

By midmorning, with the sun high in the sky, they were already exhausted, hungry, and thirsty, when a train approached. The sound, which had been growing louder, began to lessen. The train was slowing, and by the time it was passing them it was barely moving at all. "Jump on," Oxana shouted. Kolya, reaching for the train railing, dropped his walking canes. He bent over to grab them, but the train lurched, and he was thrown against the railing and hit his head. Oxana, grabbing him, fell against the railing and nearly lost her grip. Both managed to get through the door and inside one of the compartments as the train picked up speed. They slipped into a couple of empty seats, but the conductor was already coming down the aisle, demanding to see their tickets. Oxana made a pretext of searching her bag, pretending to have misplaced them, but the conductor was not to be fooled. Uttering a few obscenities, he told them he would see to it they were put off at the next stop, which happened to be Odesa's central rail station, their exact destination.

Even before the train came to a complete stop, Oxana and Kolya jumped out, determined to deny the conductor the satisfaction of throwing them off, and set out for Vera Veranitzskaya's mansion. They stopped several times to rest, before the familiar towering roofline finally emerged from the stately trees. They approached the gate, only to discover it was chained shut, and the silk cord to call the butler was not there. Peering through the wrought-iron fence, Oxana saw that the flower beds were trampled over, several shutters were loose and banging against the house, and one windowpane in Vera's boudoir on the second floor was smashed.

"Privyet," Oxana called. "Anyone here?" There was no answer.

"It seems abandoned," Kolya said.

"That's impossible. Vera would never abandon her home."

"Privyet, Privyet," Oxana called.

"Mama, there's nobody here."

"Privyet, Privyet," Oxana continued calling, rattling the chain.

"Mama, let's go."

"Someone must be here. What's happened to Vera?" Oxana pushed once more on the iron gate. A policeman down the street blew his whistle, and Kolya took hold of Oxana's hand and led her away. They retraced their steps back into the city center to Primorsky Boulevard, Odesa's famed promenade along the Black Sea.

"I'm sorry, Kolya," Oxana said, watching the docked boats and ships rocking in the cool, saltwater-smelling sea breeze. "I was so hoping Vera might help us. I can't imagine what's happened to her."

While Kolya gazed across the harbor, Oxana scanned the storefronts on the opposite side of the boulevard until she spotted what she was looking for—one of the government-run Torgsin stores, billed as catering to foreigners but in reality, thinly veiled government-owned pawn shops, eager to pay cash for valuables that would later be sold at a profit.

"Wait here. I won't be long." Oxana crossed the street.

A sales representative eyed her cautiously when she came through the heavy glass door. She pulled Vera's icon out of her dress pocket and laid it on the counter. "Not much of a market for this stuff these days," he said. "Only the old folks want them, and they've already got all they need."

"It's real gemstones and solid gold."

He held the icon up to the light. "I'll give you fifty rubles."

"Fifty? It's worth at least ten times that."

"Lady, it's not worth anything until someone comes along to buy it. Fifty rubles is a good offer."

"I can't accept less than five hundred rubles."

"I'll give you sixty."

Oxana was fingering Jakob's ring in her dress pocket. *It's all I have from Jakob. How can I part with it?* But as soon as she posed the question, she found the answer—*Kolya. Jakob also gave me Kolya, and he is far more important than a piece of jewelry.*

"How much if I add this?" Oxana laid the ring on the counter.

The sales agent eyed the ring. "A hundred for both."

"Four hundred, no less."

"I can give you two hundred but not one ruble more."

Oxana glanced from the icon to the gold ring—*Vera, Jakob, the past*—she shook her head as if clearing a fog from her mind—*Kolya, the future.* "Three hundred."

"Alright. Three hundred. Lady, you drive a hard bargain." The store clerk counted out the money while Oxana plucked a tin of meat and a loaf of rye bread off the shelves.

She crossed the street to where Kolya was sitting. "Let's sit in the park while we eat our dinner, so you can watch the boats."

"What dinner? We don't have anything to eat."

"What do you call this?" Oxana showed him the bag with the meat and bread.

Kolya grinned and rubbed his stomach as they headed to one of the park tables. Oxana twisted open the tin of meat and tore a piece of bread from the loaf, folded the meat into the bread, and handed it to him, warn-ing him to eat slowly and only a small amount until his body became accustomed to solid food, otherwise he might make himself sick.

Oxana stared across the park to the beautiful azure sea. It was a relief to eat food, real food, leisurely and in public, without having to hurriedly swallow, worrying that a search brigade might suddenly appear at the door and grab even the crumbs off the floor. She watched the pedestrians hur-rying along the street, remembering how she and Vera had once regularly spent hours along this very boulevard, shopping for all sorts of extravagant merchandise—dresses, shoes, hats, ribbons, soaps, perfumes. Why had she needed all that? What had it added to her life? Happiness, true happiness, lay with her piano playing, with her beloved Irina and Jakob, and now, most of all, with Kolya.

They both were full before they finished their sandwiches, and Oxana wrapped the uneaten portions and put them in her bag. The sun had already set, and people in the park appeared to be preparing to spend the night. Some lay alone, face down. Others were huddled near trees. A few had a tattered blanket for cover while some had nothing but their clothes.

"It's fine with me if we sleep right here in the park," Kolya said.

"Kolya! You read my mind. I'm so sorry. I was certain we would be sleeping in Vera's mansion. Let's hope the police don't take offense."

———

Kolya was already awake when Oxana opened her eyes. He was acting fid-gety, and when she asked what was wrong, he confessed his dire need for a toilet. Confessing a similar need, Oxana gathered up their belongings and they crossed the street toward a coffee shop where, despite the early hour, they could see the owner sweeping the street in front.

"The café's closed," the man said.

"I'm sorry, sir, but my son is in need of a toilet."

"We don't serve beggars."

"Please, sir, we're not beggars. We are simply in need of toilets."

"You spent the night in the park. You're filthy dirty and you smell. That makes you beggars. Now be off."

"Mama, I can't hold it. I need to go now," Kolya pleaded, nearly crying.

Oxana pulled a fifty-ruble bill out of her purse. "I should think this is enough to buy both a cup of coffee and a trip to the toilet. And I expect my change."

The man stared at the bill. "Yes, of course. My—a fifty—you don't see bills like this very often these days. Toilet's at the back, help yourself, and I'll get the coffee brewing right away."

———

As Oxana ambled down the impressive seaside promenade with Kolya at her side, the previous evening's twilight-lit romantic vistas gave way to the grim realities of daylight. Long queues had formed in front of nearly every shop.

"Why are they holding on to each other's belts?" Kolya asked Oxana.

"It's to keep from falling down in case one of us faints," one of the men in line answered, overhearing Kolya's question. Oxana apologized, but the man replied, "No harm in asking questions. Times are tough. The sooner he understands how things work, the better."

They paused on a sidewalk bench to eat the last of yesterday's meat and bread, and a young girl, maybe sixteen or seventeen, carrying a baby, approached with her hand out. Her emaciated body was literally skin and bones and her clothes were little more than filthy, tattered rags. The baby was wrapped in a dirty blanket and was so silent and unmoving, Oxana wasn't certain if it was alive. Oxana handed the girl a piece of bread and she chewed half of it, spat it into her palm, and fed it to the baby. Taking nothing for herself, she tucked the other half into the baby's blanket and walked over to a queue of customers and began begging.

Oxana listened as one of the men in line berated the girl for not having a job. Oxana gasped when the man slapped the girl's face. She maintained her grip on the baby, but the bread Oxana had just given her fell to the pavement. Oxana stood, not certain if she should intervene, watching the girl bend over to retrieve the bread scrap. The man kicked her and she fell forward. Oxana ran toward the girl as several people in the queue also rushed over to her. "She's dead," one woman said. Oxana called to a policeman standing a short distance down the street. He slowly came toward them. Oxana started to explain to the officer what had happened, but he ignored her, grabbed the baby, and walked away.

"What about the girl?" Oxana called to him.

"Leave her," the officer replied, without turning around. "They'll pick her up tonight when they bring the trucks in."

Oxana returned to the bench where Kolya was still sitting. She stuffed the last of the meat and bread in her bag and noticed he was crying. She touched his hand gently, but he turned away and they proceeded down the boulevard in silence.

Staking out a spot on the sidewalk where there appeared to be the largest concentration of shoppers, Oxana laid out four dresses her mother had sewn, calling out every few moments, "All for sale—good quality, cheap prices." A few women paused to look, and one woman, after closely examining the fabric and the needlework, bought two, but only after bargaining Oxana down to a ridiculously low price.

By late afternoon the pedestrian traffic was thinning and Oxana was folding the remaining two dresses to put them back in her bag when she saw a woman about her age coming down the street. *Who is that? I think I know her.*

The woman came nearer and Oxana could not help but stare. She was, of course, now much older and her hair was shorter, but her face was the same as Oxana remembered. "Kolya, I think that's Xenia," Oxana said.

"Who's Xenia?"

"She was Vera's maid and we were friends."

"Xenia, is that you?" Oxana called to the woman.

"Oxana?" the woman said, stopping to stare back.

"Yes, it's me." They hugged and exchanged the traditional kisses.

"How great to see you. I can hardly believe it's you, but where is Vera?" Oxana asked. "We went by her house earlier and it appeared to be abandoned."

"It's not entirely abandoned," Xenia said. "I still live there, but Vera was arrested and taken away."

"Arrested?" Oxana cried. "Oh, God. What happened?"

Xenia explained that Bolshevik agents had stormed all the mansions around Vera's, and all the wealthy people, including Vera, were arrested—enemies of the people, the officers said—and Xenia had no idea where they had been taken. She said the soldiers moved into the house and all the servants, except her, fled. The soldiers eventually left, and she was now there all alone and wasn't sure what would happen next.

Oxana stood listening with her mouth open, hardly able to believe it.

"And how about this handsome young man standing here beside you?" Xenia said.

"Forgive me. I was so excited to see you I forgot my manners. Xenia," Oxana held out her hand toward Kolya, "this is my son, Kolya."

"Pleased to meet you," Kolya said.

"Likewise," Xenia responded. "So where are you staying?"

"We don't actually have a place to stay," Oxana confessed.

"Then you must come and stay with me, at Vera's house. It will be just like old times, and I want to hear all about your life since you left Odesa, and especially how you came to be a mother."

"It's a long story," Oxana said, taking Xenia's arm.

"I like long stories," Xenia said, laughing, "and besides, we have the entire evening." Oxana and Xenia, with Kolya following behind, talked the entire way to Vera's house.

Oxana was shocked when Xenia unlocked the door and led them in. The carpets were muddy, some of the furniture was overturned, and the upholstery was torn. Empty vodka bottles were strewn about, the wallpaper was stained, and the main hallway stank of urine.

"Is it still here?" Oxana asked, heading down the hall toward the music room.

"There it is," Xenia said, pointing to Vera's grand piano. "I covered it and pushed it against the wall before the soldiers came inside. It's about the only thing in the house they didn't either steal or destroy."

Oxana removed the covering and played a few notes. The wood was badly scratched, but the keys, hammers, and strings appeared to be in excellent shape.

"Play it," Xenia said.

"Oh no, I'm far too rusty to do it justice," Oxana answered, "but Kolya plays. Kolya, play something for us."

Kolya sat on the bench, and as soon as his fingers touched the keys,

Oxana's eyes welled with tears as memories of the past came flooding back. Kolya played a scale to warm up, and Oxana remembered how she too had warmed up with a scale during her first meeting with Vera. Kolya's beautiful music pouring out of the magnificent instrument reminded Oxana of how much in awe she had once been, in awe of Vera, of the piano, of the house and the servants, and how she had so easily slipped into Vera's life of luxury and ease, how natural it all had felt at the time, but now seemed so distant and extravagant.

"That was beautiful," Xenia said when Kolya finished. "You are very gifted, like your mother."

"But starting tomorrow, you must practice," Oxana said, "and as soon as you are ready, we will go to the music academy, my old school, and see about getting you a scholarship."

———

Oxana, Kolya, and Xenia sat in Vera's dining room, lit only by candles— the electricity had been cut off months ago, Xenia had explained—eating boiled potatoes and cabbage from Xenia's small garden, served on the few remaining pieces of Vera's china that had not been either stolen or broken. Oxana smiled as she listened to Kolya talking and laughing with Xenia.

The room still exuded a faint, faded air of the grandeur she remembered so well, and gazing at the empty chair at the head of the table, Vera's chair, Oxana could almost see Vera sitting there overseeing the dinner, nodding to the servants, ensuring every action was executed with precision, grace, and elegance.

Xenia had taken Oxana's old room, so she offered Oxana and Kolya two adjoining guest bedrooms. The beds were bare mattresses, but Xenia pulled old sheets out of a cupboard, explaining the soldiers had taken all the satin linens with them.

The next day, as promised, Oxana took Kolya to the Odesa National Music Academy, her old school, hoping to enroll him as soon as possible. While waiting in the front office for the receptionist to appear, Oxana's eyes lit on a poster tacked to the wall. Heinrich Neuhaus would be performing a concert at the music academy. The moment of déjà vu made her gasp.

Kolya must play for him, Oxana thought, staring at the poster. *This is his golden opportunity, just as it was for me . . . except I failed my golden moment. But Kolya will succeed. I know he will.*

"Kolya," Oxana said, turning to him seated in an armchair. "You must study with Heinrich Neuhaus."

"Was he your teacher here?" Kolya asked.

"Oh, no, no. Heinrich Neuhaus teaches in Moscow."

"Then how can I study with him? Are we going to Moscow?"

"I hope so. I certainly hope so."

The receptionist appeared and confirmed that Neuhaus was indeed coming to play a concert. Oxana hurried Kolya out of the room without even asking about enrolling him.

The next days passed in a flurry of practicing and lessons. Oxana chose the pieces Kolya would play for Neuhaus and coached him every morning. He spent his afternoons practicing, and then, after Xenia's dinner of boiled cabbage and potatoes, he performed the pieces for Oxana and Xenia. Oxana insisted he treat these evening performances like his actual audition, even making him wear an old butler's tuxedo Xenia had found for him in a closet.

Kolya dropped into bed each night exhausted, while Oxana and Xenia talked and laughed by candlelight for long hours, reminiscing.

On the night of Neuhaus's concert, Oxana was a nervous wreck throughout the program. Despite the nearly sold-out hall and Neuhaus's magnificent playing, she could not concentrate on his performance. She was focused on her desire to get him to listen to Kolya, hoping and praying everything would work out.

Oxana convinced the ushers to allow her and Kolya backstage afterward, claiming they wanted autographs. Oxana introduced herself to Neuhaus and shook his hand. He was exactly as she remembered him—short, with a small moustache. He smiled and said hello, giving no indication he remembered her. She was not surprised. Why would he remember her? Even her name had changed. She was now Oxana Rostova. The Oxana Stepaniaka who had once played for Heinrich Neuhaus no longer existed.

"And this is my son, Kolya," Oxana said. Neuhaus shook Kolya's hand, and Oxana blurted out, "Maestro, he would like to play for you."

"Many wish to play for me. I'm sorry, but I haven't time for them all."

"Please, Maestro. Please listen to him."

"Who is his teacher?"

"I am, Maestro."

"Not a good sign when the mother is also the teacher."

"Please, Maestro—listen for five minutes. It's all I ask."

"Before I agree to hear your son, you must answer me one question, and you must speak as his teacher, not as his mother. Is he truly talented?"

"Yes, Maestro, he is very talented."

"Then bring him to the academy tomorrow at ten and we will see if what you say is true."

———

Oxana, Xenia, and Kolya—who was dressed in the ill-fitting butler's uniform—arrived well ahead of time and nervously waited. At precisely ten a.m., Heinrich Neuhaus entered the room, greeted them, and asked Kolya to begin.

Kolya played a prelude and fugue by Bach, just as Oxana had during her audition so many years earlier, and when he finished, Neuhaus said nothing, only nodding for him to continue. Kolya launched into one of his favorites, Beethoven's *Appassionata* Sonata and again, at the conclusion, Neuhaus said nothing, only nodding slightly.

He doesn't like it, Oxana thought, twitching in her seat and wringing her hands. *He's only trying to be polite.* Kolya played two Chopin selections and finished with Liszt's Second Hungarian Rhapsody. Neuhaus remained silent with his eyes closed while the reverberations from the roar of the crashing octaves faded away. Oxana could hardly remain seated. *He didn't like it. He doesn't know what to say. He was right. I'm an overbearing mother.*

Neuhaus opened his eyes and turned to Oxana. "Does the boy play the Chopin Fantasy?"

"Yes," Oxana managed to utter.

"Then please play it for me," Neuhaus said to Kolya. Oxana was perplexed. Why, after already hearing so much music, would he request one

more piece? Neuhaus sat in silence while Kolya played, giving no indication of his opinion of the performance.

Kolya brought the piece to a dazzling conclusion, and the old master rose slowly from his chair, took hold of Kolya's hands, and turned to
Oxana, "This boy is a pianist by the grace of God. He plays with a maturity
beyond his years." Looking into Kolya's eyes, he continued, "You are des-
tined to be one of the finest pianists in Russia, if not in the entire world."
Oxana was too nervous to sit any longer and was not even certain she
had heard Neuhaus correctly. "I would love for him to be in my class in
Moscow." Neuhaus paused. "But I cannot accept him."

"Cannot?" Oxana gasped. "Please. You must take him."

"Oxana Rostova, our political situation is very difficult. I've been told
that no one from Ukraine is to be invited to Moscow. If I disobey, I will
lose my job and my career. I cannot take the risk."

"But . . ." Oxana's voice trailed off. She could think of nothing more to say.

"I'm sorry," Neuhaus responded.

"Kolya, come now," Oxana said, gathering their things and trying to
control herself. "We must be going. The great master is very busy, and we
must not waste his time—"

"But politics is not without loopholes," Neuhaus interrupted. "I was
not forbidden from inviting Ukrainians to Leningrad, only Moscow. My
esteemed colleague Vladimir Sofronitsky would, I'm certain, be very happy
to take your boy into his class at the Leningrad Conservatory. You can
travel immediately?"

"Yes, yes, we can travel tomorrow. The sooner the better. Spasiba, spasiba, Maestro. Yes, Leningrad, a lovely city. Spasiba, Maestro."

"Then I will wire him today, and he will be expecting you."

"But Mama, how will we get permission to travel?" Kolya asked.

"Don't worry about that. I'll think of something," Oxana whispered.

They stepped out of the room, but Neuhaus called Oxana back in.
"Oxana Rostova, you think I don't remember you, but I do. You once
played for me, although your name then was not Rostova."

For a moment, everything stopped, and Oxana felt as if she were frozen
in place, unable to move or even think. How could this great musician
remember a mere student he had heard only once, years ago? It seemed

impossible. Oxana nodded, not daring to speak, fearing the geyser of emotion pulsing through her body might erupt at any moment.

Neuhaus continued. "Do you know why I requested that your son play the Chopin Fantasy? It's because even after all these years, I remember every note of how you played it. I have never since heard an interpretation to equal yours, and I wanted to see if he has what you had. Your son plays it exactly as I remember you playing it. I'm sorry I could not invite you to Moscow. I wanted to. Your talent was tremendous and you would have been my finest student. But then, as now, I was not allowed to bring a Ukrainian into Moscow. But now we can give your boy the education he deserves, and that you were denied."

Oxana tried to shake his hand but was trembling too hard. Heinrich Neuhaus patted her on the back and led her out of the room, standing in the doorway while she made her way down the hall with Xenia and Kolya. Before they turned the corner, Neuhaus called out, "This time, we will do things right."

━━━━━

Oxana was explaining to the ticket agent that because she and her son had an invitation to Leningrad, she was certain they needed no further permission. "Passports are the law, ma'am. No exceptions," the agent repeated, while the complaints from the people in line behind grew louder. A police officer emerged from the crowd.

"Officer, allow me to introduce myself. My name is Oxana Rostova," Oxana said, holding out her hand. When the officer reached to shake, she discreetly placed a wad of rubles in his palm. She knew the risk she took, and her heart was pounding in her chest. The officer appeared flustered, but much to Oxana's relief, stuffed the rubles into his pocket.

"Sell the lady the tickets," he said to the agent, and stepped back into the crowd.

With tickets in hand, Oxana and Kolya hurried to the track and quickly boarded the train. Despite the sunshine, the interior was dark, and they stood a moment to allow their eyes to adjust. "Why are the windows painted black?" Kolya asked as they made their way to their seats.

"Who knows? Maybe they don't want anyone to see what is outside the window."

As the train left the station and picked up speed, Oxana reached over and held Kolya's hands. "You know I was only a few years older than you when I left Peterstal for Odesa. It was a great opportunity for me, and now you have a similar opportunity. This is not to be taken lightly. You must work hard. Hard work is the only path to success. Never forget this, Kolya." *And now I sound just like Mama*, Oxana thought, recalling the lecture her mother had given her and the powerful sense of responsibility it had instilled in her. She wanted to impart to Kolya a similar sense of responsibility. Becoming a pianist was no easy task. Only the very strongest succeed.

They rode in silence, half dozing, until the train began slowing. It came to a stop, and a group of soldiers entered the car, demanding to see passports. Oxana, trying to steady her nervous hands, handed the soldier their tickets.

"I need to see your passports. No one travels without passports."

"I'm sure they're here somewhere, Officer," Oxana said as she fumbled through her bag while Kolya stared at him. "They must've been stolen."

"They weren't stolen. Don't try to pull that trick on me. Get off the train," the soldier shouted, and the officers behind him raised their rifles.

Oxana and Kolya grabbed their things and stepped out the door and into the sunshine, stunned to discover they were standing on the platform in Peterstal.

Others were being forced out of other train cars as well, and the officer ordered everyone to stand in a line.

"Bring the criminals over here!" someone shouted. Oxana recognized the voice.

"Oxana Nikolaevna, what a surprise to see you," Andrei Bilyik said, coming around the side of the train. "And this must be your talented son I've heard so much about."

"Why were we ordered off the train? We have tickets . . . we're invited to Leningrad. I demand we be allowed to travel."

"Always demanding," Bilyik said. "Mother Russia makes generous offers which you refuse and then you make your demands. Why are you so ungrateful?"

"Please allow us to reboard the train and continue our journey."

"You will not be continuing your journey because you are both criminals. You have no passports, which means you do not have permission to travel. You boarded the train illegally."

"I beg you to allow—" Oxana began.

"Proceed according to orders," Bilyik shouted to the officers behind him. "I have no more time for this woman's nonsense." Bilyik went inside the depot as the train pulled away from the station. A soldier ordered the men to one side of the platform and women to the other side. Kolya stood frozen, and the soldier jabbed him in the back with his rifle, shouting, "Men over there! Now! Move!"

"Mama?"

"Stay beside me and keep calm."

Another train consisting of only cattle cars pulled into the station, and one of the soldiers unlocked the doors. Men and boys leaned out, panting for fresh air. "We're thirsty and hungry," several called out, and the soldiers pointed their rifles at them.

"Men onto the train," an officer shouted.

"Mama—" Kolya whispered.

"Officer, he is only a child. He needs to stay with me."

"Men on the train," the officer shouted louder and waved his rifle at Oxana.

"But officer—"

The soldier pushed his rifle barrel into Oxana's face. "Are you deaf, lady? I said men on the train."

"Do as the officer says," Oxana said, putting her arm around Kolya's shoulders. "You're a young man already. Have courage and be strong, and no matter what happens, as soon as you arrive in Leningrad, you must go to Professor Sofronitsky. When I arrive I will do the same, and that is where we will meet up."

"But Mama—"

"No tears."

Oxana watched Kolya climb into the car along with the others, keeping his eyes on her. She waved and mouthed the words "be brave" just before a soldier slammed the doors shut and locked them.

"Women, turn around," an officer shouted as the train slowly pulled away from the platform. Oxana obeyed.

Shots rang out.

The women on either side of Oxana fell, face forward. Only a second later, she felt the bullet strike her in the lower back, and there was an explosion of light as the pain seared through her.

Chapter 32

As soon as he was inside the train car, Kolya pushed himself against the outer wall so he could see through the slats. "Mama!" he screamed, hearing the shots and seeing his mother crumple to the ground, just before the train rounded a bend. "Mama!"

He slumped to the floor and looked around. Men and boys were crowded against each other on rows of plank seats along both sides of the railcar while many more were either standing or sitting on the floor. The stench was nearly overpowering, and Kolya pinched his nose and breathed through his mouth. Sitting with his head between his legs, whimpering and staring at the dirty floor, he felt a pat on his shoulder. "I'm Vova," a boy a few years older said, crouching down beside him. "My real name's Vladimir, but I hate it, so everyone calls me Vova. I heard the gunshots and your scream."

Kolya stared at the boy, saying nothing.

"I'm sorry about your mama," Vova continued, sitting beside Kolya. "What's your name?"

"I'm Kolya."

"Hello, Kolya." Vova extended his arm, and the two boys shook hands. "Nice to meet you. That's my papa, over there." Vova pointed to a middle-aged man seated on the floor with his back against the wall. His head was tilted back and leaning to one side. His eyes were closed, but his mouth was open, and Kolya assumed he was also breathing through his mouth to avoid the smells.

"He was a teacher, but the Bolsheviks said he wasn't a good Communist—that he was subversive and needed to be reeducated. When they came to get him, Papa demanded I come along because there wasn't anywhere else for me to go."

Vova pulled a small wad of bread from his pants pocket. "Are you hungry? You can have this. It's for my papa, but he's sick and can't eat." Kolya shook his head, but Vova insisted. "You should eat it. They won't give us any more until tomorrow."

They rode in silence, Kolya watching the countryside go by, at least the little he saw through the slats, while Vova stared across at his father. Several hours had passed when Kolya nudged Vova, who had fallen asleep. "I need a toilet," he whispered.

Vova pointed to one of the buckets on the floor inside the door. "It's the one on the right," he whispered. "The other one is our drinking water."

Kolya stood in front of the bucket and opened his pants. "What the hell ya doing?" a man yelled. "Can't you see it's full? Piss over there." Kolya followed the man's pointing finger, shuffling deeper into the car. The floor was wet and soiled with feces, and the smell was horrible. Turning to face what he thought was the wall, Kolya suddenly realized it was bodies piled on top of each other, nearly to the roof. He began to retch and quickly pushed his way back through the crowded car.

After several more hours, the men began to settle for the night. "You can sleep beside me," Vova said. "There's not enough room on the benches, so we sleep on the floor. It's not so bad if you mound up the straw to make a pillow."

Kolya was awakened by the screeching brakes as the train came to a halt. A gust of fresh air blew into the car when the doors opened, and the sunshine allowed Kolya to fully see how extremely crowded the car was with men and boys shoulder to shoulder. One soldier climbed in, grabbed the latrine bucket, and dumped it out the open door while others stood on the station platform with rifles aimed to prevent anyone from escaping. Another soldier entered to hand out slices of bread from a breadbasket he held under his arm. A man lunged toward the basket, and one of the guards jumped into the railcar and hit him with the butt end of this rifle, cutting a gash across his face. "Take that, you pig!" the guard shouted. The man fell, moaning, his palms pressed against the wound as blood streamed through his fingers.

The breadbasket was empty before the soldier got to all the men. "Our bellies are empty," some complained. "We need bread."

The guard pointed his rifle. "Shut up or I'll fill your belly with lead and you'll never need bread again."

Several more soldiers climbed into the car and began tossing out the bodies Kolya had seen piled against the wall. Vova's father was still sitting in the same position as yesterday, and the soldiers picked him up and threw the corpse out the open door. "Bye, Papa," Vova whispered, wiping his eyes.

"I'm sorry," Kolya said and put his arm around him.

The soldiers jumped onto the platform and slammed the doors shut. Someone shouted and the train began to move. Kolya and Vova sat beside each other the entire day. There was nothing to do, and Kolya had no sense of the passing of time.

"Why can't you walk right?" Vova asked as they peered through the slats, trying to inhale fresh air.

"I don't know. My mother never told me, but I heard people talking. They said my father hit me when I was a baby because he wasn't my real father. I don't know who my real father is, and now I don't have a mother either." Kolya started to cry.

"I'm sorry," Vova said. "My mama's dead too." Kolya nodded and wiped his cheeks with his coat sleeve. Vova nudged him with his elbow. "I've got something for you, to cheer you up."

"What?"

"Just a minute. I have to go get it." Vova pushed his way into the crowd of standing men, returned a moment later, and handed Kolya a piece of bread. "Here, for you, my little friend. Compliments of Comrade Stalin, but eat fast," he whispered.

"My bread's been stolen," one of the men suddenly shouted. "Someone took my bread."

Vova smiled and winked at Kolya. *Eat fast*, he mouthed.

As the train rumbled on, Kolya tried to play one of his pieces in his mind, to break the boredom. At first, he had a hard time concentrating, but after a few tries, he closed his eyes and, imagining he was sitting at a keyboard, played an entire section.

"Are you a piano player?" Vova asked. "You're moving your fingers like you're playing a piano."

"My mother taught me. I'm supposed to go to the Leningrad Conservatory. That's where we were headed when they forced us off the train."

"My mama was a piano player," Vova said. "She tried to teach me, but I didn't really take to it. My papa said I should be a writer. He said I could be the next Dostoevsky. Do you know Chopin?"

"Everyone knows Chopin."

"My mama played Chopin. It was beautiful." Vova rubbed his hand across Kolya's head, tousling his hair. "You remind me of Chopin. I think that's what I'll call you. Chopin, my new friend."

Kolya and Vova passed the hours sitting beside each other, Kolya rehearsing his piano music in his mind while Vova peered through the slats in the wall. They could not see the position of the sun and so they waited until eventually it grew dark and knew that another day had passed.

"He's counting the days," Vova said, pointing to an old man across from them as a glimmer of early morning sunshine began to stream through the railcar slats. Kolya and Vova watched the man carve a slash, his seventh, into the wall of the car.

No one knew where they were headed or how long they would be confined, but it was apparent they were heading north. A cold wind was now blowing through the slats. "It'll be warmer if we lie against each other and cover ourselves with both our jackets," Vova said one night. The next night, two older men offered to huddle with them. All through the train car, men were huddled two and three together for warmth, with only their sweaters and jackets as covers.

———

"Hey, Chopin," Vova whispered. "Look outside. It's snowing."

"We're crossing the Urals," one man mumbled. "They're taking us into Siberia."

The train came to a stop and the doors opened. Kolya and Vova leaned out, peering, but there was nothing—no village, no train station, not even a platform, only the snow-covered, wide-open landscape. Several trucks filled with soldiers pulled up alongside the train. "Out of the train," one of the officers shouted, and the men began tumbling to the ground. Some, too weak to stand, fell and had to be helped up.

"What's happening?" Kolya asked as Vova held his hand so he could jump to the ground without injuring himself. "Are they going to shoot us?"

Before Vova could answer, the officer yelled, "March" and pointed his gun toward the east. The men instinctively formed a line and began moving—but where, they had no idea. The temperature was well below freezing, and many were wearing only their shirts and pants. Kolya leaned on Vova for support, and when they rounded a bend he saw a large lake. The shoreline was frozen over, but there was open water farther out. "Bath," the commanding officer shouted. "Government orders—everyone—to maintain health."

Some started to protest that the water was too cold, but the officer fired his gun into the air. "Shut up and do as I say. Into the lake! Everyone!"

Kolya, wearing a shirt and pants, the only clothing he had, stood shivering, watching as some of the men hesitantly pulled off their outer layers and stood in their underclothes.

"In! Now!" the officer yelled again.

"Stay beside me," Vova said, shedding his shirt and pants. "I'll make sure nothing happens to you."

Kolya slowly undid his buttons and removed his shirt. His hands were shaking.

"Chopin, you better hurry. There's no point in hesitating. It's not getting any warmer."

Kolya looked away when Vova stepped out of his undershorts and stood facing him completely naked. "I can't take off my pants. I'm embarrassed," Kolya said.

"Don't think about it. Everybody's embarrassed. Let's just do this quick and we can get our clothes back on."

The men and boys continued stripping until everyone was entirely naked and shivering. Some went in slowly, with teeth chattering and arms wrapped around their bodies, while others ran to the water and dove in.

"I can't swim. I'm afraid of the water," Kolya said, hobbling along beside Vova, keeping his hands in front to cover himself.

"I'll hold you up, Chopin. Don't worry. I won't let you drown."

No soap or towels were provided, and after a few dips the men emerged from the freezing water and pulled their clothing back on as quickly as they could. The column was marched back to the train cars and the doors were slammed shut. Kolya and Vova sat shivering in their damp clothing while the train picked up speed.

———

Kolya awoke to Vova nudging him. "Wake up, Chopin. I think we're here."

"Where?" Kolya mumbled.

"Where they want us to be, I guess."

The train had not moved for several hours, and squinting through the slats, Kolya saw a depot. Soldiers were moving about outside, and from what he could hear, they were apparently waiting for another regiment to arrive. Trucks pulled up to the station platform and more soldiers climbed out. "Welcome home," one of the soldiers called out, opening the doors of their railcar, and the others laughed. The sign along the platform read "Vologda."

The snow was nearly knee high, and the soldiers jeered as the coatless, hatless, some even bootless men jumped from the railcar into the snow. "You'll be warm soon enough, once you get to work."

Kolya could not lift his legs high enough to get through the snowdrifts. "Lean against me, Chopin," Vova said, putting his arm around Kolya's waist. "I'll hold you up."

The column advanced slowly, and at first it appeared they were heading into the city. "Maybe they're taking us to a hotel," Kolya said.

Vova laughed. "I think you're dreaming, Chopin. You need to wake up."

The column of men came to an intersection in the road and the soldiers directed them toward the river, away from the city. "So much for your nice, warm hotel, Chopin," Vova said and laughed again.

They had been trudging through the snow for nearly an hour when the thick stone walls and towering steeples of a monastery came into view with hundreds of people swarming about. Kolya had been shivering the entire time, and Vova pulled him in tight and wrapped his jacket around him. "To the left. To the left," a guard shouted when the men reached the entry gate.

"Stay with me," Vova whispered as they made their way across the monastery courtyard, where another guard pointed them toward the larger of the church buildings. The door was standing open despite the cold air, and Kolya could see rows of bunk beds four high, up and down the entire nave, crammed so close there was hardly room to walk. He and Vova entered. The room was dark and nearly as cold inside as outside.

The men were ordered to find a bed, and Kolya followed Vova down a side aisle. The bunks were filled with men, women, and children, all lying on top of each other for warmth. Vova pointed at an empty bed at the far end, near the church altar.

"Bottom one's taken," an old man barked. "Take the top ones."

"But he can't climb," Vova said, pointing at Kolya's legs.

"I said, bottom one's taken. Take the top."

"It's fine," Kolya said. "I can climb up."

"What's this place called?" Vova asked the old man.

"Prilutsky Monastery, but don't get too comfortable. It's a transfer point. Only us old people and the young ones are allowed to stay. Tomorrow you'll be sent into the forest to cut down trees. They call it a special settlement, and as far as I know, no one has ever come back."

Kolya and Vova climbed into the top two bunks. There was no bedding, only a layer of straw. "How do you like your hotel bed, Chopin? Is it all warm and cozy?" Vova laughed.

"There's buckets of drinking water over there, if you're thirsty," the old man called up to them, pointing, "but I wouldn't drink it. They don't boil it. Best you find some clean snow and suck on that." Kolya rolled on his side, intrigued by the images on the ceiling and walls. The plaster was cracked and crumbling, but the frescoes were still surprisingly vivid and colorful.

"Food!" a guard yelled. Kolya and Vova followed as everyone climbed out of their bunks and crossed the courtyard. The dining hall was a large room with a fire in the open stove, and people moved slowly through the food line, trying to soak up as much of the heat as possible. Each person was handed a piece of bread and a bowl of watery soup, and they made their way back across the courtyard to their bunks to eat in silence.

Kolya did not sleep that night. There was constant noise—children crying and mothers trying to soothe them, snoring, many were ill and lay moaning, and sounds of vomiting and coughing echoed across the church nave. Toward daybreak, Kolya's stomach was hurting and he went out to the latrine area, which was nothing more than a fenced-off portion of the cemetery behind the church building. He had picked up a couple small tree branches to use as walking sticks and was balancing on them, pulling up his pants, when he spotted a group of boys running toward him.

"Looky there," one of the boys shouted. "A new little kulak, fresh off the train." One of the older boys rammed his fist against Kolya's chest and knocked him to the ground. "You're wearing some awful nice clothes, boy. I sure would like to dress like you rich kulaks. I think I'd like your shirt and pants for myself. Take them off."

Kolya, struggling to his feet, did not respond and did not make eye contact with any of them. "I said take them off! Now! And your boots too." Kolya leaned over to untie his boot laces, and the boy grabbed at his shirt and ripped it off. Kolya slipped off his boots and pants and handed them over, squeezing his arms against his chest, trying to keep warm.

"Maybe I'd like your underwear, too. Take them off." Kolya hesitated, and the boy punched at him with his fist. Flinching in time to avoid being hit, he pulled his T-shirt over his head and shoved his undershorts to his ankles.

"Pick them up and hand them to me," the boy said, "and hurry up."

Kolya did as he was told and now stood before them naked and shivering.

"Look at his little pecker," the boy called to his friends. "How you gonna make babies with a tiny thing like that?" The group laughed. The boy held the underwear to his nose. "Hell, these shorts stink of piss. I'll bet you still pee the bed at night, don't you, boy?" Kolya remained silent, staring straight ahead. "Here," the boy said, throwing Kolya's underwear back at him. "I don't want no pissed-in shorts. Hurry up and put them back on. I'm starting to get sick looking at your ugly pecker." Kolya caught the underwear in midair, and when he bent over to step into the shorts, the boy whacked him across the back and Kolya fell. The boy shoved Kolya's clothing and boots into his backpack and the group ran off laughing.

Kolya quickly pulled up his undershorts, grabbed the tree limbs for support, and hurried back inside the church.

"Chopin, where were you?" Vova whispered when Kolya climbed into his bunk. His bare feet were bleeding, and he was shivering too hard to speak. Vova crawled in beside him and wrapped his jacket around Kolya. "Just lie here. I'll be back." It was now daylight outside, but the interior of the church was dark. A few minutes later, Vova climbed back into the bunk and handed Kolya a pair of pants, a shirt, boots, and a sweater. The clothing was dirty and stank and was too large. "Stuff some straw in the boots so they fit better," Vova said, "and roll up the pant legs."

Guards entered and ordered everyone to stand as they began going down the aisles, removing the dead bodies. "This one's stark naked," one of the guards yelled. "Some son-of-a bitch stole his clothes." Kolya looked at Vova, standing beside him, and Vova smiled.

They were marched into the churchyard, where trucks were waiting, and men and boys were being ordered into the truck boxes. A soldier grabbed Kolya when he stepped forward.

"He comes with me," Vova said, keeping hold of Kolya's hand.

"How old?" the soldier asked.

"I'm fourteen," Kolya lied, hoping it was old enough to go with Vova.

"Bad legs," the guard said, pointing his rifle. "He stays."

"No, he comes with me," Vova said.

"You his mother or something? Git your ass in the truck," the soldier yelled. "The kid stays."

Vova grabbed Kolya's hand and shook it. "Take care of yourself, Chopin. I'll see you in Leningrad," and he jumped into the truck box as it pulled out of the courtyard.

Chapter 33

Andrei Bilyik came out of the train depot with Ilya, the town doctor, beside him. "Fill these out," Bilyik said, handing the doctor a wad of blank death certificates. "Put anything down. Make up the names. It doesn't matter who they were. They were all guilty." Ilya stared at the row of women's bodies. In addition to his medical responsibilities, he had been ordered to assume the role of town coroner. Bilyik had demanded paper documentation of deaths, which, he said, would provide an accounting of Russia's efficiency in eliminating criminals.

Bilyik walked away, toward the town square, while Ilya bent over and rolled the first woman onto her back. She was young, maybe even a teenager. Her dress was soaked with blood. He checked for a pulse and quickly filled out a death certificate. He moved on to the next body and repeated the process, while the two soldiers beside him hoisted the first one into the back of the waiting truck.

He knelt beside the third body. He rolled her onto her back and recognized Oxana. She moaned. He quickly felt for a pulse—it was faint—and he heard a gun cock behind him. "What are you doing?" he said, turning to see a soldier pointing his rifle at her.

"I've got to shoot her. Those are my orders," the soldier said.

"Stop! Put your rifle down."

"But she isn't dead."

The doctor stepped between the prone woman and the soldier. "Why waste a bullet? She'll be dead soon enough. Besides, Andrei Bilyik promised me a cadaver, and this fresh one will be ideal."

"I don't know nothing about—what did you call it? A cadver?"

"Cadaver—a body I can dissect for science—medical knowledge."

"I don't know anything about no dissecting. Step aside."

"Do you think you give the orders here?" the doctor shouted at the soldier. "Andrei Bilyik communicated with me. I should think that is enough authority for you to follow." The soldier lowered his gun. The doctor pulled bandaging from his case and, feeling through her dress, wrapped her injured abdomen. "Careful," he said as soldiers hoisted her into the truck. "Lay her apart from the rest. I want her alive as long as possible."

Ilya quickly wrote death certificates for the rest of the bodies and climbed into the back of the truck. "Drop her at my office in the square before you haul the others away," he shouted as the driver shifted into gear and gunned the engine. While they drove the short distance, the doctor hurriedly opened her dress at the waist. Her chest had a large gash, and she had lost a great deal of blood.

"Take her into the back room and lay her on the table," the doctor said as soon as the truck came to a stop.

"She still isn't dead," the soldier grumbled as they laid her on the table. "Orders were to shoot them dead."

"Orders were to deliver one body to me for scientific purposes," Ilya said. "Now leave." He quickly closed the door and lit a kerosene lamp. He undid the temporary bandage. The wound was still bleeding, and he unlocked his medicine cabinet and pulled out supplies—cotton bandages, a bottle of rubbing alcohol, a syringe, pain medicine.

Oxana moaned and opened her eyes. "Oxana, it's me, Ilya. Don't try to talk. You are safe, for the moment at least. I'm going to give you a shot to ease your pain, but it will also put you to sleep. I'll see to your wounds as best I can. As soon as it's dark, I'll carry you to my truck and drive you to my house. I live at the commune, but I can put you in a shed and lock the door. As soon as you are stable enough to travel, I'll get you to a hospital in Odesa. You will live, Oxana—if I can keep you a secret."

"Ilya," Oxana mouthed.

"Shh," he said, putting his finger to his lips. "You must sleep until I can get you to safety."

"My son?"

"Shh. Not a sound. If you are discovered, Andrei Bilyik will have both of us shot." He filled the syringe and injected the painkiller while Oxana lay silent, eyes wide open.

Chapter 34

Kolya joined the other children assembled in the courtyard. "We have orders to send you to school to receive a proper Soviet education," a guard intoned in a monotone voice, and he ordered the children to follow him, single file, down the road.

The school was a decrepit one-room building. Kolya filed in with the other children and took a seat on one of the wooden benches. There was a curtain hanging along the back wall, which Kolya could see behind. It appeared to be the teacher's living space. Kolya sat quietly staring while the teacher, a grim-faced middle-aged woman, intoned her introductory lecture. "You are no longer kulaks. Kulaks are enemies of the people. They have exploited the toiling masses for generations, but no longer. You are here to learn the skill of collective labor and to acquire the instinct of socialism. Henceforth, you will all be equal members of Soviet society."

She sat at an old upright piano pushed up against one wall and began the national anthem. "Sing!" she shouted. "You must sing." Kolya winced every time she played a wrong note, and when she finished she asked him, "Do you think you can do better, or are you trying to draw attention to yourself?"

"I can play. My mother taught me."

"I will allow you to play for one minute," the teacher said, "to see if you are telling the truth, but if it is nothing but noise, you must stop."

Kolya sat on the bench. The ivory was missing from many of the keys.

He played a one-octave scale to try it out and heard several children giggle. One boy shouted, "He's pretending. He don't know nothing about it."

Kolya played the loud opening of a Liszt rhapsody. His fingers were stiff and he played a few wrong notes. *Mama would not be happy.* When he glanced over his shoulder to gauge the teacher's expression, he saw that the other children sat at attention, some with their mouths hanging open. The teacher hurried out of the room, and Kolya continued to play. By the time he finished, she had returned with one of the guards. The students clapped while the guard stood whispering with the teacher.

"Comrade," the teacher said, giving Kolya a stern look, "it is arranged that you may stay after school for one hour each day to practice."

"If we're all equal members of Soviet society, then why's he get special treatment?" one of the boys yelled across the room.

"Shut up, you stupid lout," the teacher said. "Ten of you would not add up to one of him."

———

Kolya fell into a routine of going to school with the rest of the children in the monastery encampment, spending the day learning very little, practicing one hour after the other children left, and walking back to the monastery alone to face a meal of watery soup and tough rye bread.

Eventually spring was in the air, and the snow had melted enough so that the road from the monastery was one long mud puddle. Returning after his practicing one afternoon, he heard a voice: "Chopin. Over here."

"Vova!" Kolya gasped.

"Quiet, Chopin. I'm here." Vova pulled aside the branches of a bush along the side of the road.

"They let you come back!" Kolya put his arms around Vova and hugged him.

"They didn't exactly *let* me. I escaped."

"What's wrong with your face?" Kolya asked, staring at Vova's black eyes and the gashes on his cheeks.

"Don't worry about me, Chopin. They roughed me up a little. It's nothing. Look, Chopin, we gotta get out of here. Everyone's sick and dying. I have it all figured out. Tomorrow, when you come by on your way back from school, duck into these bushes. Pretend you need to take a piss, just in case anyone's watching. And leave the rest up to me."

"I don't know, Vova. It seems risky. What if we get caught?"

"If they try to catch us, we make a run for it."

"But what if they shoot at us?"

"Then I guess we need to run faster than their bullets." Vova laughed. "Don't worry, Chopin. We'll be fine. We have to get out of this place and get you to Leningrad." Vova pulled back the branches so Kolya could ease out of the bushes and back onto the road. "See you tomorrow," Vova said, "and by the way, I heard you practicing. You're pretty good. I was impressed."

The next day Kolya pulled back the branches and crawled in beside Vova.

"What are these?" Kolya asked when Vova handed him two passports.

"What do they look like? They're passports for our train ride to Leningrad."

"How did you get these?"

"It took a while, but I found two boys our age, and let's just say they didn't look like they'd be needing these passports as much as we do."

"But how do we get to a train?"

"You sure are full of questions, Chopin. There's an old guy who comes along every day with a cart full of onions pulled by a horse. We hide under the onions until the old man stops, and then we borrow his horse."

"You mean we steal his horse?"

"Chopin, you need to think differently. We're going to do the guy a favor. The horse is old and doesn't have a lot of years left in her. We borrow her and the old guy can get himself a new horse. In the end, he'd probably thank us. Here's our story," Vova continued. "We're brothers. Our parents are both dead, and we're on our way to live with our grandmother in Leningrad. Let's see what your new name is."

Kolya opened the passport. "It says Vadim Repinoff."

"Nice to meet you, Vadim Repinoff." Vova reached to shake Kolya's hand. "I'm your older brother, Boris Repinoff."

Before long they heard the old man whistling, and as soon as the huge, heavy cart creaked by they dashed up to it, jumped in, and quickly dug in under the onions.

About an hour later, the cart stopped. Kolya watched the old man totter over to a tree. He sat under it, wiped his brow, took a few swigs from a vodka bottle he pulled from his pants, and soon was asleep. "Keep quiet and follow me," Vova whispered, and they slid out from under the onions. Vova crept up to the horse and untied it from the wagon. He led it a few steps away and hopped on. "Hang on," Vova said, pulling Kolya up behind him and kicking the horse's flanks. Kolya looked behind as they galloped away. The old man was still asleep beside the tree.

They rode across the open expanse, stopping only for a rest break for the horse, until they spotted a town. They rode into a small grove of trees and dismounted.

"We'll leave the horse here and walk in," Vova said. "It'll raise less suspicion, and someone will come along and be happy to find a horse for the taking. It'll be our gift."

Kolya found two tree limbs to use as walking sticks while Vova tied the horse's reins to a tree branch and they headed to the train platform at the edge of the town. The schedule was posted on an outside wall and indicated there would be a westbound train in about an hour.

"Give me your passport," Vova said, "and I'll get our tickets."

Vova went inside while Kolya munched on a raw onion from the old man's cart that he had stuffed in his pocket.

Chapter 35

Kolya stepped out of the Leningrad train station and was stunned. Odesa was the only real city he had seen, and this was entirely different—huge, thronging with people, and with magnificent buildings everywhere. He wanted to soak up as much of the city as he could before even thinking of finding a place to stay.

Walking was difficult, especially over cobblestone, and he and Vova went slowly, but seeing the city was worth the physical pain. The Neva River was a deep blue-green, and Kolya paused to stare at the dozens of boats and ships of all sizes. He had always wondered at the paradox of his fascination with water yet also his fear of it. His legs prevented him from swimming and yet he had an intense desire to be on the water.

Kolya had read about the city's many magnificent church buildings, hailed as some of the most beautiful in the world, and he could hardly believe he was actually seeing them: the Kazan Cathedral with its huge colonnaded walkway modeled after the Basilica of St. Peter at the Vatican in Rome; and St. Isaac's Cathedral, a massive neoclassical architectural gem with a gilded dome, which the Soviets had turned into a museum of atheism. But best of all, in Kolya's opinion, was the Church of the Spilled Blood. Kolya and Vova overheard a tour guide telling the legend of how the church had acquired its name because it was built as a memorial over the site where Tsar Alexander II was assassinated. Kolya gazed at the colorful architecture—a throwback to the medieval Russian style, with multiple cupolas and inlaid mosaics. He regretted that he could only dream of how spectacular the inside must be, for the church was permanently closed to the public. The Soviets had turned it into a conveniently located grain and vegetable storage building.

Kolya and Vova admired the bridges along the Moika canal and stopped to see the gigantic Bronze Horseman statue, erected in honor of Tsar Peter the Great. They meandered down the famed Nevsky Prospect, lined with all sorts of the city's most expensive shops, cafés, and theaters. Finally, they wandered into Palace Square, where the view of the Winter Palace reduced Kolya to tears. Too tired to go any farther, he sat on a bench, staring at the massive, ornate, green-and-white home to the tsars of Russia while Vova went in search of a room in a boarding house.

Completely overcome with exhaustion, Kolya was in a deep sleep when Vova prodded him awake and dangled a key in front of him. "Since it doesn't appear there is any availability at the Winter Palace, I found a place for us, unless you prefer to lodge here on this park bench."

Kolya yawned, stretched his arms, stood, and nearly collapsed. His legs were stiff, and he would have fallen if Vova had not grabbed him.

"Whoa, easy there, Chopin. How about we sit here and eat before heading out. I'm starving." Vova pulled two sandwiches out of his pocket and handed one to Kolya.

As soon as they finished eating, they resumed their trek, until eventually, with little daylight left, Vova stopped and pointed across the street to a dilapidated two-story building with about half the windows boarded up.

"Here we are, Chopin."

Kolya and Vova pushed open the front door and were assaulted by both the smell of stale air and the hiss of a mangy cat. An old woman appeared from behind a door and scowled. As Vova helped Kolya climb the staircase, she called to them, "Remember, I said I don't serve food. You gotta get yer own breakfast in the morning."

Vova slipped the key into the lock and opened the door. The room consisted of one chair, pushed up against one bed, which was pushed against one boarded-up window. Kolya rolled onto the bed and without even undressing, fell asleep.

When he woke, Vova was sitting in the chair, holding two more sandwiches. "Chopin, do you realize you've just slept twelve hours?" He handed

Kolya a sandwich and pointed to a suit that was draped across the back of the chair. "While I was waiting for Sleeping Beauty to wake up, I found this. Now you'll look like a pianist." Kolya knew better than to ask where any of it had come from.

After asking for directions, Kolya set out later that morning, dressed in his not-entirely-new suit, while Vova headed out in the opposite direction, with the plan of finding more comfortable accommodations. Kolya went along the Moika canal, turned onto Ulitsa Glinka, and soon was standing in front of the Leningrad Conservatory of Music. The building was stunning, like a palace, with an elegant old-world façade, tall windows, and ornate carvings.

Making his way up the foyer's grand staircase, he entered a receptionist's office and asked to see Professor Sofronitsky. The receptionist took him down a long hallway, opened a door at the far end, and motioned him in.

An elegantly dressed man was seated at a table, below a slightly raised platform where a black grand piano stood with its lid raised, awaiting its next performer. The man turned, and Kolya saw that he was at least a decade younger than Neuhaus.

"I am Professor Vladimir Sofronitsky," the man said, rising from his chair. He was tall and thin, with long hair neatly combed back, revealing his forehead, and Kolya immediately noticed his eyes, wide and piercing, as if he were looking right through you. "And you are?" Professor Sofronitsky asked.

"Kolya Rostov," Kolya stammered, uncomfortably sensing that Sofronitsky was staring him down, as if trying to size him up.

"Kolya Rostov?" Sofronitsky repeated several times while Kolya stood tugging on his suit—it was too tight—and nervously tapping his toes. "My friend Heinrich Neuhaus wired me long ago to expect you, but you never showed up. I had given up hope."

With no further introductions, Sofronitsky pointed to the piano. "Play something for me. Don't worry—I understand you've probably not practiced. I only want to hear how you sound, what shape you are in."

Kolya played a few short pieces, and when he finished, Sofronitsky was smiling. "Ah, wonderful. Of course there is much work to do, but you are exactly as Heinrich said. Please come at two o'clock tomorrow, and we will begin."

Kolya turned to leave. "And," Sofronitsky said, "a certain person has been stopping by asking about you and will be very pleased to see you."

———

When Kolya returned to the conservatory's foyer the next afternoon, a woman dressed in black with a black scarf covering her head was standing with her back to him, peering out the window. She turned when she heard his footsteps.

"Mama!" Kolya exclaimed, and he ran to hug her. "Mama—I thought you had been shot."

"Kolya, I was so worried. I didn't know where you were or if you were even alive."

They hugged, and Oxana kissed him on his head when he buried his face in her dress.

"But you were shot. I saw it," Kolya said.

"Yes, I was shot, but Doctor Ilya saved my life. He nursed me until I was stabilized and then hid me in the trunk of his car and drove me to a hospital in Odesa. He stayed with me, but as soon as I was well enough to travel, I told him I had to get to Leningrad to meet you. He somehow, I have no idea how, arranged for me to ride with an old gentleman who was driving from Odesa to Leningrad. It was a long trip and took many days, but I slept most of the time. Anyway, I can tell you all about it later. Right now, I want to get you home."

"Home?" Kolya asked. "Do we have a home?"

"Yes, we do. Almost immediately upon arriving here, I found work as a maid for a lady. I live in her apartment, and now you can have a room there too. I've already told her all about you. Her name is Tatiana Semenova, and you will like her. She's an opera singer—retired now, of course—and she has a lovely piano that you can practice on."

"Mama, you're a maid?"

"Kolya, don't be snobbish. It's a job that gives me, and now you too, food and a place to live. Now let's get going. We have much to talk about." Oxana put her arm around his waist. "I want to hear everything about how you've been and how you got here, but first, where did you get that suit? It seems about two sizes too small . . ."

Chapter 36

Jakob walked into the town square in Peterstal, as he had nearly a decade earlier, except this time he made no effort to conceal himself. He had been a coward for agreeing to leave with Wilhelm, had been a coward for allowing Elena Vladimirovna to convince him to leave a second time, and had been a coward for staying away so long, but this time he was here to stay.

He had spent his time roaming from one odd job to another in Odesa, Lviv, Kharkiv, and most recently in Kyiv. He earned enough money to provide himself with hot meals and a warm bed each night, and that was enough. He desired nothing more. His few relationships had all ended almost as quickly as they began, with the most recent girl leaving in the middle of the night, shouting that he needed to "find her, whoever she is, because it obviously isn't me!"

Thoughts of Oxana and Peterstal were never far from his mind. He was hearing rumors that the Bolsheviks were starving the rural farmers into submission in order to take ownership of the land and force everyone into collective farming. While no one spoke openly about this—to do so would have meant arrest and imprisonment—everyone was whispering. Jakob was beginning to fear for Oxana and hoped she was safe and healthy.

Wandering around Kyiv one day, Jakob heard piano music coming from the open window of an apartment. He stood to listen. The music was Chopin's Fantasy. He had not heard the piece since leaving Peterstal, and when the playing suddenly stopped, he was tempted to call out to the pianist to keep going.

That night, he was jolted awake in the midst of a dream where he saw the Firebird, exactly as he had as a teen at the old pianist's concert in Peterstal, except this time when the Firebird turned to reveal her face it was the face of Oxana, and she was in tears.

He tried to put the dream out of his mind as nothing more than a silly remnant of childhood fairy tales. No adult actually believed in a Firebird. Nevertheless he felt haunted by it and when he arrived at work that morning, he was carrying a small suitcase containing everything he owned.

Jakob quit his job, and within an hour he was headed toward Peterstal. He did not have an internal passport, so travel by train was impossible, but he walked, hitched rides on farm wagons, and even at one point stole a bicycle and rode a good distance.

At first, Peterstal appeared unchanged. The buildings were as he remembered, but nearly all were vacant, and except for a few limping, emaciated stragglers he did not recognize, the town was deserted.

He made his way to Fedor's farm. He had to see Oxana, no matter what, even if she and Fedor had a dozen children by now.

"Hello, old friend," he called to Fedor, who was in the farmyard, and he was about to call hello to the woman beside him when they both looked his way, and he realized she was not Oxana.

"Jakob Schweitz, is it you?" Fedor dropped his rake and came running toward him. He was much thinner than Jakob remembered, and his face was wrinkled, as if he were already an old man. Except for his curly black hair Jakob would not have even recognized him. "It's great to see you. Where have you been?"

"Away," Jakob replied, "but I'm back now. For good."

"I guess you could say I was away too," Fedor said, "for a while, and not by my choice, but I'm back now too. Let me introduce my wife, Katarina."

"Wife?" Jakob said, staring with astonishment. She appeared younger than Fedor and was also emaciated, but despite her dirty dress and messy hair Jakob could see that she had once been beautiful.

"Hello," she said, somewhat sheepishly.

"Where's Oxana? I heard you and she were married?" Jakob said.

"Have you forgotten your manners, old pal? You could start by repaying Katarina's politeness and saying hello."

"Hello, Katarina." Jakob took off his hat and bowed slightly to her, not sure if Fedor would be pleased or interpret the bow as an insult, but he let the moment pass without comment.

"Married might be a stretch, old pal," Fedor said. "She didn't turn out quite as I expected. Nothing like her sister. You got the better one of those two, I can tell you."

"What do you mean?"

"She played me for a fool, that's what I mean. The whore was already pregnant when we married, and she tried passing the bastard off as mine. When I found out, she had me arrested and sent away. But I got the last word. I came back and ran her off."

"Fedor, you can't talk like that around me," Jakob said, keeping his voice calm. "Oxana is no whore . . . and what do you mean you ran her off?"

"She's gone."

"Where to?"

"I hate to be the one to break the news, but she's dead."

"Dead?" Jakob felt his knees weakening, as if he might collapse, and he leaned against the farmyard gate to steady himself.

"She and that bastard son of hers were trying to escape. She had resisted joining the commune, and I guess the higher-ups got tired of dealing with her."

"Son?" Jakob's stomach was tightening and his hands were twitching. He was struggling to hold back tears and was certain his face was turning red.

"I'm glad they finally got her," Fedor continued. "She and that brat tried to destroy me."

Jakob stood a moment, lips quivering and hands now visibly shaking. He lunged toward Fedor and socked him in the mouth. Fedor fell, and Jakob kicked him in the stomach.

"Stop!" Katarina shouted, and she tried to pull Jakob away.

Fedor struggled to his feet, and Jakob smacked him again alongside his head.

"You always were a damn idiot," Jakob shouted as Fedor rolled in the grass, blood streaming from his nose and mouth.

"And you are a son of a bitch," Fedor spat out the words. "You were probably fucking them both, never could make up your mind. Who knows, maybe her bastard son is yours."

Jakob kicked Fedor in his groin, and he doubled over in pain. "I hope I never see you again, you sorry piece of shit."

Fedor, despite his pain, lunged toward Jakob and kneed him in the groin. "Take that as a little going-away present," he said, "and don't ever come here again."

Jakob, clutching himself, hobbled a short distance but stopped when he noticed something red half buried in a mound of dirt. He went toward it and saw it was fabric and immediately recognized it—Oxana's concert dress. He bent and tugged it free.

"Go ahead and take it!" Fedor shouted. "Maybe it'll help you to think of her while you jack off."

"Asshole!" Jakob called, stuffing the dress inside his shirt and heading down the road.

Dead? Son? He kept repeating the words over and over. Her mother had told him Oxana was going to have a baby when she sent him away, and he had assumed Fedor was the father.

Jakob soon approached the charred remains of what he recognized as the old Lutheran church. A makeshift shack had been put up next to it, and some distance away in the little cemetery, he could see the hunched form of Father Vanska sitting on a bench. "Is it true?" Jakob asked as he approached the priest. "She's dead?"

"Jakob Schweitz?" Father Vanska said. "Is it you?"

"Yes, it's me," Jakob said, sitting down next to the priest. He covered his face with his hands and burst into sobs. "Is it true?"

"My son," Father Vanska said softly, putting his arm around Jakob's shoulders. "I'm afraid it's true. She was shot by the soldiers."

"Fucking bastards," Jakob muttered, still sobbing. "I hope they rot in hell."

"God forgive me for saying it," Father Vanska whispered, "but I hope so too."

"She had a son?"

"Yes, a fine boy. And an excellent piano player, as good as she was."

Jakob leaned sideways, trying to hide his face. "I'm sorry, Father. It's just . . . I can't . . ."

"It's fine, my son," Father Vanska said, rubbing his back. "There is no need to speak. Tears are the water that God uses to wash our souls, not words."

"Is he . . . her son . . . is he . . . mine?"

"Yes, Jakob. The boy's name is Kolya, and you are his father. Oxana told me before she left."

"Oh, God," Jakob moaned. "Oh, God . . . where is he?"

"I don't know, Jakob. He was taken away when they shot Oxana, put on a train; no one knows where."

"I will find him. If it takes the rest of my life, I will find him."

"Jakob, no one knows where he was taken or even if he is still alive. Russia is a big country—he could be anywhere. You may never find him."

"But I must, Father. I must."

"Jakob, stay here, at least for a while. Visit Irina's grave and talk to her. It will calm you and help you heal. Have patience and allow God's will to unfold. You have returned. Maybe one day Kolya, your son, will also return, and if not, you will be together in heaven, along with Irina and Oxana. You must believe this."

"Yes, Father," Jakob said, drying his eyes and standing.

"Come every day," Father Vanska said as Jakob turned to leave. "I can tell you many stories of Oxana and your son. They were both wonderful people. You will be very proud."

Jakob nodded and shook Father Vanska's hand. He rounded the corner, crossed the square, and slowly made his way to the rear of the Orthodox church. It took him a moment to find Irina's grave, since it was completely covered over with grass. Jakob knelt and tried speaking but could only sob. He pulled up several clumps of sod and dug into the soil until he had formed a small hole. He took Oxana's red concert dress out of his shirt and laid it on the grass, running his hands over it to brush away the dirt. He gently folded it into a square and held it to his lips. "Goodbye," he said, and laid the folded square into the hole. He brushed the dirt on top and replaced the clumps of sod, pushing them back in place until the hole was undetectable. He lay down, resting his head on the clump of sod, and looked across to the pond at the edge of the cemetery, where three ducks—a mallard and two hens—were swimming. Jakob closed his eyes and covered his face with his hands.

Part 4

Hope

Leningrad, Russia
1941

Chapter 37

Kolya tiptoed into the dining room. He was seventeen and in the bachelor's program at the Leningrad Conservatory, having completed his pre-college training the previous spring. As Neuhaus had predicted nearly a decade earlier, he was well on his way to becoming one of the finest pianists in Russia.

Tatiana Semenova slowly buttered a piece of thick rye bread while she scanned the program for the evening's concert. Kolya surprised her by bending over and kissing her cheek. "My, my," she chuckled, laying her reading glasses on the table. "Every day you seem to get taller and more handsome. In my time, a boy with your looks could have married any princess in Russia."

"What do you think of my program?" he asked.

"It couldn't be better—Chopin and Rachmaninoff—you certainly know how to charm us old ladies. So much of the music written now is so angular, like machines pounding away, but Chopin and Rachmaninoff—ahh, like the old days, suave and genteel."

"Maybe in the middle of my Chopin I'll play a few bars of that Prokofiev sonata Sofronitsky has been pestering me to learn, to see if anyone is awake enough to notice."

"Well, I'll certainly be awake and will notice," Oxana said, entering the dining room with Kolya's lunch. "You will do no such thing. And from what I've been hearing, a few bars are about all you know of that sonata. Maybe you should work a little harder and get it learned."

"Don't worry about it. I'm doing fine at school." He smiled at her. "Mama, would you mind getting me a cup of tea? I think Tatiana would like some more too."

Kolya watched Oxana shuffle back into the kitchen. She had never fully recovered from the gunshot wound nor regained the weight she lost while in Peterstal. Her hair was prematurely gray, her skin had begun to wrinkle, and she walked with stooped shoulders, and yet, Kolya felt proud of her. *She's still beautiful*, he thought, *despite all she's been through*. As soon as she disappeared around the corner, he pulled a small box, wrapped in silver paper and tied with a stiff silver bow, out of the breast pocket of his blazer.

"Ooh," Tatiana exclaimed, clapping her hands.

"Shhh. It's a surprise." Kolya placed the box on the table beside his tea-cup, and when Oxana returned with the teapot, he jumped out of his chair and put his arms around her waist. "Happy birthday. I'll bet you thought I forgot, didn't you?" Kolya held her hand while she eased into one of the dining chairs. "Open it," he said, handing her the gift.

"Yes, open it—I can't wait to see what's inside," Tatiana sang out.

Oxana's hands had developed a slight tremor, and she slowly undid the ribbon and tore away the paper. She opened the box and pulled out a smaller package wrapped in silver tissue paper, slowly unfurling the edges. When she at last freed her gift from the tissue wrapping, she held up a sparkling silver necklace with a large pear-shaped pendant embedded with a bright blue stone.

"It's turquoise, Mama, from Turkey. Do you like it?"

"Put it on; it's gorgeous," Tatiana said, clapping her hands.

"Kolya, this is too expensive. Where did you get the money? Please tell me you didn't steal it."

"Of course I didn't steal it, Mama. Do you like it? Don't spoil the fun by thinking of money." Kolya plucked the necklace out of his mother's hand and eased it over her head.

"It's beautiful—thank you, Kolya. I don't know how you managed to buy it, but it is very special."

"I want you to wear it tonight at my concert," Kolya said, giving her a kiss on her cheek. "I need to get back to school—I'm already late."

"But Kolya, you haven't even touched your lunch," Oxana called after him.

"I'm not hungry. Don't forget to iron my shirt and tuxedo," he added, grabbing his coat off the hall tree and dashing out the door.

————

Kolya's classroom was on the conservatory's third floor, and he made his way up the grand staircase with the usual difficulty. He had seen many doctors over the years, but the verdict was always the same—his legs were permanently injured. Although the frequent spasms of pain would never go away, he had been fitted with braces, which helped to stabilize his legs so that he rarely needed to rely on his sticks.

It was a tradition to post each day's lesson schedule on the classroom door for anyone who might want to sit in and hear the lesson. Kolya took a quick glance to verify that his name was indeed listed for his two p.m. slot. He entered the room and was relieved to see no spectators today—it always added a bit of extra stress when people were listening. Like all the classrooms of the conservatory, the room was plain, with walls painted an off-white that reminded Kolya of the color of bones, as if the painters mixed their paint from the crushed skeletons of failed pianists. Every classroom had a large, framed photo of some famous musician, always severe and unsmiling, and always hanging on the wall opposite the piano, conveniently staring down to remind the students of the futility of their efforts, no matter how thoroughly rehearsed their performances were. In this room it was Beethoven who stared sternly, eager to pass judgment.

Professor Sofronitsky taught in the old Russian style, sitting at a long table below the raised platform where the piano stood. Kolya approached Sofronitsky's chair as nonchalantly as he could—he was late and Sofronitsky hated students being late—and laid his music score on the table. He bowed slightly and proceeded toward the piano. "What's this?" Sofronitsky called out as Kolya sat on the piano bench.

"It's Chopin's Fantasy."

"I know what it *is*," Sofronitsky said. "I want to know why you bring me this?"

"Since I'm playing it in the competition, I thought you would want to hear it."

"Do you not remember that last week I specifically requested you bring me the Prokofiev sonata?"

"I forgot the music at home."

"You forgot the music at home?" Sofronitsky raised his voice. "You are not a child. Can you not remember your music? I expect more from you, Kolya Rostov. I expect promptness, and I expect conscientiousness." Sofronitsky was silent for a few moments and Kolya sat at the piano, staring at the floor. "We can work through it anyway," he said, more calmly. "I know the piece very well. I don't need the score." Kolya sat a few more moments, still staring at the floor. "Well? Begin."

"I'm sorry, Professor, but I don't know it yet. I . . . I have not had time to learn it," Kolya whispered.

"So finally you tell the truth, except that the reason you do not yet know the Prokofiev sonata is not because you have not had time. When you are a student of mine you have all the time in the world, because piano practice is all you do. You have no other life. You eat, you sleep, and you practice—that is it. The reason you do not yet know the Prokofiev sonata is because you've been lazy." Kolya continued staring at the floor. "All right, if you insist, play the Chopin. Perhaps I can offer a few suggestions for improvement."

Kolya placed his hands on the keys and began. "Stop!" Sofronitsky shouted. "The first note is piano. You didn't play soft—start again—no! Stop! Are you an idiot? I said piano. Do you not know the difference between loud and soft?" Sofronitsky was in a rage. Everything was wrong. "Can't you do even the simplest thing? My dog can do better. Have you never learned to play legato? Perhaps one of our beginners can give you a few suggestions."

Kolya never said a word. Even as his hands shook and his lips trembled, he held his composure. He was not going to give Sofronitsky the pleasure of seeing him reduced to tears.

The lesson dragged on well past the appointed end time and came to a halt only when Sofronitsky had completely exhausted himself. Kolya picked his music score off the table and, on his way out, Sofronitsky quietly said, "If it is not too much to ask of such a busy young man, may I hear the Prokofiev next week?"

Kolya went down the hall, down the three flights of stairs, and out the front door. He darted down the street as quickly as his legs allowed. When he tried to hurry, his braces made him look like he was a staggering drunk, but he didn't care. His legs were hurting, and he nearly fell several times, but by the time he reached the bar he had both calmed down and slowed down.

The Matryoshka, named after Russia's famous nesting dolls, was Kolya's favorite bar. Its walls were lined from floor to ceiling with shelves of the colorful dolls, but one didn't need to look too closely to detect that the dolls on display were not beautiful hand-painted works of art, but rather the low-end, mass-produced versions the street vendors liked to foist on unsuspecting tourists.

Kolya paused inside the door to allow his eyes to adjust to the dim light and the haze of cigarette smoke. The mournful sounds of the old accordion player who always played the same songs, all in the same key and all at the same tempo, wafted above the din of the bar patrons. The bar's most enticing allure was its willingness to serve everyone who stepped through the doors, with no thought of asking for proof of age, and students from across the city came in droves to enjoy the debilitating effect of the bar's freely flowing alcohol.

"Chopin, over here," Vova called from his usual table in the back. "Come and meet my new friend, Igor." Vova and Igor already had drinks in hand, and as soon as the barmaid approached the table, Kolya ordered a shot of vodka.

"Nice to meet you, Igor." Kolya extended his hand, and they shook.

"And now he's your friend too," Vova said.

Kolya downed the vodka in one swallow and wiped his mouth on his shirt sleeve.

"Must've been a tough lesson," Vova said, patting him on the back.

"Nah, Sofronitsky loves me. Says I'm the best—he's never heard better."

"Ya, that's what I hear he tells all his students."

Kolya tapped his glass on the table to signal the barmaid for another.

"Don't you play tonight?"

"I do. It's to celebrate my mother's birthday and a run-through for the competition next month."

"Are you sure you should be drinking before a performance?"

"What's a little vodka? It gets my adrenaline flowing."

"Well, I'm sure your opera-singing girlfriend will love you—with or without the vodka," Vova said, poking Kolya in the ribs. "Chopin, you had better watch out. That Tatiana Semenova is a sly old fox. I've heard she's had lots of men. They say she was even one of the tsar's lovers. She might be planning on getting you into her bed for a little romp."

"Well at least at age ninety the chances of illegitimate children are fairly remote," Kolya said, and the trio roared with laughter.

"You know they say she must even have caught Stalin's eye," Vova continued. "How else could the old girl keep that apartment all to herself? The government has broken up all those old rich apartments and loaded them up with families. How is it possible she escaped?"

"I know how," Kolya said. "She told me."

"So, spill the beans, comrade. What's her secret?"

"She said that she told the truth."

"And what might that truth be?" Vova asked, tapping his glass on the counter to signal the barmaid for another round of drinks.

"She said that when the inspector came, he told her that by decree there had to be ten families living in the apartment, and she told him that by an amazing coincidence there were exactly ten families. He demanded to know their names and occupations, and she started in. First is old Herr Bach and his wife, plus all their children," Kolya said, imitating Tatiana's loud, high-pitched voice. "They've got so many I've lost count. Everything he does is intricate and detailed. I think he's a mathematician. Comrade Haydn and his wife also live here, but she's so dull I never speak to her and I have no idea what Comrade Haydn does. The young Mozart couple are nothing but trouble and never pay the rent. I think he's a painter. Herr Beethoven is a bachelor—typical German, horribly rude. I try to avoid him. Besides, he's deaf—can't hear a thing. I think he's a bricklayer. Then there is Monsieur Chopin, very elegant, but that horrible woman he's with—dresses like a man and smokes cigars. I don't know how he can stand her. I think Monsieur Chopin is a poet." By this point Vova and Igor were nearly crying from laughter.

"That's not ten yet—tell us the rest," Vova said.

Kolya glanced at his watch. "To be continued," he announced. "I need to get home or I'll be late for my concert." He pulled a couple rubles out of his pocket and tossed them on the table. "A pleasure meeting you, Igor," he said, and he grabbed his coat, which he had draped over the back of his chair.

"Here, let me help you." Vova jumped up, snatched the coat out of his hands, and held it while Kolya slipped his arms into the sleeves. "Chopin, try not to be late tonight," he whispered, leaning into Kolya's body until his mouth was touching his ear. "The car will be there at ten and they hate to wait. I know how you like to play encores for the old ladies, but tonight is important. Besides, it'll be past bedtime for your old opera-singing girl-friend anyway, so give her a nice good night kiss, tuck her into bed, and be on time for a change!"

Kolya headed toward the door. "And Chopin," Vova said, "wear your tuxedo. It'll be a nice extra touch that will not go unnoticed." The evening had turned windy and it was snowing. Kolya pulled his scarf tight around his neck and hurried home.

He never failed to be impressed by the lingering vestiges of old-world elegance each time he entered Tatiana's building. Despite the chain-link gate that had long ago been put across the stately entrance to keep out thieves, he liked to imagine some doorman, in a heavy blue velvet coat and top hat, standing at attention beside the tall wrought-iron and bev-eled-glass doors.

Kolya stood for a moment at the bottom of the wide circular staircase in the center of the foyer. A large crystal chandelier hung so low, one could almost touch it while ascending the steps. The chandelier had not worked for many years, and nearly all the light bulbs had been stolen, but the crys-tals remained, and he liked to imagine its beauty in the old days when it was fully lit.

Kolya went up the foyer's marble steps, amazed that they remained intact—it was probably too much work to chisel out and cart away the heavy stone—and the wrought-iron balustrade had somehow escaped Soviet confiscation. Midway up the staircase, Kolya stepped onto a small landing with two threadbare easy chairs and a low table that was miss-ing a leg and being propped up by a piece of wood. A set of imposing carved mahogany doors opened into Tatiana's apartment, which covered the building's entire second floor.

There was a rush of warm air as Kolya pulled open the heavy door. He hung his scarf and coat, opened a smaller set of double doors, and stepped into the apartment's large front room, which spanned the entire length of the building. Fifty white French-style chairs were set in rows across the center portion of the room facing Tatiana's black concert grand piano. The parquet floor, at least what remained of it—many pieces were loose or missing, so that one had to be careful to avoid tripping—was waxed to a golden sheen. His mother spent hours on her knees, scrubbing, to keep the old floor shiny.

Behind the piano, faded blue satin draperies provided a regal frame for the twelve-foot, floor-to-ceiling windows that opened on to a small balcony overlooking the street. He admired how his mother had managed to fold the drapes into their gold-braided tiebacks in such a way as to hide the holes and stains. Much of the room's wallpaper was peeling, revealing the underlayer of plaster, and nearly all the painted woodwork was chipped and scuffed. Yet tonight, with candles blazing, it was almost as if the entire room had been transported back to its former glory, the fin de siècle of Tsarist Russia.

"You're late," his mother said when she came into the room. "The guests will soon be arriving. Don't you think you should at least warm up your fingers?" She helped him out of his coat. "You've been drinking."

"It's nothing, Mama. I was with Vova and his friend—we had one drink. It's no big deal. It helps me play better."

"Kolya, don't forget that I too know a thing or two about performing, and drinking does not help you play better. You'll ruin your concert."

"Mama, Mama, always worrying." He kissed her cheek. "I'm glad you're wearing your necklace. It looks great on you." Her black dress hung gracefully on her slender body, and the iridescent blue turquoise enhanced her alabaster skin. The doorbell rang, and Kolya dashed into his room to change into his tuxedo.

At precisely seven p.m., the last of the guests were seated and Kolya stood peering into the room from behind the dining room doors. Tatiana's private boudoir—dressing room, bedroom, and bathroom—was opposite him, and all eyes were pointed in that direction, patiently waiting. Tatiana emerged, and the guests, many of whom still vividly remembered her legendary performances at the Mariinsky Theatre, stood and applauded, honored for the opportunity to pay tribute to their beloved diva. She wore a colorful, floor-length silk caftan and a matching scarf over her hair. Her face was made up in operatic fashion, heavy with eyeliner, rouge, and lipstick, and she stood in the doorway a moment, the scent of her perfume wafting into the room.

Tatiana smiled, bowed, and slowly made her way to her chair in the front row while Kolya simultaneously made his entrance from the opposite side of the room. In a bit of theatrics they had mastered over the years as a nod to the old-world elegance and sophistication Tatiana so loved, he bowed and held her hand as she gracefully descended into her seat; this moment never failed to amuse him. Only after Tatiana was seated, a queen on her throne, did the audience stop applauding and take their seats.

He opened the concert with one of his favorites, Rachmaninoff's recently composed masterpiece, the Corelli Variations. Kolya had learned it after hearing another pianist perform it in a recital, and he played it frequently. As his fingers sounded the quiet simplicity of the opening theme, he liked to imagine a butterfly on a gentle breeze, floating across the room. The audience sat silent as he played each section with increased drama until, after the final wildly difficult fortissimo variation, the piece concluded as it had started—quietly. Standing to bow, he felt humbled by the cheering audience. He had come so far from his childhood days, when he had practiced on an old upright piano in tiny Peterstal.

Kolya's program continued, alternating works by Chopin and Rachmaninoff, but despite the audience's cheering and shouts of encore, Kolya noticed his mother's unsmiling face and rather timid clapping. *Nothing escapes her. She heard my wrong notes.*

At the end, he waved his hands to quiet everyone. "Ladies and gentlemen, for my encore I would like you all to join me in wishing my mother a happy birthday." He launched into a dramatic arpeggio flourish up the keyboard, and the entire crowd, led by Tatiana's bewitching voice—still surprisingly powerful and clear—began to sing.

Afterward, the guests made their way into the dining room, where the huge table was laden with an astonishing array of Russian hors d'oeuvres, the likes of which Kolya had never seen. "Oxana has outdone herself," he heard one guest murmur to another.

His mother had prepared pickled cucumbers, herring, onions, and mushrooms. A large mound of black caviar stood in a bowl that rested on a plate of crushed ice, and next to that were plates of various salamis and cheeses, several loaves of dark rye bread, and of course, everyone's favorite, a large bowl of *olivje* salad. Kolya stood between a side table that held a dazzling array of desserts—tea cakes, blintzes with lemon slices, piroshki stuffed with pistachios, pastila, and slices of halva—and the tea trolley, with a tall silver samovar for hot tea as well as wines, beers, vodkas, and a selection of after-dinner liquors.

He watched his mother proudly move among the guests with elegance and grace, removing dirty dishes, refilling empty glasses, wiping up spills, and beaming as, one by one, each guest offered their congratulations on her son's performance. "Please eat, Kolya—there's enough food here to feed our entire army," she whispered on her way into the kitchen with yet another armful of dirty plates.

"It looks great, Mama. It must have taken you days to prepare all this food."

"I did it to celebrate your performance. Now eat!"

"I don't have time, Mama—I've got to run."

"Run? But the guests want to visit with you. I don't understand all this mysterious late-night coming and going, and I don't like that you're spending so much time with Vova."

"I'm not meeting Vova tonight. I have someplace I promised to be, that's all. Really, Mama, it's nothing. Don't worry."

Several older ladies interrupted to congratulate Kolya. He quickly thanked them and pushed through the throng, nodding to some and ignoring others as they attempted to speak to him and shake his hand. "But you haven't even changed out of your tuxedo," he heard his mother call as he grabbed his coat in the front vestibule. "You're going to get it all wrinkled."

Kolya went out the door and down the foyer staircase. Outside, he glanced up at the tall windows, blazing with light, and saw his mother gazing down at him before he stepped into the back seat of a black car parked along the sidewalk. He felt a pang of guilt, knowing his mother was disappointed that he had not stayed for the reception, but he had to do tonight's job. He had only made a down payment on his mother's necklace, and the jeweler was expecting the rest of the money in the morning.

Chapter 38

Kolya pulled his blankets over his head. It was the morning of the competition, and he could hear his mother in the kitchen. He knew she was eager to hear all the contestants and would be in the hall promptly at ten a.m. However, hearing the others would only make him anxious, so he intended to stay home to rest and do some last-minute warm-up.

For Kolya, the stakes of the Leningrad Conservatory's annual piano competition were especially high. The winners, who were usually seniors or graduate students, were nearly always catapulted into a performing career. If he could win now, as a freshman, it would guarantee a media blitz that would make him famous throughout Russia.

Arriving in the hall just ahead of his scheduled performance time, he strode to the piano when his name was announced and bowed to the judges, who sat at a long table below the stage. He put his left hand on the piano to steady his legs while he made a deep bow to acknowledge the audience's applause and to sneak in a surreptitious glance at his mother, in her usual spot—third row, to the right of the keyboard. Kolya sat on the bench a moment with his hands folded in his lap. He usually was not nervous before his performances, but today he was feeling a slight case of butterflies in his stomach.

His opening piece, a required Bach prelude and fugue, was going well, until, near the end, he lost the thread of the fugue theme in his left hand and played a couple of wrong notes before getting back on track. *No big deal*, he told himself, bowing to the applause. *Probably no one even noticed. I did a good job of covering it up.* He glanced at his mother. She was clapping, but not smiling—she had heard his flub.

Chopin's Fantasy went perfectly, without a single glitch. *Yes!* he thought as he played the final chords. Again the audience roared, and again Kolya saw out of the corner of his eye that Oxana's applause was tepid. She always told him he played with too much pedal, but she was old-fashioned—obviously, everybody else loved it.

His program ended with the Prokofiev sonata Sofronitsky had been pestering him to learn. He played a few wrong notes near the beginning and had a memory slip in the second movement, but the audience didn't seem to mind, or didn't notice, and applauded while Kolya bowed to the center, to the left, the right, and back to the center. The applause became even wilder when several girls brought flowers onto the stage, and he kissed each on her cheek as he accepted the bouquets.

Kolya slowly walked off the stage, clutching the flowers and waving to the crowd. His mother was not smiling. I'll show her. She's too stuffy. He would win despite her disapproval.

It would be at least an hour before the results were announced, and Kolya hurried out the auditorium's rear exit door. A cold wind was blowing, and he shivered as he darted down the street to the Matryoshka. He ordered a vodka, downed it in one swallow, and ordered another shot. *Everybody says I'm the best, but she always wants more and more. She's always pushing for it to be better and better. I'm already good. Why does she keep pushing me?*

Kolya downed a third shot and returned to the hall in time for the awarding of the prizes.

The contestants sat on the stage in a semicircle in front of the concert grand piano and Oxana was still in her same seat, third row, right of center. The jury chairman announced fifth place, then fourth, and third. Kolya hardly listened, certain he couldn't possibly have ranked that low. He kept glancing at his mother, hoping for some sign of approval, but she sat stoic, staring straight ahead, almost as if she were consciously refusing to make eye contact with him. Finally, the chairman drew out each syllable as he intoned, "And seeecond prrrize goooes to . . . Kolya Rostov."

Second prize? He was supposed to be first prize. He was the best—everyone said so. Kolya stood to receive his certificate and caught sight of his mother turning her back and exiting the hall.

———

After the competition, Kolya lost interest in school and grew increasingly eager for the end of the term. He blamed it on the weather—spring was late, and it seemed the dreary wintry days would last forever.

He tried to coax Tatiana to join him for strolls along the canal, but she refused, insisting it was too cold. Kolya suspected that the cold served only as a convenient cover for her diminishing energy.

The news was as depressing as the weather, and Kolya merely skimmed over the newspaper articles. Day after day, it was nothing but stories of Hitler's progress. Yugoslavia and Greece had succumbed in April, Crete in May. Only Great Britain remained beyond the Führer's grasp. Everywhere Kolya went, the war was the topic of conversation—could the British hold out? And then what? Would the Germans dare to invade Russia? The newspapers kept reassuring Soviet citizens that they had nothing to fear, but . . .

One rainy Tuesday, Kolya arrived at the conservatory even later than usual for his lesson. He was drenched but relieved to hear piano music coming from the classroom. *Sofronitsky is running overtime and won't know how late I am*, he thought. He glanced at the schedule posted on the door. Another name was penciled into his time slot.

Today was Tuesday, wasn't it? And it was two p.m.? Well, nearly two twenty, but that was beside the point. He went into the room, and as soon as the student finished playing, Kolya approached the table. "Professor Sofronitsky, has some mistake been made?"

Sofronitsky looked up. "No, no mistake has been made."

"Has my lesson time been moved?"

"No, your lesson time has not been moved, it has been *re*-moved. I'm sorry, Kolya Rostov, but I am a very busy teacher and there are many students who wish to study with me. I cannot waste my time on lazy slackers like yourself."

Kolya was too stunned to speak. He turned toward the door, but Sofronitsky called him back to the table. "Kolya Rostov, I know you probably feel I am being unduly severe, so let me explain. Do you know how difficult it is to be a good pianist? Good pianists train until their fingers are infallible, incapable of errors. They can play as loud and as fast as they desire, and they dazzle their audiences." Sofronitsky paused, and Kolya was not sure if he had finished or not.

"But then there are the great pianists," Sofronitsky began softly. "They do not play merely with their fingers. In fact, many of the greatest pianists have a disdain for finger agility. They understand that loud and fast playing alone will never move an audience. The great pianists play with their minds, and their hearts and souls. Kolya Rostov, when you played for my good friend Heinrich Neuhaus in Odesa, he heard a great pianist, and when you came here and I first heard you, I also heard a great pianist. But now I only hear the notes. I no longer hear your soul. You've squandered your talent, and now, unfortunately, you are merely a good pianist with excellent fingers, but we already have too many of those here at this school."

Sofronitsky paused again, and Kolya stood staring at his feet. It felt as if they were glued to the floor and he was trying to figure out how he was going to move them.

"One more thing I think you should know." Sofronitsky was now whispering so softly Kolya had to strain to hear him. "When my friend Heinrich Neuhaus told me about you, he said he had heard only one other pianist who played as you did. Only one other, Kolya Rostov, only one other—and do you know who that pianist was? It was your mother. Kolya, you have let your mother down. She made great sacrifices for you, and you have not lived up to your potential. That will be all. Kolya Rostov, I wish you much luck."

Kolya spent the rest of the day wandering the city, not sure what to do but very sure of what not to do, and that was to tell his mother. Even before he opened the door to the Matryoshka, he heard the mournful accordion player and smelled the cigarette smoke. He shed his jacket and looked to their usual spot at the back of the bar but didn't see either Vova or Igor. Maybe he was so late they had finally given up and left. It didn't matter. He could drink by himself. He motioned for the barmaid and spotted Vova a few tables away, with a very handsome young man. *Yet another friend. Vova knows everybody, at least everybody who is male, young, and good-looking.*

"Chopin." Vova waved. He leaned over and said a few words to the young fellow, patted him on the back, and came over to Kolya.

"Where's Igor?" Kolya asked.

"He's busy. At least he said he was busy, so I guess we'll have to take him at his word and manage without his scintillating wit and lively conversation. So, Chopin, how did your day go?"

"Not so well. Terrible, in fact. Old Sofronitsky axed me."

"Chopin, what do you mean, he axed you?"

"He axed me, threw me out of his class."

"Ouch. This calls for a drink." Vova waved to the barmaid, and she came over and set two glasses of vodka on the table.

"Cheer up, Chopin, and drink up." They chinked their glasses in a toast and downed their vodka in one gulp. "Think of it like this. In the big picture, it's no big deal. One setback caused by one teacher at one school on one day of the year. Nothing more than that. There are other teachers, other schools, other days of the year." Both tapped their glasses on the table for another round. "Chopin, tomorrow when you wake up, you can start a new chapter. And who knows, maybe it will be even better. Maybe in the end you'll wish old Sofronitsky had given you your freedom much earlier."

"He said he can no longer hear my soul and I have squandered my talent," Kolya said.

"That's pretty harsh. What does an old ogre like him know about a soul anyway? At least you apparently had one."

"Vova, I'm thinking I might go to him tomorrow and apologize and beg to be let back into his class."

"Apologize? Beg? You? Chopin, how can you even think of such things? You're probably more talented than the old goat ever was. You have nothing to apologize for, and nothing to beg for. He was rude to you. He's the one who should be apologizing."

Kolya downed a third shot of vodka. "Vova, I've been thinking about a lot of things. I don't want to do the late-night car rides anymore. I want to stop. Tell them to stop coming."

"Now you're really not making any sense." Vova put his arm around

Kolya's shoulder. He tapped his shot glass on the table and pulled his chair closer. "Chopin, you need to relax. Don't make any decisions you'll regret. You're popular, they like you, and you're making a ton of money. Are you sure you want to throw it all away? Besides, Chopin, you're not exactly a miser, always buying the latest fashions for this beautiful body of yours, jewels for your mama, gifts for that opera-singing girlfriend. It takes a lot to keep you going. You want to throw it all away?"

"Vova, I need to stop. I need to think."

"Then take some time to think. No more late-night car rides for Chopin, at least for a while. I'll tell them you're sick or something. And if I were you, I'd march into Sofronitsky's office tomorrow and tell the old codger to fuck off and go to hell, and you can even ad lib a few other expletives. Trust me, there is nothing as liberating as cussing. You'll feel so much better once you've done it. Let's drink to the medicinal value of cussing!"

They both downed another shot.

"To the medicinal value of cussing!" Kolya shouted. They banged their glasses on the counter, chanting, "Vodka, vodka, vodka," to the barmaid.

It was nearly two a.m. when Kolya staggered through the door. As usual, Oxana had left dinner warming in the oven, but he turned the oven off without bothering to look inside and stumbled into his bedroom, falling onto his bed fully dressed. He usually enjoyed being drunk—it helped him forget. He had tried so hard over the years to forget Peterstal, forget everything that had happened, but tonight, with Sofronitsky's words swirling in his mind, it all came flooding back—the relentless hunger, and what they ate; the horrible memory of it still made him want to throw up. Sofronitsky was right. His mother had sacrificed everything, had done everything she could to keep him alive. And in the midst of all their suffering, she had still found it in herself to teach him to play. She had demanded perfection, but she did it for him, so he could be the best . . . he had squandered his talent and let his mother down.

But she had let him down too. *Who is my father? Why won't you tell me, Mama? My name should not be Rostov. But what should it be?* If he was nothing more than some drunk's bastard son, what did that make his mother?

And he remembered the gunshots, his mother falling forward, the train ride, and Vova. *Vova saved me. He's my friend, my best friend—or is he?*

The black car no longer parked on the street, and Kolya now spent his evenings at home. Tatiana preferred to stay in her room, so his mother would take a dinner tray to her, then Oxana and Kolya sat at the large dining table by themselves. They spoke of trivial things—the rain, the latest concerts, the dreary winter, and how nice summer would be, but each thread of conversation eventually trailed off and lapsed into silence. Kolya was too ashamed to talk to his mother—too ashamed both of what he had become and what he had failed to become—and the weight of all that was left unsaid bore down on both him and his mother until it was unbearable, and they retreated to their rooms with an unbridgeable abyss between them.

Chapter 39

Sauntering slowly along the Moika canal, Kolya savored the sunshine and clear sky. It was June 21—the summer solstice—the beginning of Leningrad's White Nights, when the sun barely dipped below the horizon before rising into a new day. Kolya paused to admire the sapphire-blue water and to inhale the forsythia and jasmine that had burst into bloom and enveloped the city in an intoxicatingly lush perfume. Everyone he passed seemed in good spirits, even greeting strangers as they bustled about, as if the festive mood was contagious.

Kolya pulled open the door to his old standby, the Matryoshka, and entered. The bar was full and noisy, and as he jostled through the crowd to join Vova and Igor at their usual back table, every conversation he overheard was about Hitler and the war. Vova already had a shot of vodka waiting for him, and Kolya downed it even before sitting down.

"Hitler will never attack us," Vova was saying to Igor. "He's too smart for that. He would never repeat Napoleon's mistakes."

"But what if he does?" Igor said.

"Then we fight," Vova replied. "I'm not afraid to fight."

"I'm not either," Igor added.

"I'm not afraid to fight either," Kolya said, joining the conversation. "But I'm sort of afraid of dying. What do you think happens when you die?"

"Nothing. That's what happens," Vova said. "You just stop being. That's all. You just stop."

"I think you go to heaven when you die," Igor said. "But I suppose living in heaven is not much different from living in Russia. You're still going to have to do what you're told."

"Wow, Igor. You're sounding like some kind of philosopher. I'm impressed," Vova said.

They tapped their glasses for another round.

"Even if Hitler does invade us," Kolya said, "I don't think he would ever come to Leningrad. Why would he bring his army here—we have nothing but old palaces and churches. He would try to take Moscow."

"The Germans will never invade," Vova said. "Stalin won't let it happen. He'll cut some deal with Hitler."

"That depends on what Stalin hates more: Hitler's socialism or the West's capitalism," Igor said. "I guess we'll have to wait and see."

The bar had become even more crowded and was so noisy, conversation was nearly impossible.

"We need to upgrade," Vova announced, "to celebrate this beautiful night. Let's go to the Europa." They paid their tab and headed toward Nevsky Prospect. At the hotel, bands were playing in both the bar and the dining room, and people were even dancing in the lobby. They ordered drinks and waited for a table to open up so they could sit.

Soon a trio of young ladies from Azerbaijan who were staying at the hotel approached them. The six of them talked, drank, laughed, and Kolya even attempted to dance, although it mainly consisted of one of the girls holding him up while he swayed to the music and kept insisting he was not drunk.

During a break in the music, one of the girls leaned toward the boys and whispered, "How about we continue the party in our room upstairs?"

"What sort of men do you take us for?" Vova asked, winking at Kolya.

"You seem like adventuresome types," she replied.

"What if we prove to be a complete disappointment?" Vova continued, with Igor snickering beside him. "Besides, I don't think my friend Igor here has even gotten his first hard-on yet—he's still waiting for that glorious moment."

"Perhaps one of us can help him achieve this monumental goal," the girl continued, while her two friends laughed.

"Well, ladies, stay right here while we make a short visit to the gents to discuss your intriguing proposal." Vova stood, and Igor and Kolya followed him. As soon as they were out of sight of the girls, they looked at each other, nodded their agreement, and headed out the front door. Kolya's head was spinning and his stomach was churning.

"I have to stop," Kolya said. "I think I might be sick."

"What? Those girls got you that excited?" Vova said.

"I think I've had too much to drink,"

"There's no such thing," Vova shouted, just as Kolya leaned over and threw up on the sidewalk.

"Whoa," Igor said. "Maybe we've had enough for one night."

"I'm fine," Kolya said, wiping his mouth on his shirt sleeve. "Let's go."

"You heard the man," Vova said, putting his arm around Kolya's shoulder to steady him. "Let's go."

They stopped off at a couple of small bars before eventually ending up at the Hotel Astoria on Ulitsa Bolshaya Morskaya, near St. Isaac's Cathedral, for nightcaps, or rather by this point morningcaps. They fell in with a crowd of university students and proceeded to talk, sing, and drink until eventually, with the sun already high in the sky, the three stumbled down the sidewalk, leaning against each other for support.

———

A few hours later, his mother was shaking him. "Kolya, wake up," she said. "You have to get up and hear what they're saying on the radio."

His head hurt and his stomach was churning. He mumbled that he was too tired and turned toward the wall.

"Kolya, right now. Get up. Come hear the news," his mother said, tugging at the blankets.

"Fine, sure. What's the big deal?" Kolya pulled on the pants he had worn the previous evening. They were suspiciously damp—had he spilled a drink or gotten so drunk he peed himself? He couldn't remember anything. He stumbled into the dining room, where Tatiana was sitting in front of the radio.

"Men and women, citizens of the Soviet Union—the Soviet government and its head, Comrade Stalin, have instructed me to make the following announcement: At four a.m., without declaration of war and without any claims being made on the Soviet Union, German troops attacked our country, attacked our frontier in many places, and bombed, from the air, Zhitomir, Kyiv, Sevastopol, Kaunas, and other cities. The government calls upon you, men and women, citizens of the Soviet Union, to rally even more closely around the glorious Bolshevik Party, around the Soviet government and our great leader, Comrade Stalin. Our cause is just. The enemy will be crushed. Victory will be ours."

Tatiana put one hand over her mouth and wept while making the sign of the cross over and over, muttering, "I'm too old to endure another war. There've been too many already. I'm too old, too old."

"Kolya, go to the bank right away," his mother said, "and withdraw all our money. Then go to the store and buy all the food you can carry. Hurry, before everything is gone."

Long lines had already formed at the bank by the time Kolya arrived. He stepped to the end of the line, but within minutes, dozens were already behind him, pushing, shouting, frantic to get inside. Police arrived to try to calm the crowd. "What's taking so long?" many shouted. "We have to get in before they run out."

Kolya had been in line for more than an hour when he finally stepped up to the withdrawal window. The teller was a young girl, and her hands were shaking so that she could hardly count the bills. Kolya saw that her cash drawer was nearly empty, but he was able to withdraw his funds.

Back on the street, he had only gone a short distance when he heard an angry uproar and turned. A bank manager had appeared on the steps. "Go home," he was shouting. "We have run out of money. There is no more. You must go home."

Some in the crowd raised their fists and yelled profanities as the police pushed people out of the line. "Go home," the officers shouted. "Go home. Maybe in a few days there will be more money."

There was also a long line outside the grocery store, two blocks from Tatiana's building, and Kolya joined at the rear. The line moved very slowly, and it was more than two hours before he was allowed inside the store. His legs were hurting, and he was afraid he might collapse, but the store shelves were rapidly emptying, and he randomly grabbed items and stuffed them into Oxana's large canvas shopping bag. The store clerk didn't even tally the items for an accurate cost, but only briefly glanced into the bag and named a price. Kolya had to drag the bag along the sidewalk to get home—it was too heavy to carry.

He dropped the bag of groceries on the floor and collapsed into a chair, but his mother shoved the money he had given her back into his hands. "You must go out again. Buy more. All you can." Kolya's legs were shooting spasms of pain, and he hobbled into his room and grabbed his walking sticks.

By the time he got back to the grocery store, it was locked up. He hobbled another two blocks to one of the city's most elegant department stores, hurried past the racks of expensive clothing and down the stairs to the lower-level food section, and again grabbed all he could carry.

That evening, he and his mother were sorting the various packages, cramming everything into tins and jars to ensure nothing would fall prey to mice, when Vova's shrill whistle sounded from the street below.

"Please, Kolya, not tonight," his mother said. "Wasn't last night enough? Must you go out again?"

"I'll stay here with you, Mama." Kolya kissed her cheek. He had not kissed his mother since her birthday, when he had given her the turquoise necklace. "I'll just go see what they want."

"We've got to celebrate," Vova said when he came down to the street. "Igor and I are now soldiers. We just joined."

"We're going to fight those German bastards until they're driven out," Igor shouted.

Kolya declined, turning to go back inside.

"Suit yourself. But you'll be missing a lot of fun," Vova shouted after him.

His mother was half reclining on the threadbare sofa in the front room when Kolya came back in and sat beside her. "Mama, there is something I need to tell you. Professor Sofronitsky threw me out of his class. I no longer have a piano teacher."

"I've been wondering when you were going to tell me."

"You knew?"

"Of course I knew. I know everything about your musical life. It's the other things in your life that I know nothing about."

"How did you know?"

"Professor Sofronitsky telephoned me. He told me before he told you. He said he had great respect for me as both a mother and a musician, and he wanted me to know about his concerns for you. I told him that I also had concerns and then I thanked him for the phone call."

"I'm sorry, Mama, for not telling you."

"Kolya—there seem to be many things you have not told me, and your silence hurts."

"Please, Mama, don't say that. I don't want to hurt you, but there are things I can't tell you. I'm sorry, but I can't. Let's try to be happy. We have a nice life here with Tatiana. I've made enough money so you can buy everything we need, and so I can buy you nice things. You never had nice things in Peterstal. Let's enjoy life for as long as we can, without worrying. Maybe the war will be short and we'll get through it without too much trouble."

His mother closed her eyes and lay still for a long while, holding her arms tight against her body, and Kolya recognized, for the first time, that she was in pain.

Without moving or opening her eyes, she said, "I wasn't angry with you for losing the competition. I know you think I was, but I wasn't."

"Don't think of that now, Mama. It's unimportant. There will be other competitions."

"I was disappointed—disappointed because I couldn't hear your inner voice, your passion. When you played, I only heard your fingers."

"That's the same thing Professor Sofronitsky told me. He said I squandered my talent and that he couldn't hear my soul."

"I respect Sofronitsky very much," she continued, speaking softly and slowly, "and what he told you is both true and not true. You have not squandered your talent. You have simply put it on hold for a while. It will reappear when the time is right. As for your soul, you have not lost it, but you seem to have misplaced it. Kolya, you will find it again."

They remained still, the silence broken only by his mother's heavy breathing as she lay with her arms clasping her body. Kolya thought she had fallen asleep and he was about to get a blanket to cover her when she began to speak. "Since you made a confession, I also need to make one. I have kept something from you as well. I've been seeing a doctor. I am quite ill—he says I'm dying." Kolya stared at her, not sure he understood what she had said. "I have had pain ever since the gunshot wound, and now it appears I have cancer. My doctor says there is nothing that can be done. Tatiana knows—I told her—and now you know too." Oxana leaned her head back and closed her eyes.

Kolya remained seated, frozen in place, unable to move, unable to think or speak.

His mother opened her eyes and turned toward him. "Please play for me, Kolya, like you used to, like back in Peterstal."

"Of course, Mama, I'll play for you," he managed to whisper.

"Fantasy," she said. "Yes?"

"Yes."

Kolya stepped to the piano. For the first time in many months, maybe even years, he felt an intense need to play. He needed to hear the music, to lose himself in the actual physicality of making the music, needed to feel the intimate connection between his hands and his emotions, his fingers producing whatever his heart dictated.

He was quickly absorbed by the music and soon was playing the final chord. He held the keys down for a very long time, feeling like he was about to fall off the edge of a steep cliff, but as long as he held on to that last chord, he could stave off the future, stop the passing of time. As long as he held on to the keys, the war would not happen, his mother would not die, and their happiness would last forever. It was the act of lifting his hands from the keyboard that would break the spell and cause his entire world to crumble.

His mother was asleep and he knelt beside her, weeping silently, holding her hand, listening to her heavy breathing.

Chapter 40

Kolya met Vova and Igor at the train station the next afternoon. It had been only twenty-four hours since the invasion, and Vova and Igor already had their deployment orders. Kolya wished he was going with them, but there was no point in even trying to enlist—he would never pass the mandatory physical exam.

"Take care of yourself, Chopin," Vova said, and all three hugged. "Igor and I will be back in no time." As the train began to move, Vova leaned out the window and shouted, "Hitler's ahead of schedule. Napoleon didn't invade until the twenty-fourth." Kolya laughed and waved, somehow sensing he would never see either of them again.

Calls had gone out for all able-bodied citizens to join the efforts to prepare to defend the city. Kolya enlisted in one of the civilian units assigned to digging ditches, stringing barbed wire, and laying land mines, but his stiff knees made the work impossible. Whenever he tried to bend over or carry a heavy load, he fell, and by the end of his second day he was dismissed as more of a hindrance than a help.

———

"What about this?" his mother said while eating breakfast and reading the newspaper. "The Hermitage is planning to evacuate their entire collection, and they're needing workers to help pack everything up."

Kolya agreed it might be work he could do, and as soon as he finished eating he went to apply. Walking along Admiralteyskaya Prospect, he was surprised at how quickly the tenor of life was morphing into a wartime atmosphere. Workers were already building a huge wooden box around the massive Bronze Horseman statue. Pausing to watch the workers, Kolya thought of the legend that as long as the Bronze Horseman stood, the city would not be conquered by enemy forces. He hoped the legend would prove to be true.

He continued toward Nevsky Prospect, where many of the shops, bars, and restaurants were already emptying out their supplies and getting ready to close up. Windows in many of the buildings were already covered with strips of paper to prevent the glass from shattering if they were broken. The inhabitants of one building along the Fontanka River, trying to be artistic, had taped their window strips into elaborate scenes of palm trees with monkeys.

The doors to the Hermitage were wide open and workers were rushing in and out. Kolya stepped inside and asked about filling out an application.

"What application?" one of the workers said. "There is no application. We have plenty of work for everyone. Start over there." Kolya wasn't sure where "over there" was.

"Hey, over there," the man repeated, pointing to a long table in the center of the room. "You can put in the stuffing as soon as they get it off the wall."

Two workers had lifted a huge canvas away from its hooks and were wobbling unsteadily as they descended the ladder. They carried the painting to the table where Kolya stood, and several staff members carefully removed it from its frame.

"It's even more beautiful up close," one said, gently lifting the frame away from the canvas. Kolya leaned in for a closer look. "It's Rembrandt," the worker said. "*The Holy Family*—one of our finest—priceless." They carefully placed the canvas in a wooden box and told Kolya to pile layers of paper on top for protection.

Worried he would do something wrong and harm the painting, Kolya slowly and carefully placed each layer until one of the curators yelled from across the room, "Hurry up, put the covering in. At the rate you're going, it will take five years to pack these paintings, and I don't think the Germans are willing to wait that long."

As soon as Kolya finished, the crate was whisked away and another crate, with another painting, was put on the table.

Day after day, Kolya covered priceless pieces by Titian, Rubens, Velázquez, El Greco, and Da Vinci with cotton padding and filled the crates with wood shavings before the carpenters nailed the boxes shut.

Kolya and his mother's evening conversations became more lively, a pleasant change from their earlier painful, silence-laden attempts to converse. Kolya described how he had spent an entire day wrapping the Russian crown jewels and packing them in crates. "It was like they were cheap souvenirs being sent to some tourist shop," he told her.

"I'm happy you're working at the Hermitage," she said. "As a mother, I can see things a bit sooner than others can."

"What do you mean, Mama?"

"When you describe your work, I hear your voice and see your eyes." She coughed and Kolya got her a glass of water. "These things do not lie. I can once again see your soul. You are going to be fine, Kolya, and that makes me very happy."

He did not bother to tell his mother that he had received a note saying the conservatory students and faculty were being evacuated to Tashkent in Uzbekistan, and he could go with them. He simply crumpled it up and tossed it into the trash. Leaving his mother and Tatiana behind alone was unthinkable.

———

Each day, Oxana read aloud the news reports of the unbelievable speed of the German army's advancement. By early July, with the Germans already within 275 kilometers of Leningrad, Kolya was going to the museum early in the morning and staying late to prepare the first trainload for shipment to Siberia for safekeeping.

Now and then, Kolya stopped at the Matryoshka on his way home. He found it amusing that the bar had packed away their cheap nested dolls as if they were every bit as precious as the Russian crown jewels, but without

Vova and Igor, and with the dust-covered shelves bare and the old accordion player gone, he found it dreary.

Making his daily trek along the Moika canal, to and from the Hermitage, Kolya thought of the irony that during one of the most beautiful summers he could remember—with warm, dry air; clear blue skies; and trees and shrubs blooming prolifically—everyone was rushing around completely consumed by the flurry of war preparations. It was so beautiful that late one afternoon Kolya rode the train out to the park surrounding the Pavlovsk Palace, the former home of Tsar Paul I, just to admire the rows of linden trees alive in gold, purple, and dark red along the park paths. Kolya paused to observe the carpets of mushrooms under the trees and overheard several babushkas—ever superstitious—exclaiming, "Many mushrooms, many deaths," as they shook their kerchiefed heads at the bad omen.

———

One day in late August, the museum director called everyone into the main hall. "You may stop working," he announced in a flat, emotionless voice. "As of today's report, the German army is within fifty kilometers of the city. The railroad is now under German control, and there will be no more trains out of the city." He turned and left, leaving everyone silently staring at each other, until someone said, "Well, that's that. I guess we can go home." Kolya watched the workers take off their aprons and gloves and slowly file out the door.

Oxana was too weak to leave the apartment, and with his work at the museum finished, Kolya spent his time sitting with her. The radio was reporting that the German army was within ten kilometers, and even the slightest sounds—a car horn honking or the shout of someone on the street below—caused him to sit up in a near panic. *Is today the day? How will they come?*

On September 4, his questions were answered. Kolya was in his room, reading, when bombs began falling. He ran to the window and saw utter pandemonium on the street. Cars whizzed past with horns honking at anything in their way. People were rushing out of their buildings onto the sidewalks. In the gaps between the deafening roar of exploding bombs, he heard screaming.

He opened the door to his mother's room. "So today it begins," she whispered. "Go check on Tatiana."

Kolya knocked on Tatiana's door, but there was no answer. *She can't possibly be sleeping through this noise*, he thought. He knocked again and asked to come in, but still there was no answer. He inched the door open to peek in. She was not there.

There was a knock at the front door. "Is this the home of Tatiana Semenova?" a police officer asked when Kolya opened it. Kolya nodded, and the officer told him to come outside. "I need a positive ID." Kolya followed the officer. They stepped out the front door and Kolya's legs buckled. He slumped to the sidewalk, gagging, leaned over, and threw up. Tatiana was lying in the street, covered in blood, her face smashed beyond recognition. It was only by her dress that Kolya was certain it was his beloved Tatiana.

"She just stepped in front of the car—didn't even see me," cried a man, leaning his head out the car window. "I couldn't stop in time—it's not my fault."

Kolya struggled to his feet and wiped his mouth. "What should we do?" he asked the policeman. More bombs exploded, much closer than the others, and everyone instinctively ducked their heads. People were running down the sidewalk, and some were even running in the street without stopping or even seeming to notice the dead body.

"Do? Nothing, that's what we should do," the officer said, straining to be heard above the pandemonium. "I only need you to verify her identity so I can report it. Is it Tatiana Semenova?"

"Yes, officer, but we can't leave her lying in the street, we—"

The officer cut him off. "Can't you see we're at war? There are casualties all over the city. Right now, the ambulances are picking up the wounded. The dead will have to wait."

The stopped car was blocking the street, and the cars backed up behind were honking their horns. Several drivers who had gotten out of their cars to see what the trouble was took hold of Tatiana's legs and pulled her to the edge of the sidewalk. As soon as the body was out of the way, cars started speeding past.

Kolya's stiff legs made kneeling impossible, but he bent over and tried to pick Tatiana up. She was too heavy, and he fell over into the street and was nearly run over. A horn honked. "Idiot!" the driver yelled, "Get the hell out of the street!"

He crawled back onto the sidewalk and pleaded for help, but no one stopped. A bomb exploded and the flying debris cut a gash in his forehead. Feeling faint, he went back into the building and up the steps.

"Tatiana's been hit by a car," he shouted to his mother. "She's dead, down on the sidewalk. I can't move her." Blood was running down his cheeks, and Oxana ran into the kitchen for rags. "I don't know what to do," Kolya continued, while his mother frantically dabbed at his bloody forehead. "It's too gruesome. I don't know what to do," he kept repeating as they descended the circular stairway and stepped out the door. He stopped, stunned, when he looked to the spot where Tatiana had lain only moments ago.

"Where is she?" Kolya said. "What happened to her?"

Cars were speeding by, and the only signs that a horrible accident had occurred mere minutes earlier were the still-fresh pools of blood on the road and sidewalk.

"Has anyone seen a body being taken away?" Kolya asked the people hurrying by, while his mother stood, holding her hands to her mouth. No one seemed to have any idea what he was talking about and ignored him as if he was crazy, until finally, one old man hobbled across the street. "A truck loaded with corpses passed by," he said. "The workers slammed on the brakes, tossed her into the back, and sped away." He seemed astonished by their efficiency and repeated several times, "It only took them thirty seconds—thirty seconds and they were gone."

Another round of bombs exploded. Kolya put his arms around his mother to shield her from flying debris and led her back inside.

"Where was she going?" Oxana asked.

"I don't think she was going anywhere, Mama. I think she did exactly what she intended to do."

"That can't be true. Tatiana would never take her own life. She must have been frightened and wanted to go somewhere. Why didn't she call for one of us to go with her?"

———

They stood in the doorway that evening, gazing into Tatiana's suite. Her jewels were long gone, sold off as the years wore on and her bank accounts became depleted, but everything else was there—closets full of elegant dresses, shoes, hats, fur coats and muffs, silk scarves and caftans, and even old opera costumes. Kolya noticed a piece of paper folded in half with Oxana's name written on it in a hasty scrawl, lying on the dressing table. He handed it to his mother and she read it aloud.

> My dearest friends,
>
> I am tired of living. I cannot endure another war. The bombs are terrifying. I leave everything to the two of you, my dear Oxana and Kolya. Thank you for your wonderful care. May you be safe.
>
> Tatiana Semenova

Oxana folded the note and tucked it into her pocket, and she and Kolya stepped out of the room. He gently closed the door behind them. It felt like a sacrilege to disturb anything, as though a part of Tatiana was still there, taking a few last looks before making her final departure.

Kolya stood gazing out the large windows while his mother reclined on the sofa. In the twilight, the street below was surprisingly serene, almost as if the carnage of the day's bombs had been nothing more than a bad dream.

"I once was standing here gazing out when Tatiana came into the room," Kolya said. "She asked me what I was looking at, and I told her I wasn't looking at anything in particular. I was enjoying the view. She said her maids often liked to look out the window too, and they always said the same thing, that they were enjoying the view. I asked if she ever stood here enjoying it, and she said, 'My boy, I have never stood inside looking out windows. I've always been a part of the life that was happening down below on the street.'"

"That was Tatiana." His mother laughed. "Never an innocent bystander. She was one of life's guilty participants. I'm going to miss her very much."

"Nor was she one to slip quietly away in her sleep," Kolya added. "I guess she wanted to go out with more drama, like a modern-day Russian Tosca. I'm going to miss her too."

Chapter 41

Kolya lay in bed, counting the seconds of silence between the whistling sound of each bomb as it hurtled toward its target, and the roar of its explosion. He dressed and poked his head around the door to his mother's room. "We're safe—for now. It sounds like the Germans are targeting the eastern side of the city."

She nodded but said nothing. He helped her sit up and slip a robe over her nightgown. He held her by the waist as she stood and proceeded unsteadily into the kitchen. Sitting at the table, sipping coffee, they discussed what they should do for Tatiana. Oxana said they should try to invite her old friends for a small service in the apartment, but Kolya quickly squashed that idea. "You couldn't possibly entertain guests—you hardly have the energy to get out of bed, and Tatiana's friends are all nearly as old as she was. It wouldn't be safe for them to come."

His mother nodded. "I suppose you are correct, although I wish I could do something to honor her memory."

"I think the only way we can honor her memory is by staying alive," Kolya said, "which means you need to go back to bed and get your rest, while I do the breakfast dishes."

The bombing kept up all morning and into the afternoon. Without knowing from one moment to the next if it was over, Kolya found it impossible to concentrate on anything else. There were periods of silence, but before long the whistling of the falling warheads began again.

At last, in the late afternoon, the air raids stopped. Kolya picked up the telephone to call for a cab, but the line was dead. *The Germans have cut the phone lines*, he thought. He put on his jacket, went down the circular stairway and out the front door. Kolya stood on the sidewalk a long while and was nearly ready to give up when a taxi finally came toward him and he waved it down.

"Why you want to go to a morgue?" the driver said. "Aren't there enough dead bodies on the streets for you?" The driver took Kolya to several local morgues, but everywhere it was the same story. The staff was overwhelmed and there was such chaos and confusion he could hardly get anyone to stop long enough to talk, and when he did, no one had any idea where Tatiana's body had been taken. "No time for paperwork," he was told by one clerk. "The dead are removed, and that's that."

It was dark by the time he headed back to Tatiana's building. The streetlights were turned off to limit visibility for the German planes, and Kolya had to lean out the taxi window to tell the driver where to turn. "It's war now," the driver said when Kolya handed him the fare. "Take care of the living and forget about the dead. Leave them for God to take care of."

His mother was already in bed, and Kolya stared at the large calendar hanging beside the stove while he reheated the plate of dinner she had left for him. Each New Year's Day, she had dutifully replaced the old calendar with a new one, but Kolya had never given it any thought, until now. He remembered the old man in the train, marking a notch for each day the train rolled on, and how, back in Peterstal, Gregor made a mark on a post in the barn every time it rained. Kolya had thought this sort of recordkeeping was silly, but he now understood. It was an attempt to make sense out of a senseless world. Maybe Gregor's rain tracking was a way of reassuring himself that there would always be another rain, and hence, enough grain to keep them all alive during the coming winter. Perhaps the daily log of the old man in the train was his way of accepting that, while the trauma of his fate was beyond his control, it was a trauma that would eventually come to an end—the horrors would not be eternal.

Kolya found a red pen and put a large X on both September 4 and 5. *This too will end.*

Sipping coffee the next morning, Kolya marked his red X as soon as he heard the planes, well aware of the grim reality that each day might be his last to check off. What if their building was bombed? Would they be engulfed in flames, buried in rubble when everything collapsed on top of them? He thought of how close he and his mother had been to death before—starvation in Peterstal, his mother shot, his captivity and escape. Would their luck hold? Or was their time up?

During a lull in the bombing, Kolya glanced out the window. Columns of black smoke were coming from the direction of the Badayev warehouses, a huge complex of old wooden buildings that held most of the city's food supplies for the coming winter. He decided not to tell his mother.

———

Food rationing had been implemented as soon as the Germans surrounded the city. While standing in line to receive the daily bread allotment one day, Kolya detected the unmistakable increase in the tempo of the relentlessly broadcast tick, dubbed the "Leningrad metronome." The government had set up more than fifteen hundred loudspeakers throughout the city as a public warning system. When all was safe, a slow, monotonous tick, tick, tick was broadcast, but when an incoming air raid was detected, the tempo gradually increased.

Kolya nervously watched the others in line, certain they were hearing it too—Leningraders' ears had become acutely tuned to even slight deviations in the rhythm—yet no one reacted, reluctant to give up their positions after having already stood in line for several hours. Within minutes, sirens began to wail, and the speakers blared "*Vnimaniye!* Attention! Air raid! Air raid!"

Everyone dashed down the street while medical assistants posted on street corners frantically waved their arms to guide people to the nearest bomb shelter. Kolya took off, despite his stiff legs, toward Bolshaya Morskaya, ignoring the medical assistants and fleeing the crowds. He was risking arrest—it was illegal to ignore orders to go to the bomb shelter— but he had to get home to be sure his mother was safe. The whistling of the falling bombs was ear-piercing, and as each bomb detonated, the street shook as though there was an earthquake. Kolya crossed Admiralteyskaya Prospect and dove for cover under a park bench just in time to see several buildings collapse into a heap of rubble.

He crawled out from under the bench, pulled his coat over his face for protection, and raced home, despite the debris—bricks, plaster, pieces of metal, shards of glass—flying all around him. The air was darkened by thick clouds of smoke, and several times he tripped and fell. His legs were bleeding and aching, but he kept going.

Turning the final corner, he was relieved to see his—Tatiana's—building was still standing and not on fire, but nearly all the windows were smashed. He tore up the steps and shoved open the apartment door, yelling, "Don't move, Mama, don't move." Oxana was lying on the sofa in front of the window and had pulled a blanket and pillow over her head to deaden the noise of the bombing.

"I'm fine. I'm fine," she kept repeating.

"Lie still, don't move." Blood was beginning to soak the blanket. Kolya tossed the largest pieces of glass off her and then picked up the four corners of the blanket and, lifting it away, flung it out of the gaping holes of what had, only moments before, been the apartment's tall, beautiful windows. Kolya ran into Tatiana's bedroom, grabbed a bedsheet, and ripped it into strips to bandage his mother's cuts. When he finished, his mother took over, bandaging Kolya's bloodied hands until they resembled huge bear paws.

"Well, I guess that settles the question of piano practice, at least for a few days," Kolya said.

―――――

Kolya needed to find a workman to board up the broken windows. The beautiful autumn was giving way to what was appearing to be an early winter, with cold nights and daytime temperatures hovering only a few degrees above freezing. Wood was scarce and all but impossible to obtain. Kolya told the workman to use some of the apartment doors, but they proved too heavy and unwieldly, and the workman was only able to tack up pieces of cardboard. The cardboard kept blowing loose, and the large main room was too chilly and drafty to use, so Kolya and his mother confined themselves to the apartment's servants' area—the kitchen and their two bedrooms. Amazingly, the city's electrical generators were still running, although for how much longer was anyone's guess, and Kolya moved his mother's bed into the kitchen beside the stove and kept the oven on. It was the only source of heat.

He hurried out early to get in line long before the bakeries opened—by the time they opened, the lines snaked down the street and the wait was much longer. Despite wearing three or four layers of clothing it was impossible to keep warm, and he would hop from foot to foot, beat his chest, rub his arms, and blow into his gloves to try to keep his blood circulating.

Kolya added black Os to his calendar when the first snowfall occurred on October fifteenth—unusually early. There were heavy snowstorms almost daily, and Kolya's calendar, with its red Xs and black Os, soon looked like a checkerboard as he tracked the progress of the two conquerors, moving in tandem, inching toward their as yet undefined, but nevertheless inexorable goal.

By the beginning of November, Kolya stopped going out to collect their food rations so he could spend all his time with his mother. She could no longer rise from her bed, and she lay with her head covered by pillows, trying to drown out the incessant noise of the exploding bombs. Her doctor had prescribed morphine for her pain, but she took it sparingly, saying it made her even more tired and sleepy. Kolya prepared meals from the food she had collected and stored ever since the June invasion. He knew it was foolish to forgo the rations and deplete their precious supplies, but his mother did not have much time left.

One day, she was breathing heavily and would open her eyes for a few moments but then close them again, seeming to fall back to sleep. Kolya heated water, added a few tea leaves, and held the teacup to her lips. She swallowed a few sips before choking and pushing the cup away. Holding her hand, he felt her body temperature dropping and her pulse slowing. He offered more tea and she took a few more swallows. It revived her somewhat, and she turned toward him. There was an almost pleading look in her eyes, yet also an absence, as if she were seeing past him, already entering another world.

"Do you want some food?" he asked. She said nothing. "Do you know who I am?" Still nothing.

But then she began to speak, so softly that Kolya had to lean in to hear. "I love you, Jakob. I have always loved you."

"I'm Kolya, Mama. Your son, Kolya. Jakob was Aunt Irina's husband."

She held up one hand like she was reaching for something, and Kolya took hold of it. She clasped him tightly, "Jakob, forgive me—I did wrong . . . tried to make up . . . your son . . . music . . . forever."

Kolya pressed her hand to his lips, "I'm Kolya, Mama. Jakob didn't have a son. Remember? You told me Aunt Irina died before the baby was born."

She was gasping for breath, her eyes staring blankly, her words barely audible. "Jakob . . . son . . ." Her lips continued moving but no sound came out. A few moments later she closed her mouth and stopped breathing. Kolya ran his fingers across her eyes to close the lids. He laid his head on her breast and wept. There was no one to call and nothing to be done. He was now utterly alone.

Kolya lay on his cot in the kitchen beside his mother's body that night but hardly slept. He was wearing his heavy winter coat and covered himself with blankets but was still cold. The silence in the apartment was unnerving. He had become accustomed to his mother's heavy breathing, but now there was only the soft sound of the wind blowing through the smashed windows.

It was still dark when Kolya rose and knelt beside Oxana's bed. Her face was tranquil, her body rid of the excruciating pain. "Goodbye, Mama," he whispered, carefully wrapping the bedsheets tightly around her. He retrieved the turquoise necklace he had given her for her birthday and draped it around her neck, adjusting the stone so it hung perfectly across her chest. He went into Tatiana's room for the colorful wool blanket she always kept folded across her bed. He wrapped the blanket around his mother, pulling it tight to keep it from falling away. He kissed her lips, in the old Russian tradition, before covering her face and fastening several of his belts around her to hold everything in place.

Lifting his mother's body off the bed—she was surprisingly light, maybe even less than fifty kilos—he carried her into the front room. With the wind blowing freely through the open windows, it was well below freezing, and snowdrifts had formed across the parquet floors she had so meticulously scrubbed.

He brushed the snow off the sofa near the piano and laid his mother across it. He sat at the piano, wiped the snow off the keyboard, and pushed away the snow underneath so his feet could use the pedals. Rubbing his hands together and blowing on them, he bowed his head a few moments, then slowly, softly, began to play Chopin's Fantasy. His fingers were stiff and cold, but as the somber sounds filled the room, a warmth emanated from within himself, and his mind was flooded with memories—Peterstal, Gregor's kindness and love, the hidden food that kept them alive, loading the piano into the back of the wagon to get it back to his grandmother's house, his mother's determination that he become the best pianist he possibly could be, and the moment he learned his mother had survived the horrible gunshot.

Kolya played the final chords—not fortissimo as Chopin indicated, but pianissimo. "You were the great pianist," he whispered. "You deserved to study at the Leningrad Conservatory with Sofronitsky, not me, and you deserved to win the competition." He bowed his head and made the sign of the cross three times across his chest—and then slowly lowered the fallboard.

He carried his mother's body across the room and out the door to the landing. Using his walking sticks for balance, he slowly made his way down the spiral staircase, holding his mother's shrouded head and easing her securely wrapped feet down each step.

The snow was no longer cleared from the streets. There was no gasoline or diesel fuel, even for the snowplows, and children's sleds were the only means of transporting goods. Kolya did not have a sled, but the family in the apartment on the ground floor, with three young boys, had hung theirs in the foyer to make it available to everyone in the building.

Lowering the sled from its hook, he placed his mother's body on it. He secured her with a belt and tied the sled's rope around his waist so that his hands were free for his walking sticks.

The sun had begun to rise and the sky was a rosy pink. It was at least minus ten Celsius, maybe even colder. The sled was difficult to pull through the knee-deep snow, and Kolya had to move slowly to keep from falling.

He made his way down Ulitsa Bolshaya Morskya until he reached the intersection with Nevsky Prospect and turned onto the famed boulevard. There was no bombing, and the city was enveloped in complete silence. Other people were out, also towing sleds with wrapped bundles eerily similar to his, but they passed each other in silence, looking away as they did.

Hour after hour, Kolya slowly trudged along, swinging his legs to keep the sled moving, watching his shadow shortening and then again lengthening as the sun passed overhead before beginning its descent. His hands and feet were numb from the cold, and by late afternoon he was losing his concentration and fell several times. At one point he paused and braced himself, afraid he might faint from hunger, but he urged himself onward. His mother wouldn't have stopped if it were his body on the sled. She would keep going—and so he would too.

It was dark when he finally neared his destination. *Just a little farther, a little farther.*

He paused a moment to gaze at the ornate mosaic of Jesus above the arched entryway before he ducked through it and entered the grounds of the Alexander Nevsky Monastery, a sprawling complex of churches and monastic buildings. Once inside the gate, Kolya veered off the main path to avoid being seen and made his way along the monastery's outer wall, toward the Tikhvin Cemetery, one of the most famous cemeteries in Russia, inching along quietly in case someone was watching. The cemetery was reserved exclusively for wealthy and important people, and he would be forced out if discovered. Kolya made his way to the area where the musicians were buried, passing the graves of Glinka, Mussorgsky, and Rimsky-Korsakov—until he arrived at the tomb of the greatest of them all, Oxana's favorite, Pyotr Ilyich Tchaikovsky.

He sat on the bench in front of the grave. His mother had brought him here after they first arrived in Leningrad, insisting they pay homage. Beside the statue, a large lilac bush had been in full bloom when he and his mother had visited, and she had admired its wonderful fragrance.

Tchaikovsky's bust, atop a stone pillar, was surrounded by two angels, with a large cross extending heavenward. One of the monument's angel figures was covered by snow, and small piles of snow lay across the bust of Tchaikovsky, nearly obscuring his face.

The lilac bush was almost covered with snow. Kolya lay on his side—kneeling was too painful—and, stretching to reach under the bush, he pushed back the accumulated snow until he cleared an area in the very center. He untied his mother's body, slid it off the sled, and with one arm holding aside the lilac branches, eased her into the cleared area. He pushed the leafless lilac branches back into place and shoved the snow over his mother's body until the shroud was completely covered—no one would spot anything inside the branches, and he was certain that by the time the snow melted, the bush would be leafed out enough that it would be impossible to see under it.

As he pulled the sled back on the path and swished at the snow with his boots to obliterate any trace of footsteps or sled rungs, large, fluffy snowflakes began to fall, and soon it was snowing heavily.

With tears running down his cheeks, Kolya stood a long while, imagining how his mother would eventually become one with the bush, and how, each summer, the throngs of admirers paying their respects to Tchaikovsky and sniffing the fragrant scent of the lilac blooms would forevermore also be enjoying Oxana's beauty, unknowingly paying their respects to another of Russia's great musicians.

Chapter 42

8 November 1941

Dear Mama,

I'm writing you a letter! Are you surprised? Let me explain.

The Secretary of the Kirov Party Committee has announced that everyone should write diaries. He wants us all to document our experiences now during the German blockade, so I am going to structure my diary as a series of letters to you. Then, when it's all over, I will bring this to you under your lilac bush and you can read it and know everything!

They even have a name for us here in Leningrad. We are the Blokadniki—people of the blockade. Maybe eventually they will hand out medals to all of us and we can travel around Russia giving speeches congratulating ourselves on how brave we were!

When I bring this to you, you will see that it is Tatiana's diary, with her name embossed on the cover. Isn't it beautiful? I think everything Tatiana had was beautiful. I miss her, but not as much as I miss you.

I will tell you the funny story of how I found this diary. I was searching through Tatiana's desk for something to write on and found it in one of her drawers. Oh,

I thought, this is going to be good. Can you imagine all the juicy stories Tatiana never told us? So, I opened the diary and the first page was blank. I turned it over and the next pages were also blank. I flipped through the whole book and it was completely empty. She had not written a single word! The sly old fox took all her gossip with her to the grave.

So now I will write my story in her book. I'm sure my diary will not be nearly as fun to read as Tatiana's would have been, but I will try not to be dull! You always said I must not bore my audience with my piano playing, so I think you would agree I should not bore with my writing either.

And Mama, please don't worry. You always worried about me, but now you can be at peace. I can take care of myself. I'm not afraid of anything!

Your son,

Kolya

9 November 1941

Dear Mama,

The good news is that it is so cold even the German planes are grounded. The bad news is that it is so cold even the German planes are grounded!

What—you don't like my joke?? I guess you're right— it's pretty bad! But seriously, the bombing has stopped, for now anyway. They say it's too cold for the planes' engines. Most days now are well below zero and there are big snowdrifts everywhere.

When you were sick, I didn't want to tell you too much of what was going on, but now I can fill you in. Our food situation is very bad. The government has reduced the rations five times since September, but it's not their fault. There isn't enough for everyone. I now get about four grams of bread per day, about two slices, and the bread is very poor quality. I think only about half of it is actual flour. One of the women in line said the bakers have been ordered to use fillers like malt and hemp, and even sawdust, to try to make the flour last longer, so you can imagine how delicious it is.

Like most things under our "wonderful" Soviet government, there is a lot of black-market trading. I'll try not to get involved in that unless I'm forced to. Right now, I divide my bread into three portions, and then at each meal I soak the bread in water to make it seem like more, like you taught me in Peterstal. So I am eating three meals a day, like a king!

Remember how I laughed at you when we bought all that extra food and stashed it in Tatiana's pantry? I guess after Peterstal you wanted to be sure we never went hungry again. Well, now I am not laughing, I am thanking you. I locked all the food in Tatiana's safe, the one in her bedroom where I think she used to store her jewels. Anyway, people are now stealing every bit of food they can find, but your supplies are secure, and I only eat a little at a time, when I am feeling very hungry. I will try to make it last as long as I can. Who knows how long this war will go on?

So even now, Mama, you are still taking care of me. You don't need to worry about me—rest now, and in the spring, you can enjoy your lilacs!

Your son,
Kolya

15 November 1941

Dear Mama,

I have not written for a while because I was working up the courage to write this letter. What I am about to tell you is the most difficult thing I have ever had to say to anyone. I hope you will forgive me.

Do you remember when you said there were things about my life that you didn't know anything about, and I said I couldn't tell you? The reason I couldn't is because I was too ashamed. Remember the black car that came to get me late at night? That was when I went to my job and how I made my money. So, brace yourself, here is my story.

Whenever I got into the car, there was never anyone else but the driver. He was pretty old, and I never knew who he was. Except for a few times, it was always the same man. He always tied a handkerchief across my eyes so I couldn't see anything, and I was told that if I ever took it off, they would hurt me, so I never did. I don't know where we went, but it was not always the same place because sometimes the drive was quite short and sometimes it took a long time. Sometimes when the car stopped the driver would take me inside some building, but I never knew where I was, and sometimes the driver told me to stay in the car and it happened there. People—men—did things to me. That was my job. That was what they paid me for. Usually it was only one man, but sometimes there were two or three.

They would open my pants and feel inside my undershorts. Sometimes they kissed me and sometimes they put their mouth on me or massaged me. They never hurt me, Mama, I can swear to that. I would lie back and think of different things until it was over.

I knew it wasn't right, but I did it for the money and I did it for you. I wanted you to be happy and have a nice life with lots of nice things. I didn't want us to ever again live like we did in Peterstal.

Please don't hate me for writing this—but sometimes it felt good and I didn't really mind what they were doing—but most times it was boring, just a job. Vova set it up for me. He said I was beautiful and could make a lot of money, but last spring I told him I wanted to stop doing it. I didn't want to be a dirty person any longer.

I will never do it again, Mama, I promise.

So now I'm sure you hate me and I understand. Maybe I hate myself. I think I will stop writing now, as this is enough information for one day.

Your son,
Kolya

16 November 1941

Dear Mama,

So, if you've recovered from what I wrote yesterday, there is a little more I might as well tell you. Then you will know it all. Vova and I were together too. I guess you could say I was his boyfriend. It wasn't really love, I guess it was sort of a fun infatuation. Vova had lots of boy lovers—I was only one of many—and I guess we got tired of each other. But I let that get in the way of my music making. I drank too much and I didn't practice and now I realize what I have lost I can never regain.

See why I couldn't tell you these things? I know how this hurts you, and I didn't want to hurt you. I don't ask for forgiveness. I am only writing this because I feel I owe it to you to tell you the truth.

Forgive me for saying it, Mama, but you kept secrets from me too. The day you died you were delirious, and you said you loved Jakob. You said he had a son, but you told me Jakob and Irina's baby died. So who was Jacob's son? There were so many things you never told me. What happened after you came back from Odesa, and why did you marry Fedor if he was not my father?

I guess we were both deceptive.

I miss you, Mama.

Your son,
Kolya

2 December 1941

Dear Mama,

I'm not feeling so cheerful today. Everyone always says I have a happy disposition, but these days it's hard to be optimistic. It is very bad here. The temperature has been down to minus forty Celsius, and there has been no electricity in the entire city for many weeks now. There is no fuel to burn for heat. I wear as much clothing as I can put on. If you saw me right now you would laugh. I'm wearing Tatiana's old fur coat on top of my woolen one, and I have several of her scarves wrapped around my neck and face. It's funny how no one thinks of how they look anymore. Everyone wears the warmest things they can find, so you almost can't tell the men from the women.

I'm sorry about my scribbly handwriting. My hands are sore and chapped and they hurt. I wear three pairs of gloves to keep from freezing my fingers since that would be the end of piano playing for me. Maybe it is already the end, but I try to hope I still have a future.

Your son,
Kolya

10 December 1941

Dear Mama,

Now, in addition to going out every day for food, I also have to get water since the water pipes have all frozen solid. Finding water is not as easy as you might think. Everything is frozen over, all the canals and the Neva, everything. Some people dig holes in the ice on the Neva, but the water is not clean. There is a well only two blocks away with a small shed built around it for protection and that is where I get my water, but there is always a queue and some days the wait is quite long. The bad part is that they are now storing dead bodies in the shed. When it's my turn to go in, I try not to look at the bodies piled against the wall, but of course it's impossible to not notice. Some are not even covered and you see faces staring at you, even with their eyes open. Many of the people go in pairs so they are not alone in the shed with the bodies, but I am too embarrassed to ask anyone to come with me. A young man should be strong and unafraid, so I go in and out as fast as I can. I'm glad you don't have to see this.

Your son,
Kolya

11 December 1941

Dear Mama,

My hands are red and very sore, but I will try to write. I can tell you a little more about our water situation. I can only carry one pail for drinking, and I use a rope to hang the pail around my neck so that my hands are free to use my sticks. I never take a bath anymore or even change my clothes. It's too cold to undress, and none of my clothes have been washed for a long time so if I did change it would only be from one set of dirty clothes to another! I'm sure I smell, and I think everyone else smells too, but it's even too cold to smell people! I don't shave anymore either, so I have a long beard. I would like to think it makes me look handsome, like the tsar, but I think I look more like Rasputin!

As you can guess, there are no working toilets anywhere. Everything is frozen up. So we improvise. At first I used a pail, but it was too much work to always take the pail outside and dump it, so now I go outside. Everyone, men and women, does it like this. The bread we get makes people sick, and if they have to, they go right in the street, even with other people watching. It's disgusting, I know, but there are no other options. God help us—we are all becoming like animals. When will this hell end?

I miss you, Mama.

Your son,
Kolya

18 December 1941

Dear Mama,

Do you remember Yevgeny Fedorov's family in the first-floor apartment? They let me move into one of their rooms, and I'm a little better off. It was getting too cold in Tatiana's apartment, and it was too hard for me to go up and down the steps, especially when I tried to carry water, plus it is much shorter to go outside to relieve myself.

They have only their rations for food and it's not enough, so in exchange for a room, I share a little of your food from Tatiana's safe. It's getting low, but don't worry, I'm careful to only take a little at a time. I don't know what will happen when I run out. Only God knows how long this horrible siege will last.

I let Yevgeny chop up some of Tatiana's furniture to burn for heat. I don't know what we will burn once that is all gone. One day I was so cold, I burned my music books! First, I put in Bach, and it was so dry it burned immediately. Next, I put in Beethoven, and the fire became very lively with lots of sparks and even a few small explosions. Then I put in Chopin and the fire glowed so evenly and beautifully. But when I put in my French music, Debussy and Ravel, it did not burn at all—too much perfume! It's a joke, Mama—but I think we will have to burn everything trying to get through this winter.

Your son,
Kolya

25 December 1941

Dear Mama,

Today is Lutheran Christmas. I remember how you always insisted we celebrate it, but today there is no celebration. I will eat my bread dipped in water, like every other day of this horrible winter. I am thinking of you and wishing I could eat one of your delicious meals!

Your son,
Kolya

~~10~~ 11 January 1942

Dear Mama,

We are all very hungry and I think of food all the time. There is nothing left in Tatiana's safe. Everything has been eaten. You were such a good cook, and I think of all the times I didn't eat because I didn't want to get fat. Now I would give anything to be fat. How stupid I was, so vain, always thinking of my appearance and what others thought of me. Now none of that matters. I don't look into a mirror anymore. Everyone has yellow skin and lifeless eyes. I'm sure I am no different. We all stare at each other and wonder who will live to see tomorrow.

I miss you, Mama.

Your son,
Kolya

~~15 16~~ ? January 1942

(Sorry, Mama, I don't exactly know which day it is today.)
Dear Mama,

Some people I don't know have moved into Tatiana's apartment. Their building was bombed and burned, and they were wandering in the streets with nowhere to go. Somehow they found the empty apartment and moved in.

It's a mother and two children. I asked the children where their father was, but they didn't know. They seem very ill. Both children have huge, bloated bellies, and I am not sure if they are boys or girls. They are very small, but their faces look so old, I have no idea what their ages are. They never talk, they just sit and stare. I should try to be friendly, but I don't know what to say. I know they are starving and will not live long and there is nothing I can do.

They remind me of the starving people in Peterstal. I had hoped all those horrible images were permanently erased from my mind, but now it has all come back. I was so young and you protected me, but now I see what you went through. I am reliving the same hell you lived. Maybe I deserve it.

God bless you, Mama. I miss you very much.

Your son,
Kolya

16 January 1942

(I asked Yevgeny Fedorov what day it is.)
Dear Mama,

I checked on the people upstairs, but I don't think they are going to live much longer. It was wrong of me to write, yesterday, that I had nothing to say to the children. Of course there is nothing I can do for them, but my God, they are only children! Do even they deserve this— deserve to starve and die? Today I sat with them and we told stories and even played a few games. Their names are Zinaida and Anna, so they are both girls!

We are all stranded in this frozen desert and there is nothing anyone can do for any of us, except God, and even he seems to have evacuated the city.

Your son,
Kolya

20 January 1942

Dear Mama,

It is very depressing, so maybe I will try out a new joke on you. The good news is that it has warmed up enough that the Germans have resumed bombing, but the bad news is that it has warmed up enough that the Germans have resumed bombing.

It's now the shortest days of the year. The sun doesn't rise until nearly nine and sets at three, so we barely have six hours of daylight. There is not even one drop of kerosene left for a lamp, or anything else to burn for lighting, so I sit in the dark and play music in my head, like I learned to do on the train after you were shot. It's very good for my concentration and forces me to stop thinking about how hungry I am. I can play through entire pieces. I hear every note.

I have sad news to report. Yevgeny's wife, Elizabeta, the lady downstairs from Tatiana's, where I am now living, died yesterday. Yevgeny came home last night and found her lying in bed, so I helped him take her body to the morgue. We tied her to the sled and we both pulled so it was not too difficult, but still, by the time we got to the morgue it was nearly closing time and we had to rush. We stacked her on top of a pile of corpses, and I am trying not to think about what will happen to her. At least we got her there and didn't have to dump her somewhere, the way so many people are forced to do.

So now I am going to try to take care of their boys since Yevgeny has to go to work to keep his Category I ration card.

It's funny how we are in the center of one of the most beautiful and sophisticated cities in the world, and we are all living like cavemen! There is nothing beautiful or sophisticated about anything anymore. Dead bodies are everywhere—even lying in the streets. People die while they are walking, or while they are standing in line for rations. Sometimes the bodies are nearly naked—people take the coats and shoes and even the pants and shirts, if they are not too dirty or torn. I suppose someday this will all sound so terrible, but for us it is our way of life.

What has become of us? How can we look at dead bodies and feel nothing? We should feel sorrow or sadness, but we don't dare. There is too much, and if we allowed ourselves to feel emotions we would be overwhelmed. We must keep going, keep living somehow. I wonder which of Dante's circles we have descended to already and how many more are there? I'm glad you don't have to see this.

I miss you, Mama.

Your son,
Kolya

25 January 1942

Dear Mama,

I spoke too soon about warm weather. Yevgeny said yesterday the temperature was minus thirty Celsius. My life is now a triangle of duties. I help the Fedorov boys, I stand in line for bread, and then for water. It takes the entire day to accomplish these three tasks. I go out before dawn to get in line for my bread rations because sometimes the bakeries run out and then that's it—you wait until the next day. So you see why I try to get an early start. Our ration cards are more precious than gold. If anyone faints or falls and drops their card, it's immediately snatched up by someone else and then you go hungry.

The ration cards are handed out in ten-day cycles and there were still six days on Elizabeta's card when she died so the children had an extra portion, but when her card is done . . . who knows . . .

Your son,
Kolya

3 February 1942

Dear Mama,

The last few days have been a disaster. German artillery shells struck the typographical center where the ration cards were being printed, so now, none of us whose cards ran out have gotten our new cards, and the bakeries will not give us any bread without cards, so we have had nothing to eat. The family upstairs is suffering terribly.

Your son,
Kolya

5 February 1942

Dear Mama,

More bad news. Yesterday I went to check on the family upstairs. The mother was sitting in that chair Tatiana used to love. She was staring straight ahead, and when I tried to talk to her, she had no response, so I touched her arm and she was frozen solid. The two girls were in bed, and little Zinaida was also dead. Anna was still alive, so I picked her up to bring her downstairs. She cried when she saw her mother sitting in the chair. I felt so sorry for her.

I shook a few bread crumbs out of my coat pocket and put them in hot water for her to drink. She is so small. I thought she was about five or six, but when I asked, she said she is twelve. It's odd how all of us adults seem so much older than we are, while all the children look so much younger (their bodies that is, in their faces they too look old). So, after I fed her, I took her to one of the new orphanages the government has established. They fill up almost as fast as they open, but I would be lying if I said that all the children are taken in by orphanages. Many wander the streets alone until they die, either from starvation or the cold.

Mama, I cried today after I left Anna. I have not cried

for a long time, maybe not since I left you under the lilac bush, but today I cried. I don't think I can take much more. I miss you terribly, Mama.

Your son,
Kolya

7 February 1942

Dear Mama,

After I came back from the orphanage, I had a long talk with Yevgeny Fedorov. I told him all about it, and he begged me to take his boys there as well. It is of course illegal since they are not orphans, but tomorrow I will do it. Yevgeny explained to the boys that they will have to say their papa died. At least they will get a bowl of hot soup every day, which is more than they are getting here. I can't stand to see them suffering any longer.

God help us. I miss you, Mama.

Your son,
Kolya

?? February 1942

(I don't know today's date.)
Dear Mama,

I am all alone now. You, Tatiana, Zinaida and her mother, and Elizabeta Federova are all dead. Anna and the Fedorov boys are in the orphanage, and Yevgeny Fedorov now spends his nights at the factory. So, except for me, the building is completely empty.

I think I will die soon. I am starving, but maybe I will not wait for that ending. It's for the best. I deserve to die. I have wasted my entire life. I wasted your delicious food because I was vain and wanted to be attractive. You sacrificed everything so I could come to Leningrad, and I squandered my opportunities. Professor Sofronitsky threw me out of his class because I was too lazy to work and to show up on time. I lost the competition because I was arrogant and cocky. Neuhaus said I had the potential to be the best pianist in Russia and I threw everything away. I wasted it all.

If there is a God in heaven, Mama, pray for me. There is nothing left for me on this earth.

Your son,
Kolya

Dark Winter, 1942

Dear Mama,

It is late, maybe past midnight, and I thought of you all day today. I went upstairs and stood for a long time in Tatiana's front room. It is now nearly filled with snow and the piano is completely buried.

I kept thinking of the night of my concert. You had worked so hard—the chairs filled with people eager to hear me, candles everywhere, Tatiana in her colorful caftan and you in your black dress wearing the turquoise necklace—I could see it all. I stepped into the dining room, and there it was—the table loaded with food, the dessert side table, the tea trolley, everyone smiling and so happy.

And I remembered our days in Peterstal. People were so kind and nice to us—Gregor, who really was a father to me, and Maria and Arkady with Aloysha and his brothers, and Father Vanska, and Ludmilla and Slava Domitovich. There were so many who cared about me and encouraged me, and I have let them all down.

That night of the concert, when I left, I left behind everything that was good in my life—you and Tatiana, my audience, the delicious food and the beautiful room, but in a way I also left behind all my supporters from back in Peterstal. And why? Just to crawl into that car so some anonymous, depraved, lust-filled man would give me money?

When they forced us off the train and shot you, they made a mistake. They should have shot me instead. Now I will correct their error. Tonight, I am going to bring my life to its rightful conclusion.

I miss you so very much, Mama. I would sign as your son, but I don't deserve this noble distinction.

Kolya

March 1942

Dear Mama,

Well, as you can read, I didn't do away with myself. Maybe God talked me out of it, or maybe it was you. How perfect suicide would be for a person like me. I am arrogant, selfish, self-centered, and egotistical, and suicide would release me from doing the impossible work of becoming a better person. Still, perhaps I can go on living and try.

Starting today, I am going to go to the orphanage every day to volunteer. It's on Vasilievsky Island, across the Leytenanta Shmidta Bridge, so it's a long way, but if I think of the children the time goes faster and I do not feel so cold and sore.

I've gotten to know the staff at the orphanage, and they tell terrible stories. In one apartment, two little girls were found scrounging for food while their dead mother sat in a kitchen chair. Another worker told of how she was nearly finished with her search of an empty apartment when there was a noise coming from a basket full of dirty laundry. She pulled the clothes back only to discover a little boy hiding. He told her he had pulled the clothes around him to keep him warm while he waited to die.

There is a small piano at the orphanage, and I have been teaching the children a few songs. They really seem to like it and it makes everyone happy. Even some of the staff will start singing, and if you saw us at that moment, you would not know what we are going through.

God help those innocent children, and may God help me to help them as much as I possibly can. Maybe it is not yet too late, and I can still become the son you tried to raise.

Your son,
Kolya

March 1942

Dear Mama,

It's finally getting warmer, thank God, and the days are getting longer. Also, our rations have increased slightly, so we are a little less hungry. But I also have other good news. I am going to play with the orchestra. Shostakovich has completed his seventh symphony and titled it "The Leningrad Symphony," in honor of our struggles, and Maestro Karl Eliasberg wants the symphony performed here. The Philharmonic was evacuated before the siege, but the Radio Orchestra was not, so he is trying to gather the orchestra back together, even going to the musicians' homes to locate players. Of course, many died, so they are now asking anyone who can play an instrument to join, even pulling soldiers out of the army to join the orchestra. Shostakovich wrote a piano part into the symphony, and that is where I come in. I volunteered to play it. We already had our first rehearsal, but it had to be stopped after less than one hour because some of the musicians fainted from hunger. So now they are feeding us extra rations and giving us hot bricks to heat our hands while we are rehearsing. The music is quite difficult, but we will give it our best. I will write more about it after our next rehearsal.

I miss you, Mama.

Your son,
Kolya

Chapter 43

Kolya heard faint voices and opened his eyes. He could see two nurses in the hallway outside his room. His head was bandaged and he was still wearing his clothing, even his coat, but everything was stained with blood. He tried to sit up when one of the nurses came into the room. "Hello, comrade," she greeted him. "I see you are awake."

He tried to speak, but all that came out was a gargling sound. His throat was filled with phlegm.

"Stay quiet and rest," the nurse said. "You will live, but you're seriously injured and have lost a lot of blood. You were found buried in rubble after a building was bombed. I've given you a sedative to keep you calm, and tonight you will be leaving under a mandatory medical evacuation order so you can receive proper treatment." The nurse patted his arm and pulled the door shut behind her.

Kolya drifted in and out of consciousness, not sure where he was nor what the nurse had meant by a mandatory medical evacuation order, or where he was being taken. Later—Kolya had no idea how much time had passed—another nurse came into his room with a stretcher. "You will be taken to Lake Ladoga along with the rest of the medical evacuees," the nurse said, lifting Kolya onto the stretcher. "From there, trucks will drive you across the ice road to the other side of the lake. Our troops have secured the area, and a train will take you to a hospital."

The nurse rolled the stretcher outside, and several nurses lifted it into the back of a waiting truck. The box was filled with patients, most of them unconscious. "Best of luck, comrades," the nurse said, closing the truck box. "May your journey be safe."

The drive was long. Kolya tried to sleep, but the roar of the engine and the jarring from the rough road kept him awake. It was completely dark when the truck finally stopped. "Where are we?" Kolya asked the patient beside him, an older man also with a bandaged head.

"Refueling, I assume, before heading across the lake."

Kolya managed to sit up enough to pull back a flap of the canvas covering and saw they were part of a caravan of trucks. Someone shouted, "You're off!" Within moments the engine was roaring, and the truck was moving at top speed. Despite the darkness, the driver drove without any lights.

The night was suddenly lit by a flash of bright light followed by a bomb explosion.

"Damn Germans," the patient beside Kolya said.

There was another flash of light and, in that brief moment, Kolya saw a hole open up in the ice up ahead, and one of the trucks drove right into it and disappeared beneath the water.

"Hang on," the driver shouted, and without decreasing the speed, he veered sharply to the left. The stretchers banged together, and the patient beside Kolya was nearly thrown on top of him. Despite the roar of the engines, Kolya heard screaming. Several more explosions lit up the sky, and then there was calm. He drifted back into unconsciousness.

Part 5

Happiness

Moscow, Russia
1958

Chapter 44

Kolya knew he would never forget the day he received the letter. He carried it, unopened, in his pocket all afternoon. If the response was a no, it was, in all likelihood, the end of his performing career, since he was barely under the age limit of thirty-five. But if it was yes—dare he even hope?

After dinner that evening, he poured a glass of wine and sat in a chair. With hands shaking, he finally slit open the envelope. He pulled out the letter, trying not to look at it, but his eyes saw the first word—Congratulations—and he started to cry. He had been selected to be a member of the Soviet contingent for the first Tchaikovsky International Piano Competition.

He had already prepared as never before for the audition, but now that he was in the actual competition, he upped his practicing even more, determined to give his absolute all. Memories of placing second in the conservatory competition and disappointing both his teacher and his mother, because of his arrogance and complacency, still haunted him. He was determined to not repeat his mistake.

Kolya intended to follow his usual pattern of not hearing any of the other contestants, but the rumors of the Americans, especially of one contestant by the name of Van Cliburn, piqued his interest enough that he decided to sit in and listen.

It was, however, one of the other Americans—Harry was his name—that caught Kolya's attention. He was, like Kolya, older than most of the contestants, and had a certain way about his music making that strongly appealed to Kolya.

After his performance, Kolya went backstage. "I vould like to congraz-zulate you for ze lovely piano play," Kolya said to Harry, in what little English he had picked up from pirated Hollywood movies, extending his hand to shake. He was stunned when Harry replied in near-perfect Russian. Harry explained that his family had emigrated to America when he was only a baby so he had no memories of Russia, but his family always spoke Russian at home while he was growing up.

Both men passed into the second round, and Kolya was again impressed with how Harry got exactly the right sound when playing Russian music, almost as if he were more Russian than the Russians.

That evening, Kolya, along with the rest of the contestants, paced up and down the hall outside the auditorium, pausing every few moments to glance toward the bulletin board outside the ticket office. "Results are in," someone suddenly shouted, and the contestants crowded around, pushing, trying to read the list of names that would pass into the final round.

Standing beside Harry, and already knowing that neither of their names was on the list, Kolya watched Harry struggle to decipher the Cyrillic spell-ing of the names.

"I guess that's that," Harry finally said. "You win some, you lose some."

"Is this an American expression?" Kolya asked. "Here in Russia, you either win or you die."

"Ouch, that sounds harsh," Harry said.

Kolya laughed. "Don't worry—it's only a joke. When I was a child, my uncle taught me to tell jokes. I think it's fun, but no one ever laughs."

"How about I buy you a drink, and you can tell me some more jokes. See if you can get me to laugh."

Several drinks later, and without the impediment of a language barrier, Kolya was amazed at how easily the conversation—ranging from Russia's missiles to Mozart's fingerings—flowed between them. It was as if they were already kindred spirits who had somehow known each other their entire lives. Talking with Harry felt like the old days of talking with Vova.

———

Over the next few days, now that they were relieved from the pressure of practicing, they met daily. Harry's descriptions of life in America only served to solidify thoughts Kolya had been having for a long while already—it was time to leave the Soviet Union. He loved teaching, but it was impossible for a music teacher to earn enough money to have a nice life. It was concerts—especially concerts outside Russia that paid in foreign currencies—that allowed for all the extra luxuries.

The final day of the competition, before the awards ceremony, Kolya and Harry met for lunch. When they were finished eating, Kolya put his fingers to his lips to signal Harry to be quiet, and said, "Come with me. I want to show you some flowers." They walked across the street and into the park, and when Harry asked why he wanted to show him flowers, Kolya whispered that it was not about flowers. He glanced around to be sure they had not been followed before saying, "In Russia, all conversations with foreigners are listened to. I'm sure the officials have heard every word we've said to each other. Out here we can talk in private. The government at least has not managed to bug the trees and flowers—not yet anyway, but they will, eventually!"

"Yes, so far only Mother Nature can bug the trees and flowers," Harry replied.

Kolya groaned. "I'm sorry, but I'm afraid your jokes are even worse than mine." They both laughed.

Kolya kept his voice lowered to a whisper. "I want to ask you something, but you must keep it secret and not tell anyone."

"Sure, I'll keep it a secret . . . unless you're about to tell me you're planning to rob a bank or murder Van Cliburn before they give him his gold medal tonight."

"No, no bank robberies or last-minute murders."

They both laughed again.

"Harry, I'm going to defect to America. I want to live like you, with freedom—to travel, say whatever I want, read whatever I want, and play concerts wherever I want. I don't want to spend the rest of my life always requesting permission and then worry whether permission will be granted. I don't want to live here in Russia any longer."

"Defect? Isn't that dangerous?" Harry asked.

"Yes, it's dangerous. I'm a Soviet artist, and it embarrasses the government when we want to go to the West. The Communists want to project the image that everything in Russia is the best . . . so why would anyone want to leave? Tonight will be a great embarrassment, but they're caught in a trap. Along with everything else, the government controls the media so they can keep saying Russia is the best, even when we aren't, but the competition has been open to the public, and it's clear that the American is the best."

Kolya laid out the plan he had already carefully worked out. He had a concert the following week in Amsterdam, at the Concertgebouw, which he already had permission to play. "You said you are going to spend some time traveling in Europe before returning to America," Kolya said. "Perhaps you would like to come to my Amsterdam concert?"

"I would love nothing more. Of course I can make it."

"Well, in that case . . . at the end, during the applause when I'm on the stage, the KGB officer they assign to travel with me will be backstage, so it will take him a few moments before he knows anything is happening. I will leap off the stage, and would you be willing to be there to catch me?"

"Sure, I will not fumble."

"Fumble? I don't understand?" Kolya said.

"Drop the ball, like in football," Harry explained.

"Oh God, American jokes. This will take some getting used to." Kolya laughed to hide the fact that tears were beginning to form in his eyes—the gratitude he felt was overwhelming—but he was having other feelings as well, feelings for Harry that he had not had since Vova.

"I must ask one more favor," Kolya continued. "I also need you to arrange to have a taxi waiting and to ask you to help me get immediately to the American embassy. I know this concert hall, and the American embassy is around the corner. The KGB will have a car outside to take me back to my hotel, so we'll need to move fast, but once we are inside the embassy, we'll be safe."

The next day, Kolya and Harry stood outside the Moscow Conservatory's main hall and made sure people saw them say goodbye, with hugs and the traditional three kisses. They also made certain they were overheard saying how much they were going to miss each other, and they both promised to write and maybe, at some future point, they might once again cross paths.

Kolya's Amsterdam concert was sold out. He had programmed two sonatas, by Rachmaninoff and Prokofiev, in the first half and, as he stood and bowed after each, he gazed into the audience, trying to spot Harry. *Maybe he's late or has run into traffic. He'll be here soon.*

Kolya paced in his dressing room during the intermission as the minutes ticked by. *Where is he?* He was certain Harry would come backstage. The stage manager rapped on his dressing room door. "Lights are down."

Kolya sat at the piano, staring at his hands and hoping this would work. If it didn't, and the KGB discovered his plot, he'd spend the rest of his life teaching in outer Siberia—or worse. He launched into the opening notes of Mussorgsky's Pictures at an Exhibition and soon was caught up in the momentum of the piece.

Nearly forty minutes later, with his fingers sounding "The Great Gate of Kyiv," the last section of Mussorgsky's gargantuan composition, Kolya breathed a sigh of relief—only a few more minutes and he'd be free. He stood and bowed to acknowledge the roaring applause, and to gaze into the audience, but no Harry.

Kolya bowed a second and a third time. He sat at the piano and began an encore, a Chopin nocturne, certain that Harry would show up. The quiet ending faded away, the audience clapped, Kolya stood to bow—and still no Harry. *This has to work. I can't go back to Russia. There is no life for me there. Harry, where are you? Please don't fail me—we agreed to do this together. I thought we were friends.*

Kolya quickly returned to the piano bench and started a second encore—a Scarlatti sonata. As soon as his fingers touched the keyboard, he realized his mistake—he should have chosen something longer, but he was too rattled to think clearly and had launched into the first piece that popped into his mind. If he only gave him enough time, Harry would come.

The audience once again erupted into applause, and Kolya once again stood and bowed. The applause was dwindling, and he felt the beginnings of a panic attack coming on.

What am I going to do? This whole idea was nothing more than a fantasy. It was never fated to work out. I need to go back home, back to Russia.

Turning to leave the stage, a vision of his mother suddenly appeared before him, blocking his way. He jerked to a halt. Her face was stern and unsmiling. She said nothing—only stared at him with a penetrating glare—and then she was gone.

Kolya was terrified and his mind was racing, but at that moment he had to do whatever it took to succeed with his plan. It's what his mother would do. With very little applause coming from the audience, he turned back to the piano, quickly sat on the bench, and launched into Chopin's Fantasy. He heard groans. Out of the corner of his eye he saw some people heading toward the exit.

They could leave if they wanted to. He would play to an empty hall if he had to. He'd play as long as it took for Harry to come.

With the last notes of the coda's bravura ending still reverberating, Kolya slowly rose from the piano bench, completely exhausted, stepped in front of the piano to take his bow—and there was Harry, waving his arms and mouthing, *jump, jump*. Kolya grabbed his walking sticks on the floor beside the piano and leapt off the stage. Harry caught him and pushed people aside until a path cleared. Within moments Kolya and Harry were out the side door and into the taxi.

"You're in the wrong lane!" Kolya shouted when the driver pulled into the street. "The American consulate is the other direction. Turn right! Turn right!"

"There is no right turn," the taxi driver responded. "All the streets here are one way. First we go left, then we go left again, and we come back."

"We have to get out—this won't work," Kolya told Harry, opening the door and swinging his legs out.

Harry made no move to exit the vehicle. "What do you mean it won't work? It's only a short way. We'll be there in a few minutes."

"Get out—we have to run," Kolya insisted. "The traffic's too heavy. By the time we go around, the KGB will know what we're doing. They'll stop the traffic, even create an accident. Hurry—we have to go now."

They jumped out of the taxi and began navigating their way across the street, now packed with both cars and pedestrians exiting the music hall. The traffic in the southbound lanes was stopped for a red light, and they quickly rushed across and darted into the oncoming traffic in the northbound lanes, dodging cars. Kolya was using his sticks to balance himself as he swung each leg forward, and Harry got ahead of him.

Kolya tried to go faster but was afraid he might fall and be run over. He called to Harry, and Harry backtracked and grabbed his arm. They made it across the street and entered the southwest side of Amsterdam's lush Museumplein park. The siren of the KGB vehicle, stuck in the backed-up traffic, was blaring, and the KGB agents were honking and leaning out the windows, yelling for the cars to pull aside to let them through.

"Run!" Kolya yelled. "We have to run."

Harry took off, but Kolya fell. Harry raced back to help him up. One of Kolya's legs was bleeding and he was gasping for air.

"Keep going!" Harry yelled, grabbing Kolya's arm and pulling him to his feet. "I'll help you. You can do it."

Kolya took a step forward and again fell to the ground. His legs felt like they were on fire. The siren of the KGB car was getting louder as it came toward them. Harry grabbed hold of Kolya by the waist and swung him over his shoulder. "Keep going," Kolya pleaded, urging Harry on. "Just a little farther."

As they neared the embassy's elegant wrought-iron gate, the KGB car came roaring up behind them. Kolya was afraid the agents might ram into them to knock them down, but the KGB car slammed to a stop when two American guards stepped out from behind the gate. "I am Russian! I am requesting asylum," Kolya called out to the guards.

The Russian agents jumped from the car and ran toward Harry and Kolya, but the embassy guards blocked their way. "Step back!" one of the soldiers shouted, pointing his rifle at the agents. The Russians ignored him, and one of them reached to grab hold of Kolya's arms.

"Step back!" the guard shouted again, and he fired a shot into the air.

The heavy wrought-iron gate slowly swung open, and as soon as there was enough of a gap to allow them in, Harry, with Kolya still draped across his shoulder, slipped inside. Both collapsed on the driveway.

Chapter 45

Harry and Kolya were both hired as piano teachers at the community college in Harry's hometown as soon as they arrived in America, even though Kolya did not yet speak English. They also soon realized they were in love and decided to live together as partners.

As the years wore on, they talked about applying for positions at larger, more prestigious schools, but they were comfortable and content, and thoughts of uprooting quickly lost their appeal and faded.

On the eve of 1992, Kolya and Harry toasted each other with champagne—they had been in America for thirty-five years. Harry had retired and Kolya, about to celebrate his sixty-seventh birthday, was contemplating retirement. He was also contemplating, now that the Soviet Union had dissolved and Ukraine was an independent nation, a trip to Peterstal. For years, Kolya had been yearning to return to his roots, and at the stroke of midnight, with the ball dropping in New York's Times Square, Harry handed Kolya two plane tickets.

Harry died suddenly a short time later, in a grocery store. Kolya was pushing the cart and Harry bent over to pick up a watermelon. He suddenly dropped the watermelon and half turned toward Kolya before falling face forward. The doctor said it was a massive heart attack and that most likely Harry was dead before he hit the floor.

Kolya was devastated and called off the trip back to his homeland. He could not imagine making the trip without Harry. But, after several months, one of their friends invited Kolya out for dinner and over the course of the evening managed to convince him he should go, that Harry would want him to. And so, in late summer, Kolya boarded a plane at New York's JFK airport and flew to Kyiv. A taxi took him to the train station, and several hours later he was standing in Peterstal's central square.

It was a hot August afternoon and Kolya recognized nothing. An old man was sitting on the bench outside the train depot, and when Kolya told him that he had grown up there, the old man seemed eager to tell the history of the town—the school and Orthodox church had both burned, and the general store and the Stepaniak blacksmith shop had been torn down and replaced with newer buildings. The old man, pointing them out, seemed pleased with what seemed to Kolya like typical nondescript, Soviet-era, cinder block buildings. Kolya crossed the square and went around the corner, but there was nothing but a gaping hole where his grandmother's house had stood.

He walked to Fedor's farm, but nothing remained. The Domitovich house was also gone, replaced by a long, low-roofed building that appeared to house several families. Maria and Arkady's house, where he had spent much of his time with his best friend Aloysha, was still a mound of ashes, unchanged from the day the Bolsheviks burned it after evicting Maria and her three boys.

Kolya slowly made his way back into town and noticed an ancient-looking man sitting near a hut where he was sure the Lutheran church had once stood.

Kolya went over to him. "My name is Kolya Rostov."

The old man stared with glassy, watery eyes.

"My mother was Oxana Rostova. Did you know her?" Kolya said. "Her maiden name was Stepaniaka, and my grandmother was Elena Vladimirovna Stepaniaka."

"Oxana Rostova? Oxana?" the old man repeated several times.

"Who are you?" Kolya asked.

"I'm Father Vanska."

"Father Vanska!" Kolya exclaimed. "I didn't recognize you! It's me, Kolya! Do you remember?"

"Kolya? Yes, I remember him. They took him away. He's not here."

"Do you remember my mother? Oxana?"

"Oxana? She's not here either."

"I know," Kolya said. "I'm her son."

"I remember her son. He was a pianist, like her, very good."

"That's me. I'm Kolya, her son."

"Her son? Go south, about three kilometers. He can tell you everything."

"Who can tell me everything?"

"Three kilometers south, first farm, it's Jakob Schweitz."

"Jakob Schweitz? He's my uncle, my aunt Irina's husband. Is he here?"

"Three kilometers south, first farm. Irina's not here. Oxana's not here either. They shot her. No one knows what happened to the son. They took him away. He was a good pianist. Like his mother."

"I'm the son."

"No. They took him away. You go three kilometers south, first farm. Jakob Schweitz will tell you. He knows everything."

"Spasiba, Father Vanska. Spasiba. God bless you," Kolya called as he hurried down the road.

Finding the farmhouse, Kolya knocked at the door. There was no answer, but a man emerged from the barn.

"Hello," Kolya called.

"Who are you?" the man asked, walking stiffly toward Kolya, as if in pain. Kolya guessed he was at least eighty-five, maybe ninety years old.

"I'm Kolya Rostov. Oxana Rostova's son."

"Kolya Rostov? Oxana's son?"

"Are you Jakob Schweitz, my uncle? Aunt Irina's husband? I saw Father Vanska and he told me you were here, although he seemed confused. I think he's senile."

Jakob laughed. "Yes, Father Vanska is senile, and yes, I am your uncle. Come inside." He led Kolya into the house and offered him a chair. "This isn't the house Irina and I lived in. That one's long gone, burned down. This is my brother's old house. Care for a shot?" He handed Kolya a glass of vodka.

"*Za zdorovie*," Jakob said, downing his vodka.

"*Za zdorovie*," Kolya repeated the toast, also swallowing the vodka in one gulp. "I'm sorry I never met you. Mama said you went away after Aunt Irina died."

"Your mama was right. I was gone a long time—too long. I'm sorry I never came back to meet you."

"Mama used to take me to Aunt Irina's grave."

Jakob wiped his brow.

"That's our old piano," Kolya said, pointing to the upright standing against the wall. "That's the piano I played growing up."

"You want to try it? But I'll warn you, it's pretty beaten up. They were about to tear down your grandmother's house, and I managed to get it before they turned it into a heap of rubble."

Kolya stepped over to the piano and tried a few keys. It was out of tune.

"Do you know Chopin's Fantasy?" Jakob asked.

"You know about music?" Kolya was surprised.

"I know a little, mostly what your mother and grandmother taught me."

Kolya sat and began to play but soon heard sobbing. He glanced over and was embarrassed for the old man.

"Do you know who my father is?" Kolya asked when he finished. "Mama never told me. I don't know why, she always acted like it was some deep, dark secret. Father Vanska said you can tell me everything."

"Yes, I know who your father is—it's a long story." Jakob wiped his eyes. "But first play it again—Chopin's Fantasy. Please, play it again. Then we can talk."

Author's Note

The most amazing aspect of the Holodomor—the man-induced fam-
ines that allowed the Soviet government to "break the backs" of the
kulaks (private landowners) and collectivize agriculture—is that it never
happened. Robert Conquest, in his groundbreaking book *The Harvest of
Sorrow*, writes, "Deception was practiced on a giant scale . . . every effort
was made to persuade the West that no famine was taking place, and later
that none had in fact taken place."

Anne Applebaum, in her outstanding book *Red Famine*, concurs: "In
the official Soviet world, the Ukrainian famine, like the broader Soviet
famine, did not exist. It did not exist in the newspapers; it did not exist in
the public speeches. Neither national leaders nor local leaders mentioned
it—and they never would."

Ms. Applebaum continues, "It was not taught in the school systems,
and every effort was made to control all public speech. One Ukrainian
Red Army soldier, during one of the obligatory 'political instruction' classes
asked the teacher a question about the famine. He was sharply told, 'There
was no famine and there cannot be, you will be locked up for ten years if
you keep talking like this.' Students and workers sent into the fields were
told to 'sew up our mouths.' At work no one spoke of the famine or of the
bodies in the streets, as if we were all part of a conspiracy of silence."

The Soviet government went to great lengths to cover up the facts.
When the 1937 Soviet census showed a shocking population decrease of
over eight million people, Stalin simply abolished the census, declaring it
"badly organized and unprofessional." When asked about the death tolls,
Nikita Khrushchev declared, "No one was keeping count."

Since 1991, after the fall of the Soviet government and Ukraine's independence, official documents have become accessible, and historians have begun their investigations. Robert Conquest is certain that across Russia, the combined death toll between 1930 and 1937 of peasants and those arrested who died in prison camps exceeded fourteen million people. He has further inferred that five million of those deaths were the direct result of the man-made Ukrainian famine of 1932–1933. At the cost of this catastrophic loss of life, Stalin's goal was accomplished. By the end of the 1930s private ownership of land had ceased to exist. Across the entire USSR, the government had confiscated all land.

Members of the family of this book's author were among the perished.

Requiescat in Pace

Acknowledgments

If it takes a village to raise a child, it surely must take an entire city to write a book. I have received more honest, helpful, and insightful encouragement than I probably deserve, and I am grateful for all of it. To even begin to name names is also an exercise in leaving so many deserving individuals unnamed, but I feel compelled to point out my gratitude for the critiques of early drafts that were provided by Dr. Adam Prince and T. J. Beitelman.

This book would not exist without the many instructors, classes, and workshops I enjoyed at the Loft Literary Center in Minneapolis, Minnesota, and specifically the instruction and support of Peter Geye. Peter is warm, kind, and extremely generous, but also, like all good teachers, tough and demanding.

My editorial team at Greenleaf has been fantastic, especially Ava Justine, whose Polish heritage made her a perfect fit for this book.

Last, I am thankful every day for my dearly beloved life partner, Reid Smith. He did not live to see this book to completion, but I think he would like it.

About the Author

LaWayne Leno is the author of two internationally acclaimed musical biographies, *The Untold Story of Adele aus der Ohe* and *Roses of the Prairie*. He was raised in rural North Dakota, studied piano with Oxana Yablonskaya in New York City, and completed his education at the University of Mary in Bismarck, North Dakota. He currently resides in the Twin Cities of Minnesota.

www.ingramcontent.com/pod-product-compliance
Lightning Source LLC
Chambersburg PA
CBHW050520110726
47899CB00005B/1529